Bolan saw no saving grace in the Brethren's manifesto

They were neither patriots nor loyalists. The secretive organization sought to destabilize the America that had nurtured and empowered it. Bolan would have been among the first to accept that America had her faults. No nation on earth could put hand on heart and claim to be perfect.

The Brethren pushed its agenda by highlighting the nation's woes and employing indiscriminate violence to throw the population into panic.

The line had been drawn, and the Brethren had stepped over, not caring who was drawn into the line of fire.

And that brought them into Mack Bolan's sights.

Don Pendleton's Mack Bolan®
Patriot Play

A GOLD EAGLE BOOK FROM
WORLDWIDE®

TORONTO • NEW YORK • LONDON
AMSTERDAM • PARIS • SYDNEY • HAMBURG
STOCKHOLM • ATHENS • TOKYO • MILAN
MADRID • WARSAW • BUDAPEST • AUCKLAND

First edition March 2008

ISBN-13: 978-0-373-61522-3
ISBN-10:   0-373-61522-1

Special thanks and acknowledgment to
Mike Linaker for his contribution to this work.

PATRIOT PLAY

Whomever goes to fight monsters should
take care not to become a monster himself.
> —Friedrich Nietzsche,
> 1844–1900

I will fight the monsters on their own terms, facing
them with fire and blood, but I refuse to become
one of them, and will retain my humanity and stand
before them as a man.
> —Mack Bolan

For those who fight the good fight

PROLOGUE

The Federal Reserve banks in Boston, Cleveland and Atlanta were the first to be hit, and the method for each assault was the same. Plain panel trucks were driven as close as possible to the buildings, then the drivers left the vehicles and walked to waiting cars. These vehicles drove away and, once clear, the large explosive bombs inside the panel trucks were detonated by remote control. The totally unexpected attacks on Federal Reserve buildings caught everyone by surprise. There was no kind of warning. No time to evacuate. The explosions were large and created serious damage to the exteriors of the buildings, despite the protective concrete barriers that had become part of city architecture. With each explosion the barriers were severely damaged, and the powerful blasts hurled deadly chunks and smaller fragments toward the buildings. Unknowing members of the public were caught in the horrific blasts and so were security personnel within the blast radius.

Boston had twelve dead, and twice that suffered serious wounding.

In the aftermath of the Cleveland attack the toll was higher. Fourteen dead and close to thirty suffered wounds that ranged from minor to critical.

Atlanta sustained twenty dead. The number of wounded totaled eighteen. The Atlanta dead included eight schoolchildren on a field trip.

All three blast sites were quickly cordoned off so that police and emergency services could gather evidence. The FBI and Homeland Security became initially embroiled in a territorial standoff in Boston. In the meantime the Atlanta Homeland Security team established a swift command center, and their preliminary examination of the epicenter of the blast revealed very little as to who might have been responsible. Twelve hours after the explosions there was little evidence coming from the three sites to enable any of the agencies to issue anything of value.

The remains of the panel trucks had been meticulously gone over by everyone involved—FBI, Homeland Security and the CSI teams from each of the three cities. The CIA ran checks to see if there were any similar scenarios. Nothing was found to link the vehicles to any organization or group. It was found that the license plates were phony, created for the job, as were the plates on the cars that picked up the truck drivers. Locating the escape cars proved to be futile. Again it was surmised that false plates were changed soon after the vehicles had fled the scene.

The panel trucks had been stripped down to the bare bones before setting out for the banks. The engines had been made so anonymous it was difficult to establish where they had come from in the first instance. They had been built from various spare parts and were not even the standard engines for the model of truck used. Someone had spent a great deal of time and effort to custom rig every part so there was little chance of identifying them. The effort expended on disguising the vehicles indicated intelligent thinking and a group with a sound financial base.

The explosives used to create the bombs carried by the trucks were identified as ammonium nitrate, an agricultural fertilizer that was available at hundreds of retailers across the country, and nitromethane, a highly volatile motor-racing fuel. The motor fuel, though not as common as a retail commodity, was available in large quantities. The mixture of the two elements was a familiar one to the FBI. Designated ANFO, it had been used before in the manufacture of explosives. The fragmented detonators, located after diligent searches and painstaking reconstruction, were also found to have been built by hand from raw materials. From the blast radius it was estimated that the bombs would have been in the region of three thousand pounds in weight.

Three days following the attacks on the FRB buildings, similar attacks took place in three more cities. This time, though the locations differed, the destruction was just as horrific. In Detroit, Newark and Norfolk, panel trucks in the parking lots of large department stores were detonated. The blasts tore up through the underground garages and caused the collapse of crowded shopping floors. There were more deaths and severe injuries. The subsequent investigations revealed identical vehicle and bomb specifications. As with the three original bombings, very little steady evidence emerged.

TEN DAYS LATER in Washington, The President of the
United States dropped the last of the reports on the
bombing incidents on his Oval Office desk and sighed
wearily. His mood was a mix of anger and revulsion,
and a growing frustration. Nothing he had read in the
many documents even hinted at forward progress in the
ongoing investigations. The only consistent theme running through the reports was the clashes between agencies: the disagreement when it came to sharing
information, each agency jealousy guarding its own
turf, reluctant to divulge sources and, maintaining policy, not trusting the others in case there were security
leaks. The President made a mental note to once again
instruct the groups to cooperate with one another, knowing even as he did that the complexity of the matter
would only increase once the heads of the agencies dug
in their heels. CIA, FBI, Homeland Security would all
claim that sharing information was not a wise move
because it jeopardized their sources and protocol demanded these remained within the particular depart-
ments of each agency. The same would be pleaded by
other agencies and they would all climb on the same old
carousel. They would quote precedents and legalities,
the intrusion into human rights, losing sight of the big
picture. Coupled to that was the increasing public
clamor for the government to do something to stop the
terrible events taking place. The media, the President's
detractors, even his staunchest political allies, were asking the same questions: what was the administration
doing? Why hadn't the people behind the attacks been
tracked down?

   Alone in his office the President was asking himself
the same questions. In truth, he had no answer. If the

combined agencies were unable to track down the callous murderers of U.S. citizens, where did *he* go? And if they came up with suspects? He knew the lengthy processes that would have to be gone through before anyone dared move on the evidence.

The President was left with his final card. It was one he had played on other occasions, when the lawful and traditional agencies found themselves facing a blank wall, and it had always returned him with a winning hand. America's commander in chief saw his way clear. The people behind the attacks had showed they held themselves above both the law and had no conscience when it came to killing Americans on their own soil. They played by their rules, ignoring the suffering they caused and as yet had made no kind of statement as to why they were committing their evil acts. The President needed to counter the threat with his own force. A force that would play by *their* rules. He had no concerns about playing down and dirty. The people behind the attacks had set the agenda. Now they could reap what they had sown. The President's duty was clear. He had to protect American lives, and at the moment he was failing to do that. It troubled him greatly. He grieved for the dead and their families and for the country he had sworn to defend. The time had come for decisive, no-wavering solutions.

The President picked up one of his telephones and punched in a number. He heard it ring out. It was answered immediately.

"Good morning, Hal," the President said. "I need to speak with you urgently."

CHAPTER ONE

Stony Man Farm, Virginia

Mack Bolan leaned back from examining the spread of photographs on the conference table. He had no words to express what he was feeling at that precise moment. At the head of the table Hal Brognola remained silent. There was no need for words. The stark reality of the images said it all. Men, women, and especially the children, spelled out the sheer horror that had been visited on them. Bolan forced his gaze from the photographs to look at the wall screens where video footage of the first three attacks was playing. Aaron Kurtzman, Stony Man's chief of cybernetics, had obtained official footage taken by the FBI, CIA and HS. It was distressing video, not sanitized for TV news channels. The silent viewers in the War Room steeled themselves as the presentations rolled across the screens. This was not the first time Bolan and Brognola had watched this kind of graphic horror. They were both experienced in seeing the results of human atrocities, yet each new experience hit hard. Professionals they might have been, but foremost they were caring human beings, and the suffering inflicted on the dead and the injured would not be dismissed lightly, if at all.

"Aaron is still collating intel he's gathered from various agency databases," Brognola said. He was forced to clear his throat and repeat the latter part of his sentence as he was still affected by what he had been watching. "Jesus, Mack, who are these bastards?"

"We'll find out, Hal." Bolan was scanning the spread of images on the table.

"I can tell the Man you're on board."

Bolan nodded. "You can tell him that whoever these people are they're the walking dead men. No compromises on this, Hal."

"Amen to that," Brognola said. "I got the distinct feeling that under all the protocol the President is well and truly pissed off."

"TELL ME you've got *something* for me, Aaron."

Kurtzman swung his wheelchair away from his workstation and rolled it across the Computer Room to his steaming coffeepot. He topped up his mug, taking a swallow of the rich brew before he spoke.

"You do realize just how much data I've had to go through to get your break? CIA. FBI. HS. Local PDs. Every damned security and law department offer different views. There's more speculation than Imelda Marcus had shoes. And all I have to do is pick you somewhere to start."

Bolan absorbed the minor rant with good grace. Aaron Kurtzman's sardonic nature was ingrained. It was as much a part of the man as the coffee he imbibed in vast quantities. Grouchy he might be, but Kurtzman was the most skilled and professional cybertech Mack Bolan had ever known. He ran his department and his cyberteam 24/7 with consummate ease, though he liked to make out he was understaffed and denied access to quality equipment. The truth was, he had the best electronic data gathering and analytical setup in existence. On top of that he was the most accomplished computer expert around. He proved it each time he went to work, employing his own programs to take sneak-and-peek looks into data systems operated by the CIA, FBI, NSA and just about any agency that employed electronic systems. Kurtzman's backdoor incursions were strictly illegal in the lawful world. That did not deter him in the slightest. Missions often depended on having up-to-the-minute data. Lives depended on Kurtzman accessing certain information, so his systems-breaking programs were vital.

"I couldn't find much on the MO of the attackers. They did as much as they could to stay anonymous. No released statements claiming responsibility, which is highly unusual. One of the things these dirtbags love is saying who they are and why they did the deed. This is new. Publicity-shy terrorists."

"There has to be a reason for that."

"I wish I knew what."

"Aaron, anything?"

Kurtzman grunted. He spun his chair to face his workstation, placed his coffee mug on its spot and ran his fingers over his keyboard.

"This," he said.

On one of the larger monitors Bolan saw a blowup of a photograph that had been taken at some gathering in a large hall. On a raised platform a group of men were semi-posed as the picture was taken.

"We are looking at Jerome Gantz. Officially he's a suspected bomb maker. Four or five years ago he was mixed up with various radical groups. The FBI tried to tie him in with a couple of bombings, but there was no real evidence and then someone handling the case screwed up and Gantz walked. Then he fell off the map. Most likely he hired out his skills but stayed out of sight. I was running some checks on current home-grown antiestablishment groups. I came across some press photographs, and there was Gantz. That's him. The one losing his hair and talking to the tall guy in the business suit with the eye patch and limp arm."

"Who is he?"

"The one who could make this our clincher," Kurtzman said. "Liam Seeger." He waited for Bolan to make a connection.

"Should I know Seeger?"

"If you're into militia groups. Seeger is head honcho of…"

"The Brethren."

"Give the man a prize."

"How old is the photo?"

"Two months," Kurtzman said. "Taken at a Brethren rally in Jersey City. Seeger made one hell of a speech tearing into the administration. He accused the government of being more concerned about interfering with foreign regimes than problems at home. He threatened a wakeup call that would show how ineffective the administration is. Something that would show Americans they needed to rethink who should be governing the country."

"Gantz at Seeger's rally. You tie that in to the recent attacks?"

"It was Gantz's early bomb construction detail I remembered. Same mix as now. It was stated in FBI files that Gantz liked to make his own explosives. Ammonium nitrate and nitromethane. Designated ANFO. And background detail said he preferred to construct his own detonators. The FBI believed it was his signature."

Bolan studied the images.

Jerome Gantz.

Liam Seeger.

The Brethren.

It read like an unholy Trinity.

Or was it a coincidence?

Bolan was not a great believer in chance favoring such a coming together. He did believe that the combination needed to be checked out, if only to eliminate them or to prove they *were* tied together.

"I'll need everything you can get me on them," Bolan said. "This is too much to ignore, Aaron. Have any of the other agencies flagged this yet?"

Kurtzman shook his head. "I pulled this together from different sources. Nobody picked it up because the agency types are playing true to form and not sharing information."

"Keep it in-house for now. Give me a chance to go in without having to look over my shoulder. And in the meantime keep looking."

"You've got it, Mack. Give me an hour to pin down locations and numbers. I'll give you names to go with the faces in the picture, as well."

IN HIS QUARTERS Bolan geared up, packing clothing in one bag and his weapons in a larger, leather holdall. He phoned Barbara Price and she set in motion orders for paperwork and credentials that would identify Matt Cooper as a Justice Department special agent. With Bolan's alter ego already in the system it took only a short time for his package to be produced. He was on his way back from the armory, with extra clips of ammunition for his weapons, when Price intercepted him. She held a manila envelope out to him.

"Your secret agent kit, Mr. Cooper," she said, falling in step beside him. "Tell me something—do you live up to your cover qualifications?"

Bolan smiled. "Miss Price, what do *you* think?"

"Me? Oh, above and beyond the call of duty from what I can recall."

"Personal recommendations always welcome."

Brognola was approaching from the other end of the corridor. "You two better come with me," he said without a trace of humor.

Bolan fell in beside the big fed, Price close behind.

Brognola was fumbling in the pocket of his jacket, pulling out a pack of antacid tablets. He eased one from the pack and put it in his mouth, which meant he was fretting. He led them to Kurtzman's Computer Room where the cyberteam was gathered at their boss's workstation. There was someone else Bolan recognized— Carl Lyons, commander of Able Team.

As Bolan stepped up to the workstation Lyons glanced up.

"Carl."

"Looks like I called in on a bad day," Lyons said.

"This came in a short time ago," Kurtzman told them.

On the wall monitor was a replay of an earlier TV report. The picture was of a fenced compound, identified by the rolling text at the bottom of the picture. It was a National Guard depot in southwest Arizona. The metal mesh gates had been breached and when the camera panned around it showed smoking buildings and bodies lying on the ground.

"Two of our anonymous panel trucks," Brognola said, "drove in through the gates and up to the buildings. Only a four-man squad of National Guardsmen manned the site. When they confronted the trucks they were cut down by autofire. The panel trucks must have been left outside each of the storage buildings and set off remotely. Vehicles were stored inside one building. The second was the armory. Both were razed to the ground by the truck bombs. It's already been established that the explosive used was the same as the previous attacks."

"Makes you wonder where they'll hit next," Huntington Wethers said.

"Hard to figure," Carmen Delahunt replied.

"Is there a deliberate plan to show they can go for anything they choose," Brognola asked, "or are these just random hits?"

"Hey, look at this."

They all turned at Akira Tokaido's call. He indicated a TV news flash. Two more attacks had taken place at National Guard bases. One in Oregon, the next in Nevada. The strikes had the same MOs as the Arizona site.

"The only difference here is the fact they gunned down their victims rather than letting the bombs kill them," Bolan said.

He turned to Price. "Is transport ready?"

"Mack," Lyons said, "you got room for a partner?"

"Barbara, can you organize some more cover documents?" Bolan queried. "For both of us in case we need to stop anyone being nosy."

"Go to it," Brognola said. "Carl, you up for this?"

"Able's on stand-down. I've nothing that can't wait."

"This could be a hot one."

Lyons smiled. "You know how I hate the cold, Hal."

CHAPTER TWO

Bolan was behind the wheel of the black Crown Victoria from the Farm's motor pool. Lyons had the Stony Man file on his lap, going through the mass of documentation Kurtzman had prepared. He had been reading for the first hour of their drive, saying very little and falling silent as he went through the photographs of the bombing victims. Bolan left him to absorb the data until Lyons was ready to talk.

"The Brethren looks to be more organized than most groups. Upmarket compared to your usual militia-survivalist gathering."

"Yeah. They have a lot to say. Their rallies pull in big crowds. Seeger is known as something of a recluse. He only shows his face in public at meetings, but he has his finger on the public's pulse. He knows exactly what to say to get a positive reaction. From what Aaron dug up, the Brethren always come away with sizable cash donations."

"I guess it has to be said there are a lot of unhappy people out there," Lyons commented.

"We have dead and injured people now," Bolan said, and left it at that.

Kurtzman's data had provided them with a location for Jerome Gantz. The man hadn't been active in the past few years. He'd either quit the anarchy business or he had simply been keeping his profile under the radar.

If Gantz hadn't been building bombs, where did he get his money from? Kurtzman posed. According to his financial records, Gantz had been living on welfare and handouts—which wouldn't enable the man to afford his current home. The cyber warrior vowed to dig deeper.

Gantz had rented a house on the Atlantic shore of Massachusetts just outside a small hamlet called Tyler Bay. The area was well off the main highway, a slumbering spot that once had a thriving fishing industry. Large fishing fleets now dominated the business. Over the more recent years Tyler Bay's family-owned boats had failed to stand up to the competition. There were no more than half a dozen boats left. The town lived off the catches from the small fleet, tourism and associated businesses.

Bolan and Lyons arrived in midafternoon. The narrow road leading into the town brought them to a point overlooking Tyler Bay, which had an Old World charm to it. The road led through the town with a few cross streets intersecting.

"Nice enough spot if you want to stay hidden," Lyons said.

Bolan didn't respond. He drove the car down the slope that brought them into Tyler Bay along the main street. Beyond the town the Atlantic stirred restlessly. A steady breeze pushed the gray water toward shore, frothing whitecaps on the waves. Rooms had been booked for them at the Tyler Grand Hotel. It was set in the middle of town, on a cross street, and Bolan drove off the street and eased the vehicle into a slot on the hotel parking lot.

Misty rain was starting to drift in from the curving bay. When Bolan opened his door he felt the chill in the air. Lyons turned up the collar of his jacket and grimaced at his companion.

"I'll take Malibu anytime," he rumbled.

Bolan popped the trunk and removed his bag, slinging the one with their weapons over his shoulder. There was a second, smaller bag alongside Lyons's, which held a big-screen laptop. They made their way to the front entrance and up the wooden steps leading inside. The lobby was spacious, and looked as if it came from an earlier era, but the bright-eyed young woman behind the desk was definitely from the twenty-first century.

"Welcome to the Tyler Grand, gentlemen. Would you be Mr. Cooper and Mr. Benning?"

"Yes, ma'am," Lyons said, his mood lightening for the first time since leaving Stony Man.

The woman smiled. "Miss, actually."

"Don't mind him," Bolan said. "He's really just an old-fashioned boy."

"Straight off the farm?"

"In a manner of speaking."

The woman pushed the register across the desk for them to sign in. She watched Bolan sign and write Washington in the home column. Lyons did the same.

"Vacation?" she asked.

"We just needed to get out of the city," Lyons said.

He patted his bag. "And take some pictures and write an article on Massachusetts for our magazine."

"Sounds interesting."

"You'd be surprised how city dwellers enjoy reading about places like Tyler Bay."

The woman handed them keys. "Really? Oh, nothing happens here. Now you go up the stairs to the first landing, turn left along the corridor. Is there anything you need?"

"Pot of fresh coffee for two would be nice," Bolan said.

"I'll have it sent up to your room, Mr. Cooper." The woman found herself staring into Bolan's blue eyes. A faint flush colored her cheeks for some reason. "About ten minutes? Will that be satisfactory?"

"Fine," Bolan said, smiling gently.

BOLAN LEFT HIS DOOR open while Lyons took his main bag to his room, then returned with the laptop.

"That was a fast move, Mack."

"Sorry?"

"That girl at the desk was hooked."

Bolan shook his head. "Carl, are you developing a wild imagination?"

Lyons grunted and crossed to the oak desk near the room's window, which overlooked the street. He unzipped the bag and took out the laptop and a compact color printer. When Stony Man personnel had booked the rooms, they had asked for ones equipped with Internet access. Surprisingly the Tyler Grand had them in all rooms. Lyons connected the laptop and printer and opened the e-mail.

"I'll check with Aaron," Lyons said. "See if he has a data update."

Bolan stowed the bag holding their weapons in the wardrobe, then opened his clothing bag and took out the slim leather folder that rested on top. Inside were sheets of paper with the Stony Man-created *American Routes* logo on the top, the magazine he and Lyons supposedly wrote for. He placed them on the writing table, along with a few pens and a compact digital camera.

Lyons watched him. "Very professional."

"In case anyone gets curious."

"Uh-huh. You mean like Little Miss on the desk."

"Like covering our backs. Small town, Carl. Visitors are fair game. Something to talk about and talk can get overheard."

"CHIEF HARPER? IT'S ME. Those two guests just booked in. They're in rooms 8 and 12. Cooper and Benning. What do *I* think? Something about them doesn't gel. I mean, they're supposed to be writers for some travel magazine but I don't know. Very assured. Confident. To be honest I think you should keep an eye on them. They're in a black late-model Crown Victoria. It's parked in the hotel lot. Yes, I'll let you know if I find out anything else."

The young woman replaced the handset. As she did a teenage girl walked by the desk, carrying a tray with a pot of coffee and cups.

"Room 8?" the girl asked.

"That's right, Lana."

LYONS SCANNED THE TEXT from Kurtzman. He was about to call Bolan over when there was a knock on the room door. The coffee had arrived.

"You ordered coffee, sir?" Lana asked as Bolan opened the door.

The soldier reached for the tray. "Thanks. Carl, you got any cash?"

"No need, sir, it's my pleasure. Enjoy your coffee." Lana reached out to pull the door closed as she moved away.

Bolan placed the tray on a side table and poured two cups. He took one to Lyons, who pointed at the message on the laptop:

Been running satellite sweeps. Checked Gantz's place. The house overlooks the beach. A motor cruiser has been anchored in the bay near the house for the last few hours. Managed to get visuals of the cruiser's name. Running a check on who owns it as a precaution. Still pulling in any intel I can find to do with the Brethren and any names that come up, especially Gantz. Feed you whatever looks interesting.

Lyons erased the message, then pulled up a two-page document that featured Tyler Bay. The article was in unedited text and ended halfway along a sentence. He left it on the screen.

"So what do we do now?"

"Wait until dark then check out the Gantz place," Bolan said. "Hey, this coffee is okay."

Lyons had wandered over to the window, cup in hand. He leaned forward as something caught his attention. "Mack, take a look at this."

Bolan joined him and they watched a blue-and-white police cruiser roll into the hotel parking lot and stop next to the Crown Vic. Bolan saw the uniformed driver lean across and tap into his onboard computer.

"He's checking us out," Lyons said. "Either Tyler Bay has a superefficient force, or we are being checked for other reasons."

"I'm guessing Little Miss has been reporting in."

Lyons grinned. "Sorry, Mack, looks like she isn't lusting for your body after all."

"Another disappointment I'll have to live with," Bolan said.

Lyons stayed at the window and watched until the Tyler Bay Police Department cruiser backed up, swung onto the street and drove off. He remained where he was, and his patience was rewarded when the cruiser did a U-turn and parked farther along the quiet street.

"He's staking us out."

"Let's give him a long wait," Bolan said. "Won't be dark for a few hours and we aren't going to leave until it is."

"IT'S JOHNSON on the radio for you, Chief."

Jason Harper, the town's chief of police, pushed aside the report he was reading. "Patch him through, Edgar."

He pressed the button on his desk set. "Go ahead, Scotty."

"I've been sitting here for nearly five hours, Chief, and those guys haven't moved. Can hardly see the damn hotel anymore. It's dark and the fog's rolling in real fast from the bay. You want me to stay on?"

Harper checked his watch. "Give it another half hour, Scotty, then you can go home."

"Okay, Chief. See you in the morning."

Harper figured he'd done his duty where the newcomers were concerned. It looked as if they were what they claimed to be. The check on their vehicle had linked them to the *American Routes* magazine based in Washington. Maybe their article would stir enough interest in the town to pull in a few more tourists. Lord knew Tyler Bay could do with them. There wasn't much else to the place now. The few boats that still fished the local waters didn't bring in much money and once they quit… Harper didn't like to think about that day.

He leaned back in his seat, hearing the creak of the frame. He locked his fingers behind his head and stared across his cluttered office. The office and its contents, including himself, needed a damn good overhaul, Harper thought. Hell, the whole building needed an overhaul. The place had been around since the 1950s and that was a long time. Not that much ever happened in Tyler Bay. A tired little town, slowly fading away. Harper had been in charge of law and order for twenty years, and the department remained the same as it always had. He and his small force went through their routine day after day, though Harper sometimes wished something might happen just to break the monotony. He knew that was nothing more than wishful thinking. The folk who inhabited the town were decent and law-abiding, and he didn't want anything to happen that might bring harm to them. There hadn't been a major, or—come to think of it—a minor criminal incident since Homer Sprule had taken his shotgun and threatened a guy from the IRS when there had been a mix-up about tax assessment. It turned out there were two Homer Sprules in the county, and the IRS had sent the inspector to the wrong address. Harper chuckled when he recalled that incident. It came to him that had been more than eight years ago. He sighed. Some hot town, Tyler Bay.

He pushed to his feet and reached for his hat. Passing through the main office he called out to the night deputy that he was going home and if anything came up needing his attention that's where he would be. Outside he zipped his uniform leather jacket, turning up the collar. He could feel the damp fog against his face as he crossed to his parked department SUV. Once inside he fired up the powerful engine and turned out of the parking area. He flicked on his lights and turned up the radio so he could keep a check on anything coming in. With only four cruisers to patrol the town and surrounding county, Harper wasn't expecting even a trickle, let alone a flood. He expected just another Tyler Bay Thursday night.

HARPER DECIDED TO STOP and have something to eat. If he didn't it would mean he'd have to get himself something after he got home. The thought did not appeal to him. Harper had fended for himself since his wife had died seven years earlier. He'd managed okay, but when he worked late he couldn't face cooking a meal, so it was easier to head to the diner on Main Street.

The diner had only a couple of customers in one of the booths. Harper acknowledged them as he made his way to the counter. He preferred sitting there because it gave him the chance to see Callie Rinehart. She was a special lady in Harper's opinion. Very special. Redhaired, with striking green eyes and a laugh that hit the spot every time he heard it. Her husband had skipped out on her three years back, and the only time she'd heard from him again was in the form of divorce papers from somewhere in Nevada. She and Harper had first got together at the Tyler Bay Founders' Day celebration twelve months ago. Since then they had formed a cozy relationship. Neither had made any definite commitment. They went out, spent time either at his or her place, and took things on a day-to-day basis. It suited them both. Work time was erratic for him and Callie, so they used what time they had available. Like tonight.

Harper climbed on the stool he always used and waited for Callie. He smiled when she appeared, carrying the large china mug she kept for him. He watched her fill the mug with steaming black coffee and place it in front of him.

"Chief."

"Callie."

She smiled. At thirty-six she was an attractive woman. Harper was fascinated by her facial structure. High cheekbones, a wide, generous mouth and the most even white teeth he had ever seen. There were times he questioned why she could be attracted to a forty-two-year-old man, admittedly not at his physical best. He didn't question it too deeply. He considered himself a lucky man to have been blessed by knowing two exceptional women in his life.

"And they say the art of conversation died the day television was invented."

"Not true, ma'am."

She touched his hand where it lay on the counter. Even that quiet gesture made him feel better. "You want me to stop by later?" she asked. "I'll bring apple pie."

"Shame on you, girl, tempting an officer of the law."

"Whipped cream to go with it."

"Damn, there goes a twenty-year unblemished record."

"I didn't realize you could be bought so easily."

"We all have our price."

Callie turned and called through his order. He always had the same when he came in at night. Steak and eggs, with fried potatoes and beans. It was his first meal since coming on duty. He seldom ate during the day, not having the patience to leave the office or to break off a patrol.

A few more customers came in while Harper ate, so he didn't get much more time to spend with her. He heard someone mention the fog was getting thicker. He finished his meal and had another coffee. Callie took his money and brought his change.

"See you later, Chief."

"You watch that fog when you leave," he said.

"Going straight home?"

He nodded. "Yeah, I need to tidy up before you call."

"No need to do anything special just for me."

"I just need to clear out all the beer cans and fast-food cartons."

Harper gave her a wave and left the diner. The fog was getting thicker. The illumination from the street lighting made his SUV glisten where the moisture from the fog had layered the bodywork. As he unlocked the vehicle, Harper heard the mournful sound of a foghorn. Glancing to the east side of town, he caught a glimpse of the hazy lighthouse beam coming from the point.

He had just reversed from the curb, turning the SUV around, when his radio burst into life.

"Chief? Chief, this is Edgar."

Harper picked the mike off the hook. "Go ahead."

"I just had a call from out the point. Someone swears they heard gunshots coming from where that fellar Gantz lives."

CHAPTER THREE

"Cruiser's gone," Lyons said.

He had watched the police vehicle move off and head through the intersection. Lyons had remained at the window for a few more minutes just to be certain. Both he and Bolan were dressed in dark clothing, carrying their handguns under zipped jackets, while Bolan carried a small carryall that held his night-vision monocular. Slung from Lyons's shoulder was a compact case that resembled a digital camera. Inside was a GPS unit that held the coordinates they would need to pinpoint Gantz's home.

They left Bolan's room and made their way down to the lobby. Little Miss was no longer behind the desk. A male receptionist glanced up as they walked by, then returned to his copy of *Soldier of Fortune*.

Bolan carried the bag with additional weapons, which he deposited in the trunk. Lyons got behind the wheel of the Crown Vic and drove them out of the hotel lot. He passed the GPS unit to Bolan. Kurtzman had provided them with a map that would guide them to the area where Gantz lived. The map became even more helpful as they encountered the fog rolling in from the Atlantic. They had about eight miles to cover once they were clear of the town, as Gantz's house was located on the coast in an area known as Tyler Point.

"Think Gantz will spill what he knows?" Lyons asked.

"He'll spill," was Bolan's reply. He recalled the images in the photographs he'd viewed back at Stony Man. The callous disregard that had been displayed by the group behind the bombings was deeply imprinted in the soldier's mind, and he refused to even attempt to blur them. He wanted them to remain sharp because they were the driving force behind his mission: to locate the bombers and bring them down.

Executioner style.

Bolan used his cell phone to check in with Kurtzman at Stony Man.

"Nothing new for you, Striker. That fog you have down there is delaying any new intel on Gantz's place. Satellites are blocked out."

"Just keep an eye out," Bolan said.

"I've got a trace running now on Gantz's telephone. Nothing yet, but we might pick something up. He might have used his landline to call an associate. If you get close to him, see if he has a cell. More likely to have used that to make an indiscreet call."

"Call you later."

LYONS ROLLED the vehicle off the narrow tarmac road that passed by the Gantz house. He cut the engine and they went EVA. Once they were out of the car, Bolan checked the GPS unit and read the digital display.

"That way."

They followed the directions of the unit, taking care to check the ground. The terrain at this proximity to the coastline could prove to be difficult and more so in the enveloping fog. According to the information received from Kurtzman earlier, the house was set on the edge of the beach and the water. From the tarmac a side road led directly to the house. From the location on the GPS unit they were left of that side road and within a couple hundred feet of the property. He switched off the unit and returned it to Lyons. They moved in the direction of the house.

Bolan, slightly ahead of Lyons, held up a hand to halt them. He dropped to a crouch and used the night-vision monocular to check the area. The green-toned image, surprisingly clear and bright, showed Bolan a large 4x4 vehicle parked at the side of the road. He also pinpointed a man in a long leather coat, cradling a stubby submachine gun in his arms, leaning against the side of the 4x4. Bolan passed the monocular to Lyons. The big ex-cop took a look, then tapped his partner on the shoulder and passed the device back.

"Looks like he's on his own," Bolan said. "But don't take that as gospel."

Though he couldn't see Lyons's face when he spoke, Bolan was sure he was smiling when he said, "Think he'd like some company?"

"Nobody enjoys being out in the cold."

Lyons slipped away.

BOLAN STOWED the monocular in the shoulder case, slung it across his back, then moved in closer to the beach house. He made his move as fast as he could without creating any giveaway sound. He reached the wooden front porch and crossed it to flatten against the wall to the right of the door. He slipped the 93-R from its shoulder holster. Just to his right was a window. Bolan turned toward it. What he saw decided his course of action.

And then the rattle of autofire came from the direction of the 4x4 and Lyons.

From inside the house raised voices reached Bolan. There was muttered conversation; the sound of boots on a wood floor, coming in the direction of the door next to Bolan.

The door was yanked open and an armed figure came into view, a raised MP-5 in his hands.

The gunner came through the door without checking his perimeter. Bolan hit him full in the face with the Beretta. Flesh split and blood welled up immediately. The guy slumped against the door frame, his weapon forgotten in the world of pain that engulfed him. Bolan hit again, harder this time, and the groaning man went to his knees, then flat to the porch as the Executioner caught him around the neck, applied pressure and a hard twist that snapped his spine. Bending over the prone form, Bolan snatched up the MP-5, pushed his Beretta back into its holster, then checked the load for the weapon he had acquired.

Turning, he kicked open the door and stormed into the house, his weapon tracking in on the men standing over the battered and bloodied form of Jerome Gantz. They swung around at his noisy entrance, realizing he wasn't one of their own, and went for their holstered weapons. One of them also raised a handset he was holding and began to yell into it. His commands were drowned by the harsh crackle of the SMG in Bolan's hands. He drove hard bursts into the guy with the handset, then swept the muzzle around and took down another hardman. That left one standing, and he had his handgun clear and opened fire the moment he spotted Bolan. The Executioner, ducking low and breaking to the left, had already moved, forcing the guy to track in again. Down on one knee, Bolan swept the guy aside with a sustained burst that blew the life from his body and slammed him to the floor in a mist of blood.

From outside the house Bolan heard the stutter of an autoweapon. Then a brief pause was followed by the unmistakable boom of Carl Lyons's Colt Python. Two shots rang out before silence fell.

"On the boat. There are more on that boat," someone whispered, the words slurred and spoken by a person in terrible pain. Bolan turned and met the pain-filled eyes of Jerome Gantz. His captors had stripped him to his shorts and tethered him to a wooden kitchen chair using fine wire around his wrists and ankles. Blood was seeping from where the wire had cut deep into his flesh, and the wooden floor around the chair was spattered with blood. Gantz's face and body had been beaten to a bloody wreck. Blood dripped from a baseball bat on the floor close by. The white bone from his shattered left cheek gleamed through the split flesh. His lips were pulped, and bloody teeth hung by shreds from his gums. A bleeding gash lay open on his exposed skull. Livid red marks showed over his ribs and around his knees the flesh looked swollen and pulpy.

"The Brethren?"

All Bolan got was a tired nod from Gantz before the man's head lolled forward against his bloody chest.

A sweep of the open-concept room, which extended from living area to the kitchen, showed that someone had thoroughly trashed the place. Broken items littered the floor; every drawer and cupboard hung open; the furniture in the living area had been overturned. The TV had been tipped to the floor and smashed, and so had a CD player.

Lyons appeared in the doorway, taking a look around the interior before stepping inside. His Colt Python was back in its holster, and he carried an MP-5 he had taken from the outside guard.

"Somebody is really pissed at him," he said, his tone matter-of-fact and holding no trace of pity for Jerome Gantz's condition.

"The Brethren," Bolan said.

"Coop, tell me why we're bothering to save this dirt-bag's life."

Bolan was about to reply when he heard a distant raised voice. It came from the beach side of the house.

Gantz's warning: *On the boat. There are more on that boat.*

Bolan jabbed a finger in the general direction of the rear entrance. "We need to clean house first."

It was enough for Lyons. He followed Bolan toward the door that exited onto the rear porch. The soldier paused for a heartbeat, reached for the handle and jerked the door open. He ducked low, went through and to the right. Lyons was on his heels, moving left away from the lighted rectangle of the open door.

Their exit was accompanied by wild bursts of auto-fire. The rear porch was hit by heavy fire, wood splintering and shredding under the salvos. A window shattered, glass blowing into the house.

The sea breeze that had pushed the fog inland had dispersed a greater part of it on the beach. Both Bolan and Lyons were able to pick out the moving silhouettes of the men behind the guns from where they now lay prone on the sandy beach. Bolan raised himself to a semicrouch and turned his MP-5 on the shooters, his calmly delivered volley cutting a bloody swathe through them, while Lyons's SMG added its own deadly noise. Men went down yelling and screaming until there was none left standing except the single guy tending the inflatable raft that had brought the killing crew to shore. He witnessed the deaths of his partners and decided enough was enough. Turning, he shoved the inflatable through the incoming surf and threw himself on board, struggling to use the single oar. He might have made it if he hadn't pulled the pistol holstered on his hip and fired warning shots in the direction of the beach.

Lyons snapped in a fresh magazine from his confiscated weapon and returned fire. The MP-5's 9 mm slugs shredded the rubber of the inflatable and cored into the shooter's body. He fell back into the deflating folds of the boat and went down with it.

Bolan made his way across the beach. He could just make out the dark bulk of the waiting boat riding the soft Atlantic swell. It showed running lights at bow and stern. He reached for the night-vision monocular and took it from the pouch slung across his back. When he peered into the lens he could see a clearer picture of the cruiser. The dark shape of men moved back and forth.

And the dull gleam of misty light running the length of a gun barrel—a .50-caliber machine gun, was aimed in their direction. Bolan didn't hesitate. He turned and ran in Lyons's direction, hit him side-on and they thumped to the sand an instant before the boat-mounted machine gun opened up. The solid sound of the auto-fire, slightly dulled by the enveloping fog, hammered at the air. The intermittent flash of tracers told Bolan they were being fired at by professionals. The slugs pounded the sand, showering the men as they crawled away from the line of fire. Then the trajectory rose and the fire was hitting the house, pounding its way through the wooden structure, a long and incessant blast of fire that had no other intention than that of rendering the house into a wreck. The bloodied image of Jerome Gantz flashed through Bolan's mind. Whatever had happened to the man before Bolan arrived would now be completed. He had no illusions—the directed gun-fire was intended to make sure Gantz was dead.

Someone was determined to kill the man.

The question was, why?

With everything that had happened it appeared more than likely that Jerome Gantz *had* been the man behind the design and construction of the massive bombs used in the devastating public attacks.

For some currently inexplicable reason Gantz had been singled out for some kind of reprisal action. Torture? A savage beating? For something the Brethren wanted and now that they had failed, the death of Gantz was the final act. The seemingly overt act of destroying his home knowing Gantz was inside and helpless proved that thought.

The hellish beat of the .50-caliber machine gun ceased abruptly. As Bolan raised his head, he heard the rumble of a powerful engine, the throbbing pulse of the screws as they pushed the cruiser away from the shore. He shoved to his feet and grabbed for the monocular, taking a hurried scan of the departing boat. He saw its stern as it disappeared into the fog, and picked out the shape of a man leaning against the stern rail. He was tall, the pale oval of his face indistinct. Bolan did see the cap of white-blond hair above the face. Short cut, almost spiky. It was an image he wasn't about to forget.

The image was lost in the fog, as was the beat of the engine.

Damn. Bolan lowered the monocular and turned to see Lyons impatiently brushing damp sand from his clothing.

The twin beams of powerful spotlights penetrated the shadows, pinpointing the two men. A hard voice broke through the gloom.

"Put down the weapons and raise your hands. I've got a 12-gauge Winchester. Don't do anything that will cause it to go off."

Bolan caught Lyons's stare. His Able Team partner had a look on his face that said it all.

CHIEF HARPER MOVED across the beach, staying to one side of the light coming from his cruiser. He could clearly see the two men facing him. They fit the description of the guests from the hotel he'd received earlier in the afternoon. He kept the shotgun on them as he closed in. It was with some relief he saw them drop their weapons to the sand, keeping their hands in clear sight.

"There more weapons under those jackets? Just in case, open them."

Bolan exposed his Beretta. "We're not going to make any trouble here. Check our IDs and you'll understand."

"IDs for what?"

"Let me pass mine across," Bolan said. "No tricks, Officer."

"It's chief of police. Now what about the ID?"

Bolan used his left hand to unzip the inner pocket of his leather jacket. He fished out the small ID wallet and held it for Harper to see.

"Toss it over."

Bolan did as he was instructed and Harper crouched to pick it up, his eyes never moving from his suspects. He scanned the plastic-coated ID inside. He checked the photo against Bolan. Then he glanced at Lyons. "You got the same?"

"Yes, Chief. I'm Benning. My partner is Cooper."

"Justice Department? Special agents?"

Bolan nodded. "We're working undercover and came here to talk with Jerome Gantz, but it looks like we were a little late."

"Where is Gantz?"

"Inside the house and in a bad way. We interrupted his visitors, who were beating him. Soon as they saw us all hell broke loose."

"That's what I heard?"

"There were more on a boat anchored off the beach," Lyons said. "They hit the house with a .50-caliber machine gun."

"Thought I recognized the sound. It's something you don't forget."

"Chief, we should check to see if Gantz is still alive," Bolan said.

Harper hesitated for a few seconds, then lowered the shotgun. "Go ahead. I need to call for assistance." He held out the wallet for Bolan to take. "I think we need to talk, Special Agent Cooper."

Bolan retrieved the guns he and Lyons had dropped on the beach. He nodded to Harper as he walked by and headed for the bullet-riddled house, Lyons alongside.

"Hell of a start," Lyons muttered.

As soon as they were inside, stepping across the littered floor, they saw Gantz. The man and the chair he was bound to had toppled over. Bolan crouched beside Gantz and checked him out. He had caught a couple of the .50-caliber shells. The large projectiles had ripped his left side open, leaving large and bloody wounds. Blood had already formed a large pool across the wood floor.

"Is he dead?" Lyons asked.

Bolan, checking for vital signs, shook his head. "Still breathing."

"I'll get Harper to call for medical help."

Bolan nodded. He stayed beside the unconscious Gantz for a while, aware that there was little he could do for the man. The bullet wounds had caused severe damage. Even if he was admitted to hospital it was going to take a miracle to keep him alive.

He wandered around the rooms, not even certain what he was looking for. His search failed to turn up a cell phone. Also Gantz wasn't going to leave quantities of his bomb-making ingredients lying around the house. Or even manufacture them on the premises. Vehicles arriving and departing from the area would have been noticed in a quiet town like Tyler Bay, which would explain the hit team coming in from the water.

Gantz would have built his bombs somewhere else, at a spot where regular traffic would be expected. Maybe some kind of industrial site. A place where there would have to be the kind of equipment the panel trucks could be adapted for their intended use. It wouldn't be an easy place to find, considering the number of such sites there were across the country.

Bolan took out his cell phone and contacted the Farm, asking for Kurtzman.

"What's the miracle I'm expected to perform tonight?"

"We're at Gantz's house outside Tyler Bay. He already had visitors, but not the kind who bring a bottle of wine to accompany a meal."

"Understood. Gantz?"

"He'd been tortured when we arrived. We mixed it with the visitors. The upshot is they hit the house with a .50-caliber mounted on that boat you spotted in the bay. They used it to get to Gantz's house. Must have been waiting for dark and the fog to cover their approach. Gantz took a couple of shells. He's still alive but critical."

"Where do I come in?"

"Gantz couldn't have made his bombs here. There has to be a manufacturing site somewhere."

Bolan heard the big man's deep sigh.

"Haystacks and needles just registered," Kurtzman said. "That's a hell of a request."

"I realize that. I'll go through the place here to see if I can turn anything up that might help."

"How about a confession written down and personally signed by Gantz?"

"If I find it, you'll be the first to know. Aaron, patch me through to Hal. And thanks."

"For what? I haven't done anything yet."

"I have faith in you, buddy."

Brognola came on the line. "Is Massachusetts in flames yet?"

"A small part of it is smoking."

"I knew it. Tell me the worst."

Bolan gave a detailed report of the Tyler Bay episode. He made it clear to Brognola that they were attempting to gain further information so he and Lyons could make their next move against the Brethren.

"Gantz name them?"

"He named them, I got the feeling the affair between them is over."

"A .50-caliber round or two is a hell of a way to end a romance."

"Hal, these people weren't about to do it easy."

"So why were they working the guy over if he was with them?" Brognola's tone became irritable.

"A fallout? Maybe he had a change of heart after the bombings. The number of dead and injured might have hit home. He could have been attempting a shakedown. Asking for more money. Threatening the Brethren with exposure if they didn't pay up. We need to ID these people. Hal, we're all making guesses right now."

"Yeah, I know. I wish we could make the right one."

"Early in the game. I understand why you're touchy. We all know the Brethren could stage more bombings before we get to them."

"Yeah, sorry, Striker."

"No apologies needed. I'll touch base later. Right now we have the local law to keep on our team."

"You need any backup just yell."

"Will do."

LYONS CAME FROM OUTSIDE, with a pair of hand cutters Harper had supplied from his vehicle's tool kit. He handed them to Bolan, who severed the wire around

Gantz's limbs, freeing him from the chair. He covered the unconscious man with a blanket. Lyons went back outside as a precaution, prowling the area with the restless energy that never seemed to leave him.

Chief Harper joined Bolan inside the house. "I have my people on the way. They'll seal off the area. And I radioed for an ambulance. It has to come some distance. I called the Coast Guard to check the area. The trouble is, by the time they reach the bay that boat will be long gone. Coast Guard is busy tonight with all this fog."

"Best guess is they'll find that boat empty and drifting."

"My thoughts, too."

"Best we can do is try, Chief."

"How's Gantz doing?"

"Touch and go. Those .50-calibers didn't do him any favors."

Harper eyed the big man, sensing there was a reason he wasn't showing much feeling over Gantz's condition. "Something I should know, Agent Cooper?"

"Tell me about Gantz."

"Not much to tell. He turned up a few months back. This place had been rented out to him for twelve months. He only showed his face in town a few times. All we got from him was he was here to rest after an illness. The man wasn't what you'd call talkative."

"He have any visitors? Did he make trips away from the area?"

"Only a few visitors, but he did make a fair number of trips away from town in that SUV parked out front. You ask a lot of questions, Agent Cooper."

Bolan smiled. "I suppose I do. It's necessary, Chief.

We need to get a line on the people Gantz was involved with."

"And who are these *people?* Not the friendly kind, from what's happened here tonight. Or is this a need-to-know operation?"

"We believe Gantz may have been involved in the recent mass bombings."

"The Federal Reserve banks and the department stores? And those National Guard units?"

"The intel we have is moving more and more toward Gantz being involved."

Harper took a slow look around the room. "Son of a bitch wasn't making the bombs here?"

"Most likely he worked out his details here, then took trips to wherever they actually constructed the packages."

"How did you tie him in?"

"Gantz was involved in making similar kinds of bombs some years ago. Back then he was never convicted, and appears to have been keeping low ever since, but recently he was seen in the company of a radical militia group."

Harper digested the information. "Come to think of it, Gantz did make some of his away trips days before the recent attacks."

"He make any trips out of town since the attacks?"

"His last one was a couple of days ago. Hell, you think he was setting up more bombs?"

"It's what we have to find out, Chief. I'd be grateful if you could arrange for photographs and fingerprints of all the dead. I need to get them to the lab for positive identification."

"I can do that. We might be a small department, but we have the equipment. I'll call for my guy to do it for you."

CHAPTER FOUR

Stony Man Farm, Virginia

The digital and fingerprint images sent from Bolan were in the system, being scanned by the FBI's AFIS recognition program. Kurtzman also had them being scanned by military databases and any other recognition systems he could work into his search. Huntington Wethers was taking his turn watching the scans running across his monitors. It was just over an hour when he got his first hit.

"We got one," he called.

Kurtzman rolled up to Wethers's workstation as a hard copy slid from the printer. He snatched it up and scanned the information.

"There it is," he said. "Henry Jacks. He's done time for assault. Over the past ten years he's been associated with three different militia groups. Guess who he's been with the last three years? The Brethren. He hates the government and doesn't agree with anything they do. He has been quoted as saying *'when we burn you down, it will be a new day for real Americans.'*"

"*His* burning days are over," Wethers said.

"Let me run a check on known associates," Kurtzman said. "We might hit lucky."

It was quickly found that Jacks's two closest friends were both members of the Brethren, and a cross-check revealed they had both died in the assault on Jerome Gantz's Tyler Point home.

Carmen Delahunt, who had been quietly monitoring her data input, called for Kurtzman's attention. "A news service in Washington just received a claim from a group calling itself America the Free. They are saying they are responsible for the recent bombings, and there are more to come."

"New name to me," Kurtzman said.

"I just ran a trace through FBI files," Delahunt said. She was former FBI herself, so her knowledge of their procedures was a great help to Stony Man. "There's no data on such a group. But the information they included in their claim is pretty close to what the FBI has on the bombings."

Kurtzman pondered on that. "Okay, Carmen, you stay on that for a while. See what else you can find on America the Free. There's something odd in this. Let's see if we can dig it up."

Kurtzman relayed the current information to Bolan and advised they were continuing with the identification of the others involved.

Tyler Bay Hotel

ADDITIONAL INFORMATION came through the laptop, and it was Bolan's turn to check the screen when another Brethren connection popped up. He found himself staring at an image that took him back to the Gantz house and the boat retreating into the fog shrouding the bay.

The image stared at him from the screen. A long, lean-featured face. The stare was hard and direct, and above it the hair was pale and cut short. It was the man Bolan had seen at the stern rail. He had been right at the time—it was a face he wouldn't forget. He called Lyons to take a look.

"He's the one I spotted on the boat just as it pulled away. Deacon Ribak. One of the Brethren's top lieutenants. Ex-Army Ranger out of Fort Benning, Georgia. Served thirteen years. Last couple of years his personal politics clashed with the Army's. He refused to change his views and took a discharge a couple of years ago. Joined the Brethren six months later and has been with them ever since. He's a trained professional, Carl. He's seen a lot of hard action." Bolan ran his fingers down the column that detailed Ribak's military career. "One hell of an asset for the Brethren."

"I still don't get why they hit Gantz. What they did screams interrogation. If you want the guy dead, it can be done quick and easy. Unless you want him to tell you something."

There was a knock on the door. Lyons turned and flattened himself against the wall, his Colt Python in his hand, as Bolan crossed the room and cautiously opened the door. Chief Harper stood on the threshold.

"Come in, Chief," Bolan said, more to warn Lyons to stand down.

Harper stepped inside. When Bolan closed the door the cop saw Lyons putting his weapon away.

"Don't tell me you guys sleep with your guns under your pillows."

Bolan smiled. "I keep mine in my hand and one eye open."

"Damned if I don't believe you."

"What can we do for you, Chief?"

"Quit the 'Chief' crap. The name's Jason."

"Coffee?"

Harper nodded. "I feel like I've done a week's shifts in one night."

Lyons handed him a cup. "You mean, this isn't normal for Tyler Bay?"

"Hell, no. If it was, I'd been retired and gone by now. I came to tell you I had a call from county hospital. Gantz is still in surgery. The outlook isn't too good. Apart from the damage those big .50s did, he has broken ribs on both sides of his body and two kneecaps more mush than bone. Lower jaw totally shattered and most of his teeth are gone. That crack on his head split his skull clear open."

"Your officer get anything from him?" Bolan asked.

If Harper thought that was coldhearted he made no comment. He simply shook his head. "Edgar stayed with him all the way to the hospital. Gantz didn't say a thing. Edgar didn't leave his side until they wheeled him into the operating room. He's still there in case Gantz survives. Not that it seems likely."

"Something to look forward to," Lyons said quietly.

Harper rounded on him. "Son, I figure you've had a tough time tonight, but every man deserves a little Christian pity when he's down."

"You think so?" Lyons snapped. "Get out of small-town U.S.A. and smell the real world, Chief."

Bolan stood between them. He put a big hand on Lyons's shoulder. "Doug, go and cool down, okay?" He met Lyons's anger with a calm manner that stood the Able Team leader down. He turned aside and crossed the room to stare out the window.

The soldier faced Harper. "You heard about the bombings and saw the TV reports cut and dried for public viewing. We had the official versions. No hiding the results of those explosions. Every little detail. Men, women and especially the children. Innocent victims. Americans like you and me, Jason. Going about their business and not expecting what happened to them. It doesn't leave us much room for pity when we realize this was done by Americans to Americans. We have to deal with the aftermath, and have done so before. There are times it's hard to distance ourselves. Sometimes we succeed. Other times we don't."

Bolan's quiet explanation had its calming effect on the cop. Harper drew a hand across his tired features, staring into the blue eyes of the big man who seemed to have total control of anything that came his way. He was unaware it was the way Mack Bolan dealt with tangled emotions. The ability to move away from crisis moments and bring his natural skills as a mediator into a tense situation. It served Bolan well. He employed the same emotion to clear his own anger when faced with a mental struggle.

Over his years of conflict he had learned long ago there were times he needed to detach himself. Not to completely forget the evil his enemies employed, but to put them on standby while he refreshed his mind and body. The things he had seen he would never fully forget. That was an impossibility even for the Executioner. It was not something he wanted to forget. As long as he had his memories of the terrible things witnessed in the past, he remained strong for his battles in the future. Mack Bolan was human. A caring human being. He understood the deep and dark acts his enemies were capable of. He was also aware of his own strengths, which kept him fighting his War Everlasting.

Harper glanced across to where Lyons stood at the window, shoulders hunched and taut as he struggled to contain his anger. "Could be maybe I have been here in Tyler Bay too long. Backwater town. Nothing much happens. Worse thing about it is, I like it that way." He looked at Bolan. "Hell of an admission for a professional cop."

"You keep it that way, Jason. So we can all remember there are places like Tyler Bay. That there are still sane and safe places in the middle of the madness. That's something we all need to hang on to."

"I guess so." Harper went across to Lyons. "Rough night for us all, son. Best excuse I can come up with right now."

Lyons turned to face him. "No sweat, Chief. I blow hot too fast sometimes."

"Way I hear it, you got more right than anyone to do just that."

Incoming mail made itself heard on the laptop. Bolan opened the message.

Boat was on a charter from a marine rental company up the coast. It was paid for with plastic. I accessed the details. It was charged to a company in Philadelphia. South Star Investments. Operated by a guy called Arnold Petrie. Hope you are sitting down for next piece of info. It took me some time unraveling all the strings but I came up with a name that rang dim and distant bells. Ran it again until a name came through. Thin link, but the guy fronting the Philly company has a connection, albeit skinny, to the Eric Stahl Corporation. You owe me big-time, big guy.

IN THE MORNING, following breakfast, Bolan and Lyons checked out and drove to a final meet with Chief Harper.

"I was going to give you a call," Harper said as they walked into the station house.

"Good or bad call?" Bolan asked.

"I figure it depends how you feel on the subject. I just spoke with my officer at County Hospital. Gantz died around 2:00 a.m."

"Can't say I'm heartbroken. Not after what the guy did."

"I guess not," Harper said. "Bad way to die though." He glanced at Lyons. "No offense meant, Agent Benning."

Lyons shrugged. "You sow what you reap," he said, and that piece of philosophy got him a puzzled look from Bolan.

"I got the number you gave me," Harper said. "If anything comes up I'll pass it along. Likewise if anyone comes asking about Gantz. By the way, I've got the house sealed off if any other agencies show up. Like you told me, I'll refer them to your contact." Harper reached down and opened a drawer in his desk. "Almost forgot. One of my deputies found this in the pocket of one of Gantz's jackets." He held out a plastic bag containing a slim cell phone. "You must have interrupted his visitors before they made a full search of the house. Think it might be useful?"

"We'll know that after I send it to our people." Bolan held out his hand. "Missed it myself. Appreciate your help, Jason."

"Any time, guys. Tyler Bay always likes to give visitors a welcome." He grinned. "Your kind of visitors, I mean."

"You sure as hell did that, Chief," Lyons said.

"Take care," Harper called as the two walked out of his office.

Watching them go, Harper shook his head. Some night, he thought, then realized he'd forgotten all about his date with Callie. He grabbed his hat and hotfooted it to the diner.

CHAPTER FIVE

Liam Seeger liked to believe he had been born a rebel, despite being born into a wealthy family. Since early childhood he had fought against authority, and as the years passed he'd developed this persona until it was like a second skin. He joined any group if it had a hint of being radical. In school, then university—those years had been his best—he battled the establishment wherever it existed, doing everything he could to embarrass it and his family. He had only been twenty-three when he became involved in a subversive movement that saw conspiracy in all aspects of government policy. He read articles, he watched documented evidence and he spoke to antiestablishment figures, steeping himself in the lore. His conversion to becoming a dedicated antiestablishment figure came during marches and rallies that denounced government policies and the fragmentation of America. Seeger saw this happening across the country. Dissatisfaction. Mistrust. The betrayal of the nation by a cynical and manipulative administration that ran rife through all levels of society.

His own struggle against the administration became personal when he was involved in a violent demonstration against America's foreign policy. During the physical struggle against an overwhelming police presence, someone fired a gun and the police responded. Seeger was hit when a riot shotgun was discharged. He took part of the blast in his face and left shoulder and arm. The aftermath was that he lost his left eye from the injury and his arm became partially disabled from the wound. Worse he developed an antisocial attitude and became a recluse. He ran his battle against *them* from the basement of his house. The authorities closed ranks against his claim for personal injury, and his claim for compensation was thrown out of court. It was not for the money. It was the principal of the matter and to simply prove to Seeger that his theories were justified. The attitude of the establishment demonstrated to him that he had been correct all along. The result catalyzed his struggle against them, and he threw himself into aligning himself with groups working along the same lines. It brought him into contact with diverse members of the antiestablishment community. Seeger met them, heard their stories and threw himself fully into the struggle. He created the Brethren from a small, struggling militia group, using the not-inconsiderable money that had come to him after the early deaths of his parents. He gained more money when he sold off the family tool-and-die company and plowed it into building his reclusive home in the Colorado mountain country and establishing a permanent base for the Brethren in even more isolated Colorado high country.

As far as Seeger was concerned, the country was becoming a shadow of its former self. Pride in America was receding. So much was happening. America was waging a struggle with itself; the greed for money against the struggling lower classes. Against a powerful and increasingly repressive federal authority that had abandoned the nation to further its own global-militaristic agenda. Instead of looking after Americans the government machine reached out to dominate the world with its military actions and its need for oil. It silenced its critics. Smothered protest and manipulated the media. Liam Seeger, by the time he was in his forties, had become a man the antiestablishment groups listened to. From his residence in Colorado, standing in splendid isolation, Seeger was the head of an amalgamation of groups that now came included beneath the Brethren umbrella. Formed as the Praetorian Guard of militia groups, the Brethren showed the way for other groups to follow. He had recruited well, choosing only people who held not only his beliefs, but with the same passion. Using his natural skills at oratory and organization, Seeger made the Brethren a group to be envied. His persuasive skills kept donations flowing in. The creed of the group was assertive action, not the sterile bleating that came from other militia groups. Seeger had formed the Brethren to actually do something positive to destabilize the government.

In the early days the Brethren carried out low-key operations against federal targets. They were small and more of an irritant at first. But then the Brethren's strike teams hit out at larger targets. They stole equipment and arms. Seeger sought and recruited men with professional skills that would become vital when his long-term operation became ready to launch. It was big, ambitious enough to create the situation that would lead to a massive rejection of federal authority, and if it went to plan, oust the government by showing it was helpless when it came to protecting the American public.

The deeper he went into his intentions the harder Seeger worked to bring it to fruition. He saw a desperate need to hit out at the establishment, to split it wide open and to make it look ineffective in front of the American public. He was aware that what he was planning would become nonnegotiable. Once the operation actually got under way there would be no turning back. It would be a one-way street. Full commitment would be expected from everyone involved. He received this assurance from his people, and that solid confirmation gave him the confidence to move ahead.

The plan took many months to conceive and move forward. There were people to put in place, covers to establish. He had to recruit specialists who would help to create the tools the Brethren needed to go ahead with the planned strikes.

A bonus came in the form of an anonymous benefactor who gave his support through an intermediary named Harry Brent. From what Brent explained, the benefactor hated the government with a passion. He would do what he could to aid the Brethren. He had contacts that would help bolster the group's continuing need for finance. This was demonstrated by the first of a number of donations of diamonds from a source in West Africa. Brent explained that the diamonds had been obtained cheaply because the source was dealing illegally. Through Brent's continuing brokerage the diamonds were sold for a considerably higher sum. The infusion of such a large amount of cash realized Seeger's dream of his planned attacks to be able to come sooner rather than later.

The attacks, which would result in death and injury on U.S. streets, did nothing to quell Seeger's intentions. The sacrifice of a few to benefit the many was not a new concept. It had happened before and would again. The dead could rest in the knowledge they had helped to wrench the future of a nation from the hands of a repressive and heartless government.

Through Brent, Seeger's benefactor had been taken off guard when he first heard of Seeger's plan. He came around to accepting it very quickly though when Seeger expanded its potential. The benefactor had agreed that he would stay in partnership with Seeger, but remain a sleeping partner until he saw the outcome. He would provide assistance that would help to draw in more financial assistance and personnel through covert organizations and deals. Seeger had no objections. Money was still needed to fund the Brethren and its schemes. On top of the supply of illicit diamonds from a West African, there were weapons. Brent had his own man named Jack Regan, who gave the Brethren a solid source for guns and allied equipment.

The months passed, details were worked out and people put in position. The manufacture and distribution of the bombs took place in secrecy, so that the attacks could be coordinated to the minute.

The day came for the first strikes. The bombs were delivered and did exactly what they had been designed for. Shock and outrage followed. There was panic. Again, as intended. The second and third strikes followed, increasing public unrest as the administration in Washington, fed by its agencies, was in the dark as to who and why. The outcome was a total success as far as Seeger was concerned and in his isolated compound in the Colorado mountains, they celebrated this initial assault of their war against the federal government.

Seeger's satisfaction, however, was shortly to be interrupted by news of a betrayer in their midst. One of their own had initiated his own campaign. The reason was the most bitter pill to swallow—sheer greed.

Jerome Gantz, the bomb maker. The man who had concocted the compound, manufactured and placed the detonating devices, had turned against them. He had engineered the theft of four million dollars' worth of the African diamonds, and though his scheme had been uncovered, the diamonds had not been recovered. The money the diamonds would have brought represented a significant contribution to the continuing campaign. Gantz may have been the best at manufacturing the explosive devices Seeger wanted. Unfortunately for him his skills as a thief left a lot to be desired and his complicity in the double-cross was exposed by one of Seeger's security people. A team had been sent to Gantz's Tyler Point home to get the information of the diamonds' whereabouts. The mission had failed due to armed interference and Seeger's military commander had returned empty-handed. Because of the seriousness of the events Seeger had called a council of war at his Colorado home.

The meeting had been convened hastily, following the Tyler Point incident. By the time the attendees were gathered, it was midday. They waited in the well-appointed lounge of Seeger's home. From the lounge windows lay a wide panorama of timbered land and distant mountains. It was lush country, quiet and unspoiled.

Food and drink had been prepared and laid out on a large table for everyone to help themselves. With the mood that hung over the gathering more drink than food was taken.

Deacon Ribak, who had been in charge of the aborted mission on Tyler Point, was the least affected. His attitude was considered almost cavalier by some of the gathering, but Ribak himself saw it in a less disastrous light. He was seated in one of the deep leather armchairs, a drink in one hand and a chicken leg in the other, watching the hushed conversation with amusement.

The door finally opened and Zac Lorens came into the room just ahead of Seeger. As always, Lorens was immaculately dressed in a suit and neatly knotted tie, his thick hair neatly brushed back from his high brow. Being second in command, as well as lawyer to Liam Seeger, was a position Lorens prized highly and he was never slow in reminding others of his position. The first thing he did was fix his stony glare on the seated Ribak. It was admonishment for daring to sit in the presence of Seeger. It was lost on Ribak. He sat defiantly, refusing to be intimidated.

Liam Seeger strolled into the room, glancing at the assembly, and his imperial air almost demanded a fanfare. He was dressed in casual clothing. As with everything he wore, his clothes fit his lean frame perfectly. A black patch covered his empty eye socket, and the hand of his crippled arm rested in his jacket pocket. He scanned the room, pausing briefly on Ribak, then sat.

"We all know why we're here," Lorens said, taking the lead. His words and his scathing look pinpointed Ribak. "The disastrous screwup at Tyler Bay."

Ribak placed his chicken leg on the plate beside him on a side table and emptied his glass of wine. He used a paper napkin to wipe his lips and hands before looking in Lorens's direction and feigning surprise. "You talking to me, Lorens?"

He changed tack instantly. "Nice glass of wine, Mr. Seeger. Just the right temperature."

Lorens's face had become flushed with rage. "You know damn well I'm talking to you, Ribak, and you will address me in the correct manner."

"Lorens, this isn't the Army and you sure aren't an officer. Now I came because Mr. Seeger asked me. Any problems I'll answer to him."

Lorens took a step forward until Seeger's outstretched hand halted him. "Zac, go and get yourself a drink. The rest of you, take a seat."

Seeger allowed the moment to pass before he addressed Ribak. "Actually, Deacon, I do feel an explanation *is* in order."

"Yes, sir, I agree. The operation was running smooth. We waited until dark. Shore party went into Gantz's house and followed procedure. Beringer was in charge. He radioed that they had Gantz and the interrogation was under way. At that point Gantz was holding out. He refused to give Beringer the information, and they couldn't find what they were looking for in the house. Next thing I heard was automatic fire. Hell of a lot. I got a message from Beringer that they had been hit by unknowns and they'd taken casualties. Whoever it was came storming out the rear of the house and took down the beach team. We opened up with the .50-cal. It didn't go our way. So I called the assault off and we got the hell out of there. Nothing else we could do, sir."

"So you ran," Lorens said, unable to hold back.

"You ever been under fire, Lorens? I doubt it. Little

pink-skinned lady-boy like you would dump in your pants if one of Mr. Seeger's saddle ponies farted behind you. Now my assault backfired on me and I lost half my team, but don't you ever accuse me of running, or I swear I will rip your fucking throat out here and now." Ribak had leaned forward in his chair. He caught himself and sat upright again. "I apologize for my outburst, Mr. Seeger. Shouldn't have let myself get upset."

"No problem, Deacon," Seeger said. "What is more important is, do you have any idea who the intruders were? Could they have been a government agency? FBI? Homeland Security? Anything like that?"

Ribak admitted he had no idea. "They came at us out of the fog, weapons up and firing. No warning. No announcement. FBI will normally throw a challenge first. These people just hit us hard and fast. I can't give you an answer, sir."

"Perhaps they represented the group Gantz was negotiating with?" Lorens suggested, neatly bringing himself back into the conversation. "We can't ignore that possibility. Gantz must have known that what he'd done was liable to bring retribution if we found out. We *did* find out, and maybe Gantz had a team around to offer protection."

"Could be, Mr. Seeger," Ribak said. "Could be a coincidence, but they damn well showed up fast when we went to work on Gantz. He was in to us for a lot of money. He'd want backup."

Seeger appeared amused at Ribak's comment. "As usual, Deacon, you are a master of understatement. Only you could class four million dollars' worth of diamonds as a lot of money. But as you say, it is a possibility that both you and Zac have a valid point."

"You want it checked out, sir?"

"It needs checking out, Deacon. Only this time just send a small force. No more than two or three. Let them do some discreet gathering of information. Find out if Gantz is alive or dead. Where he is. And we had better check out Mr. Petrie in Philadelphia, too. In case he was involved."

"I'll get straight on it, sir."

Ribak took his leave from the meeting. Lorens waited until the door had closed before he turned to Seeger. The Brethren leader lifted a hand briefly.

"Deacon was man enough to accept the failure of his operation, Zac. I cannot, in all truth, censure him for that. And he is our best man when it comes to military know-how. Let's move on, shall we?"

Lorens understood he was being instructed to back away from the subject. He dismissed what he had been about to say.

Seeger nodded. He turned to the rest of the group. "A failure, gentlemen, but one we can learn from. As Deacon has admitted, he was caught unprepared being confronted by an unknown force. If this force was part of the group aiding Gantz in his theft of our diamonds, then we have the answer. However, the possibility it was some government agency means we should ask ourselves how and why. Had Gantz tipped them off himself in the hope of escaping our wrath? Or was it an unfortunate coming together of opposing sides by a simple twist of fate? We know this government has its insidious tentacles spread far and wide. It intrudes into every aspect of American life. They monitor the communications networks. Bug phones and have spy cameras everywhere. Maybe they had prior knowledge of our intent. We will check every possibility. Foremost we must learn a valuable lesson. Not to take anything for granted. Trust no one we do not know. Consider every stranger a potential enemy. If we allow ourselves to become too confident we invite betrayal, and as we all understand, this administration feeds on betrayal. Turning American against American. They do it with such deceit that the masses have no idea how they are being manipulated."

Lowell Rogerson, commander of the northeastern Brethren unit said, "The bombings showed how lax the authorities are. It's thrown them into total confusion. But it will make them more vigilant. They're going to be watching out for us next time. Perhaps this incident with Gantz proves they are becoming more alert."

"A good point, Lowell. We do need to be sharper. On your other point, though. You feel they'll be watching out for us? Their blind spot is the fact that they have no idea where, when or how we strike. If we keep changing our targets, I don't see how they can anticipate."

ERIC STAHL GLANCED UP. "Well, is he still a believer?"

General William Carson smiled. It made him look like a hungry wolf ready for the kill. "Eric, that one-eyed idiot is ready to march up Pennsylvania Avenue right this minute. Believe me, son, Seeger is close to pissing his pants with the pure joy he's experiencing, according to Ribak."

"He's saving America. Allow him his moment."

"He'd be advised to make the most of it." The general filled his tumbler with more of Stahl's malt. "Oh, you don't mind?"

"You can take the whole bottle, Bill. Now let me ask you something. Is this really going to work? Dropping the whole of the blame for the atrocities on the Brethren? You can't see any backfire coming our way?"

Carson had already taken up his seat again. He swallowed a mouthful of his drink. "Not going queasy on me, Eric?"

"Not at all. Just my cautious side rearing its head."

"We have that arrogant prick just where we want him. Let him and those weekend soldiers run around making all the noise they want. Come the day, with the whole country up in arms and screaming blue murder because the President is wavering, that's when we make our move. With the President having lost support, the public demanding his resignation, he'll be on his own. If he tries to bring in the military, we stall him. Let his own statutes create delays to prevent him getting his assistance. We use your communications setup to blanket the country with the news he's ready to quit. Force him to resign. Then *I* get the military to move. We take control. Have the streets full of armed troops. Planes overhead and we also send in cleanup companies to blast hell out of the Brethren's compounds. Every damned one of them. No quarter. We put them down like the rabid dogs they are. When it's over we produce the evidence that links them to the bombings. Once they're dead and gone, who is there to point the finger?"

"I can think of one."

"Not that one-man band running around poking sticks into wasp nests? Eric, he's doing us favors. Think about it. Who is he going after? The Brethren. Every strike he makes it's more likely to draw attention to them. Not us, because we're not even in the picture at the moment."

"Assume he makes a connection. Starts to move on us?"

"Then we employ our usual tactics and call in our people. Let them deal with him. Pulls the heat off us so we can move ahead. Trust me, this is what I do for a living. Jesus, Eric, nigh on thirty years. I think I have it worked out by now."

Stahl didn't doubt that for a second. The career of General William "Bull" Carson was second to none. The man had joined the Army a year under the enlistment age and had seen combat before a year passed. Even at that young age he had proved his worth. His career went from strength to strength. His reputation for taking orders, coupled with a no-compromise attitude when in combat earned him quick promotion. He rose through the ranks as easily as some men breathed and thrived on challenges. Men under his command would walk through fire and brimstone for their commander. His tough stance in battle earned him the unofficial title Bull Carson. He accepted the name with pride, and it served him well as he pushed and fought his way to the top. Carson treated his men fairly, but expected the best from them, and to see him bawling out an offender for some misdemeanor was never forgotten. Once the reprimand was done with, it was over. Bull Carson never held a grudge. He would hand out his verbal punishment in the morning, and he would be seen sharing a drink with the man the very same night.

Eric Stahl had known Carson for more than ten years. He respected the man's military judgment, and found that Carson had similar feelings about the state of the nation. Carson was secretly incensed the way America was going. He despised the slide into too many wars.

Too many interventions abroad while the U.S.A. was struggling at home. He viewed the current administration as weak, opting for the quick fix instead of tackling problems over the long term and settling them once and for all. He sensed the U.S. Military machine as being betrayed. Given too much to handle with not enough resources. Sending young Americans to die in dusty streets thousands of miles from home, often never quite sure just what they were fighting for. And when the despots of those countries were caught and put on trial he had to watch them playing their sick games in the courtroom. Demanding this and that, refusing to acknowledge the courts and throwing tantrums. Vast sums of money and hours of wasted time were expended on these people. The courts backed down and let the ranting prisoners claim their human rights had been violated. *Their* human rights. These complaints coming from men who had no problems with human rights when they slaughtered men, women and children of their own countries. There would have been no human rights concerns if Carson had his way. The tyrants would get swift justice if he had his way; a merciful 9 mm bullet in the back of the skull and the matter would be settled.

Carson had not earned his high rank by bucking the system. He knew the right time to stay silent and when to raise his voice. He also knew that his beloved America needed help within its borders. The hell with the rest. Let them squabble and fight, kill each other over some damned religious incident. His concern was the U.S.A. It needed a leader with a hard line, who would not bow to the namby-pamby decrees of the PC brigade, a President who would toughen the line and say enough.

Clamp down on excesses and channel money and time into the ills of the nation. The trouble was the mass of Americans only had the two main political parties to choose from and at the end of the day they were interchangeable. Politics had become a brightly colored, yelling, screaming circus at election time. It was bigtime entertainment, with millions of dollars cast to the wind. Candidates toed the party line, made promises that were little more than verbal placebos and once the raucous din settled down everything returned to what it had been before.

Carson watched and quietly fumed, and in his own mind understood the way to change things was by direct action. His association with the then Senator Eric Stahl made him aware he wasn't the only man with a vision for the country. Drastic, yes. Needful, yes. Carson had seen Stahl's attempt, and failure, over the Zero affair. It had been a wild, and in Carson's eyes, brave attempt to set things right. Stahl had lost his senatorial status, while Carson had watched from the wings. He knew one thing. Eric Stahl would not let his desires drift away. Carson and Stahl had worked together over the years, the general dealing with many of the weapons contracts that went Stahl's way. He saw no reason why that should end.

Stahl Industries produced fine ordnance for the military complex. The two men had shared many weekends together at their country retreats and the practice continued. During long evenings, over dinner and drinks later, they had discussed their feelings concerning the fate of America. Piece by piece, like a jigsaw of the mind, the overall picture revealed itself to the pair. With quiet determination they drew their plans, each coming up with a new angle, a different slant, until the battle plan was complete. Complex and requiring deep planning, the scheme was bold, had parts that needed strong nerves and stomachs, but would, if successful, present them with their one and only opportunity to succeed.

Carson sat on his own on a number of occasions, long after Stahl had retired, going over the plan. He asked himself questions that veered toward his personal loyalties to country and President, first accusing himself of a traitorous act, then countering with the justification. The suggestion he might be turning away from America and becoming nothing less than a terrorist himself gave him long, sleepless nights. In the end his conscience cleared itself of that accusation. He was not turning away from America, he was making a sacrifice so that America could be strong again in body and mind. He understood that to achieve that, there would be a need for sacrificial action. Drastic as it was, it had to be seen as a wake-up call, incidents that would make the American public suffer; incidents that would frighten and put them in a panic because the government would not be able to stop them.

The President would be seen in a weak position, the leader of the most powerful nation on Earth having to stand by while the nation cowered beneath the shadow of some unknown threat laying waste to sections of the country. As the incidents increased, the less in control the Washington administration would appear. It would go on until Stahl and Carson decided the right moment had come. Their moment. Then, Stahl would use his substantial radio and television links to put to the people that enough was enough. The President was failing and it was time for a new leader, one who would not flinch from the harsh realities. At the same time military forces acting under orders from General Carson would make their planned strikes at the Brethren. It would be an overwhelming surgical strike against the militia group, destroying their compounds and routing their forces. In the aftermath conclusive evidence that the Brethren had been responsible for the attacks on the nation, painting them as heartless radicals intent on uncalled-for death and destruction, and the current administration had allowed it to happen through ineptitude and a reluctance to make a strong defense.

In his reflective moments Carson had admitted, only to himself, that it was a reckless and dangerous action he and Stahl were contemplating. So much could go wrong. But he reminded himself that through his military career he had witnessed, and had been involved in, similar wild actions. Some thought up by others, many of his own. But war required decisive and off-the-wall decisions. The very nature of war begged for operations that had to come from moments of sheer audacity, simply because the moment required just that. In combat situations, with the tide flowing in opposite directions to what had been planned, instant decisions had to be made. And many of those instant solutions worked, changing the status quo. Veritable losses had been changed to resounding victories by quick thinking.

In the end Carson made his decision. However chancy the moment, it had to be taken. The need of the nation outweighed the fate of those trying to make a difference. It was as simple as that. The facets that went to make up the fabric of the action, unpalatable as they were, had to be faced. General William "Bull" Carson was prepared to shoulder that responsibility. He would live with the burden and face the consequences, and God, in his own way.

"Your man Ribak. He'll keep us updated on what the Brethren is doing?"

"Don't you worry about Deacon. He might be a hard-assed, insolent son of a bitch, but he'll do whatever I want. I recruited him because he's just the right man for the job. Seeger believes Ribak's one of God's chosen soldiers, come down off the fuckin' mountain to train his rednecks how to fight. They're just a bunch of loonies. Give me a single squad of *my* trained boys and we'd wipe that sorry-assed bunch of yokels off the face of the earth without raising a sweat."

"I'm confident you could," Stahl said. "My real concern is this man taking on the Brethren. I'm sorry to bring the matter up again, Bill. I'm starting to have a familiar feel about him."

"No need for apologies. Better to be concerned than to just ignore any kind of threat. From what you're saying, is there a chance you might know who he is?"

"I may be wrong. If I am, I'll apologize in advance, but if I'm right we could have more on our hands than we thought a few minutes ago."

STAHL HAD ALWAYS been known as a hard-liner. The epithet neither embarrassed or fazed him. His views on the way America was going were well-known and had been printed in newspapers and magazines for years. Stahl, the industrialist, commanded his massive armament industry with unlimited zeal. He was a powerful man, still so even after he had been forced to step down from his senatorial position following the Zero fiasco. Because the administration was required to keep Zero out of the public and global eye as much as was humanly possible, Stahl's involvement in the failed attempt to gain control had been kept under wraps. Eric Stahl, always one to grasp any opportunity, plea bargained and promised to remain silent if he was freed from any kind of prosecution. The concession was that he stood down from public office. Stahl was disappointed. He had enjoyed the privileges the position granted him, but he reasoned that at least he was maintaining control of his vast business empire, and that would still give him the opportunity to carry on with his personal agenda—that being the toppling of the U.S. government. He reasoned that he could still do that without the need to be in office during its inception. When the time came Eric Stahl would assume the mantle of commander in chief and take charge of the country.

There was no doubt in Stahl's mind he was the man for the job. His vision of a superior America, powerful and able to quell any threat, was no mad scheme. He understood the discontent that ran throughout the nation. Past administrations, through weak leaders and feeble policies, had plunged the country into a state of malaise. No one dared stand up and point the finger. Even after the terrible events of 9/11 America was still in the grip of terrorism. Attempts to crush the opposition had resulted in the disastrous war against Iraq. That still lumbered on, with more U.S. troops, equipment and money being poured into the country. Stahl had watched and listened, and to his dismay he saw very little that promised it would be over soon. More American lives would be wasted under the guise of cleansing Iraq and establishing democracy. Afghanistan was still very much in the headlines, with the supposedly defeated

Taliban once more raising its brutal head, while at home bad government policy was doing nothing to ease the condition of the country.

Staying below the radar had been Stahl's wisest move. Walking away from a prison sentence had allowed him time to regroup his thoughts, step away from direct involvement with the Third Party, despite it having been more his creation than any of the other members. He made it clear he was doing it so there would be no slur on the party, and they could maintain their campaigns in good conscience. Once he had severed his links he was able to let the dust settle and concentrate on his business empire. Washington had much on its mind, and an ex-senator soon lost out to other more pressing matters at home and abroad. Stahl still had powerful friends, mainly in the military-industrial complex, and a number of those still favored his vision of a harder-edged, defiant America. Stahl decided that taking his time and rethinking strategy was an advisable concept.

The emergence of the Brethren had been a gift for Eric Stahl. He had heard about the isolationist, antigovernment group. He dug into the history of the organization, learned everything he could about the people and their policies, and after assimilating the facts, realized that here was a group he could assist in their aims and at the same time strengthen his own position.

The first and most important thing to establish was his need to remain anonymous. Stahl had reasoned from his investigation into the Brethren that its manifesto encouraged the use of extreme violence as a means of exposing Washington's weakness when it came to protecting its citizens and its organizations. Stahl had no problem with that kind of methodology. Shock tactics were needed to make the American public aware. If a few civilians had to be injured or die, to hammer home the need for a stronger administration, so be it. But it also called for a careful orchestration of the program. So until the country was backed against the wall Stahl decided he would remain in the shadows, ready to step in at the critical moment.

He recruited a go-between, Harry Brent, someone who could bridge the gap between benefactor and recipient. His in-depth investigation of the Brethren showed that their main obstacle was obtaining enough funding so they could run their program of violence. As with any complex plan, money was a deciding factor. The Brethren needed money. Stahl would help them get it. From the start he realized he could not do this openly. He would have to organize a means by which the organization could receive its much-needed funding without his name being known.

His scheme involved using illicit diamonds purchased directly from a source in West Africa. A subsidiary of Stahl Industries had been approached in the past by agents of rogue African groups looking for hard cash. The concept was simple: illicitly mined diamonds of both industrial and high quality were offered at a low cash price. These could be resold on the European and American markets for a much higher yield. The African sellers had no way of getting to these markets because of their status, so they were happy enough to take a percentage of what the diamonds were worth. Through his contacts Stahl's intermediary was able to set up meetings with a chosen seller and arrange for regular purchases. As an added incentive, Stahl brought in an arms dealer, Jack Regan, who would offer to supply ordnance to the rogue groups for their internecine struggles over tribal territories at subsidized prices. Stahl's involvement was as a benefactor who wanted to help the Brethren, providing he remained anonymous.

It worked. For a few months. The Brethren benefited from the large cash amounts the illicit diamonds brought in. It enabled them to bring forward their planned demonstrations of the government's inability to protect the nation and its people. Through his go-between, Stahl learned about the Brethren's command structure, the people within the group and how it worked. Stahl read about and watched on television the results of the group's indiscriminate strikes. He was also able to witness the dismay, the anger and the frustration of America's people. Faced with these savage acts they turned to local and national representatives, demanding something be done. Which only encouraged the Brethren to commit more destructive acts, emphasizing how ineffectual the administration had become. America was under siege within its own borders, and no one seemed to be able to even point their finger at who was behind the strikes, let alone stop them.

Police units were deployed as show of force. There were localized riots against these units, purely from frustration by members of the public who had no other way of showing their emotions. Racial attacks increased as rumors spread that the strikes were the responsibility of extremist terrorist groups within the U.S. These attacks were repelled by the police, and it soon developed into American against American. The Brethren found its membership increasing as individuals responded to the call, as did many other militia groups.

Much of the rumormongering was initiated by the Brethren itself, though the group was careful to only issue statements espousing its shock at the cruel strikes. There was never any suggestion the Brethren was involved, only that its members were repulsed by such attacks against America. But its spokesperson reminded the public it had been warning of such violence. The propaganda was cleverly worded, designed to discredit the government and to raise the Brethren's credibility as a group to be listened to.

Eric Stahl devoured the reports with relish. He was finding his shadowy participation with the Brethren to be paying off handsomely. His covert activity was bringing his day closer. That time was not due yet. Not until the voice of America demanded a change. When the great mass of the people became overwhelming, then he would put into motion the second strategy.

CHAPTER SIX

Clear of Tyler Bay, Bolan headed for the interstate and picked up speed once he was on the highway. He estimated a four- to five-hour drive, depending on conditions.

"Apart from the disturbance last night, that was a nice town," Lyons observed.

"You'll tell me next you could live in a place like that."

"Why not?"

"Too cozy for you, Carl. You need noise and color. A place where the action buzzes."

"Whoa, whoa, where do you come up with that profile?"

"Carl, I know you too well."

"Yeah? Well there's no need to spoil my illusions so early in the damn day."

"Okay."

"By the way, are we being politically correct today? Or are we going in hard?" Lyons asked.

"The Brethren has already shown its disregard for

law and order," Bolan said. "How high does the body count need to go before we get the message?"

"I'm getting the feeling it's leveling out already, Mack."

"Carl, no illusions on this. We're in a war situation here. Plain and simple. The Brethren has declared that, so we respond in kind. Search and destroy. Go for everything that has the Brethren written on it."

Bolan glanced at his partner. His expression told Lyons all he needed to know. The Able Team commander settled back and checked the Philadelphia city map he'd taken from the rack back at the hotel.

"Pedal to the metal, Chief. Let's go see a man about a boat rental."

Bolan handed Lyons the plastic bag holding the cell phone. "See if you can get anything from that. It'll give you something to do and stop you from making funny remarks about my driving."

Lyons switched on the phone and began to go through the various functions. In the phone number list there were no more than half a dozen saved contacts. The recent call list only had three registered. Lyons used his own phone and contacted Stony Man. He spoke to Price and quoted the information from Gantz's cell.

"Have Aaron check these numbers. See if he comes up with any names for us."

"Will do. Anything else?"

"Let you know. We're on our way to Philly. Update when we make contact."

IT WAS EARLY AFTERNOON. The sky over Philadelphia had a sullen, cloudy aspect. It didn't promise a great deal, but then Bolan and Lyons weren't in vacation mode. Both were aware that the Brethren could launch another attack anytime, anywhere within the United States. That very thought motivated them as Bolan drove into and through the city, Lyons guiding him from the Philadelphia map he had open.

South Star Investments was painted on the door, directly above the name Arnold Petrie, CEO. The office suite was on the fourth floor of a building that housed a collection of business enterprises with less than exciting prospects in their immediate futures.

"This place makes tacky look good," Lyons muttered as he and Bolan emerged on the landing from their walk up the stairs.

"You never learned that appearances don't always tell the full story?"

Bolan leaned on the handle and pushed the door open. There was an outer and an inner office. The outer office held a desk, chair and a row of filing cabinets that looked straight out of the showroom. On the desk a computer showed a dead screen. Papers were strewed across the desk, a pen dropped in a hurry lay on top of them. A nameplate sat at the front edge of the desk: Val Paxton, Assistant. The door to the inner office was ajar and hurried movements could be heard coming from the room beyond.

Lyons closed the main door behind him and locked it. He took out his Colt Python and held it down by his side. Ahead of him Bolan, Beretta 93-R in hand, stood at the door to the inner office. He extended his right foot and nudged the door wide open.

Arnold Petrie's office was well furnished. Everything looked new: thick carpet on the floor, pale wood desk large enough to act as a dining table. The executive chair behind it was the best money could buy. A large-screen laptop sat on the desk beside two telephones.

The lone man in the office was throwing files into a box. A wood filing cabinet against the wall had all its drawers pulled open.

"We seem to have chosen the wrong day to make our investments, Mr. Petrie," Bolan said conversationally.

"Sorry, we're closed for business," the man said over his shoulder.

"You are Arnold Petrie?"

"No, I'm Homer fuckin' Sim—"

Lyons heeled the office door shut with a bang.

Petrie spun, saw his visitors and the weapons they were carrying, and froze. The man was haggard, pale and unshaved, heavy dark rings beneath his eyes. His striped shirt was half unbuttoned, and the tie he wore hung askew. Arnold Petrie was displaying the symptoms of a man haunted by events and scared the aftermath was about to catch up with him.

"Sleepless night, Petrie?" Bolan asked.

"Must have something on his mind," Lyons said.

"Who the hell are you two? And what's with the guns?"

"We have business with you," Bolan said.

"And the guns," Lyons continued, "are there because we might want to shoot you."

"Shoot me? You can't just walk in and threaten…"

"It might be a good idea if you sat down, Petrie. We could be here for a while."

"Is this a holdup? You guys after money? Hell, you'll be disappointed if you are. This office is for investments. All done over the phone or Internet. No cash involved."

"I understand your kinds of investments, Petrie. Tell me, how are share prices in agricultural fertilizers doing at the moment? And nitromethane? Should be rising, the amount your people have been buying."

Petrie's expression gave him away. He backed toward the desk, suddenly leaning across it to snatch up a handgun resting in an open drawer. As fast as he was, he looked slow when Lyons moved, crossing the space between himself and the desk in two long strides. His left hand swept around and slapped the pistol out of Petrie's hand.

"Miserable son of a bitch," Lyons growled.

He caught hold of Petrie's shirt, hauling the man away from the desk and across the office. Unable to control himself Petrie slammed into the filing cabinet. The unit toppled under his weight and the man rode it to the floor where his head snapped forward and impacted against the side, breaking his nose. Petrie rolled off the cabinet, blood streaming from his nose.

"Easy," Bolan cautioned. "Right now we need him conscious."

Lyons backed off, expending his energy by going through the box Petrie had been packing.

"Broke my fuckin' nose," Petrie mumbled.

Bolan rounded on the man. "You want him to break something else?" Petrie's wide-eyed stare was answer enough. "Talk to me, Petrie, I'm all that's between you and my partner."

"Tell you what?"

"You hired the boat that delivered the thugs who attacked Gantz. Why was the Brethren angry with him? *He* can't tell me because he's dead."

"Dead?"

"See how it's getting bigger? Now you're an accessory to one more murder."

"Look, all I did was arrange the boat rental."

"Copping a plea already," Lyons said. "Same song you dirtbags sing when you get caught. It isn't going to wash this time, Petrie."

"Gantz is dead because the Brethren sent a bunch of hard-asses after him," Bolan said. "You're included in anything they did. Just the same as being involved with the bombings. It puts you right in the frame, Petrie. Multiple deaths. Attacks on federal property. That means a long, long stretch. Even if they could keep you alive permanently, you'd never be let out of prison. No parole. Just a single cell where you'd be lucky to even see daylight." Lyons turned from the box and showed Bolan a leather-bound personal organizer he'd located. "If it was left to me I'd make it quick for you and do everyone a favor."

"You can't pin this one on me. All I did was act as middleman. Gantz sent me a list of what he wanted and I filled it. Arranged delivery. That's all. I didn't know what he was going to do with that stuff…"

"The hell you didn't," Bolan said. "Petrie, you knew about Gantz. What he did. You're in up to your neck."

Petrie wiped blood from his face, glanced from Bolan to Lyons and back. "I want my lawyer. I have my rights. This is harassment."

Lyons smiled. "Dirtbag, you have got this so wrong. We're not even cops. Don't play by their rules. With us you get no favors."

"So why should I cooperate?"

"Because right now you are on panic street," Bolan said. "Ready to skip town and hide. Tell me I'm wrong,

Petrie. Tell me your business partners have decided to move on and they don't want to leave any loose ends around."

"Jesus, you don't know. One prick upsets their arrangements, and they figure the best thing is to close down here and move somewhere else. You don't know what these people are like."

"Bombings, indiscriminate slaughter. I think I know exactly what they're like. Killing you isn't about to make them lose any sleep."

"Look, all I understood was that Gantz had stolen something from the Brethren. Something they wanted back. Whatever it was had pissed them off. That's why they went after Gantz. But things didn't work out the way they wanted. They got hit, and Gantz was taken out of their hands. Why am I telling you when you already know?"

Petrie slumped against the wall, silent, not even making any more attempts at stemming the flow of blood from his nose.

Lyons wandered into the outer office. When he returned he asked, "Where's your assistant? Val Paxton. I get the feeling she left in a hurry."

"Val? What about her?" Petrie refused to meet Lyons's eyes.

Bolan leaned in close, his voice hard. "Where is she, Petrie. Quit stalling."

"I told her to get out. Go home and stay clear until she hears from me."

"Son of a bitch," Lyons said. "You knew the Brethren might come calling so you threw her out on the street to look after herself? Nice move, Petrie. This isn't going away and you damn well know it," Lyons snapped.

Bolan had a bad feeling about the woman. "You called them. The Brethren. Laid it on them that Val knew about Gantz's double cross. You gave them some story that would put them on *her* trail and leave you with enough time to skip town."

Whatever else he was, Petrie had no chance as an actor. He tried and failed to conceal his guilt. "It was her or me," he said.

"I'd say you just bombed out of Philadelphia's Employer of the Year award," Bolan said.

Lyons began to thumb through the personal organizer until he located the page with Val Paxton's employment information. "This is where she lives? And her phone number?"

"Yeah. She won't answer. I told her whatever she does, not to answer the phone. She trusts me. She'll do what I told her."

"Going to be one hell of a shock when she finds out what you've been up to here. Or does she already know?"

"She has no idea. I hired her because she has experience in the investment business. I worked this office as a genuine agency and that's all Val knew it as."

"Your Brethren associates won't be taking any chances," Bolan said. "If they're putting a hold on their dealings in this town, they'll make a clean sweep. And that *will* include you. Once they deal with Val, you'll be next. I guess you already figured that by the packing you're doing."

"You handle things here," Lyons said. "I'll grab a cab and get across to Val's address. I spotted a cab rank just around the block when we drove in."

Bolan nodded. "Stay in touch."

Lyons holstered his revolver and left the office without another word, leaving Arnold Petrie alone with Bolan.

THE APARTMENT BUILDING where Val Paxton lived was thirty years old, well maintained and five stories high. The cars parked at the curb fitted the area—except for the large, dark blue SUV wedged in between a Honda and a three-year-old Buick. Lyons's cabdriver established that when they drove by and he spotted the Suburban.

"That's something you don't see around this neighborhood every day. Somebody won the lottery, or else the pushers are marking new territory."

Lyons asked to be dropped at the far corner of the block, paid the cabbie and started walking back to Val Paxton's building. He went up the steps, then took the stairs to the second floor and checked out numbers on doors. When he came to Paxton's door, he reached inside his jacket and loosened the Colt Python.

That was when he picked up a scuffle of sound from inside the apartment—a man's demanding voice, followed by the unmistakable protest from a female seconds before the sound of a slap.

Lyons hit the door with his foot, just below the lock, and it flew open and banged against the wall. The Python was in Lyons's hand as he dived into the apartment, landing on one shoulder and rolling, coming up on one knee. The .357's muzzle tracked across the room, Lyons making his scan of who was there: three men, one young woman on her hands and knees, long ash-blond hair hanging over her face, her clothing disheveled and torn.

The Able Team leader leveled his revolver, swinging around to cover the trio of men. One guy had an autopistol in his left hand and he aimed it toward Lyons.

The room echoed to the heavy thunder of the Python as Lyons triggered a 180-grain slug. It hit the pistol man in the chest, coring through to puncture his heart before exiting through his back. The brute force of the shot kicked the guy backward. He struck the edge of a chair and went down hard.

The man's partners went for their own handguns in the space of a couple of seconds, but their actions did nothing to save them from Lyons's second and third shots. He took one guy in the left shoulder and the third in the throat. He went down instantly, making a bloody mess on the carpet.

The guy with the shoulder wound started to yell. Lyons, his mood ugly, pushed to his feet and slammed the Python's steel barrel across the guy's skull, dropping him to his knees where he collapsed facedown on the floor. If he had been conscious he would have seen Lyons standing over him, the Python aimed at the back of his skull, a wildness in his eyes that only faded when his finger eased off the trigger. The rage inside had almost made him pull that trigger. Lyons knew his limitations. One of them was his short fuse. It was liable to land him in trouble unless he managed to control it. Most times he did, but the temptation was always there, lurking, waiting to push him into the abyss.

He holstered the Python, crossed to the door and closed it. He knew someone would be reporting the shooting, so time was running on a short string. Lyons bent over the young woman and eased her to her feet. As she came upright, the blond hair fell away from her face and Carl Lyons found himself staring at one of the most beautiful women he had ever come across. The hair framed a pair of blue eyes and a mouth of exquisite loveliness. Thin, arching brows drew attention to the eyes that were scrutinizing Lyons with an intensity the Able Team leader found disturbing. The only distraction he noted was the bruise on her left cheek and a trickle of blood from the corner of her mouth.

"Val Paxton?" He received a nod. "No time now. Just listen. Do you have a coat?"

"Well…yes… Why?"

"Go get it. Fast."

Lyons gave her no time to question him. He turned and checked each of the men on the floor, searching for keys for the Suburban parked below. He found them on the second attempt. As he stood he heard a shocked gasp from the woman. She had taken her first clear look at the bodies.

"Oh my God."

"You want to end up like them?" Lyons asked bluntly.

"No."

"Then do what I tell you. They didn't drop by to sell you life insurance. Now get that damn coat and let's get the hell out of here."

The harshness of his words seemed to have an effect on the woman and she turned, breaking into a run, and vanished into what Lyons assumed was her bedroom. He spotted a large shoulder bag lying on the floor and snatched it up. When Paxton reappeared, dragging a knee-length, all-weather coat over her torn blouse, Lyons thrust the shoulder bag into her hands.

"What the hell do women put in these that makes them so heavy?"

He didn't wait for an answer, just caught her arm and propelled her to the door. The hall was still empty but Lyons heard raised voices, especially the shrill cry of a woman demanding her husband phone the police. They took the stairs fast, and it was only Lyons's iron grip that kept Paxton on her feet. They reached the door.

"Dark blue SUV at the curb to the right. We go straight to it and get in."

On the sidewalk Lyons walked her to the Suburban and used the remote to unlock it. He opened the passenger door and helped her in. Slamming the door, he walked to the driver's side. The powerful engine caught on the first try. Lyons dropped the transmission into Drive, released the hand brake and edged away from the curb. Beside him Paxton sat hunched over, clutching her bag as if it were a life preserver. Her head was down and her long blond hair had fallen to cover her face again. Lyons concentrated on getting them as far from her apartment as possible. He figured she needed some time to absorb what had happened, so he left her to it. He drove steadily, observing the speed limits and watching the traffic lights. The last thing he needed was to be stopped because he'd jumped a red light.

Lyons took his cell phone from his pocket and speed-dialed Bolan. His call was answered on the second ring.

"Hey, Matt, how's it going?"

"Petrie's not playing the game. He decided he has nothing more to say. So I'm sending him away with a couple of marshals. See how he likes a nice, quiet isolation cell. You?"

"I walked into some opposition. They played hardball but they won't anymore."

"The woman?"

"Alive. Right now I'm cruising Philly in a borrowed four-by-four, looking for a spot where we can catch our breath."

"Keep in contact."

"Will do."

Lyons broke the connection and slid the cell back into his pocket. He sensed movement beside him.

"Who are you?" Paxton asked. "Police? FBI?"

Lyons fished out his ID and showed her. "Somewhere in between," he said.

"Justice Department? Mr. Benning—or should I call you Agent Benning? What is going on? Who were those men in my apartment? The men you shot, by the way."

"First you can call me Doug. And those men I shot were about to *shoot* me. Hey, are you okay? Looks like they were giving you a hard time."

She nodded. "It hurts, but I'll survive, and thanks for what you did. I wasn't being ungrateful. It isn't every day I get roughed up and then witness an OK Corral gunfight in my apartment." She pulled her coat around her and Lyons could see she was shivering from delayed reaction.

"You know the city well?" Lyons asked.

"What?"

"Val, I am lost. Can you get us somewhere where we can sit and talk?"

She stared through the windshield, acquainting herself with their surroundings. "Take a left at the next intersection. Stay on it until I tell you where to go."

TWENTY MINUTES LATER they were seated in a fast-food restaurant off Island Avenue. They sat at a table, drinking coffee, watching the rain stream down the window. It had started to pour as they'd left the vehicle.

"I can see why Pennsylvania is so green," Lyons commented. He was finding it hard to say anything serious, since Paxton had spent a little time in the restroom, tidying herself up. The long hair and makeup hid the bruise on her cheek and she had cleaned the blood from her lips. He figured she had to have been carrying a complete makeover kit in the shoulder bag. *I can see why Pennsylvania is so green. Carl, you're babbling like a teenager on his first date.* He cleared his throat and took a swallow of his coffee.

"That's a new line," Paxton said. She was smiling at him, and he was pleased to see it reached her eyes. Then she got serious. "Agent—Doug—please tell me what's been happening. I don't understand any of it and to be honest I *am* scared."

"How long have you worked for Petrie?"

"Arnold? Around four months. Why? Is he in some kind of trouble? I never saw him like he was this morning. I hardly had time to start work before he rushed in and told me to go home. Not to come back and not to contact him. When I asked why, he got really upset. He said that when I got home I wasn't to answer the phone if it rang. Under no circumstances. It was important I did what he said and not ask questions. To be honest he scared the sh— I mean…"

"Yeah, I get your meaning. Listen, Val, did he take any calls while you were in the office?"

"One, just before he sent me away. He sounded a little scared. I don't know who it was calling because he transferred my phone to his so any calls went directly to him."

"And when you got home?"

"I couldn't understand any of it. I sat around trying

to figure out what to do. Arnold had frightened me. And confused me. In the end I thought I'd better leave the city for a while. Go and stay with my sister in Portland. I mean, Oregon is a long way away from Philly." She paused. "You think that's a good idea?"

Lyons nodded. "I need to ask you about the men who came to your apartment."

"Oh, those men. They knocked and, like an idiot, I opened the door. I know it was a stupid thing to do, but I guess by that time I wasn't thinking clearly. No excuse, I know, but..."

"Forget that. Just think back. What did they ask?"

"They came in, looked around. Asked if I was alone. The one who had the gun in his hand when you showed up—I guess he was in charge—started to ask me questions about South Star Investments. Who visited Arnold. What they talked about. As if I knew. There were people he took into his office and closed the door. I just got on with my work. I told him I had no idea what was talked about behind a closed door. Then he started asking me about diamonds. I mean diamonds. I guess I got a little annoyed then and told him I had no idea what he was talking about and maybe he should go shove his questions. That seemed to make him mad. I realized I shouldn't have said that. And that...that was when he started to slap me around." She tugged her coat tighter around her as she was reminded about her rough treatment.

"He ripped my blouse and said if I didn't tell the truth he could do more than just hit me. He started asking about diamonds again. Who I was working with. He kept going on about diamonds. When I told him I had nothing to do with any diamonds, he really hit me." Paxton touched her fingers unconsciously to her bruised cheek, her eyes moist. "I fell down. The next thing I knew guns were going off and you were there." She reached across and touched Lyons's hand. "I just realized I haven't thanked you properly for what you did for me."

"You already did."

"I did? When?"

"After we left your place."

"I guess I must have been really shook up. Even so, it needs saying again."

"No need."

"Yes, there is. I hate to even think what might have happened if you hadn't come through that door when you did. Doug, do you understand all this? What's all this thing about diamonds? If you do, tell me."

Lyons made the decision to bring her into the loop. Explaining Petrie's involvement might jog her memory and revive some dormant memory of something she had seen or heard. She had shown herself to be a bright young woman. Maybe she was even smarter than Lyons imagined. It was worth the risk, knowing what could happen if the Brethren started the bombings again.

"Petrie has got himself involved with some bad company. He operated the investment business purely as a cover to hide his real business."

"Okay, I'll put the fake business on hold for later. So what was the real reason he was there?"

"He is part of a militia group operating outside the law. They were behind the recent bombings across the country. Petrie assisted in the operation. From what we've learned so far it appears he could have been behind the purchase of the raw materials that went into making the bombs."

Paxton became very quiet, staring out the window. It was some time before she spoke. "But all those people were killed. So many of them." She turned to look Lyons directly in the eye. "Are you telling me I worked for a man who was part of that?"

"Yes."

"Even after what happened to me today, it's hard to believe Arnold was part of those terrible acts. Doug, why are they doing it? Murdering Americans? It doesn't make any sense."

"It does to these people. They want to prove a point. Val, they have grievances against the government. They see conspiracies in every corner. So they create panic and unrest and show that the government can't even protect its own. Then it justifies their manifesto."

"Since those bombings, people are certainly nervous. You can sense it sometimes out in the streets. A car backfiring can make them stop and wonder if they should run for cover."

"Exactly what the bombers want."

Paxton was shaking her head. "Then why doesn't the President do something about them?"

"Because we're only just rooting out who is at the back of all this. There's more than just a bunch of redneck militia involved. We have to drag them all into the light or they'll disappear and simply regroup at another time."

"This is like something out of a movie. A dream. No, a nightmare."

"No, Val, it's real. We're trying to cut these people off from organizing more bombings. I need anything you can tell me."

She took a breath and reached for her coffee. "I wish

I did have something to give you." She stared into her empty cup. "Could I have some fresh coffee?"

Lyons went to the counter and bought two more cups of coffee, then returned to the table. He slid Paxton's over to her.

"How are diamonds involved?"

"A man named Gantz was attacked and later died from his injuries. That was in a little town on the coast. Gantz was the guy who built the bombs for the Brethren. They found out that Gantz had stolen something that belonged to them. From what you say it sounds as if Gantz stole the diamonds."

"What do diamonds have to do with an organization like the Brethren?"

"It's too early to figure that one out, and not really why I'm here right now."

The woman tasted her coffee, stared into the cup for a moment. "There is something I want to tell you. Something I just recalled. It might not have anything to do with what you're looking for."

"Right now I'd listen to someone quoting from the weather forecast."

"I recalled something I overheard some weeks back. I was passing Arnold's office and he'd forgotten to close the door fully. I'm not in the habit of listening in on his telephone conversations, but this time I couldn't avoid hearing. He was agitated, almost arguing with someone. Arnold said something about a delay with the next delivery to the farm." She sipped at her coffee, wincing when the hot liquid touched her bruised lip. "It means something—doesn't it?"

Lyons nodded. "It might. Did you pick up anything else?"

"I heard the name Lorens. Then a reference to a Pelman's Farm. That was it, Doug, I'm sorry."

"No need. You maybe just handed me the piece I've been looking for."

Lyons took out his cell phone and called Bolan.

BOLAN FINISHED HIS CALL and experienced a genuine moment of satisfaction as he turned to Arnold Petrie, who sat in sullen silence behind his desk. Right at that moment he looked like a man who had suddenly lost everything. It may have been the fact he had been caught in a conspiracy. Or it could have been the steel manacles and chains tethering his wrists and ankles, and the presence of the two federal marshals standing watch over him.

Hal Brognola had put the federal machine into top gear following Bolan's call. He had contacted the Philadelphia U.S. Marshals Department and arranged for Petrie to be taken into immediate custody. The marshals had arrived quietly, entering by the rear of the building after parking in the adjoining ally. Once they had restrained him, Petrie slumped into a sullen silence.

"No fun anymore?" Bolan asked.

"It never was supposed to be," Petrie said. "We have a real agenda." For a moment his bravado returned. "It won't stop."

"It has for you and Gantz." Bolan ignored the sneer that curled Petrie's lips. He had been holding back what Lyons had told him, but decided it was time to play his holdout card. "We have Lorens and Pelman's Farm. And let's not forget the diamonds."

This time Petrie's face did go pale. His surprise was genuine. "How did you…" He stopped himself but knew he had just confirmed Bolan's expectations.

"You figured you were the only one with good intelligence? By the time the marshals here have you processed and tucked away in your new home, we'll be moving on the farm."

Petrie lost it, lunging up out of the chair and stumbling to his knees as the manacles and chains toppled him. He was screaming wild obscenities at Bolan as the marshals moved in. They handled him with practiced efficiency.

Petrie stared wild-eyed at Bolan. "I'll be back on the streets before you can spit. Then we'll see who comes out on top."

"You want us to take him now?" one of the marshals asked.

"Yes. Just remember. He has no communication with anyone. No phone calls. No lawyers. Nothing. Keep him isolated until further notice."

"As of now he doesn't exist."

"You can't do that," Petrie said. "I have my rights, goddamn you."

"So did those children you blew into pieces in Atlanta, Petrie. They had rights. They were just starting to live their lives. You took everything from them. Think yourself lucky all you lose at the moment is the ability to shout your garbage to the world."

It was a relief when the doors closed and Petrie's demands faded.

Activating his cell phone, Bolan got through to Kurtzman at Stony Man. "See what you can pick out from Petrie's telephone accounts." He gave the office number to Kurtzman. "We have a lead to why the Brethren were mad at Gantz. No full details yet but the buzzword is diamonds."

"Let me run that around the office, see if it generates any ideas."

"Run a search for a Pelman's Farm in the Pennsylvania area. I'm certain it's around here somewhere. If not, extend the search. Most likely it will be a leased property and you might even link it back to Stahl."

"That's interesting," Kurtzman said. "We've been running down Gantz's credit-card purchases. Came across a number going back a few months. For gasoline. He filled his tank a few times at a gas station on the fringes of Lancaster County. So I've already punched that information into Petrie's file and it came up with a possible just before you called. Ties in nicely. Petrie took a yearlong lease on a farm just inside Lancaster County. Pelman's Farm."

CHAPTER SEVEN

Lyons had pulled back into traffic when he and Paxton left the diner. He had been half listening to her instructions on how they could get back to meet up with Bolan when his instincts warned him to keep watch on an SUV two cars behind. Same model as the one he was driving, black instead of dark blue, but with plates that had a similar number sequence.

"Sit tight, Val. I'm going to do some bobbing and weaving, just to convince myself of something."

"Sounds ominous."

For the next few minutes Lyons made several turns, keeping them casual, but in his own mind testing for the driver in the black SUV. The guy, staying back, made exactly the same turns and after the fourth deviation Lyons didn't need any further convincing.

They were being tailed.

"How did they find us so fast?" Paxton asked when he explained his maneuvers.

Lyons didn't answer immediately. He was watching the tail vehicle. "Only thing I can figure is they must have onboard tracking devices so they can coordinate positions car to car. Which isn't good news for us."

Paxton swayed as Lyons cut around a red Ford. "You mean, they'll be able to find us wherever we go?" She made an angry gesture. "Even all the way to Oregon?"

"I wasn't planning on driving you there myself," Lyons snapped, then caught the wry smile edging the woman's mouth. He felt a surge of anger that surprisingly mellowed and he was forced to grin himself. "I need a pathfinder to get me out of the city and instead I get a comedienne."

"So what can I tell you?"

"I'd be happy with the quickest way out of town."

"I'm thinking, I'm thinking. Hey, are they liable to shoot at us?"

"What do you think?"

"I'm thinking I must have done something bad to get into a fix like this. And all you have is that gun you used earlier?"

"Yeah." She didn't make any comment at that, but it did remind Lyons that he was slightly under-armed if it did come to a shootout. "Val, take a look in the rear. There may be other weapons they had with them when they came to your place."

With some struggling, accompanied by muttering, Paxton climbed over and onto the rear seat. She checked around and Lyons heard her give a pleased sound. "I think there's something here," she said. "Holdall on the floor. Let me look inside." Lyons heard the sound of a heavy-duty zip being opened. "My God, who are these people, *The A-Team?*"

"I wish," Lyons said. "All those guns being fired and they never hit squat in five seasons. Bunch of clowns."

"I don't think your TV viewing habits are going to be much use to us, Doug." She took a look out through the window. "Okay, two blocks down take a left, then first right."

"Yes, ma'am," Lyons said.

Lyons was sharply aware that no matter where Paxton directed him, their pursuer would stick with them and it was not beyond a possibility of other vehicles joining the chase if they were also equipped with the tracking devices. He followed his companion's direction and thirty minutes later the city had shrunk behind them and the residential tracts were starting to thin out. In the distance Lyons could see the green swathes of Pennsylvania rolling by on either side of the freeway.

Greenery meant countryside, and countryside meant fewer people and the distinct likelihood of a hostile attack.

Paxton pointed ahead. "Take the next off-ramp. We can hit a back road that goes through forested terrain."

"You sure?"

"Trust me, I know my own backyard."

"So we leave the freeway and innocent drivers in the clear, but it's more than likely our tail will shoot at us."

"What's the alternative, Agent Benning?"

Lyons didn't have an immediate answer. The thought of engaging in a shooting match on the busy freeway was not something he found appealing. At least away from those distractions he could fight on his own terms.

He saw the off-ramp and took a calculated run across two lanes of traffic for it, leaving behind screeching tires and raucous horns.

"The rain's stopped," Paxton said.

"Must be my lucky day."

"Nice that someone is having one."

From the off-ramp the woman directed him along a minor highway for a few miles, the tail car in sight way behind them. Then she indicated a hard-packed dirt road that almost immediately engulfed them in a spread of thick timber and shrubbery. Foliage slapped at the sides of the SUV as Lyons followed the track.

"You know much about guns, Val?" Lyons asked.

"Apart from not being very nice, they make loud noises and hurt people. That said, I'm glad you had one when you came to my apartment."

Lyons took that as a no. "Tell me what's in that bag?"

"Couple of handguns and I guess magazines. And a longer one. A machine gun?"

"Put it over on your front seat."

The machine gun was an FN P-90. Lyons had done some target work with the 5.7 mm weapon. It had taken a short space of time for him to get used to the different configuration of the assault rifle with its 50-round top-loading translucent magazine, but once he had absorbed that, Lyons had found the weapon's handling better than he'd expected. The P-90 had less recoil and could be fired with either hand comfortably. The empty casing, ejected from the underside, meant no problems with them getting too close to the shooter's face and Lyons had taken to the weapon with ease. On the firing range at Stony Man he had spent some long sessions with the P-90, memorizing its setup in case he found one in his hands during a combat situation, such as the one he was in right now.

"Any extra mags for it? Long plastic ones?"

"Two."

"Okay." Lyons took out his cell phone and passed it

over. "Hit number two. It's a speed dial. The guy who answers should be Cooper. Ask him what Striker means? Understand?"

Lyons concentrated on negotiating the back road, gripping the Suburban's wheel hard as the rutted road threatened to wrench it from his hands. He saw a wooden bridge ahead, spanning a wide stream. A glance in his mirror showed the other SUV had dropped back a few yards, so Lyons trod on the gas and sent the vehicle hurtling at the bridge. When the front wheels struck the heavy wooden slats, the SUV bounced a few feet in the air, the rear following suit. Powerful vibrations rippled through the SUV before it settled back on the road on the bridge's far side.

Behind him Lyons heard Paxton's voice demanding her call be correctly verified.

"Just give me you and your partner's names." She paused to confirm. "He also wants to know what Striker means to you. Really? You guys have weird jobs." She tapped Lyons on the shoulder. "He says it's his code name."

"Okay, now tell him we have a hostile on our tail and I'll get back to him when we're clear."

"Look, there's a bunch of jerks in a big black SUV chasing us, and any minute they're going to shoot at us. Okay? Doug will call you back."

"Not word for word," Lyons said, grinning, "but I figure he got the message."

"He sounded nice."

Lyons's grin widened as he tried to visualize Bolan's face when he told him that. He peered ahead and saw the narrow road curving to the right, vanishing in an overhanging canopy of branches from the trees lining either side. He took the bend, then pushed down hard on the pedal, feeling the powerful engine surge and throw the SUV into a headlong race along the rutted track.

"How is it you speed up every time you should be slowing down?"

"Doing the opposite of what I should? Confuses the enemy."

"Mmm, well I can understand how they must be feeling. It's the one thing I have in common with them."

The pursuing SUV fell in behind them once again. Glancing in his side mirrors, Lyons caught the blurred image of someone leaning out from a passenger window. No doubt about what was about to happen. Lyons floored the gas pedal a second before he heard the chatter of a submachine gun. The Suburban shuddered as slugs peppered the tailgate, then the rear window shattered, spraying glass fragments the length of the vehicle.

Paxton screamed.

"Flat on the floor," Lyons yelled.

She rolled off the seat and lay still.

The SMG crackled again, more slugs whining off the tough steel bodywork. Lyons didn't want them to get too close in case they scored a severe hit. He had few options. Keep driving hard forward, or cut off the road and into the dense foliage and maybe hit a fallen tree or drop into a concealed dip.

His remaining, and possibly most risky option, was to slam on the brakes, drawing the chase vehicle up close, which might end in a collision if the driver behind failed to react fast enough. Lyons glanced at the P-90 on the seat next to him. It was loaded and ready for use. He reached over and picked it up, dropping it across his lap, his left hand clamping hard on the steering wheel to keep the Suburban on line. He slid his fingers across the P-90 and flicked the safety to full-auto.

"Val, brace yourself, I'm going to hit the brakes in a while."

"Why?"

Autofire sent more slugs into the body of the SUV. A side window shattered.

"That's why," Lyons told her. "I'm tired of being used as a target."

"Why do I feel there's going to be more shooting?"

The guy in the SUV was getting his range now, which wasn't good news.

"Brakes," Lyons said, and stepped hard on the pedal. He felt the Suburban shudder as the tires skidded on the damp track. Glancing up, he saw the SUV behind looming large. Lyons bared his teeth in a tight grin as the vehicle dipped and lurched. He stomped on the gas pedal and took his own vehicle away again.

Behind him Lyons heard Paxton muttering, "I'm regretting having that second coffee now."

Ahead the track opened up, widening into a two-lane strip. Some distance away he saw that the tree line was thinned and open, and grass and shrubs leveled it out. The wider track would enable the pursuit vehicle to close in and even pass.

"No damn way," Lyons said.

"Say what?"

Lyons ignored Paxton's question. He did some rapid calculations in his head. He wanted to lead the SUV in close, then hit the brake again and give himself enough time to get out of the Suburban before they could recover. It was not going to be a precise operation, more catching his pursuers off guard and hitting them hard and fast.

The rattle of autofire and slugs hitting home prompted Lyons into action.

He stomped on the gas, feeling the heavy SUV surge forward, hoping that the driver behind could be caught out by the same maneuver. The pursuit vehicle picked up speed, the shooter leaning out even more as he loosed another burst at Lyons. The driver had moved his vehicle as close to the edge of the track as he could, giving his shooter a better angle. Another window shattered, and glass fell into the floor well where Paxton lay. Her choice of expletives made Lyons grin despite the gravity of the situation.

"Okay, sucker, try this for size. Braking," he yelled for Paxton's benefit.

He stood on the brakes, fighting the wheel as the Suburban slithered and bounced, its speed dropping rapidly. The pursuit vehicle grew uncomfortably large in the rearview mirror.

Lyons resisted the urge to take his foot off the brake pedal. He stayed with the vehicle until it had become almost immobile, then yanked on the handbrake, snatched up the P-90 and opened his door, rolling out onto the ground, moving quickly to the rear corner.

The pursuit SUV had fared slightly worse. Being on the edge of the track, it dropped over when the driver braked. The big wheels hit the soft grass and spun for a few seconds before the driver regained control and hit the brakes again.

The guy leaned out the window, his SMG jerking wildly as he attempted to line up on Lyons. Then he realized what was happening and swung his muzzle across the hood, firing off a burst that went wide. The slugs chopped at shrubs beyond Lyons. The Able Team commander, on one knee, raised his own weapon and laid down a steady burst that cleared the hood of the sliding SUV and shattered the windshield. The driver caught a shower of fragmented glass full in the face and eyes. He lost all interest in his driving, flinging both hands to his glass-peppered face, gasping at the sudden pain. Lyons triggered another burst directly into the passenger compartment. He took out the driver before turning the P-90 on the shooter, putting shots into his chest and throat. The shooter twisted in agony, feeling blood rush from his lacerated throat before he began to choke on it.

Seeing frantic movement in the rear of the SUV, Lyons changed position, crouching as he circled to come around on the far side of the vehicle as it came to a final, jerky stall. He saw the rear door swing open and an armed figure scramble out. The guy moved fast, dodging around the rear of the vehicle. Lyons dropped prone, searching beneath the high chassis of the SUV, and saw the guy's legs as he moved around the rear and down the side of the vehicle. He dropped the muzzle of the P-90 and laid a burst beneath the SUV, saw the geysers of bloody debris erupt from the target's ankles. The guy screamed and fell to his knees. He was struggling to raise himself as Lyons stepped around the front of the SUV and hit him with a burst that cored in through his chest to blow out between his shoulders. The guy uttered a hoarse gasp and toppled onto his back.

Lyons checked each body, moving fallen weapons

out of reach. He searched the dead men for identification, but found nothing. They were like soldiers on a mission into enemy territory, carrying nothing that could give anything away.

He used his cell phone and called Bolan.

"Situation resolved," Lyons reported. "Three dead. No identification on any of them. These guys were well armed with P-90 assault weapons. Somebody is handing them sophisticated ordnance here, Matt."

"The P-90 is only supplied to police and agency sources. Civilians aren't supposed to be able to get hold of them. Hey, is your lady friend okay?"

"Apart from being slightly mad at what's happened she's fine. Time to get her to somewhere safe before we follow up on that farm lead."

"I'll get Hal to arrange something. Petrie has already been taken into federal custody. He'll be kept in total isolation until this is all resolved."

"I need to dump this SUV as soon as I can. It has an internal tracking device. Last thing I need is another hostile vehicle picking me up again."

"Give me your location. I'll come and get you and your lady friend."

"Make it fast."

Lyons returned to his vehicle. As he leaned inside a disheveled blond head raised itself, piercing blue eyes fixing on him.

"Hey, Benning, you could have told me I could sit up again."

CHAPTER EIGHT

Pelman's Farm and the possibility of a further clash with the Brethren lay ahead. Bolan and Lyons were more than prepared. Since Tyler Bay and, more recently Philadelphia, they had accepted the inevitability of conflict with the militia group, which had already demonstrated its propensity for unrestrained violence against anyone who defied them or stood in their way.

The identification of Deacon Ribak had shown the Brethren had taken time to employ a man with military experience in addition to the ranks of the bigoted rank and file. Ribak would make sure that the militia's "soldiers" were given a degree of training intended to equip them for the battles ahead.

Bolan was not making light of the Brethren and Liam Seeger's manifesto. He saw the group as a real threat, willing to wage a savage war within America's borders. By its actions the group had become terrorists. Seeger was using the tools of terrorism, intimidation and overt violent acts, to push his intentions into the public eye. A total disregard for life and property and defiance against the legally elected administration.

Now Bolan was behind the wheel of the Crown Vic again, the car pointed in the direction of the sprawling Pennsylvania heartland. Lyons sat beside him saying little, but ready for what they might have to confront.

The city lay behind them. Val Paxton, in the protective custody of a Stony Man escort, was on her way to Oregon, bags packed, and not too happy at having to abandon her apartment. Lyons had been disappointed at her departure. Their brief and hectic time together had left him with a degree of respect for the young woman that could easily have developed into stronger feelings given time. From the way she reacted Paxton was harboring similar feelings. That had been demonstrated in the way she had held him and kissed him just before she left. And she had made certain Lyons had a contact number for her. Whether anything would develop was for another place and another time.

Bolan and Lyons had booked into a motel outside Philadelphia. They spent the night there, moving out by dawn and hitting the road.

They were waiting for final information on Pelman's Farm from Stony Man. Electronic intel was helpful, but it only went so far. In the end it was down to the operatives on the ground to deal with any situation and to make on-the-spot decisions.

Which, Bolan had thought, was what it was all about.

BOLAN REVERSED the car until it was hidden by the thick shrubbery and trees a quarter mile from the farm entrance. While Lyons went to open the trunk and offload their hardware, Bolan made a call to Stony Man.

"We're gearing up now," he told Barbara Price when she came on the line.

"You both still okay?"

"You sound worried."

"Shouldn't I be?"

"Just nice to hear you admit it."

"Now you're teasing."

"Any updated intel I need to know about?"

"I'll put Aaron on. He has some information he wants to download to your laptop. Take care, both of you."

Price handed over her phone and Kurtzman's gruff tones came on.

"I'm downloading now," he said. "While that comes through, I've got background for you."

"Go ahead."

"America the Free is nothing but a smoke screen," Kurtzman said over Bolan's cell. "Carmen has run the name every which way from sundown. Nothing. Doesn't exist. I think they created it to draw attention away from the Brethren and let them operate in the clear. I'll let Carmen run on it, see if she can extract anything that might have a scrap of truth in it.

"In the meantime, Striker, you have my word—and would I lie to you?—that your genuine, undiluted target is Pelman's Farm. If that place has grown or even planted anything since it was rented out, I will give up my famous coffee recipe without a protest. The place stood empty for nine months after the original owner died. He had no family to take it over, just some distant relative on the other side of the country who had no interest. The place was put up for lease. No takers until our friend Petrie, acting on behalf of one of his *inves-*

tors, took up the lease. Ideal situation for what the Brethren wanted. It stands well off the main highway, along a feeder road surrounded by a lot of pastureland. It's genuine rural territory out there. Closest neighbor is another farm eight miles away. Farm delivery vehicles would not be suspect, nor other traffic going back and forth. I'm sending through digital scan images of the place taken just an hour ago. Look at the close-up of the vehicle parked outside the storage shed. Familiar? Same configuration as the vehicles used in the previous attacks."

Bolan studied the laptop display as it came on-screen. The sharp images from the orbiting satellite would allow him and Lyons to work out their strategy.

"You guys need anything else?" Kurtzman asked in Bolan's ear. "I do have other work, you know."

Bolan smiled. "Thanks, Aaron. This is good stuff."

"Only good?" Kurtzman asked, sounding aggrieved. "What's wrong with superb? Excellent? Earth-shattering?"

"I know how modest you are. I didn't want to embarrass you."

"You're a funny man. Talk later."

Bolan cut the call without any further delay. The sound of a friendly voice could easily become a distraction, and the last thing he needed right now was anything pulling his thoughts away from what lay ahead.

Lyons had opened their bags. They spent the next few minutes changing into their combat gear, Bolan, as usual, choosing his blacksuit. Lyons pulled on a set of camou fatigues. They moved to ordnance: Beretta 93-R and the .44 Magnum Desert Eagle for Bolan, the big .357 Colt Python and a backup SIG P-226 for

Lyons. Their lead weapon was the M-16 with 30-round magazines. A 9 mm Uzi hung from a sling around Bolan's neck. John "Cowboy" Kissinger, Stony Man's armorer, had also sent along a 12-gauge Franchi SPAS shotgun for Lyons. Kissinger understood Lyons's preferences for the weapon and had removed the folding metal buttstock for easier handling. There was a satisfied smile on the Able Team leader's face as he thumbed shells into the underbarrel tube magazine. Spare ammunition for their weapons went into the pouches on their combat harnesses. Fragmentation and stun grenades were clipped to their harnesses, while Cold Steel Tanto combat knives were sheathed on their belts.

Bolan showed his partner the image detail on the laptop screen. Lyons absorbed the images, pointing out several positions and suggesting where they might begin their assault. His strategy mirrored Bolan's. With everything fixed in their minds, the Executioner powered down the laptop and placed it in the trunk. He closed it and used the remote to secure the car.

Lyons watched him zip the keys in one of his blacksuit's pockets. "I hope they're secure," he said. "It's one hell of a walk back to town. Especially dressed like this."

"I'll keep them safe for you, Mom."

The final piece of equipment they donned were compact com-links. Once they had the headsets and microphones in place, they ran a swift check.

"Let's do it," Bolan said.

They parted company.

Bolan headed for the west perimeter, Lyons the east. They had a distance to go and needed to move carefully in case there were lookouts. They cut a wide swath across the lush Pennsylvania landscape before closing in on the fenced property.

Easing up to the high wooden fencing, Bolan dropped flat in the thick grass and peered through the gaps in the white-painted planks. He had come in at the side of the largest of the storage sheds some thirty feet away. He noticed the heavy activity centered around the building. Parked about ten feet away from the open doors was a panel truck.

The one Kurtzman had picked up on his sat scan? he wondered.

Bolan checked out the rest of the open complex and failed to see any other trucks. Okay, he admitted, they could be inside one or more of the sheds. Or the house.

He spoke into his com-link. "Ironman, this is Striker. You seen any other panel trucks your location?"

"None," came the reply. "Few cars. SUVs. No trucks."

"I see the truck Bear picked up on his sat scan in front of my position. We need to check it out when we get inside the perimeter. There's a lot of activity around it."

"Okay."

"If it starts to move out before we reach it…"

"Got the message, Striker."

BOLAN CRAWLED ALONG the base of the fence until he reached one of the support posts. The planks were nailed to the post. Brown stains ran from the heads of the nails down the white paint, evidence the planks had been in place for some time. Bolan placed his M-16 on the ground and gripped the plank closest to him. He tested the grip of the nails. They were sound but not embedded in hard wood. Time and exposure had reduced the grip of the nails in the post where moisture had soaked in. Bolan exerted considerable muscle power, gently rocking the plank until the nails started to give. He paused, then started to pull again. This time the nails slid gradually from the soft wood, allowing him to pry the long plank clear of the post. Bolan pulled it back enough to enable him to work his way through, reaching out to bring his M-16 with him. He eased the plank back into position, guiding the nails into their original holes. He brushed away telltale flecks of white paint that had fallen from the post so there was no immediate obvious sign of entry.

The grass near the fence line was thick and uncut, concealing Bolan's presence. He didn't allow complacency to weaken him. He needed better cover than blades of grass. Raising his head, he picked out a timber stack laid out alongside a small shed. He took a longer scan of the immediate area. No one in sight. The panel truck was still the center of attention, and Bolan saw that a number of the men around the vehicle were not helping with the loading. Now that he was closer he could see they were all armed. Some carried their weapons, others had them slung. Even from where he was positioned he recognized the P-90s, which confirmed his suspicions. It was the first time he had seen farmworkers armed like these men. There was something in their manner, the way they carried themselves, that suggested these men were far removed from manual agricultural workers. If he was right, and from what he was seeing he didn't doubt it, the only harvest these men would be gathering was death.

"Ironman, I'm inside and eyeing the panel truck being loaded. There's a squad guarding it. All armed."

"Be making my way in your direction any time now, Striker. Whoa! Eyeballed a couple of armed patrollers myself. Local farm boys my ass—"

As Lyons cut off abruptly, Bolan picked up the heavy boom that could only have come from the Able Team leader's SPAS shotgun. The stuttering crackle of autofire followed almost immediately, chased by two more shotgun blasts.

Good or bad, the assault was under way, and it could only be resolved by immediate action.

Bolan forgot about temporary cover. He pushed to his feet and broke in the direction of the panel truck, its loaders and the armed squad gathered around it.

The Brethren activists spotted him before he was halfway to the truck. One of the armed men yelled a warning and immediately went for his slung weapon. A second man, yards away, already had his P-90 in his hands and he swung around to pinpoint Bolan and open fire. If he had taken time to aim and lock, he might have achieved his objective, but he failed on both counts. His instant fire was way off target, and he didn't get a second chance. Bolan raised his M-16, sighted and laid a 3-round burst into the guy's chest, kicking him back against the side of the panel truck and then to the ground. The sight of one of their own going down caused a general scattering of the loaders and the armed crew, though the first man who had raised the warning shout stood his ground, sweeping his weapon on target. He was no seasoned combat veteran and stood little chance against the honed skills of Mack Bolan. He had already dropped to one knee, settling his M-16 firm to his shoulder, and loosed a second triburst that spun the gunner off his feet. Out the corner of his eye Bolan spotted another shooter leaning out from the rear of the truck, weapon rising. The Executioner swiveled at the hip and fired. The 5.56 mm slugs punched through the thin metal of the corner panel, flattening and ripping into the would-be shooter's face and neck, slivers of auto metal piercing his flesh. The man stumbled away from the rear of the truck, dropping his weapon and clamping hands to his bloody face, screaming in pain. The second he was in full view Bolan hit him in the chest with a burst that ended his pain and his life.

LYONS HAD CLEARED HIS FENCE in a fashion similar to Bolan's. He had gained his feet, covered by a piece of farm machinery that looked as if it had been in the same spot for years. Long grass grew up around the faded paintwork and had started to sprout between section of the chassis. Aware that time was not on his side, Lyons moved toward the far end of the machine, his SPAS cocked and ready for use. He checked out the area, seeing nothing except more abandoned farm equipment and outbuildings.

That situation changed fast, as circumstances were apt to do in combat scenarios.

As Lyons conversed with Bolan, the pair of SMG-carrying men who appeared in Lyons's line of sight swiveled their weapons in his direction.

Lyons reacted with the speed and deadliness that had become second nature and let go with the first shot from the big shotgun. The target caught it chest-high, his body ripped open from waist to sternum, a bloody eruption of flesh and organs ripped from his body as he went down. His partner, shock etched across his face, triggered his own weapon, the crackle of autofire followed by twin booms as Lyons fired again. His shots almost ripped the other guy's left arm off just above the elbow, the final one placing its charge full in the target's face. With his head torn apart, the guy fell back without a sound and lay on the bloody earth.

Angry at the way his stealthy approach had been disturbed, Lyons pushed out from behind his cover and ran in the direction of Bolan's position, his ears picking up the crackle of autofire as his comrade in arms also joined the battle. As he ran, the Able Team leader thumbed in fresh shells to replace the ones he had used, his eyes searching for further enemy presence.

He was rewarded for his diligence as an open Jeep swept around the side of a large shed, raising dust as it turned in his direction. Apart from the driver there were two others in the vehicle. One on the passenger seat, the other braced in a standing position in the rear. He was staying upright by hanging on to the roll bar set behind the seats and bringing an SMG into play. The weapon chattered, the line of slugs coming uncomfortably close to Lyons, who took a reckless dive to the ground, rolling onto his front as the Jeep angled in his direction, the standing gunner turning to get a clearer shot.

The man in the passenger seat came on line as if someone had pressed his start button, bringing his own autoweapon off his lap and aiming it at Lyons. Propped up on his arms, the big ex-cop raised the SPAS and began to pull the trigger, jacking out the full eight-load capacity of the shotgun, raking the Jeep and passengers. The continuous roar of the SPAS 12 drowned out the sound of the Jeep's engine. As the muzzle tracked the vehicle and the powerful impact of the shots took their toll, the Jeep lurched drunkenly. The bloodied driver slumped sideways, the passenger clutched his mangled side and the upright gunner was thrown across the open rear of the vehicle. He fell across the tailgate, then out and down onto the ground. The vehicle stalled, the engine dying.

Lyons climbed to his feet, sucking breath into his lungs from the hard dive to the ground. He heard a moaning sound coming from the hit passenger. The guy was slumped loosely in his bloody seat, his right side showing a gaping hole that was pulsing blood through shattered ribs and punctured organs. He stared at Lyons, his face pale under the streaked blood. His breath came in rattling, sodden gasps. There was no hesitation in Lyons's actions as he drew the Python and put a mercy round through the man's skull. The driver and the rear gunner were both dead when Lyons checked them.

He reloaded the SPAS, cocked it, then moved on to join Bolan.

CHAPTER NINE

As he closed in on the panel truck, aware of the continuing presence of the Brethren, Bolan realized they were not about to quit. None of them appeared to have anything but fierce determination to keep up the struggle. Under other circumstances he might have given them credit for their loyalty to their cause, but in this instance the Brethren was waging war against their own kind, their own society and their own country, and for that Bolan could not forgive. He had memories etched in his mind of the results of what the Brethren had already done. Torn and twisted bodies. The bleak aftermath of cold and calculated strikes against federal buildings that had not simply left behind shattered concrete, but human wreckage, too, ordinary members of the public who had been caught up in the brutal destruction, swept up in the terror of the moment a child and mother, life ripped from them in the horror of the explosion. That image and others would stay with Bolan for a long time after this was all over.

The Brethren deserved no better treatment than any

terrorist striking the United States. Bolan could see no saving graces in their manifesto. They were neither patriot nor loyalist. This secretive organization was simply out to destabilize the America that had nurtured and empowered them. Bolan would have been among the first to hold up his hand and accept that even America had its faults. No nation on Earth could put hand on heart and claim to be perfect, though some might try by concealing their true intent. America struggled to satisfy all calls from its people. Sometimes it fell short and rightly so, because in the end the country was governed by human beings who tried to keep the balance while also attempting to please all groups. America was no different. She had her shortcomings despite all that the administration attempted, but there was an ongoing drive to eradicate the failures. Adding to the internal difficulties, the nation still shouldered global responsibilities, reaching out to aid those in need, and they drank greedily from America's well.

The Brethren used negativity as its basis, pushing its agenda by highlighting the nation's woes and employing indiscriminate violence and destruction to throw the population into panic. The group strove to alienate people from government, and seized any opportunity to use that fragmenting to further its own twisted cause, regardless of how many fellow Americans they killed.

That alone would have been enough to bring Bolan down on the Brethren. His struggle was in part always based on protecting innocents, those who were unable to fight back, or drawn into a conflict simply by being there. The lines had already been drawn. Now the Brethren had stepped over, disregarding who became drawn into their line of fire, and that brought them into Mack Bolan's sights.

Moving shapes revealed themselves behind the bulk of the panel truck and Bolan switched his line of approach, moving quickly to the front of the vehicle even as he picked up the scuffle of sound. He dropped to a crouch close by the front wheel, the M-16 up and ready as he took a swift look beneath the vehicle and saw two pairs of booted feet. Bolan lowered the rifle and sent a couple of bursts the length of the truck, the 5.56 mm projectiles tearing into ankles, breaking bone. The moment he fired, Bolan pushed to a crouch and moved around the front end of the truck, sensing a presence as he rounded the hood. One of the armed Brethren loomed large, taken by surprise at Bolan's sudden appearance. He raised his SMG a fraction too slowly, and the Executioner hit him with a burst from the M-16.

The slugs blew out between the guy's shoulders, leaving him gasping against the stunning impact. He stumbled away from Bolan, his eyes wide with shock and the dawning realization that he was not going to survive. He was dying even as Bolan stepped by him.

One of the wounded Brethren, leaning against the truck body, shattered ankles leaking blood, saw the black-clad figure as Bolan came into view. It was the last thing he saw just before the M-16 crackled and delivered his exit from life. There was one more man facing Bolan, his face twisted against the pain in his lower limbs, but still able to drag his handgun from the hip holster. He felt a stunning blow to his chest and the next moment he was on the ground, coughing up blood in his final moments.

Bolan took a glance around. The loading crew had

vanished inside the open shed, and he spotted movement in the shadows. Taking a moment, Bolan checked
out the contents of the panel truck. He was not surprised
when he saw the partly loaded packs of high explosives.
It seemed that the information he had gained had been
accurate. The Brethren had been preparing for yet another bombing.

"Ironman, bomb confirmed. In the truck outside
shed."

"Got you, Striker. Heading in your direction."

"Take a look at the farmhouse."

"Will do."

The crackle of weapons fire from the storage shed,
fired too close to the truck, made Bolan vacate his position and swing away from the shed's open doors. As
he ran, he plucked a flash-bang grenade from his harness. He yanked the pin, turned and over-armed the
grenade at the opening in the front of the shed. The grenade landed a foot short, then rolled. Before it detonated
Bolan threw a second, this time with better results. He
turned away from the shed, head down, and heard the
harsh crack of the grenades going off. The flash-bang
had an effect on the men inside the shed, most of whom
had been clustered just inside the open doors. Despite
not being cloistered in a perfect confined space, they
caught a degree of the grenades' power. It left them
temporarily stunned, eyes hazed, and when Bolan
swung back and breached the opening he had the advantage. His M-16 cut back and forth, taking on the
hardmen with ruthless efficiency. He left them sprawled
on the shed floor, kicking weapons aside from outstretched hands that were never going to lift them again.

The storage shed held a large amount of explosives,

blocky square packs of Gantz's explosive compound, sealed in thick plastic wrap. There were also crates of contraband weapons, some still bearing U.S. military insignia. On a wooden workbench Bolan saw timers and detonators. Farther back he saw cutting and welding equipment, as well as the remains of stripped-down panel trucks. This was where the vehicles for carrying the bombs had been adapted for the Brethren's use.

Bolan paused at the opening, checking out the area between his position and the main farmhouse. He saw Lyons cutting across in the direction of the house, and in typical Ironman fashion the Able Team leader hit the side door with his booted foot and barreled inside. Bolan sprinted in the same direction, his destination the front entrance. It wasn't out of politeness, simple expedience. If Lyons had gone in at the rear of the house, the rats he flushed out would make the front their intended escape route.

Keeping an eye out for any more combatants, Bolan centered on the front of the white-painted farmhouse. It had an upper story, the windows appearing clear, but Mack Bolan never took stock of first impressions. His apprehension proved to be correct when a dark figure moved in one of the windows. The barrel of a weapon appeared, the muzzle drawing down to pick up Bolan's moving figure. He ran a zigzag pattern for several steps, then dropped to one knee, the M-16 snug against his shoulder. The window shooter triggered fast, his shot kicking up dust to the soldier's right. Then Bolan's finger stroked the trigger, sending a burst of 5.56 mm slugs in the shooter's direction. The dark shape windmilled backward as the rounds struck him. The moment he fired, Bolan pushed forward, closing on the house's front wall, taking him out of any other shooter's angle of fire. He flattened against the boards and almost immediately heard the crackle of autofire coming from inside the building. Bolan didn't hesitate. He turned in the direction of the stoop and main door, keeping close to the wall. He reached the steps, where a covered veranda ran to the far side. The front door was flung open and a squad of gunners tumbled onto the stoop, shouting and firing into the house. The steady boom of Lyons's SPAS 12 could be heard, with the shattering of glass and hard footsteps in the background.

The lead figure erupting from the house saw Bolan and swiveled to engage him. The gunner wielded a heavy autopistol, and he opened fire more in panic than controlled resistance. Of the three shots fired only one came close enough to tug at Bolan's left sleeve. The soldier drilled three rounds into the guy's side, spinning him off his feet and dumping him hard onto the porch. Hitting him with a follow-up head shot, Bolan turned his weapon on the other figures crowding the stoop who now found themselves caught between two fires. Bolan took out one, the sole survivor catching a blast from Lyons that kicked him clear off the stoop to crash to the ground on his back, his body opened like an overripe melon.

Lyons appeared in the doorway, still wielding the SPAS. He caught sight of Bolan.

"We clear?"

Bolan didn't answer, indicating the upper story. Lyons spoke softly into his throat mike so his words were only audible through Bolan's earphones.

"More than one?"

"Hard to tell. Only one showed himself."

"You stay there and catch them when they jump," Lyons said, and silently backtracked into the house.

Easing away from the stoop, Bolan stepped out a little so he could see the upstairs windows. Apart from curtains gently moving in the breeze he could see nothing. He could hear Lyons breathing in his earphones as he slowly mounted the stairs. It went quiet after that. Bolan kept his eyes on the windows.

Then there was a frantic explosion of sound: Lyons's boots crashing against the floorboards; the splintering of a door kicked wide; distant voices; the crackle of autofire and the heavier boom from Lyons's shotgun. The window Bolan had been observing became the center of attention as a figure burst through, taking a leap onto the side roof. The guy was carrying an SMG, struggling to keep himself upright. He had momentarily forgotten about Bolan. When he remembered, he was already an acquired target. Bolan's burst caught him in the chest. The shooter toppled back against the window, dropping his weapon as he clawed at the new pain in his chest. His legs folded and he fell, rolling down the roof angle, clearing the edge and dropping to the ground. He landed hard, raising thin puffs of dust and snapping his spine.

"THIS IS JUST A BASE for their bomb cache," Lyons said. "I checked upstairs. Nothing suggests they stay here on a permanent basis. Probably just had a small squad to keep an eye on things between strikes."

Bolan took a look around himself, agreeing with Lyons's observations. The lack of furniture, and even kitchen utensils, seemed to confirm that the Brethren only used the place when they needed to. He was disappointed initially—until he walked into a small room at the front of the house and found a computer station. There was a top-of-the-line laptop sitting on a plain wooden desk. It was switched on, the screen showing a data configuration comprising dates, locations and times. Bolan sat at the desk and ran through the list. The majority of the locations were the sites where the Brethren had already detonated their bombs, but at the end of the list was a collection of similar places that had not yet been hit.

"Carl, you should take a look at this," Bolan said as Lyons appeared in the doorway.

The Able Team leader stood at Bolan's side, scanning the data, and was suitably impressed at what he saw. "Appears we got lucky."

Bolan checked the contents of the hard drive, opening a list of files. He held back from opening any of them in case they were protected and possibly rigged to erase if a password was not used.

"This is where we need Aaron's magic," he said.

He used the Internet connection and got Kurtzman to download the laptop's contents. Using his cell phone, he had a brief conversation with the man and waited until he had confirmation everything had arrived at Stony Man. Kurtzman requested Bolan return the laptop to Stony Man so his team could dig into the hard drive.

While Bolan was engaged with Kurtzman, Lyons took off to pick up their transport. Bolan had his call transferred to Brognola and gave him a full rundown on what had transpired at the farm site.

"Hal, there's enough explosives here to separate California from the mainland. It needs to be moved ASAP."

"The ATF is going to love you," Brognola said. "Let me take care of it. Give me the time to get this into motion and you'll have suits crawling all over that place. And before you ask, you and Ironman will be cleared so once the troops arrive you can leave."

"Hal, don't mention the computer we located. I need to get it to Aaron. We need every piece of information we can get."

"Will do, buddy. You two okay?"

"We got a little dusty is all. To be honest, Hal, I think the Brethren on site here were caught cold. We took them by surprise. Like they didn't expect to be disturbed."

"Complacent maybe. They had it easy for so long it started to get too cozy?"

"After Philly? I would have expected a little more resistance. Maybe we moved too fast for them. Or maybe they had local backup. Someone watching the area for them and keeping things covered. Our covert visit could have left them with their hats in their hands."

"If that's the case the Brethren didn't get their money's worth today."

"Hal, we went in by the back door, so to speak."

"Fine. But talking of backs, I suggest you and Carl watch yours. Just in case."

"Point taken."

BOLAN STEPPED OUT of the farmhouse, the laptop held under one arm. He watched the Crown Vic dusting up the approach to the house. As Lyons swung the big car around and braked, Bolan saw two sheriff's department cruisers appear at the entrance to the road.

"Carl, open the trunk." At the rear of the car they took

off their combat gear, stowing it and their weapons in the trunk, along with the laptop. Both men retained their handguns. Bolan kept his hands in plain sight. Lyons stood casually relaxed, hands on his hips, his Python tucked in his belt at the small of his back.

"Local cops," Lyons said, slamming the trunk shut. He leaned against the side of the vehicle and watched as one of the cruisers, its roof lights flashing, barreled up the road, leaving a trail of dust in its wake.

Bolan stood watching the black-and-white roll to a stop some ten feet away. There were two occupants. The driver, lean and wary, made eye contact with Bolan and held it as the man in the passenger seat pushed open his door and climbed out. He was a big man. Not overweight, simply a big man, carrying himself tall and broad. He wore a tan uniform and a leather jacket that had a silver badge pinned to it. Around his waist he wore a belt and holster. The handgun was a 9 mm Beretta and the man rested his right hand on the butt. Dangling from his large left hand was a Mossberg pump-action shotgun. He stood for a while surveying the scene, his expression changing from shocked surprise to anger. His eyes were everywhere, not missing a thing. Finally he set his gaze on Bolan, who had remained still and silent.

"What the fuck has been going on here? Who the hell are you asswipes?" His deep voice held a harsh tone.

"Which question do I answer first?" Bolan asked, leaning forward to check the badge on the man's jacket. *"Sheriff?*

"A comic, as well." The man took his hand off the Beretta, transferring it to the shotgun as he swung it to cover Bolan and Lyons. "See if you find this funny. Boys, you got one thing right. Hereabouts I'm the law."

"So, Sheriff, are you going to charge us with something?" Lyons asked. His tone was low, even, and hearing it Bolan sensed his partner's rising frustration.

"Boy, it's likely I might just put you down right where you stand."

"Without reading me my rights?"

"Right here and now, sonny, you don't have any rights. I see dead people and caught you on the property. And I don't know you from squat."

"They say education is an enlightening thing," Lyons said.

"Meaning?" the sheriff demanded.

"Right now you are about to receive some."

"What in hell are you goin' on about?"

"Right now, Sheriff," Bolan said, "you are in deep and getting deeper every time you open your mouth. So I suggest you listen."

"Son, you don't know who you are messing with. One phone call and I can make you vanish."

"This tub of lard has been watching too many cheap movies," Lyons said. "Let me slap his fat head."

"Okay, enough of this shit." Over his shoulder the sheriff called to his driver. "Boyd, call our friends. Let them know what's gone down here."

"Before you do that," Bolan said, "it might pay to understand what you've got yourself into."

Lyons laughed, enjoying the moment. "I said it was going to be educational."

"You're already down for using your weapon in a threatening manner. Also stating you might kill us," Bolan explained. "And consorting with a criminal organization."

"Say what?"

"Your driver was about to call the Brethren to tell them you have us."

Bolan's comment had the desired effect. Reference to the Brethren hit the sheriff hard. His face paled for an instant, then flushed heavily at being caught out. Bolan's call had been a calculated risk, but he had been right. Local law was running interference for the Brethren.

The heat had just been notched up to a dangerous level.

Boyd, leaning out the cruiser door, had a look on his face that warned Bolan the man was dangerous. His eyes betrayed his self-assured cockiness. In his own mind he was untouchable. And that made him doubly dangerous.

"Hell, Kyle, why don't you just put some shots in this pair and be done with it."

"Boyd, I'll decide what to do."

"You're the sheriff," Lyons said evenly, his eyes fixed on Boyd's smirking face.

"That's right," Boyd said. "Say, bub, you never did say who you are."

Bolan faced the sheriff. "Did I add resisting federal agents to my list?"

Sheriff Kyle's face flushed with barely contained rage. "Feds? Well, my day just keeps getting better and better. Hear that, Boyd? We caught us a pair of the real mothers. Government fuckin' hired guns."

"Seeger should give us a bonus," Boyd crowed. "I'll take the blond one."

He pushed open his door and started to climb out, his hand reaching for his holstered handgun. For a few seconds his body was blocked by the cruiser's door.

Lyons slid his right hand out of sight, a move that caught Kyle and Boyd wanting. As Lyons's hand reappeared, holding the big Colt, he sidestepped. His hand swung the weapon up, finger already over the trigger and he snap aimed and fired before Boyd could complete his response. The .357 boomed, and Boyd gave a screech of pain as the big slug thudded into the fleshy part of his left shoulder, spinning him and bouncing him off the side of the cruiser. He fell, blood pulsing from the hole in his shoulder.

Sheriff Kyle was shocked into inaction by the loud crack of the Python. His eyes flicked in Lyons's direction, almost as if he expected the next shot to be aimed at him. The moment his eyes moved from him, Bolan lunged forward. His left hand batted the Mossberg aside, then he slammed into Kyle with enough force to throw the big man across the hood of the cruiser. The sheriff recovered quick enough to swing a booted foot as Bolan moved in. The kick glanced off the Executioner's shoulder. Kyle rolled and got his feet under him, making an attempt to bring the shotgun back on line. Bolan launched his right fist in a powerful swing that crunched against Kyle's meaty jaw. The blow spun the sheriff over the hood again, Bolan following through to plant his open palm against the back of Kyle's skull and slam him facedown against the car. Kyle grunted and collapsed, the shotgun slipping from his fingers. Picking up the Mossberg, Bolan also took the man's Beretta from his holster.

"Let's hope it isn't a large sheriff's department," Lyons said, bending over the moaning Boyd to disarm him.

"If you don't want Boyd to bleed to death, Carl,

you'd better do something about that hole in his shoulder."

"Who said anything about *not* wanting him to bleed to death?"

Lyons moved to the cruiser and located the first-aid box stowed in the trunk. He hauled Boyd into a sitting position and started to apply a pressure pad and bandage.

Using Kyle's own issue handcuffs, Bolan secured the man to the grille of the cruiser. He stood back and took out his cell, calling Stony Man once again to report what had happened. Brognola listened in impatient silence.

"I'll make sure there's a medic in the team and Aaron can run a make on Sheriff Kyle."

"No way of knowing how deep the Brethren is in Kyle's department."

"I'm getting so I don't want to hear that damn name anymore."

"One thing's for sure. These people are reaching out. Local law enforcement now. What next, Hal?"

"I figure it's time for you to come in as soon as reinforcements arrive and take charge. We need to reassess what intel we have and decide where to move next. I know one thing. It won't be a vacation. I'll try to be there when you arrive," Brognola advised. "First I have to make a meeting with an old friend. If it works out, it might be to our advantage."

CHAPTER TEN

Lewis Bradshaw, special agent from the FBI's Office of International Operations, was a man who exuded authority. Tall, fit-looking and in his late forties, he wore his mid-gray suit as if he had been born to it. He took Brognola's outstretched hand, then sat facing him across a low table. Around them the busy lounge of the InterContinental Hotel buzzed with the comings and goings of guests and friends, unaware of the presence of two of Washington's premier law officials.

"Still take your coffee black?" Brognola asked.

"Too old to change now," Bradshaw said. He took the filled cup, leaning back in the leather seat. "How's that family of yours, Hal?"

Brognola smiled. "Fine the last time I saw them."

"Busy days in uncertain times."

The conversation halted for a few moments while Brognola cleared his thoughts.

"Lew, we've never been the type to bullshit each other. I'll say it straight-out. I know about your two dead agents in West Africa. Their investigation overlaps something my department is involved with. Off the record, talk to me about your case and I'll do my damnedest to get closure for your people because I know you can't."

Bradshaw's face remained expressionless as he mulled over the offer. He drained his coffee and poured himself a second cup. "You know what it's like working with your hands tied behind you, Hal? They say go out there and stop the perps. The terrorists. The people doing what they can to destroy us. In the same action they handcuff us and put a bag over our heads, telling us not to upset this cause. Don't tread on any toes. Beware of litigation. Oh, and by the way don't forget the first instruction to stop the bad guys, will you."

"I've been there, Lew. Right now *I* don't have that problem, so it lets me sleep at night." Brognola smiled. "That's when I actually get home to sleep."

"Does this current assignment have anything to do with the recent bombings?"

Brognola nodded, albeit briefly. "Yes. Lew, I know all about lines of demarcation, interagency boundaries and all that crap. Here and now, I just want to stop what's happening, and treading on a few toes isn't about to slow me down."

Bradshaw gave a genuine smile this time. "One thing never changes, Hal. You always did enjoy giving the finger to anything that prevented you doing what was right."

"Right is taking down the bastards killing Americans on their own streets. Blowing up young children. And murdering your agents in Africa. Our intel has pinpointed the Brethren, and my operational brief is to stop them any way I can. Lew, I need help to achieve that, so if you have anything that will give me that help, it will stay between the two of us. That's a promise, and you know I don't bullshit on promises."

Lewis Bradshaw knew only a few people he could really trust. His friend from the Justice Department was at the top of that list. Bradshaw, like any number of people in law enforcement, was up to his neck in red tape and need-to-know, frustrated by the sneering complacency of criminals and terrorists who quoted legal restrictions and their human rights while they still had the blood of their victims on their hands. He was thinking about two of his agents. Dead agents, left in the dirt of an African slum, bodies hacked almost beyond recognition. It had been Bradshaw's job to inform the families and to see the shock and disbelief on the faces of the dead agents' wives. He also understood how futile it would be trying to bring the killers to justice. His West African local contact had informed him he knew who the killers were but retribution for the crimes would be near impossible to guarantee.

Unless he accepted Hal Brognola's offer.

Bradshaw looked across at his friend. Brognola understood the predicament. He was part of the community in which they both served, and making things right was one of the most elusive matters to have to deal with.

"Can you do this?" he asked.

"They won't get away with it this time."

Bradshaw looked into the chasm that lay between the law he served and a need for punishment. For once the gap didn't seem all that wide.

"Give me an hour." Bradshaw stood. "Remember, Hal, I was never here. This discussion didn't happen."

Brognola nodded. "This time we get it done."

THE WAR ROOM conference table was partly covered by documentation, photographs and as much hard copy dealing with the mission they could gather. Wall monitors displayed more data. One, on its own, was tuned into a 24/7 dedicated news channel.

The group consisted of Bolan, Lyons, Brognola, who had returned from his meeting a short while back, Price and Kurtzman.

They were discussing an aspect of the situation that Kurtzman had been giving some deep thought.

"Diamonds. It's been bugging me since the subject cropped up, and I believe I figured it out."

"You going to share, or spend the day telling us how smart you are?" Lyons said.

Kurtzman ignored him. "The only use diamonds would be to the Brethren would be for finance. On a buy-low, sell-high basis. A few years ago this was happening with al Qaeda. They were funding their operations by taking cheap diamonds from a West African source, selling them on the black market and pushing the profits into buying weapons. The market grew until there was a clamp on illegal diamond trading. Currently there isn't the same amount of dealing, but it hasn't dried up fully."

"You found a source?" Price asked.

"Yes. And it links to our new best friends the Brethren."

Kurtzman turned his wheelchair, working a remote to clear one of the monitors. He brought up fresh images, maps and document downloads.

"I was running traces on all of the Brethren. The guy there is Max Belmont. Details of Belmont's recent travels came up. He's been making visits to West Africa over the past four, five months. Notably to this area near the coast. It's no tourist destination. Had nothing but civil unrest, number of coups over the last few years. The current administration is no better or worse than the last few. The real government is in exile, waiting its chance. While that's on the back burner the area is going downhill. Famine. Starvation. The region under siege. Mainly due to this delightful character. General Joseph M'Tusi. Local butcher, homicidal maniac cum warlord. His army roams the region doing just whatever it wants, when it wants. Any aid comes in, M'Tusi vets it first and skims off what he wants—not what he needs—what he wants. The man is a walking nightmare. The region has a diamond-mining capability. Produces good quantities of stones for cosmetic and industrial use. M'Tusi appears to have a tight rein on the production, and he doesn't seem to be making deals with the legitimate markets. Before you ask, a diamond representative paid a visit to talk with M'Tusi. The guy barely got out with his head intact. Since then M'Tusi has been left alone."

Kurtzman riffled through more paperwork and slid it across the table. "But he deals with certain individuals. Look at the one I circled."

Lyons checked the name. "Son of a bitch. Jack Regan."

"It's not the first time Regan has been involved in shady deals the SOG has locked on to. We tagged him in Santa Lorca. And running weapons over the border into Mexico. Both times he moved on before anyone could stop him."

"So where does he come in on this?"

"Maybe he's just working his usual deal supplying weapons to the Brethren. Here's intel on Regan being spotted in West Africa. In M'Tusi's region. With Belmont. I'm thinking he did some introductions for the Brethren," Kurtzman said. "Rumor has it M'Tusi's ordnance buying list has been getting bigger over the last six, seven months. He has ideas about deposing the current ruling party and needs the weapons to back his play. The area M'Tusi controls is desolate, and it doesn't have much going for it except the fact it has a rich diamond field running through it. No one has tried to move on that because M'Tusi has the region bottled up. Nothing moves in his territory without his say-so."

"I thought the diamond business was pretty well tied down," Lyons said. "All controlled by international combines."

"Tell M'Tusi that. He plays by his own rules."

"What do we figure? M'Tusi is trading diamonds for the weapons he wants, and the Brethren is cashing in with stones they got cheap?"

"There's always a market for good quality diamonds, on or off the market," Bolan said.

Bolan and Lyons studied the data. It made for interesting reading, but even Bolan was caught off guard when he viewed the images of M'Tusi's atrocities against the people of his region. His kill squads stopped for nothing. Women and children had been slaughtered indiscriminately. The photographs told Bolan everything he needed to know about the man.

"This all ties in with the intel I brought in from my meeting this morning," Brognola said. "Two FBI agents from the Legal Attaché Office were murdered a few days ago because they apparently got too close to M'Tusi and his association with illegal diamond trading. Before they were killed they sent a coded message back to their boss at home, providing information about an upcoming deal between M'Tusi and his U.S. client."

Brognola slid a folder across the table to Bolan. He picked it up. The folder and the data inside were all anonymous. Printed on plain paper. No agency titles. No hints as to where it had come from.

"Take what you need from that data," Brognola said. "The folder does not leave this room except with me. No copies. No questions. The source is reliable. That's all I can say on the subject. Make sure you get what you need. As soon as I get back to my office, that file will be destroyed."

Bolan nodded. "Understood." He did not ask any more. Brognola had his reasons. It was obvious that the intel had come from someone within the security community.

"Something else," Kurtzman said. "That cell from Gantz? We checked his call list and ran traces on the numbers. Had to break into the cell phone provider to get hold of Gantz's account. Modesty prevents me explaining how tricky that is, but we did it. Carmen followed it through and tracked the numbers. The one that got our interest turned out to be a personal landline phone. The address was for a house owned by a certain Zac Lorens, Ojai, California." Kurtzman smiled when he saw the look on Bolan's face. "*That* Zac Lorens. Seeger's right-hand man in the Brethren."

"Those calls went direct to Lorens? Could be Brethren business," Bolan said.

"Could be," Lyons said. "But it's unusual to broadcast militia business that way. I would have expected it to be done direct to Seeger's base of operations. Or are we just being suspicious today?"

"Suspicion comes with the job," Brognola said. "In this instance you guys can be as paranoid as you want."

"We can check it out later," Bolan said. "There's something else we have to do concerning diamonds first."

"WHAT DO YOU MEAN he's disappeared?"

"No other way to say it, Deke. Petrie has vanished. So has the girl he had working at his office. The team has been taken down, too. Last call we got they were following some guy who snatched her from our team at her apartment."

"It has to be the same ones who crossed us at Gantz's place."

"Who are these fucks?"

"I wish I knew. They've got some good intel whoever they are."

"Seeger is going to be—"

"He already is. And now with the farm getting hit, as well."

"How's that going to be replaced?"

"We haven't got around to figuring that part yet. Seeger's got steam coming out of his ears so I'm laying low until he calms down."

"Deke. What do we do?"

"Make sure everyone understands how serious this all is, but make them see it hasn't shut us down. We need to step back and reorganize is all. Keep our brains working and our assholes puckered. I'll talk to the man when he calms down. In the meantime work on the plans already set out."

Ribak put down the phone. He leaned back and stared at a blank space on the wall across from his desk.

If nothing else, times were getting to be interesting. Seeger wouldn't view it like that. His master plan was being frayed around the edges by whoever was working these attacks on his organization. That was the trouble with these self-styled radicals. They had tunnel vision as far as their visions were concerned. They never considered anything disrupting their operations, and when that did happen they had no real idea how to work around the problem. They saw dark clouds looming ahead and refused to see the glimmer of light in the background.

Jesus, Ribak thought, give me a military mind any day of the week.

CHAPTER ELEVEN

West Africa

Mack Bolan and Carl Lyons flew to Africa three days later and were taken from the small civil airfield to the U.S. Embassy via one of the official cars. They were met by Lyle Kellerman, the embassy attaché who had been instructed by Washington to afford the two men as much assistance as they required and not to question their presence in the region under any circumstances. As much as he resented being shut out of their business, Kellerman extended a courteous welcome to his visitors.

Bolan, as Agent Matt Cooper, apologized for the intrusion and assured Kellerman he and his partner would not involve the embassy in any of their operations. Once they had collected their luggage from the trunk of the embassy car they requested a taxi be ordered so they could move to their booked rooms in one of the city hotels.

The embassy connection had been used so that the

luggage containing Bolan and Lyons's ordnance could be brought into the country as part of the official diplomatic baggage, ensuring that it was neither checked through customs nor searched. If Kellerman had suspicions, he kept them to himself, glad that Cooper and Benning stayed at the embassy for the minimum of time.

At the hotel Bolan checked them in and they went up to their rooms. As soon as he was alone, Bolan activated his Tri-Band cell and called the number he had memorized from Brognola's sensitive data at Stony Man. His call was picked up on the third ring.

"Am I speaking to Tomas Shambi?"

The reply was slow in coming, the speaker careful not to allow himself to give too much away. "Who wants to know?"

"A friend from America."

"Where are you calling from?"

"Room 201 at the Bell Marie Hotel."

"Are you Cooper or Benning?"

"Cooper."

"Shall I meet you as arranged?"

"That would be difficult since no arrangements were made."

Bolan picked up the sigh of relief.

"I can be there in ten minutes."

"The lounge bar. By the window overlooking the street."

TOMAS SHAMBI WAS a young black man with an easy manner. He arrived at the hotel on time. At the table he shook hands with Bolan with genuine feeling. Sensing Carl Lyons's less than enthusiastic attitude, he simply nodded his greeting to the blond man. He took a seat that allowed him to face both men. The African accepted Bolan's offer of a drink and asked for a bottle of Guinness stout, explaining he had developed a liking for it during his student days in London.

"Do you know London?"

"I've made a few visits," Bolan said.

Shambi realized it was all he was going to get so he didn't pursue the matter.

"It was very bad what happened to your people," he said. "I still feel partly responsible."

"The report doesn't read that way. You gave your help when it was asked for."

"But this time they died."

"And you knew this was going to happen?"

Shambi's shocked expression was real. "Of course not. They were my friends. Would I have sent them if I had known?"

Bolan laid a big hand on Shambi's shoulder. "Then it was not your fault, Tomas. Quit giving yourself such a hard time."

Their drinks arrived. Bolan took his and turned to Shambi. "To your friends, Phil and Anthony."

"Thank you for that."

"Tell us about this deal M'Tusi has coming up," Bolan said.

"Your FBI men found out about this latest deal. In two days from today M'Tusi meets with this man from the U.S.A. to sell more of his illegal diamonds."

"This American is Max Belmont?" Lyons asked. Shambi nodded. "Do you know who else will be there?"

"A man named Kesawayo. He works for M'Tusi as his negotiator on these deals. There will also be another American there. Jack Regan. He sells weapons to M'Tusi."

"We know Regan," Bolan said. "This won't be the first time we have crossed paths."

"The meeting is somewhere in the heart of M'Tusi's territory. He knows he will be safe there. No one dares go there without his permission."

"Time to lay on a little surprise for him," Lyons said.

"He will not be alone," Shambi said. "He will have some of his men with him. M'Tusi goes nowhere without his protection squad."

"Wouldn't be a surprise if there was no one there to share," Lyons said.

Lyons's manner puzzled Shambi. He looked at Bolan for an explanation.

"Agent Benning has an odd sense of humor."

"So it seems."

"Shambi, the earlier communication explained that the exact location of the meet was still not known. Has that been resolved?"

"We will find that out once we have met with Father Agostini."

"Is that *Father* in the religious sense?" Bolan asked.

Shambi smiled. "Yes. A priest. A most unusual man, Agent Cooper."

Lyons drained his glass. "I think I'm going to need another of these. Now we have a priest standing in as mission controller. A couple more beers and I might start to see things a little clearer."

SHAMBI TURNED UP the next morning driving a battered, dust-streaked old Land Rover. He parked at the side of the hotel and helped Bolan and Lyons stow their gear.

Lyons walked around the vehicle, checking the tires and subjecting the Land Rover to a physical inspection.

"Don't worry," Shambi said, "it will get us where we are going."

"In what kind of condition is my question."

That made the young African grin. "A very pessimistic man, Agent Benning."

Bolan agreed with him. "He had an unsettling upbringing. Makes him suspicious of just about everything."

Shambi got behind the wheel and fired up the engine. It roared into life, sending clouds of smoke from the exhaust. "This Land Rover has been blessed many times by Father Agostini."

"I thought religious benedictions were a one-time deal," Lyons said.

"Ah, but this Land Rover has little faith in itself, so it requires reassurance."

Shambi's laughter almost drowned out the grinding of gears and the general noisy vibration as the Land Rover moved off.

Once they were clear of the city and rolling across the arid plain, Bolan and Lyons armed themselves with hand weapons. Shambi watched with growing concern.

"Don't worry," Bolan told him. "We need reassurance, too."

The landscape around them was dry and dusty. Vegetation was thin, what grass they saw, brown and listless. A few stunted trees dotted the way. In the far distance, to the northeast, they could see low mountains. Overhead the sky was hard blue, with barely any cloud to shield them from the unrelenting burn of the sun.

Shambi drove steadily and the Land Rover performed efficiently. It was noisy, but the engine had been well looked after.

"This vehicle has driven many hundreds of miles and never let me down," Shambi said. "When I go to see Father Agostini he helps me to look after it. He is a clever man."

"I'm starting to see that," Bolan said. "His blessing of the Land Rover comes complete with a can of oil and new spark plugs."

"That and God's help."

In the rear of the Land Rover were boxed supplies for the priest. Shambi had also brought along plenty of bottled water for them to share as they drove. He stopped at noon, parking close to a tree to gain a little shade. As they rested, Bolan took a long look around.

"Is the region like this all over?"

"More or less," Shambi said. "The people have moved away from this area. You can see why. The best land is where M'Tusi and his army live. There is water and grass. It could be used for many things but M'Tusi steals everything and kills those who even think about standing up to him."

"What about the diamonds?" Lyons asked.

"The source for them is within M'Tusi's territory. He uses the people to mine for him. Terrifies them into working for him."

"And then sells the diamonds for himself," Bolan said.

"Yes. This is what he does."

"And the profits from those diamonds fall into the hands of dirtbags in the U.S.," Lyons said.

"These are the militia murdering their own people?" Shambi asked. "Now you have it in America as we have had for many years."

"It's about to stop," Bolan said. "We cut off their cash supply, we can slow them down."

They drove for the rest of the day. Shambi stopped just before dark and they made a rough camp. The African had brought along food. Bolan took the first watch, followed by Shambi, who insisted on playing his part. Lyons completed the cycle until dawn. Before they moved off Bolan and Lyons changed into combat gear, adding the full complement of weapons and extra ammunition. Shambi had told them they were getting close to M'Tusi territory, and Bolan had no intention of going in empty-handed.

They reached Father Agostini's small settlement midmorning. It comprised a few huts constructed from corrugated sheets and shingle roofs. The mission building, a substantial structure, was part home, part church. The whole place had a calm and ordered appearance. There was another Land Rover, looking equally as battered as the one Bolan and company rode in, parked outside the mission building. As they drove across the compound, people took notice. Many of them waved at Shambi. He stopped the Land Rover at the mission building.

DURING THE LONG DRIVE, Shambi had told Bolan how the region suffered under M'Tusi's control. The man had carved out his own empire from the desolate area, using brute force and intimidation of the already suffering populace.

The prevailing conditions were just a part of Africa's problems, a vast continent that struggled in parts to rise from the misery that had plagued it for so long. And as always, it was the innocent who suffered the most. People who struggled with existence from the day they were born. Proud people, with traditions going back thousands of years and cultures that might have benefited them greatly if they had not been cursed by the men with guns, the ones who armed themselves and rode the dusty plains in their noisy vehicles, terrorizing and killing in the name of freedom. Their kind of freedom, not one that the near-starving thousands would have chosen. If choice had been the meal of the day, their bellies would have been overflowing with a freedom that meant no more oppression; food that arrived when it was promised, that was not mysteriously spirited away to the storage sheds of those in charge; medical supplies that would release the children and old ones from disease. The irony was that goods were shipped to the region, but very little reached the people who needed it. It vanished, and there was no one who could stand up and demand to know where it had gone. The few who did, suffered for their courage. Mostly they died. Or disappeared. Some were tortured, then sent back so that the people could see what would happen if they dared stand up for what was rightly theirs.

It was a situation without hope. And the innocents bore it with a courage that would have shamed their oppressors if they had the conscience that would allow them to admit their wrongs. The region's people went about their daily lives in silence, heads bowed when the men with guns came.

And their warlord, who ruled without compassion, was Joseph M'Tusi. Of all the oppressors who had walked their land he was the worst. His brutality knew no limits. He ruled by fear, by beating down any opposition with total disregard for any kind of sanctity.

Only one man seemed able to stand up to M'Tusi and remain alive.

Father Agostini. And from what Shambi had told Bolan about him, the American began to realize why even before he met the man.

As they sat in the Land Rover outside the mission, dust still swirling around them from their arrival, Lyons spoke.

"So where is this holy man?"

"From what I've heard about him, don't use that epithet in his presence," Bolan said. "He'll likely floor you if you do."

"I like him already."

FATHER AGOSTINI WAS A WIRY, brown-faced man of Italian descent, dressed in a black cassock. His lined face and sunken cheeks spoke of a life of hardship that he carried without complaint. Keen, bright eyes inspected Bolan and Lyons from beneath heavy eyebrows. He made his appraisal in silence, taking note of their combat clothing and the weapons they carried. As he assessed them, his thin hands made cups of black coffee.

"Have you come with the intention of killing M'Tusi?" he asked, his English perfect yet tinged with his Italian ancestry. Asking the question, his eyes remained fixed on Bolan.

"That is not the main purpose of our mission, Father," Bolan replied. "M'Tusi's life remains in his own hands. It will be determined by his actions."

"An ambiguous answer. My son, it raises the question, however, whether I can allow myself to became involved in your mission."

"We have no intention of compromising you."

"I feel that has already happened. Simply by you coming here I am involved."

"Then we will leave, Father."

Father Agostini laid a hand on Bolan's arm. "Certainly not. I have just made coffee. Would you deprive a lonely man some much-needed company? Please sit."

"I was serious about not wanting to bring you problems."

"And I was just testing you. To see if your intentions were serious." Agostini passed around the cups of coffee. It turned out to be hot, black, and had rich, spicy flavor. "Is it not good?"

"You don't get this at Wal-Mart," Lyons said.

"It is grown not far from here," the priest said. "Now tell me why you have come here to face M'Tusi. Shambi did explain but I want to hear it from *your* lips."

Bolan told Agostini about the bombing campaign and the involvement of the Brethren and how the illicit diamonds were being used to help finance the militia group's operations. Agostini absorbed the detail, allowing Bolan to complete his telling with the respectful manner he might conduct during a confessional.

"I have heard about those terrible bombings and people who died in America. If I was not a man of God, I might question the persistent brutality we wish upon each other."

"But because you *are* a man of God?" Lyons asked.

Agostini glanced at him. "I see you are curious at my reaction."

"Are you going to explain there's a purpose behind what happened and your God understanding?"

Agostini smiled. "I would not insult either you, or those who died, by such an explanation."

"Doesn't it come back to if there *is* a God, why would he allow these things to happen?" Bolan said. "If he does exist and has such power, then shouldn't he prevent evil taking place?"

"Tell me why *you* stand against evil."

"Because we can. We have to. If we don't, evil will swallow everything in its path."

"You see? *Because you can.* Yes. God has endowed us all with the free will to fight evil. As free men we choose to do so. It is in all men to make that choice. The individual choice between good and evil. As in life itself there are many decisions to be made and as intelligent creatures we make our own."

"You're saying that God allows us individual freedom of choice? To stand against those who have picked the wrong path?"

"If He used his power to correct every mistake, every wrong move, it would remove our ability to develop. The human race would go on without responsibility. It would stagnate. How long do you think it would survive if those things were taken from us? A world of mindless drones never faced with a challenge. Responsibility. Choice. When we act on those things it allows us to advance. To reach far beyond our expectations."

"And you believe God has put us in this position?" Lyons asked.

Father Agostini raised his hands, palms up. "My belief has given me the insight into His way. He puts us on the path and shows us that way."

"Father, you talk a good talk," Lyons said. "Almost as good as your coffee."

Agostini refilled their cups. "My sons, it appears we have monsters in our respective countries. Those who bring death and unrest and who feed from each other to satisfy their own vile needs."

"Which brings us back to why we need to shut down this diamond pipeline."

Agostini considered Bolan's argument, finally nodding. "I will do what I can to help. Even as a Christian I find it hard to hold much love for Joseph M'Tusi and those murderous followers who take great delight in what they do. I will ask God's forgiveness for my less than charitable thoughts."

"Father, I'm sure you'll be granted absolution," Lyons said.

Agostini smiled at him. "Ah, you are a hardened cynic, but this once, I am sure you are right."

As they sat and talked, Bolan and Lyons learned more of how Father Agostini struggled to keep the locals fed and ministered to their needs as best he could. He was aware of the shady dealing that went on but he was a lone individual, with little to offer except his religious conviction and a gentle hand. M'Tusi and the priest tolerated each other in an antagonistic way. Father Agostini stood up to the warlord, and the general allowed him his outrages. Regardless of what Agostini threatened, M'Tusi made it strict policy that he was not to be harmed. The African was smart enough to realize that killing a priest would attract more attention than if he slaughtered a hundred of the locals, so he pulled back from that and made it clear to his men that Agostini would not be harmed. There was another, more practical reason. As long as Agostini was around, the locals knew he would find food and shelter for them. Care for the sick at his small mission. It lent M'Tusi a degree of humanity for others to see. Carefully leaked information spread the suggestion that M'Tusi was not as much of a monster as may have been thought. Even in such a desolate and forgotten corner of the African continent, diplomacy and politically slanted spin went the distance. M'Tusi did not want to disturb that image and have hordes of interlopers entering his territory, so he confined his murderous activities to within his own backyard. That backyard comprised many hundreds of square miles of harsh, inhospitable territory. Within that tract of land lived scattered tribes in primitive villages. They survived, but only just, on what they could grow, on the cattle they raised, combating poverty and disease and the warlord Joseph M'Tusi and his army of murderous thugs.

Bolan and Lyons were apprised of the situation as they sat and listened to Agostini. The priest, worldly wise in the misfortunes of the oppressed, scraped and begged and bartered for anything he could gather to hand out to the scattered inhabitants of the area. On a regular basis he drove countless miles in his old Land Rover that he kept going through determination, faith in his convictions and, as he claimed, the wish of God. He did it all while retaining his composure, offering gentle smiles and the occasional prayer for the sick and the dying.

And now he offered to help Mack Bolan and Carl Lyons in their own crusade against evil.

One of Agostini's locals had picked up information about M'Tusi's upcoming deal with the foreigners who had come to the region before. It wasn't difficult to gain such information. It was picked up by workers in the diamond operation and passed by word of mouth. The details were not that much of a secret. M'Tusi, in his arrogance, believed he was in such control of the region that even if news of his deal leaked out to the workers and their families nothing would come of it. The region was isolated and its people so completely subjugated that talk was all they could ever rise to. Any physical resistance would lead to summary treatment, meted out by M'Tusi's vicious squads of roving enforcers.

What M'Tusi had not counted on was the silent loyalty the people had toward Father Agostini.

One man.

Struggling against the odds, but who devoted his life to looking after his flock, as he called them. The man's faith was unshakable. His determination stronger than anything they had experienced before. He came to them when they were sick. When they were starving. He ministered to their dying children and wept openly if he failed to save them. He gave everything to his people and asked nothing for himself.

When he learned about the diamond deal Agostini requested as much information as possible, making it clear that whatever was learned had to be passed to him alone and not allowed to make M'Tusi or his men suspicious. What Agostini asked was done without question and by the time Shambi arrived at the mission, along with his Americans, Agostini had the information they needed.

CHAPTER TWELVE

The village lay in a dust-bowl landscape that baked under a hot sun, undulating, rock-strewed earth that could barely sustain plant life, let alone human. The village had been deserted for a long time. Any sign of human habitation had long since been erased. A hot, gritty wind blew almost continuously, dragging along thin dust that made a hissing sound as it scraped against the flimsy sides of the huts, filtering in through the gaps, leaving a fine coating on every surface. Apart from the brittle, dried grasses and stringy bush swaying beneath the wind, nothing else moved.

The vehicles came in from the east, two of them, moving fast and leaving heavy trails of dust in their wake. They swept into the village, coming to a noisy stop in what would once have been the central compound.

Two vehicles, ex-military, badly abused, carrying combat dressed and armed Africans.

Men climbed down from the vehicles, spreading out, weapons at the ready. The dust drifted away, caught by the wind. One of the armed men snapped out a command and watched as one of his group opened a slim case and activated a satellite phone. He spoke into it, received a response and relayed it to the commander of the group.

Joseph M'Tusi, the local warlord, was dressed in military fatigues. He was a big man, six feet tall, and starting to go soft. He called himself General, the rank self-promoted. M'Tusi enjoyed the prestige it bestowed on him. It sounded grandiose and allowed him the feeling of importance it generated. In truth he was little more than a vicious gangster, terrorizing the local population through violence and intimidation. He gathered a following of brutal gunmen around him and they roamed the territory, looting, killing, raping, employing terror tactics to get what they wanted.

M'Tusi nodded in response to the message, turning to disperse his men. They fanned out across the compound, moving with casual ease. They showed an unconcerned attitude bordering on arrogance. This was their territory. They ruled it with little opposition. At this moment in time there was no one who dared to oppose them. The central government, put in power after a military-inspired coup, had ceased to be more than an irritant. Since taking power it had failed to live up to its promise and the country had fragmented, breaking into different groups, each with its own policies—mainly how much each group could make from the country. As always there were personal agendas and, more important, tribal bickering and a surprising degree of racism between the indigenous factions. So the party in power had its own problems, preferring to leave local differences to be dealt with by M'Tusi who handled any upsets with ruthless efficiency. As long as the central administration received its bounties and aid money from international organizations, it stayed out of local politics.

TO THE WEST LAY sixty miles of barren terrain before the land gave way to the Atlantic Ocean. Waterless, empty, it produced little and offered nothing but despair. Very few of the original occupants of the strip remained. Nothing would grow here in any quantity, and there was barely any game left. The local inhabitants were under constant threat from M'Tusi and his roving marauders, and stayed hidden, so anyone entering the area was unlikely to encounter much resistance.

Mack Bolan and Carl Lyons, and their guide, Tomas Shambi, traversed the distance from Father Agostini's mission overnight. By dawn they were concealed in a dry hollow at the south end of the village where they waited for the arrival of M'Tusi and his soldiers.

Bolan eased back down the dusty slope to the base of the hollow where Lyons and Shambi were waiting.

"It is M'Tusi," Shambi said.

"Glad he could make it," Lyons muttered, the bitter edge to his words unmistakable.

"So, you, too, have seen what he has done," Shambi said.

"We read his file and saw the pictures," Bolan said.

There was no forgetting the chilling illustrations of Joseph M'Tusi's past rampages through the region during the tribal slaughter, when M'Tusi led his panga-wielding squad through the area. It was not war, or combat. That was the explanation used to justify what the warlord and his followers did. In their eyes every member of the rival tribes was a threat, or potential future threat. Women and children were not spared and even Bolan, used to seeing the excesses of human barbarity, had flinched at the stark, graphic images of children being deliberately hacked to death during the purges. They were bitter images to see and impossible to wipe away.

"We saw them," Lyons added quietly.

"Every gun M'Tusi buys. Every bullet. They mean more suffering for the people," Shambi said. "And nothing is done to stop him."

"Things change," Bolan said.

"Now we just need Regan and company to show up," Lyons added.

"He will be here," Shambi said. "He deals with M'Tusi often. I have seen him in the city on a number of occasions, talking to M'Tusi's agent. The one who sets up the exchanges."

Lyons glanced up from checking his weapons. Like Bolan, he wore a long-billed baseball cap on his head against the heat. Even so he was hot and uncomfortable, a combination that did little to ease his mood. "If it goes right today, there won't be any more deals to negotiate."

"Your friend is not the kind who negotiates?" Shambi said.

Bolan smiled. "In his own way he's a hell of a negotiator."

The sound of Lyons racking the SPAS shotgun offered his only comment on the matter.

"I did not ask before," Shambi said, "but you know this man Regan?"

"We know how he does business."

"He sells death. Yes?"

"Pretty well describes him."

"Then he is an ideal companion for General M'Tusi."

Lyons raised a hand, indicating he had heard something.

"Incoming chopper," he said.

Bolan heard it now. Approaching from the north. He recognized the familiar beat of a Huey's power plant. The military workhorse he had flown in many times. This one sounded slightly weary, and Bolan could empathize with that; it was a feeling he knew well personally.

"Eyes open, Ironman," he said. "Watch the chopper in case they still have the M-60 operational."

The Huey swung into their line of sight, sucking up dust from the ground as it landed. Painted in dull, military olive-green, previous markings painted over, the chopper was old and it showed. The first thing Bolan saw was the muzzle of an M-60 framed in the open side hatch.

"Good call," Lyons said.

The 7.62 mm M-60 was a flexible, gas-operated, air-cooled machine gun with a firing rate of 550 rpm. Depending on the specific application, the M-60 weapon system comprised a pintle mount and one of two ammunition storage systems. An ammunition can bracket that mounts to the gun or the mount, the bracket held a single 200-round ammunition can. The second ammunition storage system was made up of a 500-round ammunition can and a flexible feed chute attached to the base of the mount. The M-60 had spade grips, an aircraft ring-type sight and an improved ammunition feed system. A canvas ejection control bag was attached to the machine gun to catch ejected links and cartridge cases, preventing them from being ejected into the path of the rotor blades or turbine engine intake. Either way, the weapon was provided with a controllable firing system and a plentiful load.

As the dust cleared, they were able to distinguish three figures alighting from the Huey. Jack Regan in his trademark white, crumpled suit and battered Panama hat was conversing with a lean African who wore his clothes as if he had just stepped out of a storefront display.

"That is Kesawayo, M'Tusi's agent," Shambi said. "A most untrustworthy man."

As Shambi spoke, Bolan checked out the third man carefully. Bolan had seen the face before. The image he had seen on the photo Kurtzman had put up on the big screen in the War Room at Stony Man during the briefing, a group shot of the Brethren taken by a press photographer during a Jersey City rally. The Brethren showing their public side. The man had been just behind Liam Seeger, who had been talking to Jerome Gantz, the bomb maker, just his head and shoulders exposed, but his face had registered with Bolan. There had been an expression in his eyes that stuck. He had been smiling, presenting an amiable presence, yet Bolan had seen something in his eyes that went far beyond the humanitarian facade he was presenting: cold, empty, devoid of any humanity. It was unmistakable. It had forced Bolan back, to examine the man more closely and to lock away that image for future reference. Now that recognition clicked back and Bolan was watching the man step down on African soil, still exuding the smile that did nothing to hide the dead eyes.

This was Max Belmont, the name Kurtzman had tagged the guy with. He was a Brethren political activist with extreme views on the American government.

Beside Bolan, Tomas Shambi stretched above the rim of the hollow, desperate to get a clear image of M'Tusi. As Bolan reached up to drag the young man back he caught the expression on Shambi's face. It exposed the African's barely suppressed hostility toward M'Tusi. Something that had been building for a long time. Now that the object of his hatred was in clear sight Shambi had allowed his emotions to override caution.

That abandonment had repercussions instantly as one of M'Tusi's entourage caught sight of Shambi's ducking head. He raised a warning shout that alerted the rest of the group.

In that instant any element of surprise had disappeared, and with it much of Bolan's advantage. He accepted the fact and moved on. Concerns could be addressed later.

"Carl, the chopper," Bolan snapped, and left it at that, knowing Lyons would deal with the helicopter.

"Tomas, you put your damn head down and stay down."

Bolan turned his attention on M'Tusi and his group as they moved in the direction of the hollow. Two of the leading gunmen were advancing fast, weapons ready, AK-74s, replete with customized chromed barrels and receivers. The sharp crackle of autofire concentrated Bolan's mind. He kept his head below the lip of the hollow as the first volleys slammed into the hard earth, showering him with dust. He rolled to the right, clearing his original position and brought his M-16 into play as he showed himself. He hit the pair with solid bursts, seeing the impact of the 5.56 mm slugs dust the fronts of their camou fatigues. The stricken Africans stumbled and fell to the ground, blood starting to bubble from their wounds, weapons spilling from their fingers.

Bolan moved the moment he fired, keeping his shift to the right, and as he pushed up out of the hollow he had cleared at least ten feet, forcing M'Tusi's men to change direction. Before they could counter his move he opened up again, raking the moving figures with murderous fire, the M-16 jacking out a searing stream of bursts that dropped the yelling Africans to the ground. The wild yells they employed during their attack, supposedly to frighten their enemy, did nothing to faze Bolan. He ignored the implicit threat the shouting posed and used his own energy to lay down his accurate fire.

Pausing briefly, he plucked a fragmentation grenade from his harness, yanked the pin and threw the bomb in the direction of the lead vehicle. Panic drove those near the vehicle to scatter. The grenade detonated with a hard crack, the explosion rocking the vehicle and mangling metal. Those who were still in the vicinity were caught in the blast and the resulting injuries were far more extreme to human flesh that to inert metal and plastic.

In the short moment it took M'Tusi's men to recover from the shock of the grenade, Bolan had moved again, cutting around them and then advancing on the far side of the dust cloud the grenade had created. He made out the hesitant figures of the armed Africans and took them on without a moment of hesitation, hitting hard and with ruthless efficiency. The warlord's kill squad was facing a different enemy during this engagement. Not a helpless, near starved individual, but a healthy, well-armed solider who had faced larger odds on many occasions and who refused to back down because of their reputation as killers.

CARL LYONS HAD MOVED at the same time as Bolan. His concentration was focused on the Huey and particularly the door gunner. The moment the situation went critical the gunner swung his M-60 around, seeking a target. As the first seconds went by and Bolan engaged, Lyons could see the muzzle of the M-60 wavering. The gunner was eager to join the firefight but his own people were between him and the lone enemy figure he could see. Lyons had no intention of allowing that to change. The way the gunner was acting he might open up at any given moment.

Lyons was already reaching the far curve of the hollow and once he did, his scant cover would be gone. He saw that M'Tusi's squad was concentrating on Bolan. That would allow him a little more time but once that had gone, Lyons's element of surprise would vanish.

The detonating grenade presented Lyons with his single chance and he took it, bringing into play the reckless streak he always found hard to curb. Digging in his heels, the Able Team leader broke over the lip of the hollow and ran hard in the direction of the Huey, the SPAS already rising. He wanted to be within a decent range before he used the weapon.

The grenade's effects were still being registered when the M-60 gunner made a sweep of the immediate area and picked up Lyons's moving figure. He opened fire instantly, raking the area with 7.62 mm rounds. Lyons, on the run, took evasive action, ignoring the slugs punching the earth around him. He covered a few more yards, bringing himself well inside the shotgun's effective range, then shouldered the SPAS and triggered the first shot. The blast shredded the edge of the open hatch, causing the gunner to flinch as keen shards of aluminum peppered him. The brief halt in the M-60's fire allowed Lyons to close in and he pumped out three more rounds, spacing them evenly, and saw the door gunner jerk aside when he was hit. The powerful charge from the combat shotgun tore into his upper right chest and shoulder, tearing at flesh and muscle, almost severing the guy's arm in the process. Blood and fleshy debris filled the air as the screaming gunner dropped to the deck inside the Huey. Lyons kept moving until he was able to flatten against the side of the chopper. He heard frantic movement coming from inside and gauged it was the pilot. He ducked under the M-60 assembly to the far side of the hatch and picked up on the outline of the pilot, an autopistol in his hand, as the guy pushed his way to the rear of the chopper. The moment he had a clear view of the pilot Lyons stood, leaned in through the hatch and hit the pilot with a direct blast from the SPAS that hurled the dying man back across the passenger compartment. He slammed up against the far side and pitched to the deck.

Out of the corner of his eye Lyons spotted an armed African from the main group racing in his direction. The man had an SMG in his hands and was firing as he ran, the slugs spraying the area, none coming even close to Lyons. The Able Team commander calmly swiveled at the hips, dropped the muzzle of the SPAS and blew the moving man off his feet with a single shot, the charge tearing into his midsection and spraying his insides across the dusty ground.

Lyons took brief cover against the Huey's fuselage, his fingers pushing fresh shells into the SPAS. He picked up on booted feet pounding the dirt, dropped and rolled beneath the Huey, coming up on the far side. The hatch was rolled back so he could see through the body of the chopper, and as Lyons took up position he saw one of M'Tusi's men framed on the far side. Lyons didn't hesitate. He brought up the shotgun and triggered a single round that practically took off the target's head. Swinging around, Lyons heard a burst of autofire and felt something burn across his upper left arm. He sighted the shooter and returned fire, the blast of the shotgun kicking the African off his feet and dumping him on the ground, writhing in pain from the ragged, bloody crater in his chest.

Lyons checked out the battleground. He saw Bolan's running figure, his M-16 firing repeatedly. His decision made, the big ex-cop turned to join Bolan, plucking a grenade from his harness and tossing it inside the Huey almost as an afterthought.

JACK REGAN, WITH BELMONT and Kesawayo close on his heels, angled away from the heat of the firefight. The arms dealer had pulled his pistol from the shoulder rig he wore under his white jacket. He gripped the SIG-Sauer P-226 tightly in his right hand as he ushered his companions in a semicircular direction, herding them toward the closest of the derelict village's huts. He could have wasted time cursing and ranting at what had happened, voicing how he felt at the unexpected turn of events. He did not. Regan had survived for a long time in his risky business by staying ahead of the game. If a deal went sour, the first thing he did was extract himself. Getting into the clear was the most important consideration in times of crisis. The yelling and screaming would come later. If he came out of it with his life intact, that was sufficient. The world he lived in was treacherous, violent, and prone to deceit and double-cross. The people he courted were no angels. If they had been, Regan would not have been doing business with them. He had set his rules down early on. Saving his own life was paramount. Collecting his money came a close second. If it meant losing the financial incentive, then he would accept that. A dead man had no use for money. It didn't matter how large the amount. The day the lid was nailed on his coffin it didn't mean squat if he had a billion dollars salted away. It meant a lot while he was alive and able to enjoy it. So keeping his ass attached to the rest of his body was Jack Regan's prime concern.

Kesawayo started to grumble as soon as the firing commenced. He was, as far as Regan figured, a miserable excuse for a man. From the moment he had met M'Tusi's business agent Regan had taken a dislike to the preening, arrogant man. He maintained an amiable attitude, keeping his feelings suppressed. It didn't do to get on the wrong side of the man who had a big say in how any deal went. M'Tusi, who had little idea where money was concerned, apart from spending it, left negotiations to Kesawayo. The man might have been screwing M'Tusi out of millions, but that was not Regan's concern. He didn't care as long as the deal went through and he received his percentage. So he played the game, feeding Kesawayo's vanity, and listened attentively to the man's constant and opinionated views on the world.

As he led his companions away from the gunfire, Regan was hoping, with genuine feeling, that a stray bullet might shut Kesawayo up for good. He was coming close to the point where he might do the job himself if the guy didn't shut up. He wondered why the man couldn't act like Belmont. The Brethren representative, obviously terrified, hadn't said a word since the firing began. He winced at every shot, ducking almost to the ground when grenades went off, but stayed silent and followed whatever Regan told him to do.

The trio reached its objective. Regan ignored Kesawayo, reaching out to haul Belmont into cover behind the low clay-brick wall, pushing him roughly to the ground. Belmont hugged the dusty earth with all the fervor of a man in love with a piece of dirt.

"...to know what is happening," Kesawayo was demanding.

"Looks pretty clear to me, bubba. We walked right into a fuckin' setup."

"Regan, how did you let this happen?" The tone was accusing.

Regan rounded on the man. "Me? Bubba, this isn't my screwup. It was your fuckin' high-and-mighty pretend General who arranged it. So quit talkin' down to me."

"You dare talk of General M'Tusi in such a way?"

"Bubba, he got us into this. If he doesn't get his ass shot off, we can discuss the finer points later. For now, just shut your fuckin' mouth, because I've had a bellyful of your yappin'."

Regan turned aside, edging to the corner of the hut and checked out the action. What he saw did little to ease his concerns.

THE BURNING JEEP PROVIDED a degree of cover as Bolan exchanged magazines on his M-16. Over the clatter of autofire he heard the blast of a grenade and caught the burst of flame and smoke that geysered up from the Huey. He heard the crackle as rounds for the M-60 exploded in the intense heat.

Score one for Carl.

Bolan peered through the drifting smoke, raised his M-16 and took down the closest of M'Tusi's men. He pulled the muzzle around and repeated the move on a figure angling around the front of the wrecked and burning Jeep. The African went down hard, blood staining the back of his shirt where the slugs had exited. The familiar boom of Lyons's shotgun added to the general din, and the firing from M'Tusi's squad faltered as they found themselves caught between two lines of fire.

Using the lull, Bolan freed two grenades, pulled the pins and hurled the lethal eggs one after another in opposite directions. He waited seconds after the twin detonations, then broke cover and advanced on the decimated squad, his M-16 dealing out summary death to the living and the wounded. There was little space in Bolan's mood for compassion this day. His tall figure prowled the killing field and it would have been a foolish man to have gotten in his way.

The conflict ended as quickly as it had begun. The bodies of M'Tusi's kill squad lay strewed around the area. Death had visited that African village with a vengeance and Joseph M'Tusi's fearsome reputation had been reduced to so many dead bodies sprawled in the dust.

M'Tusi himself lay in a bloody heap close by the second Jeep, his bulky torso torn and exposed from the blast of one of Bolan's grenades, internal organs seeping from the bleeding, gaping wound. The man was close to death, coughing blood, when Bolan paused to look down at him.

"Different when you're on the receiving end," the big American said.

M'Tusi stared at him. "Who are you? Why did you come here?"

Bolan reached into the rear of the Jeep and dragged out the bulky satchel he had seen on the floor of the vehicle. He knew from the sound that it contained the diamonds to be used in the exchange. Bolan dumped the satchel on the ground.

"Same reason you came, M'Tusi. Diamonds."

"To steal them? So, you are nothing but a thief."

"No. To stop you making your deal with Belmont and his associate."

M'Tusi shook his head in disbelief. "I do not believe you, American."

"It will still be the truth after you're dead. Either way, I don't give a damn what you believe."

"Kill him, kill him," Tomas Shambi cried as he emerged from where he had been waiting for the fighting to end. As he crossed to where Bolan stood, he picked up a discarded weapon and raised it in M'Tusi's direction. "He does not deserve to live."

Bolan glanced at the young man. The bitterness Shambi carried showed in his face, tears streaking his cheeks. "The man is already dying, Tomas."

"No. That is not enough. If I had a panga I would show him how it feels to be butchered."

"Then you would be a monster like he is."

"You would allow him to die peacefully? Even after you have learned what he has done?"

"You call that dying peacefully?" Bolan asked, glancing at the torn and mutilated M'Tusi.

Bolan allowed his M-16 to hang muzzle down. He turned away and walked across to where Lyons was herding Regan and his two associates out from behind the hut where they had been hiding. Regan's handgun was tucked behind Lyons's belt. Neither of the other two men had been carrying.

"I sure as hell don't know who you guys are," Regan said, "but you damn well make shit happen."

"Want me to shut him up?" Lyons asked.

"You realize what you cost me here today?" Regan went on. Despite the death and carnage all around him, Regan was now concerned about his financial losses. "Hell, bubba, I'm out a wad of cash."

Bolan hit him. Hard. The single punch seemingly came out of nowhere, catching the dealer on the jaw and putting him on the ground. Regan, dazed and hurt, wisely decided not to offer any resistance and stayed where he was.

"Perhaps you would like to do the same to me?" Kesawayo asked. He spoke in the same derisory tone he had used on Regan earlier.

The abrupt crackle of autofire burned over Kesawayo's words. He turned and saw Shambi standing over M'Tusi's body. The young man had expressed his rage by putting a long burst into the warlord's head, finally terminating his life.

"I'd suggest keeping your mouth shut, pal," Lyons

said, prodding Kesawayo with the muzzle of the shotgun.

Bolan reached out and took the bulky attaché case Belmont was carrying. It was heavy. Belmont's cold stare had no effect on Bolan. He opened the case and stared at the thick bundles of dollar bills inside the case.

"Belmont, you're a long way from home," Bolan said.

"And you don't realize who you're dealing with."

"No? A minor recruit to the Brethren's cause? That about cover it? An errand boy lost in West Africa." Bolan had pulled out the documents held in one of the case's slip pockets. Belmont's U.S. passport and visas. He held the documents up, then turned and crossed to the burning Jeep, dropping them into the flames. "No papers. No money. No diamonds. What do you do now, Max? What do you do?"

Belmont's face paled as he realized what Bolan meant. He looked around, at the dead, the burning Jeep and the wrecked Huey.

"Take the money. Just don't leave me out here."

"I already have the money," Bolan reminded him. "And the diamonds. We'll make good use of them."

"You can't leave us here. It's not…"

"You think he was going to say 'not fair'?" Lyons suggested.

"On a par with what?" Bolan asked. "Planting bombs in American cities that killed innocent members of the public as well as federal employees? Something the Brethren must be proud of. Was that what you were about to say, Belmont?"

Belmont didn't say a word. His justification for the Brethren's violent acts would not appease this man. Whoever he was, he had the backing of the U.S. admin-

istration, no doubt. Which meant he would oppose anything the Brethren stood for. Ignoring that, Belmont
found himself desperately searching for some way out
of his predicament—which he would not be in if Seeger
had not insisted he take the cash payment for M'Tusi's
diamonds personally. Seeger had seen it as a symbolic
gesture, showing the African that the Brethren both ap-
preciated and welcomed his assistance in their struggle
against the monolithic strength of the American government. It had all seemed very cozy and bound to gain
M'Tusi's trust. The stark truth had turned out to be a
world away from that. Belmont was going to be abandoned in the African badlands, an unfriendly place at
the best of times. Any of M'Tusi's faithful who still
lived were not going to be pleased that their commander
was dead, the diamonds stolen and the cash to be used
in trade missing. Max Belmont began to count his life
expectancy in hours.

    "Shambi, collect all the weapons and dump them in
the Land Rover," Bolan said.

KESAWAYO HAD REMAINED silent during the conversation
between Bolan and Belmont. He was weighing his
chances of breaking free and getting away from his
captors. Beneath the expensive suit was a warrior of
his tribe, the same tribe M'Tusi had emerged from to
become general. Kesawayo looked across to where
M'Tusi lay. No more glory, or vengeful attacks on their
tribal enemies. Lost, too, was the wealth that came from
the illicit diamond trading Kesawayo had turned into a
fine art on M'Tusi's behalf. Unless Kesawayo could
make his escape and start over. He was not such a fool.
He had salted away money from the various deals

M'Tusi and he had made. Kesawayo had always looked to the future. His own future. Loyal as he was to M'Tusi, Kesawayo had nevertheless laid aside ample funds for when the day came.

As the conversation with Belmont came to an end, Kesawayo realized that his captors, despite their fierce fighting capabilities, were not the cold-blooded killers he had first imagined. They would not kill him now. Victory was theirs, and so was the ability to show mercy. The tall American with the chilled blue eyes might have been a deadly opponent in battle. With his command of the situation complete, he would be satisfied with the result he had gained. There would be no wanton slaughter. No killing for killing's sake. There was no gain to be had by antagonizing these men Kesawayo saw. If he wanted to walk away from this place with his life intact, it would be wise to remain as he was. Silent and subservient. Let the others make fools of themselves. Kesawayo lowered his gaze and simply waited.

SHAMBI HAD BROUGHT the Land Rover after loading up with the collected weapons. At Bolan's command he placed the satchel of diamonds and the attaché case full of money in the rear.

Bolan and Lyons threw grenades into the second Jeep. The blast destroyed the vehicle. Bolan stood and watched it burn, then turned to the three prisoners.

"Time to start walking," he said.

Jack Regan, back on his feet and favoring his bruised jaw, took a long look around. "Where to, bubba?"

Bolan smiled. "Ask your buddy, Kesawayo. It's his territory."

"In this heat? How far do you think we'll get?"

"Not my problem, Regan. You play a dirty game. Now it's time to see how really smart you are."

"Hell, bubba, you might as well shoot me here and now."

"That would be a waste of a bullet, Regan. They're expensive—but then, you'd know all about the price of bullets, *bubba,* that's your business."

Bolan climbed into the Land Rover alongside Shambi, Lyons taking the rear seat. "Let's go," he said.

As the Land Rover rolled out of the village, Bolan glanced back and saw Kesawayo leading Regan and Belmont in the opposite direction. Just before he turned away Bolan caught the sun glinting on something in Kesawayo's right hand. It was the blade of a panga, one missed during the search for weapons. Kesawayo had found it on one of the dead Africans. Bolan wondered how much comfort it would give to Regan and Belmont. There was a long walk ahead. Regan and Belmont were strangers in a harsh and violent environment. Kesawayo was on home ground and might think twice about shepherding a couple of white men to safety.

In the rear of the Land Rover Carl Lyons checked the bullet crease on his arm and decided he could wait until Father Agostini's mission to get it seen to. He stretched his legs out and cradled his SPAS in his arms. "Been a short visit but a busy one, boss man. Where to next?"

"Father Agostini's mission first. Then back home."

THE PRIEST STOOD AND STARED at the attaché case of money. He kept shaking his head in disbelief. "This is for me?"

"Courtesy of the Brethren," Bolan explained. "Money

they sent to buy M'Tusi's diamonds. They changed their minds and asked if I could find a worthy cause for it."

"And I have M'Tusi's diamonds," Shambi said. "Perhaps enough to fund the return of our leader. Do you think so, Father?"

Agostini put his hands together in a moment of silence. "The right thing to do would be to dispose of both money and diamonds. But at a moment like this I can only see the good it will do. I will make sure this money is used to help my people. To buy food and clothing and medicines." He looked across at Bolan. "Is this what I should do, my son?"

"Sounds right to me."

"Of course I will have to ask God if I am doing His work in the way He wants."

Lyons couldn't hold back a grin. "Look at it this way, Father. I'm damned well sure even God needs a little help sometimes."

"I believe you could be right, my son. Perhaps this once God will look the other way."

CHAPTER THIRTEEN

Colorado

Liam Seeger had taken the news about the African incident more than badly. He was close to losing control
as he paced back and forth in his office, taking his frustration out on anything that stood in his way. The knuckles of his right hand were scraped and bleeding
following a hard punch against the solid top of his desk.

"Are we a bunch of fucking novices? Because that's
how it looks. How many more hits are we going to have
to take? Jesus, we're being sliced and diced and no one
can even get a glimpse of this bastard. He just appears,
makes his strike, then vanishes."

Zac Lorens and Deacon Ribak were the only ones in
the office with him. While Lorens had lost some of his
composure and seemed edgy, Ribak stood watching in
indifferent silence. During his years in the service he
had been bawled out by men a sight harder than Seeger
would ever be, so listening to the man's rant did nothing to faze him.

"I built this group from nothing. Made the Brethren what it is and now we are the ones being given the runaround by some loose cannon."

He rounded on Ribak. "Deke, you promised me you would stop these attacks. So why are they still taking place?"

"I don't have an easy answer, Mr. Seeger. Our problem is we have no lead to who he is, or who he's operating for. I've had all my contacts checking out agencies, looking at databases. Nothing. It's like this guy is a ghost. He comes out of nowhere and vanishes just as fast. Doesn't leave a trace. Hard to lock on to that kind of individual."

"Liam, I'm sure this man, whoever he is, can't keep this up indefinitely," Lorens said. "And we have at least gained our objectives with regard to public unrest and dissatisfaction with the government. If we keep up what we're doing I'm convinced we can still win the day."

Seeger turned on the man, his face taut with anger and frustration. "To carry on, we need all our resources intact. The diamond deal will lose us millions, and money is what we need to maintain a steady flow of weapons and equipment. Don't forget we lost four million because of Gantz and his partner. With the Africa deal lost, that's at least an equal amount. A lot of money, Zac. You don't make that up by snapping your fingers. You're a lawyer. You understand these things."

He looked across at Ribak. "Suggestions."

"We ship some of the reserve ordnance from New Mexico. And before you say anything, Mr. Seeger, I know we were going to keep that intact. Right now we don't have any choice. Without weapons and explosives we can't push ahead with any major strikes. We can't depend on another weapons buy because it will take too long to set up and transport. Use the ordnance from the New Mexico stockpile, and when we replenish, put back what we've taken. That's my advice, sir."

Seeger considered the option, knowing it was the only way forward for the present. "All right, Deke. Set it up. Make the first drop Chicago. The group there has the biggest shortfall."

"I'm on it," Ribak said, and left the room.

Lorens waited until the door closed behind Ribak. "Is it wise, Liam? To carry on with all this happening?"

"What do you expect me to do, Zac? Simply roll over and quit? Haven't we agreed this is the time? The wheels are in motion, and we have to do it now. We'll never get another chance if we allow it all to slip out of our hands. We have the reaction we wanted from the public. Protests. Action on the streets. The government not knowing what to do. Come on, Zac, this has been my vision for too many years. If we back off and let the momentum die down we've let *them* win. There's no way I'm going to let that happen."

"If that's how you feel, then we carry on." Lorens hesitated. "Look, I need to get back to the West Coast for a while. There are matters I need to attend to."

"Right now? Can't they wait?"

"Liam, *right now* is why they need attending to. I have to do these things. It's Brethren business. There are people I have to see. Things to coordinate. Make sure they don't become alarmed by what's been happening. The news will get around. We both know that. So the sooner I deal with the questions, the better. A day and a half will see it done, then I'm back here for the next phase."

Seeger was facing the window behind his desk, caught up in thoughts that occupied his full attention. "Fine. You go and do what you have to."

After Lorens left, Seeger stared at the closed door for some time. He was turning things over in his mind, assessing the way Lorens had seemed to be acting, especially when it came to mentioning the missing diamonds. Seeger, even if everyone else had missed it, had spotted an uneasy look on Lorens's face, some strange expression in his eyes. The man had not been acting himself. As with any individual with a distrust of society, albeit tinged with a little paranoia, Liam Seeger sensed odd behavior better than most. And Lorens was acting oddly. He decided, right or wrong, that he needed to act on his feelings. If he was wrong, no harm would have been done.

Seeger picked up one of his telephones. "Deke? I want you to do something else for me. Don't talk, just listen. This could turn out to be important for us *if* I'm correct."

Ojai, California

BOLAN PULLED OFF the highway and hidden his rental deep in the greenery that grew abundantly across the gently curving landscape. Zac Lorens's house lay a few hundred yards ahead, bounded by trees and dense shrubbery. The soldier climbed out of the rental car and locked it, taking a slow look around the area.

The location was idyllic. The weather made sure the Ojai valley lived up to its Mediterranean image, far removed from where he and Lyons had been a few days earlier. It was lush and green, nothing like the arid West African landscape and, at the moment, peaceful.

Clad in dark slacks, a light shirt and sport coat, Bolan presented an unthreatening figure. If anyone had looked closer, the person might have noticed the shoulder rig that carried the holstered Beretta 93-R. There were a couple of spare magazines for the 9 mm pistol in a Velcro pocket on the inside of his coat.

The Executioner moved toward the house, his mind going over the details Kurtzman had provided. Lorens's home was a spacious, ranch-style, stone-and-timber construction with Spanish influence evident in the tiled courtyard and pale stone arches that were festooned with flowers and vines. There was even a swimming pool surrounded by tended shrubs to maintain privacy, though each property in the area stood at least a quarter mile from its neighbor. Seclusion was the requirement.

Crouching behind the last barrier of shrubbery, Bolan was able to check out the way ahead. He was looking at the rear of the house, with the calm surface of the swimming pool between him and the property. The scene was silent. No movement. It was possible Lorens was not at home. He could have been anywhere. At his law office in L.A., or in court. Maybe even with his Brethren partners.

Satisfied he had not been observed, Bolan broke cover and moved quickly around the pool, heading for the expansive terrace that preceded the rear of the property. As he reached the far side of the pool, something caught his eye.

The tiled surround at the corner of the pool was wet. The pool water was fresh. And Bolan's curiosity was roused by the footprints leading away from the pool, across the terrace and to the door that led inside the house.

Footprints left by shoes, not the bare feet normally seen when someone emerges from a pool.

Odd, unless Lorens and his company enjoyed swimming while fully dressed. There was something else to wonder about. Lying on the tiles was a long pole with a metal hook on the end. It looked like the type of instrument used to hook a ceiling trapdoor for access to an attic ladder. Not the sort of thing used in a swimming pool.

Bolan dismissed the puzzle for the moment as he closed on the house. He was beginning to sense that the house was not as deserted as he had initially thought. He paused by one of the stone arches, easing the Beretta from its holster and making sure it was ready for use. He pushed the selector to 3-round bursts.

Keeping in the shadows thrown by the arch, Bolan reached the wall and flattened against it. He peered in through the side of the French doors set in the stone wall and saw a spacious lounge area, furnished with expensive fittings, tiled floor and colorful rugs.

His interest focused on the four men occupying the room. Three were armed, the pistols they carried fitted with sound suppressors, and they were grouped loosely around the fourth who was facing them.

Zac Lorens.

One side of his face was discolored by heavy bruising. His left eye had already swollen shut. His light shirt and slacks were spattered with blood from his bleeding mouth and nose.

One of the men was saying something to Lorens. The lawyer refused to look at him, and his refusal angered the man who swung the gun he was holding and clubbed Lorens across the side of the head with it. The blow drove the man to his knees, protecting his head with his arms. The brute who had hit him said something else, then drove the toe of his shoe into Lorens's side, sending him to the floor. The attacker reached into his pocket and took out a cell phone. He punched in a number and waited until his call was picked up. He began to speak. Bolan was unable to hear what was being said, the French doors effectively acting as soundproofing.

Lorens had to have heard the conversation. He made a desperate effort to gain his feet, lunging at the man closest to him and pushing him aside. Bolan saw the look of terror on his bloody face as he stumbled away from the group.

The man on the cell phone turned and raised his pistol, firing twice, the muffled pop of the weapon barely registering where Bolan stood. Both shots hit Lorens in the head. His skull split, blood fountained from the wounds as the man went down, sprawling across the tiled floor, his body going into spasm.

Bolan had found Zac Lorens, not the way he had intended, but reality tended to ignore wishful thinking.

The shooter said something to his two partners and they moved, one heading for a low coffee table, reaching for something stacked on the top. The other swung around and headed directly for the French doors, and spotted Bolan before he was able to pull back.

The guy's pistol came up and he fired three fast shots that shattered glass. Bolan felt shards tug at his sleeve as he flattened against the wall, dropping to a crouch, then leaning out again. His Beretta tracked the advancing shooter, his finger stroking the trigger to send a triburst into the room. Two of the 9 mm slugs hit the shooter in the chest, spinning him aside so that Bolan's second burst hit high between his shoulders. He went down without a sound.

More silenced shots burst through the French doors, breaking more glass and tearing strips of wood from the frame.

Bolan flicked the selector to single-shot. He picked up the hard thump of running feet, saw a shadow fall across the terrace through the French doors then move to the side. One of the remaining pair had positioned himself against the wall to the right of the doors. Leaning out, Bolan could see the tips of his shoes protruding. Small offerings, Bolan thought, but not to be ignored. He dropped the muzzle of the 93-R and aimed and fired. The end of the exposed shoe blew apart, shredded leather mingled with chunks of bone and flesh erupting from the targeted area. The hit man screamed and, wrapped in his own moment of pain, moved away from the wall, leaning forward to stare down at his bloody foot. Bolan was ready. The instant the guy's head came into view he drilled two 9 mm slugs into it. The slugs cored in and through, exiting in a shower of bloody debris.

Bolan powered to his feet, spun in at the French doors and drove his shoulder at them. The bullet-weakened frame gave under the soldier's bulk and he crashed into the room beyond. He let himself go to the floor, one hand thrown out to break his fall as he landed, rolling, hearing the subdued bark of the waiting pistol. Two 9 mm slugs plowed into the tiled floor close to his moving body. Bolan gripped the Beretta in both hands, steadying himself on his side and tracked in on the shooter as the guy swung his own weapon around for a further shot. Bolan held for a fraction longer, then stroked the trigger. The Beretta fired, twice, then a third time, each shot finding a target. The shooter came to a full stop as the slugs hit. He toppled backward, arms flailing, and fell in an untidy sprawl against the wall.

Bolan pushed to his feet. He ejected the magazine and clicked in a fresh one, cocking the 93-R as he moved around the room, clearing abandoned weapons from outstretched, still hands. No question his adversaries were dead, but Bolan was never one to push his luck.

He checked Zac Lorens. The Brethren second in command and lawyer was dead.

Bolan turned and crossed to the coffee table. He stared down at the pile of plastic bags that lay there. Water had run from the outside of the eight bags to pool on the table. Bolan reached down and picked one up. Heavy. Inside the bag were gleaming, uncut diamonds. Bolan realized where they had come from. Zac Lorens had divided the bulk of the diamonds into smaller weights, placed them in the plastic bags and dropped them into his swimming pool. Under the water the bags and their contents would have been rendered invisible. Even someone standing on the edge of the pool would have been unable to see them. Unfortunately for Lorens, his partnership with Jerome Gantz had been exposed and the Brethren had sent the three enforcers along to locate the whereabouts out of Lorens's diamonds.

Lorens's betrayal of his militia friends had resulted in his death.

The price of the illegal diamonds was rising.

Bolan picked up a muted voice. He glanced around for the source and saw the cell phone Lorens's killer had been using. He picked it up. The recipient's ID was displayed on the screen.

Ribak.

The man Bolan had seen on the boat off the beach at Gantz's house.

"Curran, what the hell is going on?" Ribak was saying.

"Ribak? Curran and his Brethren buddies can't speak. Now or ever."

"Who the hell are you? What the fuck have you done?"

"I gave them the same treatment they gave Lorens and Gantz."

"You. The fuck who showed up at Gantz's place and screwed my deal."

"Nice to be recognized."

"Son of a bitch, I am going to rip your head off your shoulders."

"Save your energy, Ribak, because this is not over yet. The farm. West Africa. You bastards wanted war, well, you've got one. This is just for starters. Tell your boss, Seeger, there's more to come. Remember what Al Johnson said. You ain't seen nothing yet. I'm coming, Ribak. The Brethren is about to become history."

"I'll be waiting. Waiting to rip out your throat."

"Just to make your day, Ribak, thanks for the diamonds. At least you were right about Lorens. He *did* have them. Your boys tracked him down and found the diamonds. Now I've got them."

Bolan shut off the cell phone and dropped it in a pocket. He spent some time going through the house. In a well-appointed study he found Lorens's laptop, open and switched on. He took it with him, along with a leather attaché case. Back in the lounge he dumped the still-wet plastic bags of diamonds in the case, walked out through the broken French doors and made his way to where he had parked his rental car and the drive back to the Air Force base and his flight back to Virginia.

RIBAK WAS OUTSIDE the house, away from anyone hearing his call to Stahl.

"How did it go, Deke?"

"Not our lucky day."

"I'm listening."

"The team got to Lorens's place. He was persuaded to admit his part in the theft of the diamonds. Lorens and Gantz knew about Moshe Bera, the man who was fencing the diamonds. They showed up at Bera's place in New York. Lorens went inside and did the deed. Killed Bera to make sure he wouldn't talk and took the bag of diamonds. Gantz was outside in the car. What they didn't know was that Gantz had been seen. When our search team asked around, someone came forward and provided a description of the man they had seen. After the realization that the description fitted Jerome Gantz, a photograph was shown to the guy. He identified Gantz as the man behind the wheel of the car. The man with Gantz had not been identifiable.

"Seeger figured it right. He couldn't understand why Lorens needed to go to California so urgently when he did. The guy wasn't having meetings on Brethren business. The team found him in his house packing bags, ready to skip. Got to say Lorens surprised me when he admitted killing Bera. I didn't think the little creep had it in him. When the boys started to get physical, he gave up the diamonds. Curran was on the phone, telling me. I suggested he retire Lorens on the spot. Next thing I hear all hell has broken loose. I hear gunfire. Then he comes on the phone. Tells me he was responsible for taking down the farm and the hit in Africa."

"Damn. So we lose those diamonds, too?"

"I'm not expecting them to be delivered by FedEx in the next ten minutes."

"How did Seeger take it?"

"He's no happy camper. Closest I've seen him to going ape shit. When I left him I heard weird noises from his office. He was swallowing his tongue and chewing the fuckin' rug. I'll leave him to cool off before I go back and calm him down. This guy is seriously out of luck right now."

"Deke, do what you can to salvage this operation. We have to keep the Brethren up and running until we have enough public outrage and political unrest to justify our intervention. If the Brethren falters, it doesn't do our cause any favors."

"I'll call you later."

STAHL PICKED UP the phone and instructed his pilot to take off. He glanced across at General Carson. "What do you think, Bill? The new plane? I thought it was time for something more up-to-date." He paused at Carson's less than appreciative expression. "Bill, is your seat belt too tight?"

"You haven't forgotten what's been happening lately, have you? The entire operation is under attack. The Brethren have lost men and weapons. The farm has been compromised. They can't manufacture bombs anymore until we find a replacement site and people. Gantz is dead, not that anyone is going to grieve over that because the son of a bitch was stealing from us. And now we've lost the fucking African diamond pipeline."

"So what do you propose, Bill? Pack up and call it a day? Abandon everything we've been planning for months?"

Carson stared out of the port beside his seat as the plane moved along the runway, picking up speed. "Of course not, Eric. You know my dedication to the cause. There's no way we can give up. Especially not at this stage."

"Then where's the problem? Bill, this is a war we are involved in. Not a weekend rally. There are bound to be setbacks. We have to ride them out and come back stronger. We lose weapons—we buy more. The same with lost men. Hire more. There are plenty out there who want to be involved in our kind of struggle. I agree that losing the bomb-making site is serious. I suggest we put that on standby until we can relocate. There are other ways of getting the public's attention."

"There is the matter of the diamonds, Eric."

"I'm hardly likely to forget that," Stahl said. "I'll have to think on that one. Come up with some other way of raising cash for Seeger."

"Good. Keep me updated." Stahl buzzed for the cabin attendant. "My usual. Bill?"

"Malt. Straight. No ice."

When the drinks arrived Stahl took his and swirled the contents around in the glass. "You had a productive meeting with your military friends yesterday."

"Oh, yes."

"Are they still solid?"

"As the proverbial rock. Once we go into full operational mode all they will need is a single call to an arranged number and they will move."

CHAPTER FOURTEEN

Stony Man Farm, Virginia

"Lorens's computer didn't give us much at first," Aaron Kurtzman said to those in the War Room. "A few names, most of which we had already. I didn't believe some-one like Lorens wouldn't have access to top-level Breth-ren information. So I put his hard drive under the microscope. There was a lot of stuff there. Deleted files, encrypted information. We sliced and diced, cut his hard drive data into sections. I sent some across to Hunt and Akira. It cut down the time it took us to scrape away at all the surface data and get to the hidden stuff."

"And?"

"Lorens had some smart moves in there. He'd really done some work hiding the vital stuff. In the end it was like working a computer game. You get through one level, and it just takes you to the next and you need to break the code to access that level and so on. If you have the passwords, no problem, but we had to find our way in through our code-breaking program. It's good, but it takes time. Lorens's main information was hidden within what's called a vault. So buried it was overlooked twice before Akira spotted it. Kind of like a tomb inside a pyramid, surrounded by false passages and fake destinations. But we—Akira—dug his way through. Once he opened the vault we found what we wanted. And it's pure gold."

Kurtzman tapped his keyboard and the large wall monitor above his workstation flashed into life. Mack Bolan studied the detailed information. There was no disputing Kurtzman's description of the data.

"There was the kind of thing we expected. Lorens's secret bank accounts. Offshore interests. He might have been a Brethren loyalist, but the guy was working his own life on the quiet. I guess he was along for the ride, but made sure he had a rainy-day fund in case things went belly-up. On the militia side he had membership lists. By the way, your local Sheriff Kyle and Deputy Boyd are both in there as fee-paying members. The lists are helpful. Names of contributors. Interesting when you look at some of those names."

"I can pass some of those along to interested parties," Hal Brognola said.

"You might want to take a close look at these two sections," Kurtzman said. "Here and here. Even after Akira pulled the data we couldn't figure what this meant. But the kid persisted and came up with the solution after working his brain to a frazzle. Deciphered, they are grid locations for weapons caches. One in the south side of Chicago, the other way out in the New Mexico desert country. Chicago is an abandoned industrial site. Workshops, steel fabrication shops. The place has been empty for a number of years. Every few years someone comes up with a scheme to redevelop but nothing gets done. So the city has written it off until they can afford to take it all apart and build on it. The New Mexico spot used to be a military base used for training in desert warfare. Cutbacks had it closed, and it got lost in the databases and forgotten about. File information says there were some storage facilities. Small barracks and office blocks. Couple of aircraft hangars. Tarmac road that leads to the main highway about thirty miles to the north. New Mexico holds reserve ordnance for the Brethren. Chicago is a local site for supplying Brethren factions around the area."

Bolan studied the detail that was displayed on one of the wall monitors. His mind was turning over the bones of the information. There could be ripe pickings if he and Lyons moved quickly. The Brethren kept in business from two main sources: money to purchase weapons and the weapons themselves. Their main money source, the illegal diamonds from Africa, had been severed. It was unlikely that Seeger would be able to replace the lost finance swiftly, if at all. The donations he received from sympathizers would be unlikely to create such amounts as had been forthcoming from the diamonds. Until he was able to boost his bankroll, Seeger would have to fall back on whatever weapons he already had in his secret caches.

If the New Mexico site was a major supply point, it needed shutting down.

And so did the Chicago base.

"Carl, you're the city boy."

Lyons smiled. "Chicago?"

"You got it."

Kurtzman swung his chair around. "I suppose that means you're going west, young man?"

Bolan nodded. "Smile when you say that, stranger."

"Oh, while you're here. Remember the motor cruiser used to let the Brethren team get into Gantz's place by the back door? It was located by the Coast Guard. It had been run aground up the coast. It was checked out, but all they found were some empty .50-caliber shell casings. No help to us now, but it ties up a loose end."

"I guess it does."

"I've got something else to make you both smile. While we were waiting for you two to come home I gathered a little satellite intel." Kurtzman provided several sets of digital photographs that would prove useful to Bolan and Lyons. "Those images are no more than three hours old. We can get you more up-to-date ones and download them into GPS units if you need."

"Thanks, Aaron."

"If Seeger knew we had this, he'd bang his head against the wall," Lyons said.

"He can bang it all he damn well wants," Bolan said. "If Seeger thought our efforts to date have screwed up his plans, wait until he hears about the next round."

"I love it when you talk dirty," Lyons said.

"Barb, can you make arrangements. Carl to Chicago. I'll need Air Force cooperation for a drop over the New Mexico desert."

"What are you planning?" Kurtzman asked.

"Night drop a few miles out from the site. I can walk in and be there by daylight. Carl, we need to liaise with Cowboy. Get him to prepare some explosive charges we can use to make sure those weapons are destroyed."

Kurtzman tapped in the command for his computer to print sets of the data and images. Behind him Barbara Price was already on one of the telephones, arranging transport for Bolan and Lyons. Stony Man was maintaining its war footing, and the troops were gearing up for their coming assault.

New Mexico

BOLAN FELT THE NIGHT CHILL evaporating as light pushed across the New Mexico landscape. He checked his position using the compact GPS unit Kurtzman had provided and saw that he was well on course for the ex-military base. It lay no more than a mile ahead. The GPS utility was proving to be more than useful.

The arid terrain around him was featureless—endless miles of undulating, sandy emptiness, the picture broken only by the occasional misshapen cactus, clumps of dry grass and mesquite plants. Some outcroppings showed here and there, but overall it was predominantly pale, dusty sand. With the daylight coming on fast, Bolan could see the wide-open sky, cloudless and clear.

His Air Force ride had dropped him ten miles out. The crew, told no more than they needed to know, had been friendly enough, but asked no questions. Bolan's jump master, a fresh-faced youngster, had said to Bolan, "Watch out for yourself, sir." That had been seconds before he had tapped Bolan on the shoulder to go and the soldier had launched himself into the cold, black night sky over the desert. His descent had been by the book, effortless and silent. He had touched down, stripped off his parachute and buried it in a hole he scooped in the sand.

Taking out the GPS unit, Bolan had checked his position, then set off toward his objective. That had been at 0420. It allowed Bolan ample time to pace his travel and arrive by daylight.

Belly down against a soft ridge of sand, Bolan used the compact binoculars he carried in his backpack and viewed the base directly ahead of his current position.

It was exactly as the satellite images depicted: a number of bleached-out buildings and a couple of hangars. The security fencing that had once closed off the base was sagging, the support posts drooping and half buried by the drifting sand. Even at this early hour, with the heat already rising, a soft wind picked up light swirls of the pale sand and swept it across the landscape.

Outside one of the hangars stood a group of vehicles, a large semi-rig backed up close to the open doors of the hangar, a couple of large SUVs and three passenger cars. Focusing in, Bolan saw a number of men transferring long boxes from the warehouse and stacking them inside the semi-rig's trailer. Moving his binoculars, Bolan saw two of the men carrying what looked like M-16s. By their movements he judged them to be lookouts. He watched for a couple more minutes, then slid away from the ridge.

The soldier stowed the binoculars in his pack. Before he closed it up again he checked the packages of explosives Kissinger had provided—blocks of C-4. In a separate container were detonators and timers, ready to be inserted into the compound. He completed a check of his weapons before he moved off. Bolan wore a combat rig over his blacksuit, holding extra ammunition for his Desert Eagle and the Beretta 93-R. A Cold Steel Tanto was sheathed against his right thigh and slung across his chest was a 9 mm Uzi.

He used the sandy ridge to cut off at an angle, circling the open frontage of the base, moving swiftly as the light became stronger. From what he had seen, all activity was going on in front of the one hangar. Bolan's easiest way in would be from the rear of the base.

He spent more time checking out the rear approach, seeing no movement and certainly no armed lookouts. Bolan closed in quickly, silently, coming to a halt at the rear of one of the buildings. He knelt in the drifted sand at the base of the wall, freeing the Uzi and cocking the weapon before he started to work his way along the side of the building and the activity by the hangar. As he came to the edge of the wall, he picked up the sounds of conversation. Flattening against the wall, Bolan leaned forward so he could make visual contact.

The doors of the trailer were being closed, the group of men starting to break up, heading for the waiting vehicles. All but two of the group appeared to be moving out with the semi-rig.

"Take it easy, boys," one of the men called. "Don't hit no fuckin' potholes."

One man, starting to climb into the cab of the tractor unit, looked over his shoulder. "If we do, you'll hear us, Dane."

Bolan, about to push to his feet, the Uzi held ready, picked up a faint whisper of sound behind him. He half rose to his feet, turning. All he saw was a dark shape standing over him, a blurred object swinging down at his head. In the final moment before it struck he told himself he had not been as careful as he should have been.

But it was too late.

Something struck him across the side of his skull. The blow pitched him forward, the Uzi slipping from his grasp. Bolan fell facedown, already close to being unconscious.

And then the day went black around him.

HE WAS REGAINING CONSCIOUSNESS as unforgiving hands hauled him to his feet and slammed him up against the hangar wall. Bolan felt his weapons being stripped from him, his harness and backpack. A hard fist slammed against his face, drawing blood.

"You see what this fuck has in his pack? Fuckin' C-4. Son of a bitch was going to blow us all to hell."

"I'll give him C-4. Shove it up his ass and light the fuse."

"Hot damn, I'll bet this is the puke who took the farm apart. An' done the Africa shit, too."

"He'll be a fed. A government fuckin' spook."

"Just the kind we're out to burn. Government assassins."

Bolan's world suddenly became intensely uncomfortable. He felt fists pounding his body, booted feet lashing out at him, heard the strained grunts and gusting breath of angry men lashing out at the enemy in their midst. He fought to stay on his feet, drawing his arms up to protect his face and head. Scuffling boots kicked up pale dust that rose and choked him.

"Rip the fuck's head off."

"Let me at him…"

"Wait, guys, wait. Back off. Come on, now, we can't kill him. We got to let Seeger know. He'll want to get this shit back to the HQ so he can talk to him."

"Hell, Dane, you damn well know how to spoil a guy's day."

The blows lessened and Bolan slumped to his knees,

head down, sucking in painful breaths. His body hurt and there was blood in his mouth. He stayed where he was, offering no resistance, aware that right at that moment he was as close to losing his life as he had been for a long time.

"You guys let me and Chester handle this piece of federal trash. I'll call Seeger and he'll tell me what to do."

"Dane…"

"Go on, get the hell out of here," Dane said. "He ain't going anywhere. You got a delivery to make. Do it."

The delivery teams moved to their vehicles, firing up the engines and dropping into formation with two escort cars in front of the big semi-rig and one tail car. They swung around and drove across the dusty compound, along the dirt track leading to the tarmac road running through the desert.

Dane stood watching them until they were almost out of sight. He called over his shoulder to Chester. "Get that storage cage opened up. Good enough for this bastard while we find out what Seeger wants to do."

Watching Dane through half-closed eyes, Bolan saw the man pick up his harness and the shoulder rig. Dane draped them over his shoulder. The man eyed the big Desert Eagle for a moment, then slid it from its holster, examining the pistol.

"On your feet, asshole." He stood and watched as Bolan pushed himself upright, swaying slightly. "Let's go, hotshot. I'll feel safer once I got you behind a locked door." He prodded Bolan in the spine with the Desert Eagle. "Nice gun. I'll hang on to it as a souvenir."

As he reached the hangar door, Bolan made to stumble over the bar step, pausing to grab for the door frame.

Dane pulled back slightly. The Executioner suddenly spun to his right, stepping away from the muzzle of the Desert Eagle, his movement bringing him on the outside of Dane's gun arm. He clamped his fingers over the militiaman's wrist, twisting hard and turning the weapon back on the man. Bolan's finger slid through the guard, over his adversary's finger and pressed the trigger. The .44 Magnum pistol blasted its big slug into Dane's side, shattering his ribs and coring on through to lodge in his heart. Bolan pulled the Eagle from Dane's limp grasp, turning and hefting the gun as he heard the man called Chester run across the concrete floor of the hangar. He tracked in and put two shots into the moving figure. Chester stumbled, coordination gone, and crashed facedown on the concrete, the SMG he was holding clattering to the floor.

Bolan bent over Dane's body and retrieved the combat harness from his shoulder. He slipped it on, ejecting the Eagle's partly used mag and replacing it with a fresh one. Walking back into the hangar, the Executioner cast around for the weapons' cache. It didn't take long. A substantial stockpile of autorifles and ammunition, all still crated in U.S. military boxes, stood on the floor of the hangar. There were also civilian weapons: SMGs and handguns; grenades and launchers. Bolan opened crates until he found what he wanted and when he walked back outside, he was carrying three M-72 A-6 LAWs.

A black Jeep Cherokee was the only vehicle remaining outside the hangar. Bolan checked it out and saw the keys in the ignition. He debated whether to blow the cache in the hangar first, then go after the convoy. He decided against it. If he blew the weapons cache first, the explosion could be noticed by the convoy and they would be alerted to possible attack. It would be wiser to go after the delivery first, then return and destroy what was sitting in the hangar. Bolan placed the LAWs on the floor of the Cherokee, then went back and retrieved his backpack with his C-4. He placed that in the rear of the big 4x4, then climbed in and fired up the engine.

BOLAN SIGHTED THE CONVOY ahead of him. Snapping his safety harness in place, he stepped on the gas and sent the SUV barreling along the road, closing fast on the tail car. He maintained his speed, intending to break aside and pass it once he was close.

Whoever was inside the tail car had to have seen who was driving the Cherokee. There was sudden movement on the rear seat. A window was powered open and a hand gripping a pistol was pushed into view. A man's head followed. He raised the weapon and began to fire at Bolan's vehicle. A couple of slugs clanged off the Cherokee's hood, one bouncing up to clip the windshield, leaving a visible chip in the toughened glass.

Bolan refused to back off. Instead he slammed his foot even harder on the pedal and felt the power of the engine throw him forward. The tail car loomed large and he swung the steering wheel to make his pass. He had to swerve to avoid hitting the tail car as it moved to block him. He brought the Cherokee back on line, and the near miss gave him an idea. He let his vehicle fall behind a few yards, then stood on the gas pedal, feeling the heavy 4x4 power up and leap forward. The gap closed with frightening speed, and then the solid front of the Cherokee slammed into the rear of the tail car, the impact pushing it forward with an abrupt jerk. Broken taillights dropped to the roadway. Bolan simply repeated the maneuver, this time increasing his speed and slamming into the vehicle again.

The tail car swung out of control, and Bolan caught a glimpse of alarmed faces inside. Tires burned against the tarmac, leaving black streaks behind. Bolan had dropped back, letting the fishtailing reach its optimum before he rammed the Cherokee into the car again, catching the vehicle sideways-on. The effect was dramatic as the force of the heavy 4x4 lifted the right rear wheel off the road. The raised wheel was still in the air when Bolan made his final strike, the head-on butt flipping the tail car over onto its side where it seemed to hang for long seconds before rolling again, onto its roof. A wide tail of bright sparks flew from the upturned vehicle as it skated along the road, windows shattering as the weight of the car buckled the roof. It rolled again, and it was like watching a slow-motion movie clip as the car bounced, turned, turned again, debris breaking from it as it suddenly described a cartwheel that took it across the road and into the sandy ground bordering the road. Smoke started to trail from the engine compartment. Moments later flame began to curl out from under the crushed, misshapen hood.

Bolan saw the crash in his rearview mirror as he hauled his vehicle back on line, feeling his seat harness pull tight. With the tail car out of the picture, he was able to concentrate on his main target, the big rig itself.

The driver of the rig, having witnessed the fate of the tail car, stepped on the gas and the big vehicle surged away from Bolan. The straight, even desert road allowed for high speed with no obstructions. It also allowed no diversions. There was no way the rig could escape. But Bolan was aware that he wasn't about to have everything his own way. Ahead of the big rig were two more escort vehicles, which he had not discounted. They made themselves noticed when they pulled ahead of the rig, and then one of them, another hefty 4x4, fell back to run alongside.

CADE CRENNA SNAPPED in a magazine and cocked the SMG.

"That fuckin' idiot," he said. "All Dane had to do was lock the bastard up. He couldn't even manage that. Keep this thing steady and I'll spread that mother all over this desert."

His partner, Lou Bukowski, nodded. "Make sure you do. This was supposed to be an easy run. No hassle, now we got that fed shit on our tail."

Crenna, working his way to the rear of the 4x4, said, "Watch me wipe him off our ass."

He reached the tailgate and pressed the button that would power down the window. Dry wind fluttered inside the rear compartment. Crenna positioned himself and raised the SMG, pushing the barrel of his weapon outside. He felt the 4x4 sway as Bukowski worked to keep it steady. Too late, he pulled the trigger, knowing his first volley was going to be off target. He saw the Cherokee slow and fall back.

"Jesus, don't you know what the fuck a straight line is?"

"Yeah, about as much as you know how to shoot."

"Funny… Shit, he's coming back…"

THE TAILGATE WINDOW of the 4x4 slid down and Bolan saw the muzzle of a weapon appear. The shooter opened up, spraying a burst of autofire that cleared Bolan's vehicle by inches. It forced the soldier to drop back out of range, and he saw the big rig diminishing as it increased speed. The 4x4 remained in its side position. With that running interference, Bolan was forced to stay back. He wasn't about to lose his quarry. The opposition had no idea what he was carrying.

He was about to show them.

The soldier pushed down on the gas pedal again, closing the gap, and pulled up close to the rear of the big rig, hiding himself briefly from the escorting 4x4. He even picked up the squeal of tires as the 4x4 braked, reducing its speed. Seconds later it came into view. Bolan was ready for its appearance. He had his driver's window down, the muzzle of his Uzi resting there. The moment the vehicle appeared, the Executioner tracked in with the 9 mm SMG. He eased back on the trigger and sprayed the rear and side of the 4x4 with a full magazine. Glass shattered and slugs cored in through the metal body panels. The shooter in the rear twisted to one side as he caught a number of the slugs, his weapon slipping from his grasp, falling and bouncing as it hit the tarmac.

The driver of the 4x4 powered his vehicle away, out of range, but Bolan had no intention of backing off now. He pulled out from behind the rig, bringing his Cherokee up close behind the 4x4. He hauled the big Desert Eagle from its holster on his belt, transferring it to his left hand. The Desert Eagle held eight .44 rounds. They stored a lot of power and Bolan knew that. He thrust the pistol out of his side window and triggered his shots through the open tailgate. One of the big slugs hit the driver, tearing through his right shoulder, exiting and shattering the blood-spattered windshield. The 4x4 swerved toward the rig, bouncing off the solid bulk of the vehicle, then angled off across the tarmac and into the soft sand bordering the road. It fell behind Bolan quickly, a heavy cloud of dust trailing in its wake.

Bolan placed the Desert Eagle on the seat beside him, reaching for one of the M-72 A-6 LAWs lying on the floor. He had no idea how long he might have before the remaining escort vehicle showed. Right then his main concern was the big rig hauling the weapons. He stepped on the brake and brought the Cherokee to a slithering halt, freeing his seat harness and exiting the vehicle. He was activating the LAW even as he stepped out of the vehicle, watching the rig head away from him. Bolan stepped clear of the SUV, shouldering the LAW and sighting on the rig. Once he had target acquisition he eased back on the trigger and felt the LAW recoil on his shoulder. The missile left a thin trail in its wake as it sped toward its target, the rocket locking on and staying there until it slammed into the trailer's rear doors. The rocket penetrated the metal and detonated inside the long container. The blast took the trailer and its contents apart in a roaring fireball, filling the air with shredded debris. The rig continued forward until the tractor swerved back and forth, twisting the burning skeleton that was all that remained of the rig. The road wheels were alight, chunks of blazing rubber flying everywhere. The moving pyre rolled on for another hundred yards before it came to a jerking halt at the side of the road.

As the drifting smoke that obscured the road ahead began to clear, Bolan spotted the remaining escort car as it slowly about-faced and started back in his direction. He leaned inside the Cherokee and picked up a second LAW, extending the tube. Stepping to the middle of the road, he raised the weapon and tracked in on the advancing vehicle. It slowed and came to a full stop as the driver recognized what Bolan was pointing at him. He turned and spoke to his partners. They were in a no-win situation. If they kept coming, Bolan would burn them before they got anywhere near. If they tried to reverse away and turn around, he could do the same. So they decided surrender was the safest option.

The driver eased open his door ready to step out. The other Brethren soldiers did the same.

They had no way of knowing this was a no-quarter situation.

Bolan triggered the LAW before one of their feet had touched the tarmac, blowing the car and its occupants into a blackened and blazing pyre. Dropping the empty casing, the Executioner gathered the remaining LAW and walked across the road until he could see the cab of the tractor that had pulled the now demolished trailer. There was a driver and his partner. One of the cab doors, the driver's, swung open and an armed figure jumped out. He was yelling his defiance even as Bolan fired the LAW. The missile struck the cab unit and turned it into a bright, full ball of fire. Debris exploded in all directions. The armed driver was still making his jump to the ground when the force of the blast engulfed him. He was hurled, screaming across the road, engulfed in flames. His partner was hurled through the shattered windshield and dumped ten feet in front of the vehicle, his body smoking and charred.

Bolan was in the Cherokee and starting to turn while debris was still raining down on the devastation that had visited that quiet desert road in the middle of nowhere.

Before he moved on Bolan had a return visit to make to the facility and the warehouse where there was still a sizable cache of weapons and ammunition to dispose of.

Then this phase of his mission would be concluded.

CHAPTER FIFTEEN

Chicago

Carl Lyons checked his watch. Time enough for him to launch his strike against the Chicago storage facility, which was located in a disused industrial site on the south side of the city. At one time the site had supported up to a dozen plants that manufactured steel goods, trailer construction and other allied industries. Now, with the downturn in the industry, this was a dead zone of dilapidated workshops and empty warehouses. Trash littered the broken concrete walkways and loading platforms. Every window in every building had been broken long ago, and graffiti colored many walls. Even the vandals had abandoned the area and left it to slowly deteriorate.

Lyons had located the industrial site, parking his 4x4 in the dark shadows beneath a mildewed arch that supported a rail track once used by the industrial site to deliver raw materials to the businesses. The rail spur line, like the industrial site, was devoid of traffic. After securing his vehicle, Lyons moved out. He wore a set of camou fatigues and carried a medium-size backpack that held a number of primed explosive compound blocks. His Colt Python rode in a shoulder rig, and he had a mini-Uzi in his hands. A webbing belt around his waist held speed loaders for the Python, extra mags for the SMG and a Cold Steel Tanto combat knife in a sheath.

Lyons worked his way across the seemingly deserted site, using abandoned equipment and scattered junk for cover. He took his time, aware that any kind of hasty approach could expose him to the Brethren. When the target of his probe came into sight, Lyons had easy confirmation that his quarry was nearby. A pair of parked vehicles stood outside the workshop, the large sliding doors open.

An armed guard patrolled the area. Lyons watched his movements, checking the perimeter of the guy's walk. It was the same distance each time. At the end of his patrol the guard paused, then turned and retraced his steps. Lyons studied the man for close to ten minutes. By the end of that time Lyons was becoming restless. He decided he had monitored the guard for long enough. He scanned the distance between his position and the building, waited his moment, then used the ample cover to work his way to the far corner of the workshop where he slipped around the corner, slung his Uzi over his shoulder and pulled the combat knife from its sheath.

The soft tread of the guard told Lyons he was coming his way. He waited until the guy stopped, prior to turning. The scrape of booted feet on the ground told Lyons the man had started to turn. He waited another couple of seconds, then made his move, coming up behind the guard. His left hand clamped over the guy's mouth, pulling his head back to expose and stretch the neck. The combat knife made its silent, gleaming arc, cutting into the throat deeply and cleanly. Warm blood surged from the wound as it gaped wide, spilling down the front of the guard's coat. Lyons hauled the struggling man around the corner of the building, his big hand still in place to stifle any cries.

With the Uzi back in his hands Lyons headed for the open doors of the workshop. He flattened against the outer wall, checking the shadowed interior. It was a maze of rusting metal, some on steel racks, more on the floor in untidy piles, the detritus of a dead era, corroding and gathering dust. On silent feet Lyons eased inside, staying close to the corrugated metal wall as he assessed the situation.

He picked up the distant sounds of voices deeper inside the building, the scrape and thump of heavy objects being moved around. Lyons probed the way ahead, picking on the talk as his guide. As he weaved his way through the abandoned clutter, the voices and the banging became more distinct. Lyons was drawn in that direction, still unable to see his quarry because of the increasingly larger stacks of rusting metal—until he reached a spot where a clear section opened out. He found himself watching a group of armed men working around a stack of boxes and crates with recognizable shapes and sizes. He had seen enough weapons' containers to know what he was looking at.

As he registered the number of armed figures in front of him, the merest sound caught his attention. It came from his left side, slightly to his rear, and Lyons knew without doubt it was not a good sign.

Glancing to the left Lyons saw a big man—genuinely big—bearing down on him. In the guy's hands was a long steel bar that he was swinging at Lyons with the clear intention of causing severe harm.

Lyons pushed the Uzi into the path of the bar, risking damage to the weapon rather than to himself, dropping to a crouch to reduce his bulk.

The guy came in fast, despite his large size, swinging the thick metal bar. Lyons heard the whoosh of disturbed air. The bar struck the Uzi and ripped it from Lyons's hands. His finger jerked back on the trigger, and the Uzi released a short burst just before it left Lyons's hands. The weapon hit the concrete floor and slid into the shadows beneath a rack of metal sheets. Lyons came up out of his semicrouch, launching himself at his attacker. His right shoulder pounded the guy's stomach, drawing a pained grunt. Lyons followed up with a solid forearm smash that impacted against the underside of the guy's jaw. It closed his mouth and he bit down on his tongue, cutting it badly. Blood began to bubble from between his lips, running down his bruised jaw and spattering his sweatshirt. As fast as the big ex-cop was, he failed to get clear enough away as his opponent let go of the metal bar to wrap powerful arms around Lyons's upper body, hugging him close and threatening to crush his ribs and spine.

The pressure was intense. The Able Team leader felt himself confined in the man's bear grip. He stared into his face, already flushed and taut with the effort he was expending. No time for lengthy deliberations. Just simple and direct action. Lyons swung his head back, then forward, with the utmost force he could sustain. His savage head butt crushed his adversary's nose and drew a strangled cry of pain. The guy's grip slackened as he focused on the pain from his nose. It was a mess, spouting blood.

Lyons broke free, slamming hard right and left fists to his opponent's face. The big man lost his balance and slumped to his knees. The former L.A.P.D. detective moved in, reaching down to where the guy knelt. He misjudged the situation and saw too late the guy snatch something from the floor. Lyons saw the length of scrap metal in the guy's right hand. The thug lashed out and the ragged edge of steel sliced through Lyons's clothing, slamming hard against his left side. The blow was solid, pain flaring, and Lyons felt blood starting to soak his clothing. He stepped back as his opponent lurched to his feet, holding the metal like a primitive sword, cutting back and forth as he threatened Lyons.

If the guy had been at his optimum performance, he might have landed a telling blow. His injuries clouded his awareness so his arm's-length slashes at Lyons passed by harmlessly, giving the Stony Man commando the chance to move in and make a grab for the guy's arm. He gripped the arm, twisted and swung the man toward him, then angled the metal strip, pushing it toward its owner. It pierced flesh just below the guy's ribs. He gave a high scream as the raw edge cut in deep, blood bubbling out around the wound. A final heave buried the metal in the guy's torso and the stricken man fell away, curling up on the warehouse floor.

Lyons drew his Python, breathing slow and easy. The pain in his left side showed no sign of easing off. He pressed his hand over the wound and felt blood oozing between his fingers. He wasn't sure whether ribs had been broken or simply badly bruised at this stage.

He leaned against the metal frame, pushing the pain to the back of his mind, and concentrated on picking up the extraneous sounds that echoed around the building.

Where had the Brethren gone?

The burst from Lyons's Uzi had scattered them to take cover.

Were they still around, watching and waiting for him to show himself so they could pick him off?

Making himself an easy target wasn't in Carl Lyons's playbook.

The Uzi had disappeared somewhere in the shadows. Lyons wasn't sure where, and he had no time to go searching for the weapon. He still had the .357 Python in his hand and at least three speed loaders on his belt. Off to his right, where the shadows were too dense for him to see, he heard the rattle of movement. A sharp sound. Metal against metal. Maybe a gun barrel scraping over abandoned machinery. Lyons pulled back deeper into his own cover, letting the darkness hide him, as well.

He waited, letting the enemy come to him.

He had learned the technique from Bolan and had honed it during many Able Team missions—letting the enemy do the approach, staying out of sight until the last moment, until the enemy walked into *his* killing ground and into *his* sights.

Right now, even from a couple of feet away, he was invisible.

And silent.

The Python was at his side, the muzzle pointing at the concrete floor. Silence settled. Lyons calmed his breathing in case the sound carried.

Now he was able to pick up the opposition's presence. From the spot he'd heard before. The hard soles of heavy boots scraping as the wearer tried to move in closer. Whoever the guy was he lacked patience, which could prove fatal.

This was a waiting game and Lyons was no novice. He turned his attention toward the shadowed spot the sound had come from, adjusting his vision, and was rewarded when he made out the denser bulk of the man's body. Maintaining his stance, Lyons noted the dull gleam of light reflecting off a gun barrel. He studied his approaching target, judging the position of the weapon to the man's outline. He pulled back as far as he could, raising the Python two-handed, and took aim. It was well within the revolver's range. A fraction of a second before Lyons fired, the guy moved again, stepping to the point where light began to materialize his face and body. Lyons didn't hesitate. He gently stroked the trigger, felt the Python push against his grip as it fired, sending its powerful .357 Magnum round at the target. The head shot knocked the target back a couple of steps, turning him as the slug cored in through his skull and shut down his brain functions. The guy collapsed, barely making a sound as he dropped, the back of his skull a gaping maw.

Lyons sank to a crouch, leaning out a fraction to increase his field of vision. He caught movement off to his left as a shadow detached from the darkness beyond a pile of stacked metal drums. The guy was faster than his dead companion and proved he had spotted Lyons by letting rip with a long burst from the subgun he was fielding. The stream of slugs ripped at the edge of the frame, creating sparks before they whined off into the beyond. Lyons had pulled back but still felt the heat of their passing.

It might have been wise to stay back under cover, but that was not Lyons's way. He chose to do the exact opposite, banking on the shooter to be curious as to whether he had hit his target. A footfall suggested he was right. Lyons edged forward and saw a dark-clad figure moving out from cover, leaning forward from his shoulder, the subgun probing ahead of him.

It was the lack of patience again, so often the catalyst that brought about misfortune. Lyons let the guy clear cover and stand exposed, peering at the shadows ahead of him and not expecting what happened next.

Lyons rose to his full height, swung around the edge of the steel frame and put two .357 rounds in the guy before he even registered he was being confronted. It was a foolish move, the last the guy would make, and another advantage for Lyons.

His target went down with a moan of protest, hitting the concrete hard, the subgun bouncing from slack fingers. By the time Lyons reached him he was struggling to suck breath into his shredded lungs and coughing up bloody froth. The big ex-cop triggered a head shot to silence the guy for good. He leathered the Python and scooped up the man's fallen weapon, frisking the guy for spares mags. He found one and slid it behind his belt, then checked the subgun, making sure it was cocked and ready for use.

He heard a rush of sound. The enemy closing in now, suddenly eager for the kill. Lyons had no objection to that, as long as it wasn't him being killed. He glanced ahead and saw the shadows bouncing off the wall.

Eager.

Too eager.

He waited in the gloom, his weapon ready, knowing they were going to walk directly into his muzzle-blast.

And they did. Coming forward, weapons up and starting to spit fire as they closed on his former position. Someone among the group was yelling orders. Another slip. The guy was simply making it easier for Lyons to pinpoint them. As they came into view, moving in a bunch, weapons still directed at where Lyons had been, he moved up to the open section of cover and triggered the subgun, feeling it vibrate in his hands as it jacked out a stream of burning slugs that caught the opposition force and sent them into total confusion. Lyons arced the weapon back and forth, holding it firm so that not one shot fired was wasted. He saw the Brethren gunners go down, bodies twisting as flesh was punctured by the lethal burst. Empty casings rang sharply as they tumbled to the concrete floor. In a matter of seconds the expectant militia became victims of their own carelessness. They fell and crashed and crumbled to the concrete, blood spurting from torn flesh, clothing shredded and weapons slipping from their fingers. Pain overtook whatever else they might have been thinking. The numbing shock of hard-driven slugs piercing flesh and breaking bone blocked out any clear thoughts about what was happening.

Lyons felt the subgun click empty. He worked the eject button and let the spent mag drop to the floor while he retrieved and clicked in his second clip. He cocked the weapon and stepped forward, the muzzle starting to spit fire again as he made certain that there would be no Lazarus rising from the dead this day, only letting his finger off the trigger when he was satisfied.

The echo of autofire faded into silence. Lyons got rid of the partly used magazine and replaced it with a fresh one from a dropped subgun. A few more clips went into his belt pouches. Lyons turned and walked away from the dead. One of the corpses had a cell phone clutched in his hand. Lyons took it, noting that the guy had been dialing a speed number. He saw the name on the screen and smiled, dropping the cell phone into his pocket.

He reached the open door to the workshop and checked the exterior. The yard still looked clear save for the two vehicles he'd seen on his arrival. Lyons turned back inside the warehouse and worked his way back to the stacked boxes of ordnance. He pulled the canvas sheet away and took his prepared explosive packages from his backpack, distributing them through the pile and setting the timers, giving himself ten minutes to get away. He pulled the sheet back over what had now become a large explosive device and made his way to the door. He stepped outside and slid the doors shut.

The Able Team leader hurriedly returned to where he had concealed his SUV. Unlocking the door, he got behind the wheel and started the engine. Lyons rolled out of the deserted industrial site, making for the service road, heading back in the general direction of the highway. Checking his watch he saw he still had a couple of minutes before the explosives detonated. Pulling to the side of the road, he took out the cell phone and checked the power level. There was ample. He tapped the speed dial number he had seen on-screen. It rang a few times before it was answered.

"Ribak?"

"Yeah. This better be good news." There was a hesitation as Ribak became aware he was having a conversation with someone he didn't recognize.

"It is for me, Ribak. *You* won't be so happy."

"Who the fuck is…" Ribak stopped, realization rendering him silent for a moment.

"Give me a little of your time, Ribak." Lyons glanced at his watch and saw the seconds counting down. "You know what they say about Chicago being a windy city? It can be pretty noisy, too. Especially today."

"What the fuck are you talking—"

The explosion was deafening even at Lyons's distance from it. He felt the SUV rock from the blast. In his rearview mirror he could see the fireball rising behind him.

"What the hell was that?" Ribak yelled.

"Don't you recognize the sound of your weapons and explosive stash blowing all to hell, Ribak? That warehouse you had in Chicago? Gone. Along with that team of Brethren watchdogs. No guns for your storm troopers. Ribak, don't you think some days would have been better if you'd stayed in bed?"

"You bastard, I'm going to take you and your partner down personally."

"You'll get your chance, Ribak. You and Seeger. Use your time wisely because it's running out."

As Ribak began to hurl his threats over the cell phone, Lyons threw it out of the window. He drove off, smoke from the demolished warehouse starting to drift across the landscape. Minutes later, as Lyons reached the main highway, he heard the distant howl of sirens as police and emergency services converged on the blast site.

He drove in the opposite direction, favoring his side and accepting that he was going to need some medical attention. He didn't like the idea of standing down. The ongoing campaign aimed at destabilizing the Brethren was going well. Losing momentum was not advisable. Bolan would want to keep hitting them. Everywhere they could and as hard as they could.

He took out his own cell phone and speed-dialed Stony Man Farm.

"That big bang in Chicago anything to do with you?" Barbara Price asked.

"What big bang in Chicago?"

"The one we just picked up coming over the wire from some TV helicopter that spotted a fireball on the south side."

"Okay, I'll come clean. Can you get me some secure medical treatment? I need a couple of stitches. I'm sure Hal can conjure up a Stony Man approved medic faster than I can. My room at the hotel."

"Yeah, sure." Price kept her voice level, but it didn't prevent Lyons picking up her concern.

"Nothing serious," he said. "Just needs looking at."

"Really? Okay, hotshot, we'll have someone make a house call."

"Thanks," Lyons said. "I'll check in later."

"You'd better."

Before he left the area and got into a busier environment Lyons parked and took off his shoulder rig and belt, stowing them in the leather carryall in the foot well on the passenger side. He slid into his leather jacket and pulled the zip high to conceal his bloodied combat suit. He moved off and cut through the city in the direction of his hotel. Using his room key card, he accessed the basement parking garage, took his carryall and used the elevator to reach his floor. Locating his room, Lyons let himself in. He retrieved his Python from the bag and slid it beneath one of the pillows on the bed. He stowed the bag in the rear of a closet, laid out clean clothing and headed for the shower. He had to soak a towel and hold it over the drying blood patch that had stuck his combat suit to the wound. He carefully peeled off the suit, gritting his teeth as the reluctant material clung to the wound edges, but he finally got it off. He stepped under the warm shower and let it sluice over him. It stung when it hit the ragged gash, and the floor of the shower became tinged with red for a while. Lyons lathered up, then rinsed himself clean. Minutes later, dried and feeling slightly less battered, he wrapped one of the towels around his body to protect his wound, then slipped on one of the bathrobes he found sealed in plastic, and rang room service for a pot of coffee.

Lyons checked his cell phone and saw that the power was starting to drop. He fished his charger out of his bag and plugged in the phone.

His coffee arrived ten minutes later. Lyons poured himself a cup and perched on the edge of the bed while he drank. His cell phone rang. It was Brognola. The man sounded weary, and Lyons knew exactly how he felt.

"Your medic is on his way. His name's Whitmore. You sure you can stay on this, Ironman?"

"Have to. Only way to knock these people down is to keep at them. Take out everything they have and cut down their people. I can't give them the chance to regroup."

"We had a call from Striker a while ago. He's on his way home. You come in as soon as you can.

"Will do. *You* had a time-out since we talked?"

"No chance. I'm about to leave for an update with the Man. He sounded irritable."

"Striker and I are moving as fast as we can. Tell him."

Brognola laughed. "Don't think I won't."

Lyons heard a tap on his door. "That might be my medicare."

He broke the connection, picking his Python from beneath the pillow, and made his way across the room. Lyons cracked the door and confronted the lean, gray-haired man in a dark suit, carrying a medical bag.

"Agent Benning?"

"You are?"

"Leland Whitmore."

Lyons stepped back, easing the door open enough to let the man inside. He locked it once Whitmore had entered. The doctor noticed the pistol in Lyons's hand and smiled briefly.

"I'm here to cure, not kill you, Agent Benning. I was told you might be a little wary."

"Most of the people I've met the last few days had it the other way 'round. I guess I'm still in defensive mode."

Whitmore placed his bag on a small table and freed the catch, pulling the bag open. Lyons's eyes never moved from the man's hand as he reached inside and withdrew…a rolled bundle. He pulled on a pair of surgical gloves.

"Let's take a look at you. Sit on the end of the bed."

Lyons sat and slipped his robe down to his waist. Whitmore removed the bloodied towel the big ex-cop had used and examined the wound. He took his time, his fingers gently probing.

"What did this?" he asked.

"Got hit by a length of steel. Guy was using it like a club."

"That would account for the ragged formation. Some dirt in there, too. You were lucky. It hasn't penetrated too deeply. Probably bruised a rib, but I'm pretty sure it hasn't done any more damage than the gash. I'll clean it up and put in a few stitches."

"Go ahead. And before you say it, a couple of days' rest isn't in the cards."

"Why did I know that was coming?"

Whitmore was thorough. He cleaned the wound, then gave Lyons a local anesthetic to numb the area so he could put in the stitches. After applying a pressure bandage he stood back and peeled off his gloves. He took a plastic bottle from his bag and placed it on the table.

"Painkillers, if you need them. No more than two at a time. And try to avoid driving if you take them. They can hit you with some drowsiness. I don't want to come out again and find you wrapped around a telephone pole."

"Understood, Doc, and thanks."

Whitmore wrote on a pad, tore off a sheet and handed it to Lyons. "Prescription for more if you need them."

Lyons pulled his bathrobe back in place. He shook Whitmore's hand. "Grateful for your help, Doc."

"That's what they pay me for. Look, I know it's not my place, but watch yourself, Agent Benning. I have no idea what your assignment is. Knowing the way you people operate, it isn't going to be a walk in the park. Just take care, son."

Lyons nodded. He followed Whitmore to the door and let him out, securing it behind the man. He checked his coffee and found the pot had gone cold. He rang room service and ordered more, plus sandwiches and a side salad. While he waited, he got out of the bathrobe and dressed. He put the Python back under the pillow, smiling when he recalled Chief Harper's remark about sleeping with his weapon. The cop hadn't been far off the mark. His order arrived, and Lyons sat and ate. His appetite was far from diminished and this time he made sure he drank the coffee while it was still hot. When he had finished he went to the door and hung the Do Not Disturb sign on the handle. Then he went to bed and slept.

"BELLER WILL BE LANDING in a few minutes, Deke. I want you on that plane. Tie up with Juan. Make sure he concludes his Brethren business in Boise, then make sure he gets back here in one piece. After that fuckup with Lorens, I don't want any more losses. Especially not my surviving lawyer."

"Begging your pardon, sir, but Zac was due to go anyhow. He had ripped us off for those diamonds."

"I don't need reminding how my so-called SIC and friend screwed me, Deke. Am I the only one around here who wants to keep this group together? You're the one with the credentials. Go do the job. Protect Juan and get him back here ASAP. Okay?"

"No problem, Mr. Seeger. Consider it done."

THEY MET in the same place. Lewis Bradshaw was on his second cup of coffee by the time Brognola arrived.

"Keeping you busy, Hal?"

"Sign of the times. You have something for me?"

"I guessed you would be interested in a report I had from West Africa. After your friends had left the country, our local contacts filed it. Nice job your people did, by the way. With M'Tusi dead, his organization has decided to fight among itself. Some problem with who should take over. From what I hear, there won't be anyone left to run it if they keep on killing each other."

"Nice people."

"The part of the report I thought you'd really be interested in concerned Max Belmont, Jack Regan and M'Tusi's broker, Kesawayo."

Brognola paused with his coffee cup halfway to his lips. "We going to have more problems with them?"

"I doubt it. Belmont's body was found in the bush. He'd been hacked to death with a panga. Kesawayo is dead, too. Skull caved in with a rock found next to him, then finished off with the same panga."

"Regan?"

Bradshaw smiled and raised his hands. "No sign. Only tracks leading away from the two bodies. He's vanished, Hal."

"Son of a bitch. We've come across Regan a few times and no matter how bad things get, he always walks away. That guy has a charmed life."

"You know the twist? He'll be fixing a deal for one of our agencies next time around. Regan is a sly fox, but knows how to turn a buck. He doesn't give a damn who pays the tab as long as he gets his cut."

Brognola didn't need telling. Or being advised that Jack Regan would show up again. That fact was as sure as day following night. "His luck will run out one day."

Bradshaw nodded. "I hope so. Hal, what do I say? You came through. Did what you promised. I won't forget it. Thanks."

"You're welcome."

CHAPTER SIXTEEN

Clair Valens sat in her car, her eyes fixed on the man she had been tailing most of the day. On and off over the past few days, too. This time, she told herself. This time it's going to pay off.

She reached beneath her leather coat to check her piece, her fingers touching the solid butt of the Glock holstered on her hip. A recriminatory smile edged her mouth as she thought how many times she had done the very same thing over the past hour. A few times, she admitted. She was edgy, aware she was flying solo on this one. No backup to keep her safe. Immediately she thought about Jackson Byrde, her former partner. He had been killed in the line of duty during the Zero affair. Not killed, she corrected. Deliberately executed as a show of force. It had been many months ago now, but the chilling memory of that day had stayed with Valens and would remain until she had full closure.

Valens was in control of what she was doing. It was against department policy for an agent to run a personal investigation and she was risking her job by doing it.

She was breaking protocol, she understood that, but it was something she could not ignore. Valens had a strong sense of justice. It was pushing her to these extremes and it would not leave her alone until she brought down the man responsible.

Eric Stahl.

Ex-senator Eric Stahl. The man who had led the Zero conspiracy; the man who been removed from his government position as a punishment. Nothing else had changed. Stahl remained head of Stahl Industries. His power was hardly diminished. The complex tangle of contacts, both industrial and military, had conspired to maintain his survival and Stahl, after a suitable period out of the daylight, had resurfaced to carry on as before. His political maneuvering appeared to be at an end, but Valens refused to believe that for a moment.

Stahl had ambition. He wanted to head the country, to take control of America. It had been the reason he had attempted to take control of Zero, the orbiting platform with its formidable array of weapons and sophisticated listening devices. A desire for such power would not dissipate following little more than a rap on the knuckles. Though she had not been privy to the deal Stahl had cut with the government, she knew the man would still lust after his supreme ambition.

Valens had used her agency facilities to maintain a check on Stahl. Her personal dossier on the man and his activities had taken a long time to assemble due to the need for absolute discretion. She told no one, which meant she had little chance of using many contacts. Once her activities were brought into the light, her chances of exposure became stronger. Even her new partner, who she trusted in every other respect, knew nothing about her personal investigation into Eric Stahl's business. Ray Curran had been a close, personal friend of Jackson Byrde. It had been hard for Valens not to tell Curran what she was doing, but she refrained from telling him. It would not have been fair to expect the man to keep her secret. She had decided to take a few days off from her accumulated vacation time and concentrate on her surveillance.

A week ago Valens had seen Stahl with a man she felt she knew but could not identify until she ran a check on the license plate of the car he was driving. Her computer scan of the plate showed it belonged to Juan Amenta. When she asked for detailed information on Amenta, she learned he was a political activist and had links with antigovernment militia groups. Amenta's background had him down as an attorney, with a practice in Chicago. Additional information brought up names of associates, which proved both insightful and left Valens with a feeling of unease.

Amenta's main client was the extreme militia group known as the Brethren. Commanded by Liam Seeger, the Brethren, with an isolated complex in the Colorado high country, ran vociferous campaigns that denounced the U.S. government, promised that the day of reckoning was due, and that the Brethren would be at the head of the popular rising of the country against Washington and the administration.

At first the Brethren's agenda seemed to be the same as many other isolationist groups who took to the secluded parts of the country, barricading themselves against the rest of society and vowed to defend their rights as Americans when the day came. Valens, while viewing these groups as more eccentric than dangerous, admitted that she also understood how they felt—alienated, fretful over the way the country was being run and cautious about the future. There had been incidents when the FBI had been forced to move against the more extreme of these groups. What they had found altered the perspective of the compounds. They had stores of weapons and ammunition, plentiful supplies of survival rations. Communication equipment and vehicular transport. Reading through FBI files she had been able to procure made Valens even more convinced that if Eric Stahl had links to the Brethren it was not because he had philanthropic desires. The Brethren, like Stahl, had a great animosity toward the U.S. administration. Stahl had even been a leading light of the Third Party, a vocal opponent of both Republican and Democrat parties. Somewhere along the line he and the Brethren appeared to have come together. Valens's conclusion did not leave her with pleasant thoughts.

She had no solid proof she could move on, nothing of any consequence that might stir federal agencies into action.

But Valens had no intention of backing off. She slowly began to build her dossier on the Brethren and Eric Stahl. She was uncertain how to proceed if and when she had what she might consider enough evidence to go on, until on a lonely stakeout of Amenta's Boise motel one night, with rain streaming down the windows of her vehicle. Amenta was in there with the man who had joined him earlier that day. Valens knew what she had to do and wondered why the notion hadn't come to her before.

Using her cell phone she called Saul Kaplan, Zero's creator and the man now in charge of maintaining the orbiting platform. It had been some time since she had spoken with him. He answered on the third ring, recognizing her voice and answering her polite query on his health and how the Zero project was doing. Kaplan paused for a moment.

"Agent Valens, I appreciate your call, but I suspect there is more to it than a polite chat about my health or Zero's performance."

"There is. I need you to contact someone for me."

"From the tone of your voice I would hazard a guess it is Mr. Belasko."

"I'm supposed to be the one who deduces things."

Kaplan laughed. "Of course. Which is why I guessed you needed to speak with someone in your own line of work."

"Can you help?"

"I have a number I can call that will get a message to the people he was involved with."

"If it's possible for him to contact me, they can use my cell phone number."

"Yes. I have that. Clair, is this something I should know about?"

"At this time I'm still checking it out. Just get Belasko to contact you. Tell him… Tell him it concerns Eric Stahl."

"Is Stahl up to his old games again?"

"That's what I'm trying to find out. Saul, please make that contact for me."

"Good enough. Clair, look after yourself. Please take care now."

"I WAS RIGHT," Ribak said. "It's the same damn car. Woman driver."

He turned from the window, reaching under his jacket for the Beretta 92-F he carried. Slipping the pistol from the leather holster on his belt, Ribak checked the weapon, easing off the safety.

"What are you going to do?" Amenta asked. "Deke, you don't start a shooting match in the middle of a motel parking lot."

"Relax, Juan, I'm not that stupid. But I'm not about to let that bitch go and maybe set us up."

"Deke, maybe she's one of your ex-girlfriends checking you out."

"Uh-uh," Ribak said. "My former girlfriends do not come looking for me. They know better."

The way he said it and allowed a smile to touch his pale lips unnerved Amenta.

"So how are you going to play this?"

"Nice and quiet. We ready to move?"

"Just about."

"Give me a couple of minutes then get out to the car and wait for me. Keep the engine running. But do it nice and steady. No rushing. We drive out easy. No fuss."

VALENS SAW THE MAN emerge from Amenta's motel room, watching as he paused to light a cigarette before moving beyond her line of sight. He walked steadily, making no suspicious moves, but Valens didn't take chances. She eased her Glock from beneath her coat and placed it on the seat beside her right hand.

Now what do you do, Clair? she pondered. One inside the room, the other somewhere out of your sight.

She knew the wisest thing would be to start the car and drive away, give it up until a better opportunity showed itself. Valens accepted that to be the best option.

Instinctively she objected to the thought. From childhood she had never gone by the safest route and even now she tended to swim against the tide. She admitted it was a failing, but each time a situation developed she refused to back off. It had dragged her into a compromising position on more than one occasion, and it would most likely do the same again if…

Her car door was yanked open. Rain blew inside, hitting her. Valens dropped her hand over the Glock even as the cold muzzle of a handgun was pushed against the side of her head.

"I suggest you don't. Choice is yours. Die now, die later."

Valens raised her hand into full view. Inside she was beating herself up for being caught so easily. No one to blame but herself. Even so, it sucked.

"Out of the car. Step easy." He made her stand with her back to him, hands on top of her head, rain already soaking her. Valens could feel the muzzle of his weapon pressed against her spine. By the movements he made she knew he had scooped up her Glock from the seat. He had to have taken her keys from the ignition because when he closed the car door she heard the blip as he used the remote to lock the vehicle. "Wouldn't want anyone to steal it. So much crime about these days."

"Tell me about it," Valens murmured.

"I like a woman with a sense of humor." He prodded her with his pistol. "See the car over there with its lights on? We're going to walk across and get in the back. No fuss. Oh, you can put your hands down now. Make it look like we're together. Fuck with me, and I'll shoot your spine out."

Valens believed him. She started across the parking lot to the waiting car. When they reached it, she opened the rear door and slid inside. Her captor joined her, closing the door. The man behind the wheel turned to look over his shoulder. Valens recognized Juan Amenta. He barely glanced at her, fixing his gaze on the man beside her.

"Now what do we do?"

"Exactly what we were going to do before Nancy Drew here joined us. Now let's go."

The car turned and rolled across the lot, making a right turn as it joined the highway. Valens slumped back in her section of the rear seat, pushing her hands deep into the pockets of her coat.

"Good idea," the man with the gun said. "We got a long ride ahead of us. Be comfortable."

In the left-hand pocket of her coat Valens worked her cell phone open and felt for the power button, which she pressed. The phone was set on vibrate alert, so there wasn't going to be any ring tones to give her away. Not that she was going to be able to answer any calls if they did come through. At least with the phone switched on her position could be tracked as long as the battery held out. Or until her captors decided to search her and found the phone.

The car was heading north. Valens tried to identify landmarks, anything that might indicate her whereabouts and could be used to track her. Okay, she was clutching at straws, but in her current position there wasn't much else she could do.

She pushed her thoughts to her conversation with Saul Kaplan. Had he been able to get in touch with Belasko's people yet? She knew she could depend on

Kaplan following through. He was a man of his word. Capable. Any man who could create something like Zero had to be smart. Let's hope you're as clever as I'm figuring, Saul, she thought.

Twice, police cruisers passed them, lights showing on the roofs of the vehicles. Not much comfort there, she decided. Beside her the man with the gun gave a pleased chuckle when the second cruiser overtook them.

"If only he knew," he said. The thought seemed to amuse him. "Cops. Just when you need one they're way out of reach."

"Do you think I need one? Am I in that much trouble?" Valens asked dryly.

"I'll let you figure that out for yourself."

THEY DROVE FOR TWO HOURS, far out of the city, the car eventually turning into a small airfield and coming to a stop outside a hangar that bore the legend Beller's Charter over the door.

"Out, lady."

The pistol was held against Valens's spine as she climbed out, pulling her coat around her against the rain. Her captor was taking no chances.

"Are we taking a plane ride? Hope the movie's good."

"Being lippy isn't making me like you any better, so quit while you still have a mouth that works."

The tone he used convinced Valens he was serious. She fell silent and concentrated on checking out the area. Darkness and the falling rain obscured much of her vision. She did spot a blue-and-white Cessna twin-engine plane on the concrete apron close by. It bore the Beller's Charter logo along its side. She had no more time to observe as the man with the gun pushed her forward and they crossed the apron, heading for the company office that was tacked on to the side of the company hangar. They stepped inside the building. It was an office-waiting room combo. A row of imitation leather couches stood against one wall. Valens was told to sit down. She dropped onto one of the couches, her hands in her coat pockets, and waited.

The man behind the battered counter, heavyset, with a beefy face, took a long look at her before greeting his other guests. He nodded at Amenta, then turned to the blond man.

"Ribak," he said. "Plane's fuelled and ready."

"I need a drink," the man named Ribak said. "You got any coffee on the go?"

"In back. Anybody else?" Amenta shook his head. "How about the lady?"

Ribak glanced across at Valens. "She doesn't need a thing. Do you, honey?"

Valens hunched her shoulders.

Amenta wandered behind the counter and into the office. Moments later he could be heard having a telephone conversation with someone. Ribak got his coffee and stood at the counter drinking it. The other man, who he called Beller, got his gear together. It appeared he was also the pilot.

Valens made her decision on what to do about her cell phone. She waited until Ribak was savoring his coffee before she closed her fingers around the phone and worked her hand out of her pocket, easing the device across the seat, pushing the phone into the overlap between seat base and backrest. She wedged it deep into the gap until it was hidden from sight. She was acutely aware her action might not achieve anything at all. On the other side of the coin there was the possibility the signal might be picked up—if anyone was searching for her.

With her maneuver completed she maintained her position and waited, offering no resistance until Ribak crossed over to her.

"On your feet."

Valens got up and they walked from the office and across to the waiting Cessna. Beller went ahead and climbed into the cockpit. Ribak pushed her in the direction of the passenger door. Once they were inside and the door secured, Amenta took the front seat, opening his attaché case to work on a stack of papers. Ribak motioned Valens to one of the rear seats.

"Wait a minute," he said suddenly.

Valens faced him. "Now what do you want?"

He grinned. "Maybe you should be a little nicer to me, honey. Where you're going you might need a friend."

"I'll keep that in mind, then."

"Smart. Now take off the coat." When she did, he tossed it on one of the seats. "Now I get to search you."

"Take your time. It doesn't look like I have any choice."

Ribak transferred his pistol to his left hand, using his right to carry out a thorough body search. "Believe me, I'm not doing this for fun."

"Don't tell me I'm losing my appeal."

Ribak caught her unflinching stare. "Honey, that's a long way off." He moved to retrieve her coat, going through the pockets before handing it back to her. "Now I got your ID. I got your gun. But I didn't find a phone. Isn't that kind of unusual?"

Valens slipped her coat back on. "Well, *honey,* if you hadn't been in such a hurry to get me out of my car you would have found it in the glove box. If you want to drop me off, I'll go and get it for you."

Ribak held her eye contact, a faintly puzzled expression on his lean face. He finally grinned. As the Cessna's engines built up power, he waved her into her seat, taking the one across the aisle from her, his pistol resting in his lap as he leaned back, relaxing. "Buckle up. Long ride ahead, *honey.*"

The word was starting to grate on Valen's nerves. She contained her feelings. There might come a time when she could express those feelings in a positive way.

Amenta went forward to speak to the pilot. The Cessna started to move quickly out to the runway. Valens could hear faint instructions coming over the radio in the cockpit. But the words were indistinct. Amenta returned to his seat and his paperwork. Resigned to her situation, Valens slumped back in her seat, wondering where they were going and who she would meet at the end of the flight.

HOURS LATER THE CESSNA made a gentle landing on a concrete runway set behind a large timber-and-stone ranch-style house. The house sat in isolated splendor with mountains in the background and rolling emptiness all around it. Daylight had come in the last hour. Valens opened weary eyes and stared out through the side window. She had no idea where they were. The moment the Cessna came to a stop, her captor told her to move. Valens pushed to her feet, movements sluggish after the prolonged inactivity of the flight. Amenta opened the door and went out first. Cool air brushed Valens's face as she exited the Cessna, still aware of the gun against her spine.

"Head for the house. Nice walk should wake you up."

"Something I need to see?"

There was no reply. Valens trailed after Amenta, pushing her hands into her coat pockets. Moving on, she casually took her hands out of her pockets, running her hands through her hair.

"No need to freshen up," her captor said. "You don't pick up brownie points for looking beautiful."

They reached the house and Valens was taken directly through to a spacious living room with a panoramic view of the mountain backdrop through a large window. The furnishing was plain and clean. Pale wood. Chrome. The floor smooth, polished pine.

There were three men waiting for them. Valens recognized one immediately—Liam Seeger, head of the Brethren. She had never seen the other two men. Glancing across the room she realized there was a fourth man, seated in a high-backed leather recliner, turned to face the scenic view. All she could see were his legs and a hand resting on the arm of the seat.

Seeger looked her over, his single eye cold, devoid of any feeling. Something in his expression made Valens shiver. He made her feel naked, as if she were spread-eagled and tied down.

"So who is she?" he asked.

Valens's escort eased the gun from her spine. He reached into a pocket and pulled out the leather wallet he'd taken from her back at the motel. He threw it to Seeger. He opened the wallet and read what was printed on Valens's ID.

"You realize who we have here? Come to think of it, why the hell *did* you bring her here?"

"It's called intelligence gathering. There was no way

I could have handled an interrogation back at the motel. Too many chances someone might have seen, or heard."

"Deke, now we have to consider getting rid of her if she becomes a risk."

"And who knows where she is way out here? Mr. Seeger, we could hide a whole baseball team in your backyard."

"Damn, Deke, it's too dangerous."

"It's dangerous falling out of bed in the morning," Ribak said. "One fuckin' agent brought out here is safer than leaving her back there where she might start talking. Look, we need to learn anything she knows. Could be she's in with that guy screwing around with us."

Seeger was still not fully convinced. He crossed to the high-backed recliner and passed the ID to the man seated there.

Valens heard him laugh gently. He leaned forward and pushed to his feet, turning to face her, studying her ID card.

Clair Valens had no idea who the man was, but the expression on his face suggested that *he* knew her.

Harry Brent, known to Seeger as the man representing his anonymous helper, was aware of Clair Valens. His employer—Eric Stahl—had never forgotten Valens's role in his defeat over the Zero conspiracy. He kept his grudge against her alive by maintaining a file on the young woman, expressing his desire to one day repay her for what she had contributed to his downfall. Stahl was one of those individuals who refused to allow past indiscretions to be forgotten. He was a vindictive man. It gave him great satisfaction when he was able to repay those indiscretions. Brent tried to imagine how Stahl would feel when he was told of her capture by the Brethren.

"Liam," he said, "don't worry about her. I know

someone who will be more than pleased to take her off your hands."

"Who?"

"My principal. Your benefactor. He knows this woman. He can persuade her to divulge anything she knows. Believe me, he'll be extremely grateful for the privilege."

Brent was smiling when he walked by Valens to help himself to another tumbler of Seeger's fine whiskey. He glanced at Ribak, giving him a brief nod.

"Let her go with Brent," Ribak said. "His people have the time to deal with her."

Seeger considered. "Lock her up in the basement until Brent leaves. I have too much on my mind to worry about her." As Ribak moved toward Valens, he asked, "She was alone? No partner?"

"She was alone. I can guarantee that. Figured she was watching us, and all the time we had *her* under observation. Her people might miss her, but there's no way they'll know where she is."

Maybe, maybe not, Valens thought. Just don't believe it's all going your way, Mr. Ribak.

Ribak took her arm and hustled her from the room, along a passage until he reached a heavy door. Opening it, he walked her down wooden stairs to a large basement room. Windowless, it was furnished as a small dormitory, with half a dozen beds and a few chairs. A small table stood against the wall.

"Toilet through that door. Drinking water at that sink. What else do you need, *Agent* Valens? All the comforts of home. We haven't gotten around to cable yet, but if you feel lonely I can always drop in so we can enjoy a conversation."

"Fine. If you do, I promise to use small words so you don't feel challenged."

"It isn't me being locked in down here, honey. I'm going back up to the big boys. I'll be thinking about you when I'm eating my steak."

Valens smiled. "That will be raw, I expect."

"Keep it up, Agent Valens. One time I'll knock that smart mouth of yours right out of your head. Just keep pushing, bitch."

He turned then and climbed the stairs, closing the door on her prison. Valens heard the door being secured. She took a long look around the basement.

Well, Clair, this time you really went and did it. Get yourself out of this little mess if you can.

Stony Man Farm, Virginia

BOLAN TAPPED IN the number he had been given for Saul Kaplan and listened as it rang and then was answered.

"Saul? It's Matt Cooper."

"Your people told me you have changed your name. Doesn't it get confusing?"

"Never thought about it that way. You needed to talk, Saul?"

"Well, really I am acting as an intermediary. For our mutual friend, the lovely Agent Valens."

"Clair? Is she in trouble?"

"She asked me to contact you as soon as I could. You are a hard man to pin down, Matt Cooper."

"What's going on, Saul?"

"Clair called and asked me to contact you. It appears she is on some kind of surveillance and felt you should know about it."

"Any names, Saul?"

"One you will recall I'm sure. Eric Stahl."

Bolan's fingers gripped the phone as he registered the ex-senator's name.

Eric Stahl wasn't someone he would forget in a hurry.

But why was Clair Valens checking him out? And if she was, did it have any connection to his association with the Brethren? More importantly, did Valens realize Stahl had an association with the militia group?

Whatever Valens's motivation for going after Stahl, it was going to involve her with the Brethren and the violent way they dealt with anyone getting in their way.

WHEN BOLAN ENTERED the Computer Room, he found Aaron Kurtzman on his own, hard at work at his computer station. The cyberwizard swung his wheelchair around as Bolan entered.

"Remember Clair Valens? Security agent working the Zero Project ? She could be involved with the Brethren through Stahl. She sent me her cell number via Saul Kaplan. I can't get an answer, but her cell is switched on," Bolan stated without preamble.

"Give me the number, Striker, and I'll track her position."

"I was hoping you'd say that."

"No big deal at this end."

"How long?"

"Hell, Striker, even I'm not that good."

Bolan smiled. He knew different. The man was *more* than good. Kurtzman had the answer Bolan wanted within a half hour.

"I have your location for Valens's cell," the computer expert said. "It's static. Signal strength has dropped a little but still strong. I'd figure it's been at the location at least a day."

"Thanks, Aaron."

"Location is a small air charter field in Idaho."

Bolan jotted down the details, then asked if there was any news on Valens's car.

"Picked this up when I ran a trace on the license plate. A car with those plates was logged into the database of the Idaho State Police. Found abandoned on the forecourt of a motel outside Boise. Manager spotted it and called the cops in because it didn't belong to any of his guests. Been there at least a day and a half. It's close on a hundred miles between the motel and the cell phone location."

"They certain it belongs to Valens?"

"No doubts. It's her own vehicle. Not an agency car. Registered to Clair Valens."

"Abandoned car. Cell phone located miles away. But no Valens. What the hell has she gotten herself into, Aaron?"

CHAPTER SEVENTEEN

Vermont

Senator Vernon Randolph rolled his SUV to a stop, switched off the engine and sat listening to the silence. He normally enjoyed the tranquil atmosphere of the lodge. Surrounded by a tract of forested acres, the building overlooked a peaceful lake and had the rising foothills of the Green Mountains in the background. The scene had a calming effect on Randolph.

This day it failed to work its magic.

The visit held a tinge of menace. Randolph knew he had overstepped himself again. His natural curiosity, coupled with a feeling of impending unrest, had forced him to continue his investigation into Eric Stahl's behavior, and now he realized he had taken a step too far.

Some might have said that Randolph's interest in Stahl bordered on the obsessive. Randolph would have refuted such an accusation. His interest in Stahl's business came about because he had long suspected the man's stance had not altered since forced out of office.

Eric Stahl was too much into his agenda to give up. He had been wily enough to withdraw from view, limiting himself to his business empire while the Zero affair slid below the horizon. Randolph saw that as nothing more than a smoke screen. Stahl would never abandon his vision of becoming a top player. It was the driving force behind everything the man did. And sooner or later he was going to step into the ring again, using a different tack, maybe, but still with the big prize his ultimate goal.

Randolph was a patient man. He went about his investigation carefully, employing tactics that kept both himself and the investigator he used well below the radar. Surviving for so long in Washington's urban jungle had taught him the art of concealment. He never became blasé about his own survival. The previous encounter with Stahl, when armed men had attacked his home, had shown Randolph exactly how far his opponent had been prepared to go to remove any opposition. He held no illusions. Stahl would go to any lengths to do the same if he suspected Randolph was dogging his tracks once again. So he conducted his covert investigation with that in mind and instructed his investigator to do the same.

The data that came his way was for the most part mundane, everyday information. Stahl appeared to be conducting himself correctly. Concentrating on his business affairs and little else. The facts did not deter Randolph. He knew his enemy and eventually Stahl would make a detour.

It happened over a period of weeks.

During that time, Randolph was fed details of Stahl's increasing contact with General William Carson. Always done quietly and away from prying eyes, except that Randolph's man maintained a close surveillance and obtained visual evidence that was presented to the senator.

General Carson's involvement whetted Randolph's interest. He understood Carson's politics and knew the man had wide-ranging influence with the three military services. He couldn't see Carson working alongside the militia group the Brethren. He was a professional soldier. The lack of discipline and command structure would not go down well with Bull Carson. He would consider them weekend warriors. But there had to be something there, a reason Carson was aligning himself with Stahl.

Randolph had spent time poring over the printed data and the few photo images his man had taken of Stahl and Carson together. His mind worked and reworked the various computations of the alliance.

And then he received a call that made a lot of the pieces fit into the jigsaw. They fell into place on the basis of what he heard.

What he heard alarmed Randolph and left him wondering how he could make use of the information.

The following morning he had another call. One that left him slumped in his armchair, suddenly feeling cold and weary and every year of his age.

His investigator, Rick Berkly, a man he had known for more than fifteen years, had been found dead in his car, in the parking lot of a downtown shopping mall. He had been shot twice through the head. What was it they called that? A double tap. Generally the mark of a professional hit.

Randolph sat and let the day grow around him, warm

sunlight penetrating the windows of his house. His mug of coffee became cold.

Damn the man, he thought. If Stahl believes this is going to stop me, he has another think coming. He had no doubt Stahl was behind Rick Berkly's murder. Guilt washed over Randolph, a sensation that cloaked him in abject sorrow at the death of his friend. A death he had brought about because of his desire to uncover whatever it was Stahl and Carson were up to. There he had been congratulating himself on exposing Stahl's covert machinations, and his faithful friend, alone and defenseless, had died trying to keep that wish on track. It was no good telling himself it was the way things went. That risk was part of such investigations. Rick Berkly had spent his days and nights out on the streets, gathering the information while Randolph had sat in comfort and safety, pulling together pieces of paper and photographs.

Now Rick was dead.

And he, Randolph, was most probably next.

That thought snapped him out of his self-pitying mood. Rick Berkly had died attempting to gather more information. What right had Randolph to sit and bemoan his own fate? His loyal friend was dead. It was up to Randolph to make sure he had not forfeited his life in vain.

He gathered every piece of information he had collated and placed it in his attaché case, then he went to his bedroom and packed a carryall with a few items of clothing and personal effects. He changed into a pair of dark trousers and a flannel shirt, pulled on a pair of walking boots, then donned a weatherproof coat and a tweed cap. He took his cell phone and laptop, picked up his keys and left the house by the door in the kitchen that led directly to the spacious garage. In the garage he placed his luggage in the late-model, dark-colored Cadillac SRX and slid behind the wheel. He started the big engine. Activating the garage door, he reversed out, closed the garage door and swung the powerful vehicle around the driveway and onto the road. It was going to take him at least six hours to reach his destination in the foothills of the Green Mountains in Vermont.

Randolph settled into the comfortable leather seat. The long drive didn't worry him. He'd always enjoyed the open road, watching the world slide by as he drove. Only before, his driving had been for pleasure.

This time he couldn't get rid of the feeling he was driving to stay alive.

It was late afternoon. Randolph, feeling a degree stiffer from his long drive than usual, pulled his luggage from the Cadillac and made his way up onto the lodge veranda. He unlocked the main door and made his way inside. Placing his luggage on the floor, he returned to the SUV and brought out the two brown bags of provisions he had picked up at the store ten miles back along the road. The owner knew him from previous trips, and Randolph had spent some time talking with the man before loading up and driving on. While he had been inside the store his vehicle was being refueled. It was something Randolph had learned a long time back. To always keep his gas tank full in this quiet backwater.

He carried the groceries into the kitchen, went to the switchbox and turned on the electricity. He did the same with the water supply, filled the kettle and put it on to boil. He spent the next twenty minutes storing the groceries and taking his carryall into the bedroom to unpack. By the time he returned to the kitchen the kettle had clicked off, so he had to drop the switch again. He spooned instant coffee into a mug and waited for the hot water. He left the brewed coffee to cool and went out to the Caddy. Before he locked it he opened the glove box on the passenger side and took out a SIG-Sauer P-226 handgun and a couple of additional magazines. He took the weapon inside and placed it on the kitchen work surface next to his mug of coffee. He picked up the mug and drank his coffee. Mundane matters occupied Randolph for the next half hour. He checked the lodge right through, making sure all windows and doors were secure. He laid a fire in the big open grate and lit it, the stacked logs beside it plentiful to see him through the night.

He considered a meal, but decided he had something else to do first. With a fresh mug of coffee beside him he sat in his favorite armchair and reached for the telephone. The soft dial tone assured him the instrument was working. He dialed a number he knew by heart and listened as it rang out. No one answered. Randolph let it ring until an answering machine clicked in.

Hi, I'm not at home just now. Leave your name, number and message, and I'll get back to you. Thank you.

"This is Vernon Randolph, Clair. I need to talk with you as soon as possible. I didn't know who else to speak to. Please get back to me. It is important."

Randolph ended the message and replaced the receiver.

"SENATOR VERNON Randolph has been trying to contact Agent Valens," Kurtzman said. "His calls came from the lodge he owns up in Vermont."

"He doesn't realize she's gone missing. Lucky you're keeping a call log on her home phone."

"Luck?" Kurtzman rumbled. "Luck has nothing to do with it. It's down to initiative and dedication."

Bolan grinned. "Right," he said. "I should have known better."

"You want Randolph's number?"

"Yeah."

Bolan took the number. "I'll check with Randolph."

The phone rang for a long time before it was picked up.

"Is that you, Clair?" Randolph sounded anxious.

"No, Senator, it's Mike Belasko."

"Belasko? Of course. You worked with Clair on the Zero affair."

"Senator, you've been trying to make contact with Valens. Can I ask why? Has it anything to do with the Brethren and Eric Stahl?"

"I know Clair has been doing some checking into Stahl's business. I wanted to warn her to take care. You see, I've been doing the same."

Bolan paused for a heartbeat. "Senator, we need to talk. Stay where you are and I'll arrange for you to be picked up."

"Mike, is Clair all right?"

"Right now I can't say. She's missing. I'm looking into it. You just wait for my partner to come for you. Big blond guy. Goes by the name of Doug Benning. Just to set the record straight—forget Belasko. It's Cooper now. Matt Cooper. Senator, are you alone at your lodge?"

"Yes. I simply left my house and drove up here. Why?"

"Expecting any visitors?"

"Are you trying to scare me? If so, it's working. Maybe I should put you in the picture. The reason I came up here unannounced is because an investigator working for me was found shot to death. He was a good friend. He was looking into Eric Stahl's current involvement with the Brethren. He must have gotten too close. I decided the safest move was to leave Washington and come up here while I tried to figure out what to do. I wanted to warn Clair she might be in danger, too."

"Benning will be on his way shortly. At least now he knows your situation."

ONE OF THE Farm-based choppers flew Lyons into the Vermont area. It dropped him a mile from the lodge, then powered down to wait. Lyons cut off through the forested area, his GPS unit guiding him in the direction he needed.

He spotted the dark SUV parked alongside Randolph's Cadillac. A single, armed man stood guard by the vehicles. Lyons stayed put and scanned the area for any other perimeter sentries. He saw no one.

Making a wide circle around the far side of the vehicles, Lyons came out of the foliage behind the sentry. He eased his way to the rear of the senator's Caddy, checking out the weapon the sentry was carrying. It was a compact mini-Uzi. Lyons waited until the guy moved, exposing his back to the big ex-cop's position, then moved quickly. The passage of his boots on the soft ground reached the sentry in the second before Lyons reached him. As the guy began to turn, the Able Team leader was already primed. He launched an unrestrained right that slammed against the sentry's jaw, snapping his head around and bouncing it off the corner post of the SUV's body, a glistening splash of red arcing across the panel. As he slid away from the vehicle, Lyons slammed his knee in under his bloody jaw, driving his head back with enough force to snap his neck. He grabbed the guy's collar and hauled the slack body out of sight behind the vehicles.

Snatching up the fallen Uzi, Lyons checked the mag, making sure the weapon was cocked and ready for use. He made a fast run for the lodge, staying low, and stopped at the veranda rail. He rolled under and flattened against the front wall, leaning to peer in through the window.

An open-plan living area that reached as far as the rear wall held three men. Two were armed with mini-Uzis like the one he had taken from the sentry. The third man had to be Senator Vernon Randolph. He was slimly elegant even in his leisure clothing. The man was seated on a wooden kitchen chair, his hands resting casually in his lap. His captors seemed to be in a heated discussion, almost as if they weren't sure what to do with their prisoner. One of them kept jabbing a finger at Randolph.

Then, for the first time, Randolph said something. The man who had been gesturing at him turned, transferred the Uzi to his left hand and without warning backhanded Randolph across the side of the head. The force of the blow threw Randolph back in his chair. It rocked and toppled over, taking Randolph with it.

Best chance you're going to get, Lyons told himself.

In his mind he was aware he had only seconds to act. Once Randolph was picked up off the floor, he would be in harm's way again. There was no time to get to the main door, which might be locked. Lyons used the only access close at hand.

He rose to his feet, backed off a couple of steps, then powered forward and smashed his way through the lodge's front window, head down and arms thrust forward to protect his face. He felt the glass and the frame shatter, sending debris into the room. In the rush of the moment he had no idea if he had cut himself on the glass, and it didn't matter as he landed awkwardly on his feet, struggling to maintain his balance. He almost remained fully on his feet but one boot slid on the smooth varnished floor and he went to his knees. The slip saved him as the guy who had slapped Randolph spun and opened up with the Uzi when he saw Lyons burst through the glass.

In the scant seconds between seeing Lyons and pulling the trigger, the shooter lost his target as Lyons stumbled. The 9 mm burst went over his head and out through the shattered window.

Lyons brought his own weapon on line, picking his target and loosing a burst that ripped into his adversary's chest. The guy reeled under the onslaught. Lyons hit him with a second burst, the final 9 mm volley tearing into his throat and lower face. The guy gave a strangled cry and fell. The second shooter had moved toward cover, searching for a spot to protect himself. He was still searching when Lyons's next burst hit him between the shoulders, coring in and enough of them finding his heart to put him down. He made an ungraceful forward tumble, crashing facedown on the hardwood floor.

It became very quiet.

A final piece of glass fell from the window frame.

Randolph slowly eased himself to a sitting position,

favoring his left shoulder where he had slammed into the floor.

Carl Lyons let the Uzi drop to the floor and took out his Python. Only now did he notice the bleeding gash across the back of his right hand. He could feel blood sliding down his face from another cut.

"Dramatic as it was, son, next time try the door," Randolph said as he climbed to his feet. He could feel himself shaking and it didn't help his condition when he saw the bloody results of his visitor's handiwork. "You have to be Cooper's friend. Doug Benning?"

"Were there any more of them? Or just the three?"

"I saw the vehicle arrive. Only three of them in it. Son, you are bleeding. Let's go through to the kitchen. There's a first-aid box in there and a third of very respectable scotch. And before you ask the scotch is for me."

Lyons followed the man to the kitchen. While Randolph looked for the first-aid box the Able Team leader went to the sink and turned on the faucet, running cold water across the back of his hand. It washed away the blood but it stung like hell. Randolph handed out antiseptic wipes and sterile pads. Despite Lyons's grumbling, the senator cleaned the gash on his cheek and when he'd stopped the bleeding he fixed an adhesive strip in place to keep it clean.

"You won't win this year's Miss Vermont beauty pageant, son, but you'll live."

Randolph helped himself to a large tumbler of the whiskey, pushing one across to Lyons, who declined and asked if there was any fruit juice. Randolph located a carton of orange juice in the refrigerator and handed it to Lyons.

"We need to move out," Lyons said. "In case they send backup."

"You think that's possible?"

"Everything is possible," Lyons said. He took out his cell phone and speed-dialed Bolan. "I had some house cleaning to do first. The senator is okay. Shaken but not enough to put him off his liquor."

"You leaving soon?"

"Very soon."

"I'll be at the Stony Man safehouse."

"Fine for some. Feet up watching TV."

"What I'm watching is no picnic. Just check it out." Lyons clicked off. "You got a TV?"

"Small one over there," Randolph said. "Why?"

"Cooper said to check it out."

Randolph switched on the fourteen-inch flat screen and flicked through channels until he found a news channel. What they saw forced them into silence.

There had been four more unexpected explosions on the streets of America. They'd been smaller than the original outrages, but still large enough to cause damage to property, and worse, to bystanders caught in the blasts. Then at least eight random attacks on police stations around the country, carried out by masked men. Overall eight police officers had been killed and as many wounded. The TV news anchor read out a statement from the America the Free group. In it the President and the administration were directly accused of being so out of touch with internal problems they were unable to combat what was happening. The statement openly accused the President as being criminally responsible for the attacks. It demanded he be removed from office. The report then went on to reveal there was already a public reaction and showed images of street protests in three major cities. People were scared and angry, the anchor quoted. Interviews with politicians presented a mix of opinion. There were those who stood by the President and others who were less than charitable. The overall mood was one of confusion, in some instances ill-concealed rage at the escalating violence and the current refusal of the government to force any action.

"Damn that man Stahl," Randolph said. "Don't you see, this is his doing?"

"You think so, Senator?"

"All part of his scheme. The Brethren do the dirty work. Kill and maim to get the public worked up. Stahl sits back until the right moment and then he'll manipulate those idiots on the Hill to reject the President and do what they can to force his resignation."

"Can't be as easy as that."

"Son, I didn't say it would be easy, but with a man like Eric Stahl holding the strings…well. Don't forget he has General Carson on his side and that man has considerable control of a damn large slice of our military. Remember we have too big of a percentage of our armed forces operating halfway around the world. If Carson could organize a military takeover, aided by Stahl and his political cronies, it would be over. The forces abroad couldn't do a damn thing to oppose it. They would be stuck out in Iran and Afghanistan at the mercy of whoever controls the military complex stateside. Those boys depend on home to send them equipment and supplies and reinforcements. Think about it, son. What's that old saying—between a rock and a hard place. My God, Stahl and that man Carson would have the President just where they want him."

"Senator, do what you need to and do it fast, we need to get you out of here."

Ten minutes was all it took for Randolph to make contact and advise what had happened. He spoke to the local sheriff's office, detailing the attack on his lodge and the result. The fact he needed his window repaired and his SUV taken care of. He apologized to the sheriff, who he appeared to know very well, that he had to return to Washington on urgent government business, but that he would be in touch ASAP.

"I'm all yours, son. Shall we go?" he said to Lyons.

CHAPTER EIGHTEEN

The safehouse Bolan had mentioned was situated fifteen miles from Stony Man. A two-story house standing in enclosed grounds had been recently purchased via the SOG, giving them a secure environment when they needed people close, without bringing them to Stony Man itself. Bolan and a two-man blacksuit team were already installed when Lyons and the senator arrived. Randolph took a quick look around the furnished living room and nodded in satisfaction.

"This is starting to become a habit," he said. "Not that I'm making a fuss, son. I recall last time. That involved some shooting and general mayhem, too. You always bring surprises to the party?"

Bolan had to smile. The senator might have been advanced in years but his mind was still sharp. "We have Stahl to thank for that. And it looks like he's up to his old tricks again. Your digging must have unnerved him. That's why he sent that snatch team after you."

Randolph's lips pursed at the mention of Stahl's name. "That son of a bitch might have been stripped of most of his political clout after the Zero affair, but he still managed to wriggle out from under. With his industrial-military contacts and his wealth, he came out a little tarnished but not a tad weaker. He retreated back into his Stahl Industries shell and, damn me, within six months he was operating like nothing happened."

"Persistent?"

"More like a man with a mission. One that he won't let go. And that makes him even more of a threat. As I mentioned when we talked on the phone, I found out that the man who has been compiling my evidence for the last months, Rick Berkly, was found dead the other day. He was a good man. Too good to die because of Stahl."

They made themselves comfortable in armchairs. Lyons, ever restless, had wandered off to make his own check of the area outside the house. A pot of coffee was produced and Bolan poured a cup for himself and Randolph.

"Power and money, Senator, they go together too well. Enough of both and a man can pretty well get away with anything."

Randolph reflected for a few moments, gathering his thoughts. "The Brethren," he said. Nothing more. He simply waited for Bolan's reaction.

"Okay, Senator, tell me what you know."

"I have some documented evidence and a deal of speculation. What I know for certain is the Brethren is not what it presents itself to be."

"An independent group representing the American people and standing up to the repressive actions of the federal government?"

"You've been reading their pamphlets."

"It's gone much further than that, Senator."

Randolph frowned at that until he realized what Bolan meant.

"I should have figured that for myself. Tell me, Matt, are there any left standing?"

"Too many," Bolan answered. "But I'm not done with them yet."

"So how can I help?"

"Fill me in with what you know."

Randolph opened his case and took out a thick file. He laid it on the coffee table and opened it, spreading papers and photographs out for Bolan. He picked up a number of printed sheets.

"This is Rick's final report. He couriered it to me the day before he died. His earlier suspicions are all confirmed, and they tally with information my other sources have fed me over the past few weeks."

Randolph pointed out a series of photographs for Bolan.

"You want to run me through these, Senator."

"Of course. This is Juan Amenta, an attorney who has advised and defended a number of individuals with less that honest leanings. He has also been active aiding members of radical militia members. Rick found he has done a great deal of work for the Brethren."

"We have a definite connection here?" Bolan asked.

"Rick found out about a discreet meeting between Amenta and a man who was later linked to Eric Stahl." Randolph indicated a number of the photographs. "Here we have Amenta with Stahl's man—who we now identified as Harry Brent—and a third individual, Deacon Ribak, all sharing a cozy coffee at a restaurant in New York."

Bolan had no trouble recognizing the third man as Deacon Ribak. "I know him, Senator. He's a member of the Brethren. We came close to exchanging shots a while back."

"Mmm." Randolph tapped the photo. "I'm not surprised at that revelation. Our Mr. Ribak is late of the military. Fort Benning. His background information told me he left the service under a cloud. But did you know he was a member of a special unit under the command of General William Carson?"

"Bull Carson?"

"The very same. We all know his stance on the way the military and the country is going. An open opponent of U.S. policy at home and abroad."

"Where does he fit, Senator?"

"Carson is a longtime crony of Eric Stahl. They've worked on military contracts over the years. They hold similar radical views and would love to change the leadership. With the shaky situation within the administration at the present, they must be rubbing their hands together." Randolph picked up one photograph. "Now I don't know how Rick got this one, but it says a great deal to me."

The image showed Stahl and Carson walking together in a secluded country setting. Walking alongside them was Deacon Ribak.

"That was taken near Carson's home in Maine. Rick's final report told me some pertinent facts. Amenta and Liam Seeger's lawyer and Brethren second in command, Zac Lorens, had a meeting some months ago. An African named only as Kesawayo also attended that meeting. My other researchers found out that this Kesawayo was the personal representative of a General Joseph M'Tusi. M'Tusi is a bloodthirsty warlord brutalizing a region of West Africa mainly for his own enrichment. It is reported he—"

"Trades illegal diamonds for cash and buys arms from a man named Regan. The Brethren had been using this to fund their operations."

Randolph smiled. "Matt, I get the feeling this is where our facts come together. Perhaps it's my turn to hear what you have to tell."

"That little pipeline has been shut down permanently. M'Tusi is dead and the connection with the Brethren severed. Lorens is dead, too. He decided to make an independent move and steal a consignment of the diamonds coming in from Africa. He worked it with the late Jerome Gantz, the guy who built Seeger's bombs."

Bolan detailed the lead up to the West African mission. Randolph listened with interest.

"The loss of so much finance will hit the Brethren hard, Matt."

"It might also push them to commit even more reckless acts than they already have. Put a man's back to the wall and it often makes him kick back even harder."

Randolph gave Bolan a concise rundown on the information remaining in his files. He didn't waste time with long words or complicated descriptions. Bolan listened and absorbed the fine detail Randolph had extracted from gossip on the hill, to information provided by his long-established personal grapevine, including the late Rick Berkly. What Bolan heard tied in with his own intel, a spiderweb of connections that provided clear proof of alliances. Clear indications that a definite plan was being drawn together with the intention of causing unrest and mistrust among the population and destabilizing the administration, leaving the way open for a possible takeover of power with Eric Stahl at the head.

"And military backup, Senator?"

"You can count on that, son. As I said, Stahl has always been in deep with the military. When you're in the arms manufacturing industry, the military is the one customer you keep close. Not just the goods. It's the big money that passes from hand to hand when contracts are up for grabs. Right now Stahl's bosom buddy is our General William Carson. Tough man. Good commander. A respected soldier. His people are loyal, so in any delicate situation he could call on a lot of military backup. He and Stahl have been conducting a great many one-to-one meetings lately. Away from prying eyes."

"Not enough to avoid you, Senator."

"My sources are some of the best. I've used them for years. They do their work efficiently and without question they are loyal to me. Too loyal in Rick's case, and it got him killed." Randolph cleared his throat. "Another thing. Stahl's involvement with the communications business. I found that out when I was running some background checks on him. Stahl has a number of small nationwide TV and radio stations tucked away in his portfolio. Quietly bought out over a few years by one of his umbrella companies. I'm sure you understand how useful they could be."

"Senator, you're quite the investigator."

"Son, I always knew reading those *Mike Hammer* paperbacks in my youth would pay off one day."

Randolph observed Bolan leaning back in his chair, his face thoughtful as he absorbed the information. He imagined the man assimilating everything he had heard and trying to make sense of it all.

"Could it be done, Senator?" Bolan asked as he refilled their coffee cups.

"Anything is possible, given the right conditions. Take the inescapable fact there *is* a strong discontent for the way the government handles certain policies. Now that isn't fantasy. It's why antigovernment groups exist. It's why militia groups were formed. They earnestly believe the government is against them and doesn't represent the citizens of the U.S.A. They hear and see what they want, and make their own interpretation. The Brethren has gone further. The group is actually already waging their war of attrition. I believe they intend to maintain their erosion principles against the administration. Strike here, there, making headway slowly by constantly refreshing their attacks on easy targets. What they do is make the government look helpless, unable to fight back, and in doing that they create the situation where the population loses faith in the administration. Matt, it could happen. The Brethren has no consistency when it comes to targets. I see that remaining their main thrust. No one will know what the next target is. Or where. The only constant will be the body count—and it's that the population will see."

Randolph's reasoning rang true in Bolan's mind. It was a surefire way of focusing the American public's attention.

"Senator, have you had any personal contact with Stahl over this?" Bolan asked.

"After last time, I'm keeping a low profile," Randolph said, "but after what's happened today it may not be low enough."

"We'll keep you here for a while and keep you informed of developments."

"Hiding me off stage? Matt, they do not frighten me."

"Senator, the last thing I would suggest is you might be intimidated by them. Believe me, I wouldn't have the nerve. But out in the open they would have the opportunity to kill you. I wouldn't like that to happen."

Randolph smiled. "I understand precisely what you're saying and I'm touched by your concern. I thank you for that, but this is more important than the safety of one elderly senator. There might still be matters I can help with. Stahl isn't the only one with contacts in the military and the administration. The people I can go to have been friends for many years. Anything they do for me is from loyalty and because they are, for the most part, honorable people. I'm quite aware that word has become something to snigger about in corners these days. But I still believe in it and I'm not ashamed to admit it."

"No reason you should be."

"Stahl buys his loyalty. That's fine up to a point. But bought friendship only goes so far. If people see the gravy train about to jump the tracks, loyalty doesn't mean a damn thing."

"And that means it's advisable to stay below the radar, Senator. We have secure computers and telephones installed in the house. Use them."

Randolph smiled. "I suppose you're right. Eric wouldn't lose any sleep if I was killed."

"Then let's not make it easy for him."

"As much as I want to rattle his cage, I understand what you're saying. I'll stay in the background, Matt, you have my word on that."

They both heard the sharp rap on the door. Bolan recognized the short pattern and put out a hand as Randolph's head turned abruptly. The Stony Man blacksuit who had been waiting in the background opened the door.

"Breathe easy. It's a friend."

Carl Lyons stepped inside. He made his way to where the pot of coffee sat and helped himself to a mug. "How far have we got?" he asked.

"I've been sent off to the bleachers," Randolph said, failing to hide his smile.

"With the information the senator has, I'll feel happier if he's here where we can keep an eye on him," Bolan said.

"Makes sense to me," Lyons agreed.

"Oh, I give in," Randolph said.

"Let me make a call, Senator," Bolan said. "Get you settled before we move on."

Randolph nodded.

Bolan stood and crossed to the telephone, having a quiet word with Lyons, who then joined Randolph. After Bolan had made his call and arrangements through Brognola he rejoined Lyons who was in conversation with Randolph.

"Isn't my disappearance from the scene going to be noticed?" the senator asked. "Don't you think it might cause concern?"

"It's something we'll have to chance," Bolan said. "And it might give Stahl something to worry over."

Randolph smiled. "Perhaps the word could be circulated I've come down with an illness. An age-related sickness."

Lyons smiled. "Senator, I only hope I look as well as you when I reach that age."

"Ha, young man, I stopped concerning myself about aging when I reached seventy. I mean, what's the point?"

"How long ago was seventy?"

"I'll let you figure that out, son."

Lyons took a swallow from his mug. "Senator, I was sorry to hear about your investigator."

"I had known Rick for a long time. He was a good man."

Lyons glanced away for a second. The death of any cop, even an ex-cop, always settled hard on him. He had been one himself and he felt the pain for them.

"It won't be forgotten," Bolan said quietly.

"Damn right," Lyons said.

"Doug used to be in the service," Bolan explained. "I guess it always stays with you."

"I understand." Randolph pushed to his feet and crossed to where Lyons stood, laying a hand on his shoulder. "Thank you for your concern."

Randolph turned to Bolan. "Like you told me. These people are not playing games. This is all real."

"Very real."

"Then you do what you have to and take them down, son. Whatever it takes. This country has more than enough to handle without a damn war at home."

"Senator, how do you see Stahl's play?"

"He will engage his political influence to raise every block he can to prevent the President from bringing in military support to defend against these acts and the threat to his presidency."

"Can he do that?"

"A man like Stahl. Oh, yes, he'll do his damnedest. Matt, have you heard of the *Posse Comitatus?*"

"Some act brought in way back that won't allow the acting President to use the U.S. military on American soil?"

"Broadly speaking, yes. Currently a great deal of its original power has been eroded because of prevailing necessity. There are ways around it, but to work that there has to be a congressional acceptance of the particular circumstances of the request."

"So is the President bound by this?"

Randolph nodded. "He has no choice in the matter. It's on the books. The *Posse Comitatus Act* specifically prevents him from using any branch of the Armed Forces before it has been brought before Congress."

"Even in an emergency?"

"Here we have the problem. What constitutes an emergency? The definition could be bandied about in discussion. Anyone against the President could argue the invalidity of the request. Get a group of dissenters and the legalities and finer points of law could tie up a decision for hours in the House. Maybe days."

"Which would be what the conspirators want? To prevent anyone coming to aid the President in the face of a hostile takeover? All he would have would be the Secret Service. And they're not an army."

"Exactly. Stahl has his cohorts box the President into a corner with no one able to come to his defense while they confuse Congress. That son of a bitch General Carson uses his influence to lock out any communication with the military. His supporters back those moves. And we have a stalemate. It leaves the way open for them to force the President to stand down because he has nothing he can fight back with. The Brethren continues its street attacks, proving again and again how ineffective the administration is. Americans being killed in their own cities is a sure way to alter public opinion. My theory would have Carson and his military then accuse the Brethren of traitorous acts against the American people. He could direct *his* strike forces to wipe out the militia and take credit for restoring control."

"A few passes by Air Force jets over the Brethren compounds dropping a few bombs and it would be over."

"That's how I see it, Matt—the Brethren being used to set the scene by their wanton acts against the country, falling into the trap Stahl and Carson set for them."

"And Stahl comes out as the hero of the hour?"

"He'll use his influence. His radio and TV stations to broadcast his offer to step in and take over. The President will be presented with an ultimatum. An act of resignation. His acceptance to stand down and for Stahl to be sworn in under emergency powers."

Bolan slammed his fist on the desk. His frustration had got the better of him for a moment. "This is crazy, Vernon. You're telling me the leader of the nation can't do a damn thing to prevent this? That he's going to be alone while his enemies gather *their* forces and do what they damn well want?"

"It's the difference between democracy and anarchy. And Stahl and the Brethren are using America's own statutes to aid them in their plan. Stahl may be a stone-cold bastard, but he's smart, too."

"With all respect, Vernon, I don't really give a damn how smart he is. In my book he's taken that one step too far. It's gone beyond forgiveness. There's only one thing I want and that is to get close enough to change his mind."

"Change his mind? My boy, I see you're using the word in an extremely loose form."

Randolph's assumption was correct.

Change translated into stop.

To shut down.

To end.

In Bolan's own parlance it had become the time to employ his much-used brand of closure.

It was time for the Executioner to act.

MORE THAN AN HOUR later Bolan tossed the final folder Randolph had handed him onto the coffee table. He glanced across the room in time to see Lyons coming out of the kitchen area with a fresh pot of coffee. Randolph had taken the opportunity to retire to one of the bedrooms and take a rest.

"Mind reader, too, Carl?"

Lyons nodded. "Anyone who can read for that long in one session deserves a fresh refill." He filled Bolan's mug, his own, then sat. "So what do we know about that we didn't before?"

"More than I wanted to. The senator has collected information that adds up to scary reading."

"What's our next move?"

"Right now we only have guesswork on Stahl's operation. Randolph's theory is sound, and I trust his judgment. But we don't have enough real proof of what he intends. We do have solid evidence on the Brethren's way of stirring the pot."

"Such as?"

"Big support in rural areas where communities have been pushed to the edge through government programs. Farmers losing out to conglomerates. Livestock producers in the same trap. Unemployment. Trading on bad times and political uncertainty. The Brethren makes sure that every time a community looks to be going under they get their people in and do everything they can to support them with cash and goods. At the same time they work on their vulnerability, get the people on the side of the Brethren. They step in at the worst time of these people's lives and give them hope, promises that the Brethren will make things right."

"So we concentrate on them?"

"Regardless of how Stahl sees the Brethren, they're still a threat in their own right. Carl, we've hit them hard already."

"So we keep doing that?"

"Yes. Weaken them. Cut them down piece by piece. Go for every target we can. Make them realize what they're doing is going to cost them. We've cut off their cash source now that M'Tusi isn't going to be supplying more diamonds. We need to keep hitting anything with the Brethren's mark on it."

"That could make Stahl nervous. Push him to make his move before he's ready."

Bolan smiled. "Now why didn't I think of that part of the scheme?"

CHAPTER NINETEEN

Stony Man Farm, Virginia

Bolan found Lyons in the War Room, alone, paperwork spread out in front of him, a mug of coffee in his hand. He sat across from Lyons and waited until the man was ready to talk.

"The more I read this stuff, Mack, the more angry I get. And before you say anything, I understand I should be able to step back and see it as a professional. Hard not to, man. I keep looking at those photographs of the kids who died in those explosions. Bad enough they had to die, but when the bastards who did it are Americans themselves…"

He trailed off, raising his head to make eye contact with Bolan, and saw his own emotions mirrored in his friend's eyes. Lyons ran a hand through his hair, frustration, a feeling of having let the dead down, a rage burning inside that was not going to die down until complete closure of the mission had been achieved.

"The Brethren will claim what they did was for the

betterment of the country, that the failure of the administration, the President, whatever excuse they tag on, pushed them to these extremes. They have grievances with the way America is governed? I have no problem with that, but the way they're conducting their argument is beyond any civilized excuse. We could beat our heads against the wall and say why weren't they listened to, or disbanded, before it came to this? The Constitution allows them the right to disagree. To put their point of view. To call the government to account. Same thing there. It is their right. Carl, our wake-up call only came *after* they did what they did. But they've gone beyond any constitutional right. Declaring war on America, just to showcase their agenda has put them in our firing line. We do what we have to in order to set the record straight." Bolan picked up a couple of the photographs. The images, stark and all too real, had the same effect as they had on Lyons. "Don't forget these, Carl. Let them remind you, but don't let them take over. Just let them know we won't forget them."

Lyons leaned back. "Okay, sensei, where do we go from here?"

"Aaron has a lock on Clair Valens's cell phone. We've pretty well accepted now that she's gone missing and it has a connection to Stahl and the Brethren. I'd like you to follow up on that. Valens is smart. She's got guts. She's also a little headstrong."

"And where are you going to be?"

"Colorado. They say mountain air is good for your health."

Lyons knew the Brethren's main compound was somewhere in the rugged mountainous region of the state. If Bolan was heading in that direction, he was about to disprove the theory about the air being healthy—for anyone who claimed to belong to the Brethren.

The Executioner's campaign was homing in on their main base.

THE EXECUTIONER wore his familiar blacksuit and tough-soled combat boots that would withstand the rugged terrain. His Beretta 93-R and the Desert Eagle rested in their usual places, and a fighting knife was sheathed on his belt. His combat harness held additional magazines for both handguns, and for his main offensive piece of ordnance—an M-16 fitted with an underslung M-203 grenade launcher. He had a number of M-406 HE rounds for that. Bolan didn't consider any other selection of grenades for the weapon. This was going to be a seek-and-destroy penetration. His mission brief was clear in his mind: locate the compound and raze it to the ground, cripple Seeger's main base and take down any of the militia who stood in his way. The Brethren had laid down the ground rules for the confrontation already. Bolan was about to return the favor.

In his backpack Bolan had an ample supply of Kissinger's C-4 packages, which he would use to bring down as much Brethren hardware as possible. There were a number of fragmentation grenades in there, as well. In a pocket of his blacksuit he had a power cell unit to set off the detonators he would fix to the C-4 once he had planted the explosives.

Following the dual strikes against the Brethren bases in New Mexico and Chicago, Bolan assumed the Colorado compound would be on high alert. He qualified that with the knowledge he was going up against a militia group, not militarily trained professional soldiers. He accepted the presence of Deacon Ribak and figured the man would have done some work with Seeger's mainly civilian members. He doubted the entire force would have combat experience and would lack the discipline of such men. Even so, Bolan did not dismiss the Brethren gunners. It was possible to get shot by an enthusiastic amateur as well as by a veteran, and Bolan had never underestimated any enemy force. It was a reckless attitude and the kind of thinking that could result in unexpected injury, or at worst death. There was also the likelihood that Seeger had drawn at least some ex-military into his ranks.

Lyons had left well before Bolan. He had a different type of mission, one that would require a different approach, so he'd moved out while Bolan was still preparing and checking out his equipment.

Kurtzman had supplied coordinates that he downloaded into the compact GPS unit Bolan would take along. From his computer, aided by satellite scanning, Kurtzman had an extremely detailed course plotted for Bolan.

The Executioner was forced to rely on Air Force cooperation for the second time. He was going to make another parachute drop into the area and make his final advance on foot. He had been hoping that Jack Grimaldi and the SOG's unique combat chopper, *Dragon Slayer,* might have been available. The helicopter, with its stealth approach facility and awesome firepower, would have made a great difference, but Grimaldi and his bird were away on an overseas mission.

With his equipment in place and his GPS formatted, Bolan received word that his Stony Man chopper was ready to ferry him to the U.S. air base where his flight

was ready to go. He made his way through the farmhouse and out into the cool night air. This current mission seemed to have become a relay of coming and
going, with little breathing space in between. On other
forays Bolan often commenced and carried out missions without ever setting foot on the Farm. This time
around, the complexities of the jigsaw had forced Bolan
and Lyons to use the SOG's facilities to the max. The
ability of Kurtzman and his team to extract solid information from different sources could not be denied, nor
the patient skills of Barbara Price. Hal Brognola, running interference and arranging backup and security
for innocents caught up in the conflict, all of them had
a hand in strategic and logistical support.

He strode to the helicopter pad and climbed on
board. As the hatch closed behind him, Bolan dropped
onto one of the seats, his pack and rifle at his feet. He
felt the aircraft surge with power, swinging briefly as it
left the ground. The pilot corrected easily, turning the
aircraft and setting his course for the air base. Bolan
leaned back in his seat, closing his eyes to snatch a little rest. He had the combat veteran's ability to catnap
at any spare moment, using the time he had. The drone
of the chopper faded as he relaxed.

Colorado

IT WAS JUST STARTING to get light.

Warmth started to chase away the chill as Bolan
gathered his black chute and bundled it together. He
worked it into a gap between two rocks, pushing the
final folds in with his foot. Crouching, he took out his
GPS unit and checked his position. His goal lay to the

west, up the unforgiving rocky slopes of the mountain. He returned the GPS to his blacksuit pocket, zipping the flap. He adjusted the straps of his backpack, freed the M-16 from his shoulder and moved out.

At the starting point of his trek to the compound the way was reasonably easy. It would become harder as he started to climb. He could see why Liam Seeger had established his base in this part of the country. The mountainous terrain was off the regular track. There were few, if any, established trails. The barren, craggy slopes encouraged little to grow hereabouts save for hardy scrub and stunted trees. It was remote and removed from any communities. People only came out here for a definite reason. In the far distance the mountains rose to meet the sky in serried ranks. Streams and rivers tumbled over ancient stones. This was vast country, primitive and with its own particular grandeur. Here, too, within this unspoiled place, the Brethren had begun to spread its poison, sending out its soldiers to spread their evil in the towns and cities of America.

But the Executioner was here now, and given the opportunity, he would cut away that poison and administer his own unique cure for what ailed the Brethren.

BOLAN LAY IN DEEP SHADOW on a ridge overlooking the Brethren's mountain base. It lay in a shallow basin, protected by jagged outcroppings. There were no fences or barriers around the hard-packed earth where four long timber barracks stood apart from an L-shaped administration building. An open-sided structure with a basic kitchen at one end and long trestle tables and benches said mess hall. Smoke was starting to rise from the cast-iron cook stoves set at the kitchen end and he could see three men working there.

On its own, standing well clear of all other structures, was a hut with an armed guard posted in front. Bolan tagged that as most likely where ordnance was kept. The armory.

To his left, clear of the buildings, were a number of heavy-wheeled 4x4s, tough, rugged vehicles for the mountainous terrain. A faint dirt trail led away from the base, angling to the southwest, which by Bolan's calculations would work its way down the slopes to the comparative flatland below. Some distance away was a camouflage net draped over what Bolan figured would be a helicopter.

He checked his watch, figuring he had at least an hour before the main body of Brethren hardmen were roused. That would allow him time to work his way into the compound and lay his charges. He had already worked out his approach, checked the couple of guards who had pulled the last detail. They were almost motionless now, listless as they lounged at their posts, wishing away the final stretch of duty. There was a faint, predatory smile on Bolan's lips as he eased from cover and began to make his silent approach.

THE ROCKS AND DUSTY BRUSH provided ample cover for Bolan as he covered the final stretch, bringing himself within the perimeter of the compound. Behind him the first of the two guards lay motionless in a spreading patch of his spilled blood. He had known nothing of Bolan's closeness until a hand closed over his mouth and the chill caress of the combat knife had cut into his throat. Bolan had dragged the corpse deep into a tan-

gled mass of thorny brush, pushing the man's dropped
weapon out of sight. Now he was within yards of the
second guard, watching and waiting for his moment.
This man was a little more alert, but only to the finger
skills required to roll himself a cigarette. He had leaned
his assault rifle against a rock where he himself
lounged, intent on forming the tobacco and paper into
a solid tube so he could have a final smoke before being
relieved. The smoke failed to reach his lips. It fell from
his fingers as Mack Bolan's knife made its second kill
of the day, the razor edge of honed steel drawn from left
to right, cutting so deeply the breadth of the blade sank
into the wound before emerging close to the right ear.
Blood rushed from the cut. Rich and hot, it coursed
freely down the shuddering form, soaking jacket and
pants. Bolan hauled the deadweight back out of sight,
repeating the action with the guard's rifle.

He sheathed the combat knife and brought his M-16
into play, a 30-round magazine in place, cocked and
ready. Bolan replayed his visual image of the compound's layout. He would need to work his way around
the ends of the barracks to reach the armory. All the
structures were raised from the ground on solid concrete
blocks at each corner and at intervals along the length
of each building. That design provided Bolan with a
two-foot crawl space and he utilized that as he worked
his way toward the armory. From the last of the barracks
he had a thirty-foot gap to cover. Open ground.

He waited, watching the armory guard pace out his
patrol. It took him around the building, then reversing
and walking back the other way. Bolan studied the guy's
beat. Slow and steady, his rifle held loosely, shoulders
down. The difference between a Brethren soldier and a

military trained guard. Easing out, using the block support for cover, Bolan watched the guard pace out his
slow walk until he rounded the corner of the building
and around the end. Bolan could still see his legs moving below the raised base of the hut.

He moved then, pushing to his feet and sprinting the
thirty feet until he was able to drop to his chest and slide
beneath the raised floor. Bolan felt sweat forming on his
face. The day was starting to warm up. He needed to
speed up his penetration and get out as soon as possible.
Turning, the Executioner crawled to the far corner of the
armory, away from the barracks and mess hall. He
waited for the steady pace of the guard to bring him to
this area, lay down his M-16 and reached out to grab
the guy around his ankles. He yanked hard, pitching the
guard facedown on the hard ground. The guy grunted
as his face was slammed into the dirt. Bolan dragged
him into the floor space and slipped the steel blade of
the combat knife into his body, seeking his heart.

Crawling out from under the armory, the Executioner headed for the front of the building and the heavy
wood doors blocking his way in. The doors were held
shut by iron draw bolts. Bolan didn't hesitate. He went
up the concrete steps and slid the upper and lower bolts,
hauled the doors open and entered the building. He had
not been wrong. The building contained a substantial
amount of ordnance that covered the range from assault
rifles and handguns, rocket launchers, fragmentation
grenades, assorted canisters of ammunition, cartons
containing plastic explosives. There was enough weap-
onry to equip a few hundred men.

Bolan didn't let himself become dazzled by the ordnance. He was not here to admire it; he was here to de-

stroy it. He slipped the pack from his back and placed
it on a wooden crate. Opening it, he removed the C-4
prepared for him at Stony Man and placed half a dozen
blocks throughout the armory. He attached the detonators that would be activated by the cell-powered pack
he carried. It would detonate them simultaneously via
a direct signal to the receivers built into the detonators.
As he placed each detonator, he switched on each power
cell, seeing a red indicator light blink into life. With his
charges set Bolan picked up his pack, slipped back out
of the hut and bolted the doors again. He slipped beneath the armory and placed a couple more explosive
packs as added insurance.

Sweat soaked Bolan's blacksuit as he placed the final
charge and worked his way from beneath the arsenal. He
stopped at the rear, hidden in the shadow cast by one of
the concrete support blocks. This would be the risky part
of his infiltration—removing himself from the compound
and trying to avoid being seen by any Brethren personnel.

He felt a trickle of sweat slide down his forehead and
find its way into his left eye, stinging briefly. In the narrow confines of the space the heat was already being
trapped, cloying, the air heavy and dusty. Across the
compound coils of pale dust drifted between the buildings, pushed by the breeze coming down off the slopes
that surrounded the compound. Bolan turned onto his
stomach, searching in the direction of the vehicles he
had observed during his entry into the compound. None
of them had moved.

That collection of 4x4 all-terrain vehicles was his
way out. He needed to commandeer one to get himself
away from the Brethren and down the mountain trail to
the flatlands.

Once he had decided on his action Bolan put it into operation. There was no point in hanging back. He checked his weapons, made sure the power pack for the planted charges was still operational. His final check was his M-16. He took an HE grenade and snugged it into the M-203 underslung launcher. He was going to need a diversion for his initial breakout. An exploding charge from the launcher, fired across the compound, would be certain to attract some attention while he went in the opposite direction.

He checked that his immediate space was clear, easing out from under the armory and standing upright. Angling the M-16 toward the far side of the compound, he fired off the HE canister. It sailed in a clear arc, reaching its zenith, then dropped. The moment it struck the hard-packed earth and exploded, Bolan turned and cut off in the direction of the motor pool. Even as he was running he loaded a second grenade and fired in another direction. He heard the blast and caught sight of smoke and dust rising beyond one of the buildings off to his right. He hit the timber side of the building immediately in front of the vehicle park, checking his surroundings. Behind him he could hear raised voices as the Brethren hardmen started to leave their barracks. He picked up the pounding of boots on the hard ground. A third grenade went into the launcher. This time he fired it over to his left. The canister cleared the low roof of one of the huts, dropped on the far side and exploded. Bolan heard glass shatter and picked up the crash of falling timber as the blast tore into the side of the hut.

He turned to make his final dash for the motor pool and almost ran head-on into one of the Brethren's gunners. The guy was half-dressed in camou fatigues, carrying his assault rifle. He hauled himself to a dead stop, recognized Bolan as not being part of the unit and made to raise his weapon. He got it to hip height before Bolan arced his M-16 around and clouted him across the side of his head with its stock. The blow was hard, snapping the guy's head to one side, and dazed him long enough for Bolan to strike again, the stock of the M-16 slamming in under the guy's chin with unrelenting fierceness. The shock of the impact broke the jaw, shattered teeth, and raised the guy on his toes before he dropped, blood spewing from his mouth. Bolan had moved long before the stricken soldier hit the dirt.

The chatter of autofire filled the air. Wildly fired slugs dug into the dirt behind Bolan. Without breaking his stride the Executioner fed a grenade into the launcher, turned and tracked in on the group of gunners on his back, between two of the huts. He triggered the grenade and it dropped in their midst. The blast threw them off their feet, bodies shredded and bleeding, the sound of the explosion echoing across the compound. Bolan caught a glimpse of more hardmen emerging from behind the closest building, pausing as they viewed the effects of Bolan's work. He took the pause to slip another grenade in the launcher, triggering it at the corner of the building. The blast ripped open the flimsy hut, filling the air with shredded wood that became keen-edged splinters ripping into flesh. As the soldiers reeled from the burst, clawing at the spearing effects of the wood, Bolan triggered 3-round bursts into them, dropping two and sending the others retreating behind the smoke billowing from the blast-scorched hut.

Bolan sprinted to the motor pool. He mentally

crossed fingers as he approached the first vehicle, hoping that the Brethren had become so comfortable and secure in their mountain stronghold they felt no need to lock their vehicles. If he found otherwise, it would delay him only for seconds to break a window. That task turned out to be unnecessary. So did his earlier expectation to need to hot-wire the vehicle. The key dangled from the ignition. In the regular military all vehicles were fitted with keyless starters. In a frantic combat situation it would have proved a disaster to have to hunt around for vehicle keys. So, whoever had organized the Brethren's military regime, would have pointed this out. Their vehicles were on standby, and Bolan thanked whoever had instilled that into the Brethren.

He opened the door, tossing his backpack ahead of him and laying his M-16 close by, and slid behind the wheel. The big engine burst into life at the first try. Bolan dropped into gear and turned the 4x4 in the direction of the west exit from the compound. Glancing over his shoulder, he saw smoke rising in the aftermath of his grenade attacks. He also saw more armed men moving in his direction, though moving with caution after viewing what he had done to the first wave. There was some desultory fire, but the Brethren gunners were shooting wild. Bolan pushed hard on the gas pedal, feeling the 4x4 surge forward. As he reached the edge of the compound, he slowed. Powering down the window, he extended his right hand, holding the detonator. The power light was steady. Bolan pushed the button.

Though the armory was hidden from his sight by the other buildings Bolan saw the rising fire of the explosion as the charges detonated, blowing the building apart and setting off additional blasts as stored ammunition and ordnance went with it. A storm of debris, some burning, rained down across the compound. The sound of the explosion reverberated around the slopes circling the base. The huge ball of flame and smoke was rising fast, the shock waves extending outward as well as skyward. The concussion reached as far as Bolan. He felt the 4x4 rock and, certain he had achieved his purpose, he stamped on the pedal and took the vehicle away from the chaos that had engulfed the Brethren's mountain compound.

As he cleared the perimeter he saw the dusty trail that led downslope, away from the base and, hopefully, away from the Brethren.

It was a hope, but it became a forlorn one. Bolan had driven less than a half mile when he caught sight of movement in the rearview mirror. He counted three identical 4x4s following him.

CHAPTER TWENTY

Locking the seat belt, Bolan jammed his foot down hard and the big 4x4 lunged forward, the tires gripping the hard-packed surface of the road. He could feel the power of the engine surging as the vehicle hurtled into the dusty morning. A glance in the rearview mirror showed his pursuers still close behind. The people driving the three chase vehicles were good. They held the 4x4s behind Bolan with ease.

Just before he took his eyes off the lead vehicle, Bolan saw a head and shoulders lean out the passenger side of the car, a stubby SMG gripped in one hand. The shooter opened fire but missed his target, the bullets flying wide. The fact they were shooting at him made Bolan realize this was going to be a hard ride. He checked the way ahead. The dusty trail stretched out in front of him, disappearing on the horizon, with little between the two points showing much in the way of cover. He was committed, with no apparent avenue of escape, so all he could do was make the best of the situation.

The soldier's attention was concentrated as the 4x4

hit a shallow dip in the trail, sinking briefly, then clearing the far side and almost leaving the ground. The vehicle swayed on its shocks, bouncing Bolan in his seat, and he gripped the wheel tightly to keep the vehicle on a straight course. Behind him the lead 4x4 took a severe shock itself as it encountered the depression and, for a fleeting moment, the driver almost lost control, the vehicle lurching, then front-dipping as the brakes were hit. The second chase 4x4 had to swerve and slow itself to avoid a collision. The momentary hesitation allowed Bolan to surge ahead and, seeing that space, he pushed down on the gas pedal again, feeling the 4x4 gather itself and then leap forward.

He heard the tinny sound as bullets struck the 4x4's bodywork. The shooter was ranging in. Taking his time to make his shots count. Given enough time and allowed to choose his moment, the shooter might lay down an even closer volley. Bolan peered through the dusty windshield, hoping he might spot somewhere he could at least make a stand. He didn't hold out much hope of seeing anything. The landscape offered little in the way of cover and whichever way he took he would be in sight of his pursuers.

A couple of minutes later he saw that the relatively flat terrain ahead was starting to fall away on his left side. The way ahead started to rise, with the shallow slope becoming steeper. Bolan kept his eyes on the changing landscape as he pushed the speed of his vehicle ever higher, feeling the ground beneath the tires changing from loose dust to uneven, broken slabs of rock. Within a quarter mile the slope falling away from the trail had become a steeply angled drop-off.

The sporadic bursts of gunfire from the lead vehicle

had ceased. Bolan didn't question why. He just concentrated on staying free and clear of his pursuers. As he drove, a sliver of a thought made itself known and Bolan allowed it to grow, forming into a notion that maybe he could do something to persuade his pursuers to back off. It was a wildly conceived idea, and he had no way of knowing if it would even work, but the way it revealed itself it would do him no harm. Driving with his left hand, he reached across and dragged the backpack close to his side, pulling the flap open and reaching inside. His fingers closed over one of the fragmentation grenades. He braced his hands on the rim of the wheel, held the grenade in his left hand and pulled the pin. Powering down the door window, he stretched out his left arm, let the lever go and tossed grenade toward the rear of his vehicle.

Bolan put on a burst of speed, distancing himself from the lead pursuit vehicle. Seconds later the grenade detonated, a cloud of dust and stones filling the void between the two SUVs. Debris rattled the rear of his 4x4. He glanced in his rearview mirror as the dust cleared and saw the following vehicle swerve violently. Whatever result he might have imagined didn't relate to actuality as the vehicle fishtailed, then lurched off the edge of the trail and vanished from sight. As Bolan pulled farther away, he heard a dull explosion and caught the swelling burst of flame and smoke as the 4x4 slammed to the bottom of the drop.

The effect of the removal of one of their vehicles brought a burst of speed from the two surviving SUVs. Bolan saw them closing fast, their speed rising to match his own, and there was a sudden eruption of autofire from the windows of the two vehicles. He felt the jarring impact as bullets struck his own vehicle. Bolan had his foot to the floor and he couldn't coax more speed from the engine.

And then the vehicle rocked as bullets struck the left rear tire. He felt the rim of the wheel strike the rocky ground, heard the altered tone from his engine as the vehicle slewed and pulled him off track. Bolan knew from experience that he wasn't going to get far with a wheel running on its rim. He could feel the steering drag against his grip. The moment his speed dropped far enough, the pair of pursuing vehicles would be on him.

He searched the way ahead. Directly ahead the terrain was still relatively flat with no cover to be seen. To his left the drop-off presented him with a steep incline layered with loose shale and rocks before it hit level ground again. Bolan made his choice the moment he saw the only possible escape route. He swung the wheel and took the vehicle over the lip of the slope, letting gravity work for him while he hung on.

The 4x4 careered down the long slope, bouncing and lurching from side to side, only its generous wheelbase keeping it from rolling over. Bolan was thrown back and forth, his body pounded by the solid impact each time the vehicle struck a hard patch. The careering, downward run seemed to go on forever. Bolan felt the impact underneath the vehicle as it struck a ridge and lifted, felt the sideways crunch as it sideswiped a boulder the size of a small car before it hit the slope again. Windows shattered and glass filled the interior. The roaring engine gave out, oily smoke seeping from under the hood. The squeal of tortured metal filled his ears. Bolan saw the windshield splinter and shatter and threw his arms up to protect his face. Hot air blew inside the cab. The 4x4 made a final lurch, clearing the slope for long seconds before it crashed back with a stunning thump. Bolan's head struck something and all went black.

HE HEARD THEM COMING out of the rocks above him, calling to one another, some even laughing as they closed in for the kill. They were filled with bloodlust, driven by hatred and an anger at the damage he had inflicted on them. That need to destroy him drove them down the rocky slope, circling to hold him in their midst, sure of their impending success, confident they had him trapped in the tumbled wreckage of his 4x4 where it lay at the base of the dusty trail.

In the wake of the crash Bolan hung loosely from his seat belt, sucking air into his battered lungs, feeling the ache around his ribs where the strap had been forced into his body. He raised his head, staring out through the shattered windshield at the fog of dust still swirling around the stalled vehicle. He was disorientated, struggling to make cohesive sense out of his situation. It took long seconds, rationality returning with agonizing slowness, and as he struggled to bring himself back he became aware of the creaking metal around him, the cooling ping of the engine beneath the crumpled hood. There was a dampness on his face, and when he touched it, his fingers came away sticky. A pulse of pain registered after that and he knew he had struck his head against something, opening a gash that was streaming blood.

Par for the course, he admitted. Then he moved, checking out his arms and legs, and apart from various aches and pains nothing seemed to be badly damaged.

Even while he was making this physical examination his mind was moving back on track, telling him he needed to think ahead. He was aware of his situation now. Armed men were in pursuit, and he knew they would be coming for him.

He needed to get out of the vehicle, prepare to face his enemy. They already knew his combat skills, so they would try to overwhelm him, take him down before he had a chance to gain the advantage. Bolan freed himself from the harness, reaching to pick up his M-16 from where it had fallen into the foot well. He booted open the stiff door, swinging out of the vehicle and snatching up the backpack that held his spare ordnance.

THE VOICES BECAME LOUDER, accompanied by the rattle of loosened stones as the pack closed in. Bolan moved to the rear of the vehicle, leaning against its body as he checked out the enemy. He made a quick count—eight. No, nine. Three of them were eager. Too eager. They moved well ahead of the rest, urging one another on as they moved rapidly in the direction of the 4x4, and leaving themselves fully exposed as they came. They were all armed with SMGs, but in Bolan's eyes they might have been weaponless. They were moving too fast to offer anything like accurate fire and on the wide span of the slope there was no cover for them.

Bolan raised the M-16 and tracked in on the closest. His finger stroked the trigger, and he put a 3-round burst into the guy. The target lost traction, his feet going from under him, and he pitched facedown on the rocky slope. His limp body tumbled for yards before coming to a graceless stop, arms and legs splayed out in an awkward sprawl. His face and head were bloody from the fall, his chest punctured from Bolan's volley. While the first one was falling the Executioner altered his aim, hitting the second guy with a burst to the chest, knocking him flat on his back. Gunner number three dragged himself to a clumsy stop, fumbling with his weapon as he tried to return fire. He managed a short burst that shattered one of the 4x4's remaining unbroken windows before Bolan stopped him with a hard burst that blew into his lungs and out through his back.

The rest of the pack stopped abruptly, dropping into smaller crouches, and began to fire on the 4x4. It was all they could do. Bolan stayed behind its cover, checking distance and angle before he began to return fire, moving the M-16's fire selector to single-shot.

Mack Bolan's skill as a sniper of extreme ability came to the fore as he fixed his first target and took the guy down with a single shot to the head. While the action was still registering in the minds of the rest of the militiamen, the M-16 had moved on, the sights acquiring the next target. It took a few seconds longer but the result was the same.

Scratch five, Bolan mentally calculated.

On the slope the four remaining Brethren thugs were realizing their fragile positions. Frantic visual searches only confirmed what they suspected.

They had nowhere to go.

Whichever way they moved, they were vulnerable.

One of the pack moved, leaning across the top of the rock slab concealing him. He began to fire on Bolan's position, laying down a protracted volley of shots that struck the grounded 4x4. It was meant as covering fire, intended to keep Bolan from taking any offensive action. After the first shots there was movement from the other Brethren hardmen as they broke their own cover and started back up the long slope.

Bolan had already moved, easing along the 4x4 and crouching at the far end, bringing his M-16 back into play. He dropped the first of the retreating men with a single shot, then picked his second target. It took two shots before he caught the guy, pitching him facedown on the rocky surface of the slope with a 5.56 mm slug embedded in the back of his skull.

The distraction shooter lost time readjusting to Bolan's move. The two men were down before he picked up his target again, and in the short span Bolan had moved. He cleared the front of the vehicle and sprinted the ten feet to take up a fresh vantage point behind a slab of flaking rock. His new position brought him farther around to the shooter's left, and he was able to see the guy. The man's weapon was probing the air, searching for Bolan. The guy fired fast, laying down hard shots that peppered the soft stone, filling the air with splinters and fine dust. Bolan edged around the rock, coming to the far side. Now he was able to view the shooter without restriction. He raised the M-16 and sighted in. The shooter's stance altered as he realized what was happening and he pushed upright from his squatting position in readiness to take better cover.

He was too slow and too late.

The M-16 crackled as Bolan jacked out two close shots. They took the shooter in the chest, spinning him off his feet to hit the hard ground on his back, his weapon flying from nerveless fingers.

And that left one.

He broke cover, scrambling and slipping as he made an attempt to distance himself from the deadly rifle in the hands of the unrelenting individual who had brought death and destruction to the isolated Brethren compound. Panic fueled his steps; terror choked out of his lungs. Sweat clogged his pores as he put everything he had in his attempted escape.

Bolan's M-16 took it all from him. Two shots, seconds apart, and the panic ceased. Terror faded to darkness, and the Brethren believer was dead before the sweat dried on his flesh.

In the silence Mack Bolan exchanged the partly used magazine for a fresh one. He dropped the magazine into the pack at his feet and slung it from his shoulder. He checked out the area, satisfying himself he was alone, and started to climb back up the long slope to where the two Brethren vehicles sat waiting.

Bolan only needed one vehicle, so he dropped an HE round into the abandoned vehicle from a safe distance and watched it blow, then burn fiercely, sending thick black smoke into the sky. He climbed into the surviving 4x4 and moved off, continuing his withdrawal from the battleground. He wondered if they would be able to spot the smoke from the compound. Or would they still be too busy trying to put out their own fires? He didn't dwell on the problem for too long. He was content that he had dealt the Brethren a hard blow. Anything that hurt them and slowed their overall plans was a plus as far as he was concerned.

As he eased the vehicle down the final grade, emerging onto lower, less harsh terrain, Bolan began to experience an uncomfortable feeling. It began as a needling sensation that quickly grew until it became a full-blown concern.

Had the Brethren given up too easily? His strike at

the compound had been hard, leaving the place a burning wreck. Something spoke quietly in his mind, telling him to stay alert because maybe, perhaps, it wasn't over yet. The Brethren had demonstrated its callous disregard for others by the bombings. Any organization capable of carrying out such attacks would not quit if the going got rough. Bolan imagined them as holding a grudge strongly, and if they were seeking nationwide domination after demoralizing the public and even the government, they would not bow out because of the actions of a single opponent.

So, the compound had been hit hard. Bolan had taken down the crew that had pursued him.

Why was he expecting more?

One answer could have been that Bolan always expected more. He never trusted dumb luck, because he didn't ascribe to the thought. His reasoning came from past experience in similar situations. His combat sense.

Bolan glanced around. Nothing.

He still didn't feel secure.

Bolan picked up the sound. It was familiar, something he had heard so many times before—the rising volume of a helicopter's rotors beating the air as it came directly for his position. He slowed the SUV, leaning out the window to pinpoint the aircraft as it powered in fast, closing on him.

It was the helicopter he had spotted under its camouflage netting back at the compound. The one he should have dropped one of his grenades on.

They had chosen their spot well. The landscape here was open, the long slopes undulating with only a few scattered boulders to break the emptiness. There seemed little chance for Bolan to make cover within the next few minutes, and he knew for sure the occupants of the chopper were not about to allow him those minutes.

Accepting the conditions, Bolan mentally moved on, seeking further options.

The descending chopper dropped to within ten feet of the ground, the downdraft from the rotors causing strong air movement that rocked the SUV and dragged up dead grass and detritus from the ground. It swirled around Bolan's vehicle, enveloping it in a misty cloud. He spun the wheel, sending the SUV on a new heading. It was only going to be a short-lived maneuver. The chopper turned in unison, the capable hands of the pilot tailing Bolan closely.

The soldier realized it was going to be more than difficult to lose the helicopter. Out here in the open the chopper pilot would have no problem keeping Bolan close as he tried to reach sanctuary. He realized his only clear option lay in taking the battle to the aircraft itself.

The question was, how?

Bolan kept driving as he swung the wheel back and forth. He did it even though he accepted it was pointless, wanting the chopper pilot to see it as a panic move.

The stark rattle of autofire broke through and Bolan saw gouts of earth erupt as a line of .50-caliber shells hammered into the ground, close but not damaging. Not yet. Once the gunner got his line of fire under control those bursts would be hammering at the SUV itself.

Bolan glanced at the M-16. It had a full magazine in place and he carried a couple more in pouches. And the M-203 launcher held the last of his HE rounds. A maneuver was forming in his mind. It was one of those thoughts that presented itself in moments of crisis. Half formed, totally illogical, but he was running out of anything else to work on, and if he didn't do something in short order those .50-caliber shells would remove any need for resistance.

A second burst from the gunner convinced Bolan it was time to take action. With his decision made he acted.

The soldier slammed on the brakes, bringing the SUV to a shaky stop. His action caused the chopper to overshoot, the pilot swinging his craft around to compensate. In that short time, with the rotor wash still dragging up dusty debris, Bolan picked up the M-16, jerked the handle of his door and rolled out of the vehicle, coming to his feet in a crouch and staying alongside the SUV as it rolled on a few yards before the stalling engine forced it to stop. Bolan was still crouching alongside the vehicle, able to watch as the chopper banked swiftly, turning to position itself at the side of the SUV again. Bolan could see the gunner hanging out of the open side door, his big .50-caliber machine gun jutting clear as he swung it around on its lintel. Knowing he had to act quickly, before the pilot became suspicious and pulled the chopper back, Bolan stood, raised the M-16, and braced himself across the hood. His muzzle drew down on the hatch opening and the dark outline of the door gunner. The M-16 began to jack out 5.56 mm slugs that found their target, aided by Bolan's sound accuracy. The gunner jerked back under the impact, his body twisting as the shots hammered his chest. Secured on a safety harness, he slumped forward, hanging out of the hatch, his trigger finger squeezing back. The .50-caliber machine gun pumped out a stream of shells that flew harmlessly skyward. Bolan heard the chopper's power increase as the pilot worked at getting out of harm's way as fast as he could, but despite his quick response there was no evading the consequences of making a direct attack on Mack Bolan.

The pilot spotted movement at the front of the SUV and saw the tall, black-clad vision of death moments before the M-16 was turned on his aircraft. The pilot was close enough to recognize the configuration of the M-16/M-203 and something told him that was not what he wanted to be looking at. He applied everything he had to the controls, felt the chopper start to sideslip, but he knew it was too late.

Bolan locked on, touched the launcher's trigger and felt the recoil as the grenade was fired. It curved in and cleared the edge of the open hatch, impacted against the compartment superstructure and exploded, blowing its charge within the confines of the fuselage. The fiery ball of the detonation and the power of the explosion tore open the aluminum carcass, sending jagged chunks of metal throughout the stricken aircraft. The pressure waves blew out the Plexiglas front canopy, and if he hadn't been strapped in, the pilot would have been thrown through. Even so, the blast embedded shrapnel in his back and shoulders as he leaned away from his seat. At the rear more heat and metal pieces found their way to the fuel tank, ripping it open and causing a secondary burn that sheered off the tail array and sent the burning wreckage in a short fall to the ground where it disintegrated in a final boil of fire and smoke.

Bolan rested his aching body against the hood of the SUV. The results of recent actions were catching up.

Battered, bruised and a little bloody, he needed time out to recharge his batteries. The downside was combat situations made no allowances for such trivia. Combatants stayed in the battle as long as the situation required. And Bolan was starting to believe that the Brethren, now that he had engaged them, were unlikely to fall back. He had no regrets. His strikes against the group may have disturbed the nest and angered the swarm. If the need arose Bolan would continue no matter what they threw at him. It was the nature of the beast, and it had formed its habits over a long time.

He picked up the M-16 from where he had placed it on the hood of the SUV and turned to climb back inside, taking a last look at the burning hulk of the helicopter. The SUV fired up and Bolan drove away, picking up his trail again, and knowing where the next confrontation would be.

"MAKE IT FAST, make it clean," Ribak said.

"Fast and clean? That's how we were hit," Ron Kemp said. "Bad. Someone infiltrated the compound and set charges under the armory. Blew it all to hell, messed with our guys, then stole one of our 4x4s on his way out."

Ribak sank back in his chair, the words echoing inside his skull. "The ordnance?"

"Scattered all over the damn place. Not a piece left in working order. Deke, whoever he was, the son of a bitch knew how to place his explosives."

That assumption had already made itself known to Ribak. "A man that good at infiltration and demolition has to have a military background."

"So who does he work for?"

"One of the agencies."

"Never met an agency man that good."

"Maybe the military lent the government on of their covert specialists. Navy SEAL. Delta." Ribak laughed. "Hell, he could be one of those fuckin' Rangers."

"Your old buddies?"

"No way. We were never that close when I was in the service. I was never one of them. Made me puke, all that 'do or die, we look after our own crap."

"Deke, what do we do?"

"Priority is to replace the ordnance. No way we're going to get far without weapons."

"Makes sense. Where do we get backup? We've lost the New Mexico and Chicago stashes. Now the compound supply. Hell, Deke, it isn't getting any easier."

"I'll organize something. Let me talk to Seeger. You get that bunch of lardasses set to cleaning up the compound and start reconstruction."

"Deke, we lost more men when they went after him. *And* the chopper that went hunting him."

"This gets fuckin' better all the time. One man? Sounds like I've been hiring the wrong people. I'll call you later."

Ribak ended the call. He shut down his cell phone and made his way to Seeger's office. The door was open, and Seeger was lounging in his executive chair, staring out the window at the spectacular scenery that served as a backdrop. Ribak tapped on the door frame and waited until Seeger swung his chair around, then related what he had been told during the telephone conversation.

"Deke, explain something to me," Seeger said. "Explain how a numerically superior force can allow one man to walk into their compound, plant explosives that destroy valuable arms, then get away in one of their own vehicles, and then take down the men pursuing him and destroy a helicopter."

"Military infiltrators are among the best operatives around, Mr. Seeger. Their training sees to that."

"This man is decimating us, Deke, tearing my militia apart. Every time he comes after us, he wins. Look what he's already done. I truly believe he'll be knocking on my front door next." Seeger gave a choking laugh. "I mean, why not? He's already in the neighborhood."

Ribak had no answer this time.

TEN MINUTES LATER Ribak stood in his own office, surveying the identical scenery Seeger had been watching. He had lit a cigarette, smoke curling in front of his face. He was angry. Not so much with himself, though he was smarting at what had happened. Seeger had been right. The son of a bitch was knocking the Brethren on its ass.

It had started at Gantz's house.

And now the Colorado base.

And each time the guy had walked away unscathed. Ribak was convinced it was the same man on each occasion. He hadn't seen him clearly at Gantz's and not at all during the other incidents. An inner sense warned him it was the same guy. He'd had help in Pennsylvania and Chicago, but the Colorado strike had been carried out by a single man.

Who the hell was he?

Ribak hadn't been joking when he told Kemp the wrong men had been hired. Give him a dozen like this elusive guy and Ribak could have turned things around without breaking a sweat.

As much as he admired the stranger's skill, Ribak had to have him stopped. Too much of this kind of damage could have serious effects on morale. Seeger wanted his militia to be involved in major conflicts. If he was going to achieve that, Ribak needed damage control. He was going to have to pull out all the stops and not worry too much about the aftereffects.

CHAPTER TWENTY-ONE

Lyons had parked a distance away from a hangar, watching the place for a while as the day brightened around him. The field was small, housing only a few hangars and outbuildings. From the background details Kurtzman had pulled, Beller's Charter was the only outfit operating from the place at the present time. Mort Beller owned and ran the charter service bearing his name. Kurtzman had even provided a photograph of Beller from his pilot's license application—a heavyset man, medium height. It was enough for Carl Lyons.

Outside it was raining, cold. Lyons was protected inside the rental car. The situation reminded him of his time on the force when he had spent long hours on stakeouts. It had been mind-numbing, waiting for something to happen, consuming fast food and drinking lukewarm coffee, the air inside the vehicle stale and the conversation staler. There were many occasions when those tedious surveillances had resulted in nothing. Lyons hoped this particular session would not be like that.

He heard the rumble of an engine and saw an expensive BMW roll in from the direction of the road beyond the field. It turned in toward the main hangar and stopped. The driver's door opened and the man who climbed out was Mort Beller. He made a dash for the small door set in the hangar, unlocked it and went inside. A light came on.

Lyons started the rental car and drove across the concrete apron, coming to a stop alongside Beller's BMW. He studied the layout for a while, familiarizing himself with the area before he opened his door and made for the office entrance. Pushing the door open he stepped inside, unzipping his leather jacket so he could get to the holstered Python if he needed it. As he closed the door behind him, he heard someone call out.

"If you want a charter today, no chance. I'm on standby." Movement in the office behind the counter preceded Beller's appearance.

His words trailed off when he saw Lyons. The Able Team leader had a good physique that showed, and his expression informed Beller he was in no mood to be brushed off lightly.

"Mort Beller."

"That a question or a statement of fact? You sound like you're here to hand me a warrant or somethin'. Should I be worried?"

Lyons slid a photograph from his pocket and laid it on the counter.

Clair Valens.

As he completed his move, Lyons kept his eyes on Beller's face. The moment he scanned the photograph Beller's expression changed. Only for an instant before he regained control but it was enough to alert Lyons.

"Who is she?"

"How the hell should I know? Maybe she's your sister."

"Considering why I'm looking for her, that could be a wrong answer."

"Hey, I was joking."

"I'm not."

The inflection in Lyons's tone alerted Beller. He might have bluffed his way out if he had possessed a stronger character. Instead he turned and headed for his office.

Lyons shook his head at the stupidity of the move. He stepped back, then vaulted over the counter and went after the bulky figure. As he went through the office door, he saw Beller reach a cluttered desk and yank open a drawer, light gleaming on the outline of a gun. Lyons crossed the office, raised his right foot and booted the drawer shut on Beller's hand. The man yelled in pain, wrenching his hand from the drawer. Blood welled from a gash. Lyons reached out and hauled the pilot around and hit him on his beefy jaw. The blow spun Beller and he sprawled across the desk, scattering the contents. He gave a groan, sliding off the desk and dropping to the floor.

BELLER OPENED HIS EYES, realized he was restrained and immediately went into a panic, struggling against whatever held his wrists to the arms of his office chair. His legs were bound, too. When he found he couldn't free himself he calmed a little, chest pumping from his exertions, and decided to look around.

He was still in his office.

His visitor was seated on the edge of the desk, watching him. Lyons had Beller's revolver in his left hand, casually swinging it back and forth.

"What the fuck is going on?" Beller demanded. He tugged at the restraints on his wrists again. Glancing down, he saw they were plastic ties and knew he wasn't about to break free. Already the skin under the ties was raw and sore.

"This should be easy for both of us," Lyons said. "I ask the questions, you answer."

Beller stared at him as if Lyons was making a joke. "Yeah, right."

"I hope so. First question. Was the woman hurt at all?"

"What the fuck kind of question is that? I don't know about any woman. Okay?"

"A problem already. Apparently you didn't get the idea."

Lyons put Beller's gun aside, then reached out to pick up the Cold Steel Tanto knife he had placed there, letting Beller get a clear look at the gleaming blade before he walked slowly around the man. Standing behind Beller, he remained silent. Waiting. Beller turned his head, trying to see what Lyons was doing. He tugged at the plastic restraints pinning his wrists to the chair arms. It wasn't long before thin beads of sweat began to form on the back of his neck, and Lyons could hear his ragged breathing. Beller finally gave up twisting his head because he was unable to see anything.

"Hey, where the fuck are you? What're you doing back there?"

Lyons leaned forward and allowed the razor edge of the knife to stroke across the back of Beller's neck. He kept the caress featherlight but it was enough for the blade to make a thin cut in the outer skin. Beller let out a startled yell, jerking wildly again, panic making him lunge against his bonds.

"Crazy son of a bitch, what the hell are you doing? Did you cut me? Fuck, you cut me. Mother…what the fuck do you want?"

Lyons moved back to face him, holding the knife in full view so that Beller could see the thin beads of bright blood on the blade edge.

"Was the woman hurt?"

Beller glared, his eyes fixed on the knife. Like the majority of people, he had an innate fear of a cold knife blade. "You bastard." He blew a hard breath from his lips. "Okay. Okay, enough with the knife. No, she wasn't hurt. But she didn't look too happy at being taken for a ride."

"Who was with her? And don't give me fake names. I know the Brethren players."

Beller realized his mouth was dry and he was ready to complain, then thought better of it when he actually took note of Lyons's steady gaze. He realized he had never looked into such uncompromising, ice-cold eyes. And he suddenly, shockingly, realized that this man was in deadly earnest.

Mort Beller had never been close to violent death in his life. His only contact was through TV newscasts. Death shown on-screen did not have the same impact and relieved the viewer of any personal involvement. Here, now, with his own mortality on the edge, Beller was experiencing the sheer terror of his own suffering in real time, and it scared him more than he might ever admit. What was even more unsettling was the fact that this blond man terrified him, standing over him with a knife he was obviously not afraid to use.

Death had never been closer to Beller than right then. Closer than Beller ever wanted it to be.

"Deacon Ribak. Joseph Amenta."

"Where did you take them?"

"Seeger's place in Colorado."

"And then?"

"Refueled and came back here. Like I always do."

"Did you go inside the house?"

"No. I never do."

"So you have no idea who else was there?"

Beller shook his head. His beefy face was dripping sweat. The cut on the back of his neck was stinging, reminding him what that knife could do. He found it hard to tear his eyes from it.

"Seeger. Does he have security outside the house?"

"There are always a few walking the grounds. Sometimes more. Hard to tell. I don't get invited in for coffee. Seeger pays me good money to fly people in or out. That's it."

"House in the open?"

"There's a wide area he had cleared same time he built the landing strip. Then it's all timber and the hills north of the property."

"What else?"

"What else? Jesus, is my name Google? I don't know. All I do is fly people in and out, like I said. I don't ask questions because Seeger doesn't like nosy people. Get curious, and he starts getting paranoid. Understand?"

"In his position I'm not surprised." Lyons paced back and forth, working things over in his mind. "Beller, have you been out there since you dropped them off?"

"No."

"So the woman could still be there?"

Beller shrugged. "How do I know? She might have been flown out by someone else."

"Only one way to find out."

The words had a chilling finality to them.

Beller was not the only one with a difficult situation to resolve. Lyons had realized using Beller as pilot to reach Seeger's home base was not a good idea. He needed someone else. That was clear. But who? Jack Grimaldi wasn't available. A solution presented itself even as Lyons was thinking about Grimaldi's lack of availability. He stepped out of the office, out of Beller's hearing, and used his cell to contact Stony Man. He was hoping the person he was considering was available.

Downright reckless?

He decided that was closer to the truth, which was pretty normal by his own standards.

He glanced across the office to where Beller sat slumped in his chair, still restrained. Lyons didn't trust the man at all. And especially not since he had made a call to Stony Man some time earlier, giving Kurtzman details he had taken from Beller's pilot's license.

Kurtzman had come back within ten minutes, giving Lyons the lowdown on Mort Beller. The man had led an interesting life. Mostly on the edge. The single item that interested Lyons was the revelation that Beller was on a list as a member of the Brethren. Said fact didn't surprise Lyons. He would have been disappointed if Beller had not been a member.

"Thanks for that," he'd said, and signed off.

Now he was calling Stony Man back again, asking for Brognola and ready to make his request. The conversation was short and by Lyons's standards reasonable.

"I'll get back to you," Brognola said.

Lyons wandered into the office and stirred Beller with the toe of his shoe. The man raised his head and returned Lyons's stare. "What now?"

"When I first came in you said you were on standby today."

"So?"

"For the Brethren?"

"Yeah."

"I figured so. They yell, you jump."

"And if I do? It's no damn crime."

"Aggression now. You should learn to control your feelings, pal. Bad vibes only generate hostility."

"Yeah? You got that fuckin' right. Hostile is just how I feel about you."

Lyons grinned. "And I thought we were getting along just fine."

"Look, what do you want from me?"

"This call you're waiting for? To fly to Seeger's place?"

"Most likely…" Beller's mouth stayed open. "Crazy bastard. You want to go there?" He saw by the expression on Lyons's face that was exactly what the man wanted. "Walk in unexpected and they'll shoot you straight off. Christ, me, too, if they figure I brought you."

"You could call ahead and let them know I'm on my way to deliver the latest edition of *The Watch Tower*."

Beller shook his head. "This is the Brethren we're talking about. They're not in this for laughs. You know what they're capable of."

"Tell me about it, Mort. Slaughter on the streets. Plain murder of noncombatants. Property destruction. Hell of a bunch you're tied in with."

"We do what needs to be done. This country is being flushed down the fuckin' toilet by the federal authorities. We're losing constitutional rights all the damn time while the government turns this nation into a fascist state. They are screwing with our constitution…"

Lyons was suddenly right in Beller's face, the muzzle of his pistol grinding hard into the man's cheek. "Those people you killed. Women and kids included. Were they screwing with your rights? Tell me, Beller, did a ten-year-old girl deny you constitutional freedom? Because you sure did deny hers."

Out the corner of his eye Beller saw Lyons's trigger finger go white at the knuckle as he applied pressure. He stared into Lyons's face and saw a murderous gleam in his eyes. He stayed silent because he didn't know what to say and felt sure the man was *that* close to pulling the trigger.

Lyons pulled back, stepped away from Beller and lowered the Python. He let go the breath he had been holding, tension releasing with it. He moved across to the desk and perched on the corner, letting the big gun hang loose in his hand.

"We came close there, Mort."

Beller still refrained from speaking. He was trembling. Sweat glistened on his skin as he realized just how close he had come to dying.

Lyons's cell phone rang. He answered and took Brognola's message, a smile crossing his face. "How long? On his way? Okay." He put the phone away. "Looks like you're off the hook, Mort. If you do one thing for me."

The phone rang twenty minutes later. Lyons picked it up and put it to Beller's mouth. His right hand held the cocked Python, the muzzle pressed hard against the man's head.

"It's me," Beller said. "I'm all gassed up and ready. Yeah. I'll be taking off shortly. See you there, Ribak."

Lyons took the phone and placed it back on the cradle.

"Wasn't difficult, was it?"

"Now what?"

"We wait."

They waited for just under an hour, until the buzz of an incoming aircraft drew Lyons outside. He watched as a blue-and-white Cessna circled the field then came in to land, taxiing up to come to a stop alongside Beller's craft. The engines died and a familiar figure climbed out and crossed to where Lyons stood.

"Benning."

Lyons nodded. "Bud Casper?"

Bud Casper, a fair-haired, lean, good-looking man in his thirties, followed Lyons inside. To his credit, Casper made no comment when he saw Beller secured to his chair, or the bruise on his jaw where Lyons had hit him.

"Have to say I kind of expected something like this. My trip with Cooper kind of set me up not to be surprised."

"Did they tell you where we're heading?"

Casper grinned. "Don't tell me it's Colorado again. Damn me, what is it about that place?"

"Don't know what to tell you, Bud."

"Least this time of year there shouldn't be any snow."

Lyons had heard about Bud Casper's first involvement with Bolan in Colorado. As well as record snowfalls, there had been an attempt to kill Casper during the mission. He had ended up badly wounded, surviving through his stubborn nature and a refusal to quit. The incidents in Colorado had been life threatening to all concerned. A longtime friend of Jack Grimaldi, the charter pilot had equipped himself well and Brognola had kept him on the books as a possible future backup pilot.

"Maybe no snow, but this could be just as dangerous."

"I told Coop last time 'round. The charter business gets to be a little quiet at times."

"You'll be sorry if you get mixed up in this," Beller said. "He tell you who we are?"

"His chief told me," Casper said. "Some sorry-ass bunch of militiamen setting off bombs in the streets. No guts to stand up and face real men, I hear. You get off on killing women and kids. Really scary."

"Mort here has showed me the course settings for our trip." Lyons picked up the clipboard Beller had previously prepared for his flight to the Seeger location. "That okay?"

Casper nodded. "Not hard to find." He traced a finger across the aerial map, nodding to himself. "I've flown over that way plenty of times. Mind, folk weren't shooting at me then."

He looked across at Beller. "That plane of yours. She all fueled up and prepped?"

"I can tell you she is," Lyons said. "I checked."

"Then we're ready to go, partner. Hey, what about him?"

"He's waiting for a trip, too. With a couple of federal marshals. They should be here any minute. Lockdown time for Mort."

Beller kept his mouth closed.

Thirty minutes later Beller's Cessna, with Casper at the controls, taxied across the field to the runway. He increased the power and cleared the strip with yards to spare, bringing the aircraft around on its heading for Colorado. Lyons spent some time in the passenger section, going through the heavy carryall he'd brought on board from the trunk of his rental car. The bag held the ordnance he had brought along from Stony Man. Lyons wanted time to check it all over and make sure the weapons were loaded and ready for use. He already had a feeling that everything else aside, his welcome at Seeger's residence would not be a peaceful affair.

CHAPTER TWENTY-TWO

Bolan's earlier call to Stony Man had updated him on Lyons's progress and his imminent arrival at Seeger's Colorado residence. It had only taken a short check via Kurtzman to get the radio frequency of the Cessna.

"What's your ETA?" Bolan asked, keying the transmit button on the SUV's com set. He let go of the button and waited for Lyons's response.

"Bud says under an hour. You?"

"According to my GPS I'll be there in the next forty minutes. I'll go EVA some way out, come in on foot and wait for you to touch down. To be honest, I could do with a time-out."

Lyons chuckled. "Getting too much for you?"

"That'll be the day. I just need to catch my breath."

"Watch yourself, Striker."

Bolan cut the transmission and concentrated on driving. The terrain, though flatter than the higher country behind him, was still rugged. He was guiding the vehicle across rough country and despite its design as an all-terrain vehicle, the ride was far from comfortable. He was still feeling the effects of his wild ride down the off-trail slope, the jolting ending and the crack on the head. His half-joking reference to Lyons about a time-out hadn't exactly been a joke. A long, hot shower, a meal and a soft bed sounded good to Bolan. The thought filtered through his mind and whispered off into thin air. His concentration centered around the upcoming clash with the Brethren. It was past due, something that had to be dealt with before the militia group carried out any more murderous acts against the American public and tried to spread what they considered a necessary message to the country. The strikes Bolan and Lyons had engineered had started to disentangle the threat the Brethren posed, but as long as the will of their leadership was broadcast, the militia soldiers would respond. If they were left alone now, they would undoubtedly regroup. Bolan was going to see that never took place. If it meant he had to take them all down and raze Seeger's residence, then so be it. There were times when rampant evil could only be totally stopped by grinding it to dust underfoot. Stopping at the citadel gates was not enough. Those gates had to be flattened and whatever stood behind them crushed, as well.

DEACON RIBAK GLANCED UP as his communications man leaned in through his office door.

"Beller's caught some turbulence," he reported. "Slowing him down some. He'll be at least another thirty minutes."

"You talked to him?"

"Well, yeah. If I hadn't, how would I know he's going to be late?"

Ribak smiled. "I asked if you talked to Mort Beller."

"Reception was a little rough but…"

"Okay. Forget it."

When the man had gone Ribak stood behind his desk. He picked up the pistol he had just been loading and slipped it into the holster on his right hip. He turned to look out of the window. Late afternoon. The day was hot and still. No breeze of any kind. The clouds in the sky were solid and unbroken. Ribak was no weatherman, but from what he could see there was no unsettling wind. He understood conditions might change at a higher altitude. Enough to slow down a flying plane? He wasn't sure, but there was enough of a doubt to caution him.

Since the strike at the high country base and the scattering of the Brethren militia up there, Ribak had been on edge. It was a culmination of everything that had happened over the past few days. There had been enough setbacks to have made Napoleon turn back from Moscow and volunteer to go and sit it out on Elba. All one way. The guy—no, two guys—who had engineered those strikes were damn good. He gave them that. They had excellent intel and used it to their advantage. And they were ruthless in their attitude. No half measures. They hit and hit hard, leaving very little behind that was of much use. Search and destroy. Take down the enemy by reducing his ordnance and his ground locations to rubble. Do the same with personnel if they put up any resistance. It wasn't the first time they had been in the field. They were running their assaults like they were in a war situation.

Ribak knew, too, it was not their last strike. He had a feeling they might well be on their way here, to Seeger's last line of defense, wanting to make it a final cut into the Brethren's belly. He touched the butt of his handgun. Let them come. It wasn't over until it was finished.

And Deacon Ribak was far from finished.

Something struck him then, making him grin as he took it in.

This had all really started back at Jerome Gantz's house in Tyler Point, when those two guys had turned up just when Ribak's team was getting at the information about the diamonds Gantz and his then-unknown partner Zac Lorens had lifted from the Brethren. From that clash the pair had moved on, picking out and hitting Brethren targets like they were toppling dominos. Ribak laughed as the thought took hold. All because of Jerome Gantz. As if he wasn't being paid enough for his work already. Lorens had been the same. The guy had already been wealthy. Both of them had just gotten greedy. Ribak had to admit that four million dollars' worth of diamonds certainly was a worthwhile sum to go for. He could almost get a taste for that kind of money himself. As far as Gantz and Lorens were concerned, long-term loyalty to the Brethren had flown the coop. The wealth the diamonds had promised had taken hold. They had gone over to the enemy.

His desk phone rang. It was Seeger. He sounded panicky. Again. Ribak was wanted immediately. When he put the phone down, Ribak realized he would be damn well glad when he could walk away from this bunch of idiots. When his assignment had been outlined by General Carson and Eric Stahl, it had seemed like a worthy challenge. The past months now felt like a stretch in prison, surrounded by wannabe hard-liners who would never had made the grade as soldiers. Oh, they were cold-blooded bastards, no argument there. Ready to plant a few bombs and take out unsuspecting civilians and shout their radical slogans from platforms. But the minute they were faced by a real soldier it was a turkey shoot. In the end the Brethren militia was only good for what Stahl and the general had set it up for— to be fall guys. Once the genuine coup took place, Seeger and his Brethren would be on their own. But only for as long as it took Carson to point the finger and burn them down.

"TEN MINUTES, Doug."

Lyons nodded. He reached for the hand microphone and turned the dial to Bolan's frequency.

"Big Bird to Striker. Over."

"I hear you. I'm in place. You ready to touch down?"

"In just under ten," Lyons said.

"I'll take position behind landing strip. Is our package in residence?"

"Might have been moved on. Couldn't confirm."

"Understood."

"We're staring to descend now. Big Bird out."

BOLAN SPOTTED the Cessna as it made a wide sweep over the area, then dropped quickly and touched down on the first approach. The aircraft rolled along the compacted strip to the far end, away from the stone-and-timber house.

The SUV's com set began to transmit. Bolan picked up the handset as Lyons's voice came through.

"You see us, Striker?"

"Got you. I'm going EVA as of now. Should be at the target in just over five."

"I'll be waiting."

"Over and out." Bolan switched off the radio and exited the vehicle. He moved into the brief cover offered by brush and timber, working his way toward the Seeger residence and keeping his eyes out for any Brethren hardmen who might be patrolling this far out. As it was, he didn't encounter anyone. Not until he was yards away from where the cleared terrain commenced just short of the landing strip.

He spotted a camou-clad guard, with an M-16 over his shoulder. The man was lounging against a tree, his gaze directed at the Cessna. Something seemed to have attracted his undivided attention, and Bolan saw him operating a com set. He was close enough to hear what was said.

"I just remembered what you said about Beller coming in on his own. There are two of them in the plane. Something else, Ribak. Neither of them looks like Mort Beller. Yeah, okay, I'll do that."

The guard clicked off and hung the com set from a clip on his belt. He brought his M-16 into play, checking the load, and prepared to head toward the Cessna.

Bolan caught hold of his jacket collar and yanked him back. The guard slammed into the trunk of a solid tree, the impact jarring him. Bolan followed through with a hard blow from the butt end of his M-16 to the guy's skull. As he went to his knees, the Executioner struck again, slamming him to the ground, gripping the guy's head and twisting it savagely. Bolan crouched beside the dead man and frisked him, locating two extra magazines for the M-16 and placing them in his pockets.

Aware that time was slipping by, Bolan followed the

brush line until it petered out, then cut across a strip of open ground, staying as low as possible until he was able to close in on the Cessna. Lyons had spotted him as he moved along the aircraft and reached the cockpit. He acknowledged Bolan's presence, taking in the man's battered and bloody appearance, his torn and stained clothing.

"Looking a little rough, aren't we?"

"You know how it is," Bolan said.

"So how do we play this?"

"I'll cut across and around this side of the house, see if I can get inside. You take the left side. Make as much of an entrance as you can. Draw attention to that side."

Bud Casper leaned around Lyons. "Hey, Coop. Still making a damn nuisance of yourself I see."

Bolan grinned. "Good to see you, too, Bud. I want you to stay with the plane. Could be we might need a fast getaway."

"You got it." He exposed the Uzi Lyons had given him.

Bolan nodded. "Give me a minute or so, then head out."

He turned then, staying low, and rounded the front of the Cessna. Lyons had made Casper run the aircraft to the extreme end of the strip where a bank of shored-up earth formed a barrier. Bolan was able to work his way around the rear of the solid bank, then cut in behind more brush, working his way toward the low wall that ran across the rear elevation of the house. He eased over the wall and waited until Lyons started to make some noise. He didn't have to wait long. The boom of a shotgun reached him and a little while later the dull explosion as the fractured fuel tank blew. That was Bolan's signal to move.

LYONS CUT ACROSS open ground, his SPAS tracking ahead of him. Armed men rushed from a side door, autorifles lifting as they spotted Lyons. The Able Team leader kept moving in their direction, his wild action making the Brethren gunners pause for an instant. If they had known Lyons, they might have expected this kind of behavior. The psychology of confrontation was implanted in Lyons's mind. He was aware that the sight of an armed, determined opponent rushing hard toward an enemy went against the grain. The militiamen would have expected Lyons to dive for cover, not charge them. By the time they took it in Lyons already had them in his sights and started to pull the shotgun's trigger, the combat weapon spitting fire as it discharged its deadly charges, Lyons firing continuously. The 12-gauge shots, made even deadlier because of the short range, ripped and tore into the targets. The first three hardmen were scythed to the ground, bloody and dying. The survivor turned to seek cover so that Lyons's final shot blasted in between his shoulders, the force lifting him off his feet and dumping him facedown on the hard ground.

Lyons took one of the grenades from his combat vest and yanked the pin. Turning, he tossed the grenade under the fuel tank he'd passed, then flattened against the wall of the house. The grenade detonated, the force of the blast bursting the underside of the tank and igniting the aviation fuel store inside. The explosion threw blazing fuel in all directions. As the fireball rose behind him, Lyons calmly reloaded the shotgun, then moved toward the front of the house.

Raised voices from ahead alerted him to more Brethren gunners heading toward him. Drifting smoke from

the burning tank blew in front of Lyons. As it began to
clear, he made out the hazy figures. Four, maybe five
of them. He raised the shotgun and hit the group before
the militiamen were aware of his presence, the SPAS
booming loudly, the close-range blasts tearing into them
with stunning force. Lyons fired on the move, ignoring
the risk of return fire, which never came. He had caught
the opposition off guard. It had been only a fraction of
time but in a combat situation hesitation walked in
league with sudden death. The law of survival in combat was to be first, fast and refuse to give any kind of
advantage to the enemy. Compassion could come later,
if it was needed. In the fragmented confusion of battle
the rule was to ignore everything but personal survival.
Forget that and the other guy won.

THE CESSNA SHOULD HAVE been empty except for the
pilot. The report from his sentry worried Ribak.

There should not have been a passenger.

Ribak felt a rise of anger when he saw a figure climb
out from the pilot's side of the cockpit and join the sol-
idly built blond man.

Neither man was Mort Beller.

"A fuckin' trick," Ribak muttered. He raised his voice
so it carried across the room. "Hostiles comin' in."

There was a lack of immediate response from the
gathered Brethren. They looked at one another, then
back to Ribak, unsure whether he was serious or simply throwing another of his unannounced tests.

Ribak pulled his jacket aside and took out his pistol.
"They're fuckin' federal agents," he yelled. "Get your
butts off those seats and let's go. Let's go."

As his command rolled across the room, there was

the distant crack of a shotgun coming from the grounds outside the house. There was the heavy thump of an explosion that sent a faint tremor through the house.

"Go help your buddies," Ribak yelled.

The gunners made a concerted effort, pushing chairs aside and grabbing their weapons. The militiamen headed for the exit, boots thumping on the floor as they crowded for the main door.

Ribak followed but didn't join them. His attention had been taken by the sound of breaking glass coming from the far side of the house opposite to where the two men had left the plane.

There was a third man.

As Ribak made his way down the main passage, he passed Liam Seeger's office and saw the man himself emerge.

"Deke?"

"Looks like you were right. We got visitors, Mr. Seeger. We are under attack."

"No. Not at my house."

"Mr.… The hell with it. Liam, are you forgetting how we have more than pissed off the federal authorities? Believe it. They are on your doorstep right now."

Ribak was convinced the strike was the work of the persistent bastard who had been dogging the Brethren since Tyler Bay. The guy, along with his sometime partner, had been slicing and dicing at anything and everything Brethren ever since the attack at Gantz's place. At the start of this day he had turned up at the Brethren high-country base and blown it all to hell. Now he was bringing his war to Seeger's home. He snapped back the pistol's slide, pushing the first 9 mm round into the breech.

Okay, you irritating mother, come see how a real soldier does it, Ribak thought.

CHAPTER TWENTY-THREE

Bolan saw a window that looked ideal for his purpose in the end wall of a section that jutted from the main house. He was angling in that direction when he picked up the murmur of voices coming from the side of the house.

Two armed figures burst into view, weapons up but not purposeful enough to track onto Bolan in time.

The Executioner's M-16 fired first, 3-round bursts dropping the pair in a heartbeat. Bolan stepped around them, reaching the wood-framed window. He rapped the butt of his rifle against the glass, then cleared the base of the frame of shards before he hauled himself over the sill and dropped into the room. It was crammed from floor to ceiling with cartons and sealed bags. A swift glance revealed the room held survival supplies, canned and sealed packs of food. Other cartons held self-heating rations and drinks. There was clothing, blankets and sleeping bags. Bolan made a quick estimate and figured there had to be enough for dozens of men. Whatever else he might be, Liam Seeger was serious in his intentions.

But at what cost?

The Brethren had showed its true colors in the actions it had taken. Indiscriminate slaughter was not the basis for a new order. It had been used before, too many times, and usually resulted in a continuation of those methods. It had no place in American society.

Bolan reached the door and eased the handle, edging the door open so he could check out the exterior of the room. He saw a corridor leading to a wider open area, and wooden stairs led to the upper floor.

Gunfire still sounded from outside. Lyons was doing his part, but Bolan couldn't expect him to keep it up indefinitely. He stepped out of the room and turned to make his way along the passage.

RIBAK SAW THE DOOR open and a tall, black-clad man stepped into the hall. Just looking at him Ribak knew this was the bastard who had been causing all the Brethren's problems. And he could see why. The guy had a presence. It showed in the way he held himself, the way he moved. His eyes were never still, and the way he carried his M-16 rifle told Ribak he was no beginner. He took into account the handguns the guy wore. They were not there for show.

It was almost a pity to have to kill the big guy.

Ribak's pistol was already on the man, his finger against the trigger. One step more…

And that was when Liam Seeger stepped into the corridor, moving so that his body blocked Ribak's target.

"Liam, move the fuck away."

Seeger ignored the command. He was focusing on Bolan. His single eye stared at the black-clad intruder. "You broke into my house. Do you know who I am?"

"Nobody important. Just a piece of dirt who murders innocent Americans because he doesn't have the guts to face them himself."

"Do you really believe that? I'm Liam Seeger. The Brethren is mine. We're going to make this country—"

"Not on your best day, Seeger. Sentence has been passed and delivered."

The M-16 crackled, the slugs ripping into Seeger's body. He gave a stunned cry as the bullets slammed him back against the door frame, then slithered to the tiled floor, his blood running red across them.

"No more," Bolan said, stepping by the body. "Your club is disbanded. For good."

Ribak saw Seeger go down, his lean body torn and bloody from the intruder's shots. He raised his hand and fired his own weapon, the shot clipping the wall just beyond.

Bolan dropped, the M-16 sweeping around at Ribak. He pulled the trigger and sent a burst that missed as his target twisted and ran, taking cover behind the angle of the wall. The soldier fired again, his slugs tearing out chunks of plaster from the edge of the wall.

There was no return fire. Bolan moved along the passage and reached the end of the wall. Ribak had gone. Up ahead the Executioner saw a door swinging shut behind someone.

Ribak was making a run for freedom.

FOREMOST IN BOLAN'S MIND was Ribak's knowledge of Clair Valens's location. The man was Stahl and Carson's spy in the camp, feeding them information of the Brethren and its plans. That might be over but the Stahl-Carson conspiracy was far from ended. They could still engineer their threat against the President and the administration. Stahl's desire for taking control was not going to fade away with a weakening of Brethren strength. Senator Randolph's intelligent summation of the alliance between Stahl and Carson had made it clear they were going to make their strike while the American public was still in a nervous state concerning the attacks by the militia. There were still isolated Brethren cells capable of causing more confusion and suffering. News of Liam Seeger's death would not reach those cells for some time, and as long as they remained committed, the strikes would carry on.

Bolan had a need to take Stahl and Carson out of the equation. He had allowed Stahl to live the last time they had clashed. He admitted now that that had been a mistake. Stahl had learned nothing from it. He had grasped his freedom with both hands, retreating into the background where he simply made a new alliance and drew plans for another round of deception and betrayal of his country. Clair Valens, harboring her own mistrust of the man, had embarked on a low-key mission of her own to expose Stahl for what he was. Bolan would not condemn her for that. She had courage and determination. Neither of those qualities was going to help her if she was in the hands of Eric Stahl.

Bolan needed Ribak alive—at least until he could tell where Stahl and Carson were, and what had happened to Valens.

The former soldier was not going to give in without a fight. And he had the advantage over Bolan. He knew the layout of the house, making it easier for him to move around.

Bolan had to think like Ribak. Would the man choose

to stay and settle matters between himself and Bolan? Or would he get out, making a quiet escape so he could return to Stahl and Carson? He would have accepted his role as undercover man for his true employers to be over now. So why remain where he might get himself killed? His place would be with the people he worked for.

There was no way he could fly out. The only aircraft available was no longer in Brethren control. Bud Casper would see to it that no one commandeered the Cessna. So that left a ground vehicle. There had to be some of them around the place. Most likely at the front of the building.

Bolan headed for the door.

In the background the sounds of autofire had lessened. There were still intermittent shots. Lyons, the one-man hell-raiser, had done exactly what Bolan had asked—engaged the enemy and kept them off Bolan's back while he went looking for Seeger and Ribak.

It was one down, one to go, and the Executioner had no intention of failing in his part of the campaign.

Bolan reached the door and pulled it open. He saw a wide, paved driveway and the hard-packed strip of a road running away from the house along a gradual incline. It would run for some ten or so miles before it connected with the regular highway running through this section of the territory.

His eye caught a moving figure, just darting out of sight around an extension jutting from the side of the house. A flat roof. No windows in the stone wall Bolan could see.

Garage?

There was only one way to find out. Bolan turned toward the garage and was close when he heard the sud-

den surge of a powerful engine. Tires burned on concrete and as Bolan rounded the end of the garage, its
doors opened and a big red SUV burst from the building. Deacon Ribak was at the wheel. It hit the paved
strip, swerved across it, then threw up reddish dust as
the deep-treaded tires dug into the compacted earth.

Bolan barely managed to pull himself back as the
SUV cruised by him. He snapped the M-16 to his shoulder and triggered a triburst that cored in through the rear
corner. The SUV maintained its course, thick dust obscuring its shape as it accelerated with surprising speed.

Ejecting the magazine, Bolan rammed a fresh one
home and cocked the M-16. He turned to the open garage and saw a number of parked vehicles. The closest
was a twin of the one Ribak had driven off in, identical
model and color. Its license plate read LS/2. Bolan
yanked the door open and peered inside. The SUV was
ready to roll, the key in the ignition.

It was no hardship to keep track of Ribak. The dust
trail left by his vehicle was clear to see. Bolan pushed
the pedal to the floor, feeling the sheer power of the
massive vehicle expend itself. As he closed in behind
Ribak, the dense dust cloud hid the man's vehicle at
times. It crossed Bolan's mind that Ribak might not
even be able to see his pursuer. The obscuring dust
cloud might work both ways. Bolan decided he might
use that to his advantage. He pulled the seat belt in
place, locking it securely, then swung the nose of his
SUV out to the side so he could draw alongside Ribak,
intending to sideswipe the other vehicle. He knew he
was taking a risk that might easily backfire. Once he
was alongside Ribak the man would have the same op-

portunity Bolan had. Regardless of that risk, Bolan nudged a little more speed out of his SUV.

Now he was directly alongside. Ribak's head turned and he stared at Bolan. Without warning, Bolan turned the wheel and slammed his vehicle into Ribak's. The impact shook both SUVs. Ribak clutched his wheel and struggled for a moment until he brought his vehicle back under control. Bolan repeated his maneuver again, sending Ribak off the road and onto the rutted ground alongside.

Bolan went after him, not allowing Ribak to recover. Again and again the soldier slammed into the SUV, battering the vehicle. He could see Ribak cursing as he fought the shuddering steering wheel. His front wheels hit a half-buried slab of rock. The SUV rose, the wheels leaving the ground for a moment, which coincided with Bolan hitting Ribak's vehicle yet again. The collision this time jarred Bolan's steering wheel from his hands and he felt his control go. He angled away from Ribak, fighting to bring the bouncing, shuddering SUV back on line. When he had succeeded he glanced around. Ribak was no longer in sight. There was a huge dust cloud behind Bolan. He stepped on his brake, slowing and swinging the SUV around to face the way it had come, touching the gas pedal to search for Ribak's vehicle.

As the dust cloud drifted aside, he saw Ribak's SUV on its right side, wheels turning, the engine still going. Bolan stopped at a safe distance, unclipped his belt and picked up the M-16. He stepped out of the SUV and stood checking out the overturned vehicle. The engine died suddenly. Steam seeped from under the hood. The turning wheels slowed and ceased moving. Bolan searched the SUV but saw nothing.

Until the tailgate door of Ribak's vehicle was forcibly kicked open. Bolan twisted in that direction, saw the blur of movement as Ribak rolled out and scrambled to cover behind the SUV.

"I want that SUV," Ribak called from his cover. "I'm going to have it sooner or later, so save yourself a lot of trouble and step away."

"Not going to happen, Ribak. Game's over. Accept it."

"I don't think I can, so I'll just have to kill you."

"It won't be as easy as killing Gantz. Or those civilians you and your Brethren buddies murdered."

"Hell, don't use that crap. We're in a war situation here. Ever heard of collateral damage?"

"Those deaths were no accidental overlap. You bastards knew exactly what you were doing."

"It's done. No advantage crying about it now."

Bolan, all the while he had been conversing with Ribak, had been moving toward the overturned SUV, a plan forming in his mind that might offer him a way out. He had pinpointed Ribak's location behind the SUV, his M-16 already lined up. He had a full, 30-round magazine in place. Thirty rounds he would be able to deliver in 3-round bursts. He stopped three feet from the exposed underside of the SUV, aimed and began to fire, moving the M-16's muzzle no more than a few inches either side of his target point. His finger worked the trigger in firm strokes, the rifle jacking out the entire contents of the magazine. Empty cartridge cases sprang from the ejection port in an almost continuous rain, gathering at Bolan's feet. He saw the 5.56 mm slugs penetrate the SUV's underside, visualizing them going on through to tear out through the roof panel.

The M-16 stopped firing. Bolan ejected the spent magazine and clicked in a fresh one, cocking the weapon and waiting.

He heard a low groan, the sound of a body slumping to the ground on the other side of the SUV. He walked around the front of the vehicle, his M-16 up and ready.

Deacon Ribak was slumped against the SUV, clutching at his bullet-riddled legs. Bolan's shots had ripped into his thighs and lower hips, the 5.56 mm slugs deformed by their passage through the two layers of metal sheeting. The malformed slugs had retained enough of their force to inflict ragged, bloody wounds. Bolan had deliberately fired low, not wanting to kill Ribak outright. Wounding had been his intention. He needed to get Ribak to tell him Clair Valens's location.

Ribak raised his head to stare up at the tall man in black. He didn't fail to notice the dried blood and the bruises on Bolan's face. Or the condition of his clothing.

"Busy day?" he asked, his face already pale from pain and the shock of the numerous wounds in his limbs.

"Clearing out rats' nests always takes time."

Ribak's hands were glistening with blood pulsing from the jagged wounds. "That was a smart move," he said. "Fuckin' sneaky, but smart."

"Dealing with people like you and Stahl tends to make me sneaky."

"I can see that."

"Ribak, where's the girl? Is she still here?"

"She'll be with him by now. Tell me something. Why was she so set on finding Stahl?"

"Old score to settle. Plus, she didn't trust him."

"I figured something like that. Jesus, she was a tough

little gal." Ribak bent forward, gripping his legs. "Carson has a house in Maine. It's where he and Stahl are running their empire-building from. That's where she is. Stahl sent his own plane for her."

Bolan didn't reply.

When Ribak lifted his head, he saw that his adversary had shouldered the M-16 and had a 93-R in his hand.

"What the hell," Ribak said. "Damned if I wanted to end up in a wheelchair anyhow."

He fell silent as Bolan moved out of his line of vision.

The 9 mm triburst hit Ribak in the back of his head. He toppled on his side.

"That was from your *collateral* victims," Bolan said.

CHAPTER TWENTY-FOUR

"Can't raise him," Stahl said. He stared at his cell phone, turning it over in his hand as if it would tell him why he couldn't get through to Ribak.

Carson picked up one of the phones on his desk and punched in a number. He waited as it rang out. "That's not like Ribak."

"You think something is wrong?"

Carson replaced his phone on the cradle. "I'll go find Brent. Get him to check it out."

Carson left the room.

"Things not running as smoothly as planned?"

Eric Stahl turned to face the speaker.

Clair Valens.

Seated in a large leather armchair, she regarded Stahl with a mocking expression on her face, despite the large, discolored bruise across her left cheek.

"It might be wise for you to consider your position," Stahl said.

"I don't worry about my position, Stahl. I do concern myself over what you and that lunatic general are planning. I include you in the lunatic reference, by the way."

Stahl leaned against the edge of the desk. "Why? Because we want to liberate this country from the incompetents currently running it?"

"To replace it with what? Stahl and Carson? Sounds like a cheap comedy duo. Or are you going to get out your manifesto and tell me how everything will be A-OK once you take charge? That all the ills plaguing the U.S.A. will vanish overnight? Bring home our troops and suddenly Iraq will become a peaceful democracy? That all those people out there who hate the U.S. will put away their bombs and guns? Take a breath, Stahl. It isn't going to happen. Right or wrong, those conditions have already been set. There isn't an instant fix."

"You fail to see the bigger picture, Clair. It's because of the way the administration has handled—actually mishandled—matters that we are in this situation. They have made terrible mistakes. Mistakes they refuse to admit to, and worst of all, mistakes they are making no attempt to rectify. It isn't simply international blunders. The country is under siege. We need to redress the wrongs done to the American people here, never mind abroad. This used to be a great place to live. The best country in the world. Now we have crime and unemployment. A loss of identity. Indecisive leadership drifting without purpose. The problems are in plain sight but no one will do a damn thing about them."

"So General Carson and ex-Senator Eric Stahl will set all this right? By stealing the presidency and imposing their kind of administration? Remember me? I've had a taste of you once before and I still haven't got rid of the bitterness."

Stahl pushed away from the desk. He strode over to hover above Valens, his face white with anger. "Bitch." He hit her across the face, the sound of the slap loud in the quiet of the room. "If we didn't need to keep you alive for the moment…"

Valens raised her head. The mark from his blow was livid on her cheek. "I don't expect to live through this, so there's nothing to lose."

She lunged up out of the chair, lowering her body and driving her left shoulder into Stahl's midsection. The impact pushed him back, and Valens maintained her forward motion until he slammed up against the desk. Stahl was sucking breath into his lungs, momentarily defenseless. He saw Valens's move coming but was too slow to stop it. Her fist slammed against his jaw, the blow solid, snapping his head to the side. She launched a second punch that struck Stahl over the same spot. Blood spurted from a torn lip. The former senator felt himself sliding along the desk, his hands scrabbling to get a grip on the edge to stop himself from falling. Before he could steady himself Valens was on him, circling his neck with her left arm and closing her grip. She pressed the heel of her right hand against the back of his skull, shoving hard. The pressure closed his windpipe and Stahl began to choke for breath. He was in pain from the solid blow she had landed, panicking through the loss of oxygen. He thrashed as they slid from the desk to the floor, with Valens curling her body against his. The strange thing was he could smell the perfume she wore. He sensed it through the gray veil that enveloped him.

"COME ON, ERIC, snap out of it. You're not dead—yet."

Stahl cracked an eye and Carson's face swam into

focus. He realized he was in one of the armchairs, sprawled back, staring up at Carson. He felt sick. His face and throat hurt, and the taste of blood was in his mouth.

"Hey, get this down you," Carson instructed. He was holding a thick tumbler in his hand. "Go on."

Stahl took the glass in a hand that was trembling. He raised the tumbler and took a small swallow. The whiskey stung his cut lip and slid roughly down his bruised throat.

Harry Brent's face moved into view. He was studying Stahl's bruised jaw. "Packs a punch, doesn't she? What the fuck did you say to piss her off?"

"You think this is funny?" Stahl's words came out in a hoarse growl. It hurt to speak. "Where is she? I hope you killed the bitch."

"Now, Eric, you need to calm down," Carson advised.

"She nearly strangled me. Calm down?"

"We have more pressing matters to attend to," Carson said. "Just to let you know, she is not dead. We still need to find out if she passed on anything that might alert the authorities first. Right now she is locked away, nursing a headache. You listen to me, Eric. Brent tried to raise Seeger's residence. Nothing. He even tried the Brethren's Colorado base. That's dead, too. Until we find out what's going on and whether any of it's down to Valens, we keep her breathing. Not to say we won't hurt her. One way or the other we need to get a handle on all this."

Stahl sat up slowly, touching his sore throat. "The strikes against the Brethren. Remember me saying I might have an idea who could have carried them out?

It occurs to me it could be the same man who interfered in the Zero Project. He and Valens worked together then. Could be he's liaising with her again."

"Who was he? An agency man?"

"It was never made clear. Mike Belasko. He was well trained. Capable. Appeared to work independently. Just like now."

"From what Ribak told me," Brent said, "this guy seems to have some good backup intel-wise. He knew where and when on Brethren targets."

"Could be a covert black ops specialist," Carson said. "I'll call around. In the meantime, Brent, you keep trying to contact the Brethren. Before you do, go and fetch Miss Valens back here. Maybe she's had time to think about her future."

Brent left the room.

Pushing slowly to his feet, Stahl crossed the room to the small bar in the corner. He splashed more whiskey into his tumbler.

"Bill, we need to assess how all this might affect our plans."

"First off, we do not let it stall us. Too much has been worked out. If we lose speed now, the whole thing could fall apart."

"Just remember the Brethren is important to what we're doing."

"I haven't forgotten that. The Brethren still figures. We have enough evidence to link them to those bombings. They have no idea we have them dancing to our tune. And the President hasn't done a great job of outing them, or even setting his various agencies on them. We're close enough to our timetable to start the ball rolling. You get your media affiliates to broadcast the material we have prepared. Make moves on the Hill to work on the political side. Let the American public see that what we have to offer, plus our ability to actually put it into action, and we have the basis for our move. We push and push damned hard."

"I guess you're right. It never was going to be an easy option."

"Hell, Eric, pour me some of that whiskey, then we'll see what that young woman has to tell us."

The lights went out.

"What the hell is going on?" Carson demanded.

In the semidarkness Eric Stahl felt a tight sensation in his chest. The whiskey tumbler slipped from his fingers. It thudded against the carpet.

"It's him," he rasped. "Belasko. He's found us, Bill."

"It could just be a power out," Carson said. Even so, he crossed the room and pulled open a drawer in his desk, taking out the Glock pistol he kept there. He checked the magazine, replaced it and worked the slide to feed in the first bullet. "You have a gun, Eric?"

"No."

"Christ, you make the damn things but you don't carry one?"

"You think I need one for a power out?"

"Eric, I said it could be. It's also conceivable that son of a bitch is here. Always prepare for what *could* happen."

"I expect the Army taught you that?"

"It did come into my basic training, but I'd already been told by my daddy. Always kept him one step ahead of the local sheriff. He might not have been much, but Daddy learned early how to cover his ass."

"I feel safer already."

Carson chuckled. "Now where the hell is Brent and that bitch?"

The door crashed open, a dark shape filling the frame. Carson moved quickly away from the oblong of faint light that was showing. He raised the Glock and fired, his two shots causing a brief flare of illumination. The figure in the doorway grunted, turning sideways and falling into the room so his face could be seen.

Carson realized he had shot Harry Brent.

BRENT WENT DOWN HARD and Mack Bolan moved with him, his body dropping to a crouch, Beretta probing ahead. He had pinpointed the muzzle-flashes and adjusted his return fire accordingly. He triggered the 93-R, felt it recoil as it spit the triburst, and heard the target grunt. The shadowed figure stumbled back, fell against an object that crashed to the floor, the hit man following it to the carpet.

Eric Stahl heard the exchange of shots, flinching at the loud reports. He knew Carson had been hit, saw the dark outline of the man fall to the floor. Then he felt something strike the side of his shoe. Faint light coming through one of the windows revealed the outline of Carson's gun. Stahl dropped to his knees and scooped the weapon from the floor, his finger curling against the trigger.

Carson had been surprised Stahl didn't carry a gun. Stahl had never seen the need. He always paid others to handle those kinds of matters for him, but not carrying a gun did not mean he was unable to use one. Over the years he had handled countless weapons at his plant's firing range during test firings. He raised the Glock, aimed and fired as the crouching man in the doorway began to straighten. He saw the figure waver and pull back from the opening. Stahl kept pulling the trigger, sending a stream of slugs at the door frame and wall until the slide locked back. He rose to his feet, unsure what was happening, wondering where the shooter had gone.

Had his shot been fatal? Or just a wounding one?

Without warning, the house lights came back on. Stahl lowered his eyes against the sudden brightness. His gaze passed over the bloodied form of Harry Brent sprawled just inside the door. Across the room he saw Bill Carson's body beside the desk, his face splashed with blood from the bullet hits in his chest and throat.

He picked up a slight sound just beyond the open doorway and panic made him realize he was holding an empty pistol. He recalled where Carson had gotten it from. The desk drawer was still open. Stahl knew that Carson would have extra magazines there, too. He had been too good a soldier not to be prepared, as he had quoted himself. Stahl broke his stance and moved quickly behind the desk, releasing the Glock's empty magazine even as he saw the two extra clips lying in the drawer.

Do it, Eric, he thought. Save yourself and it isn't over.

He snatched up one of the magazines and rammed it into the butt receiver.

Out the corner of his eye he caught movement by the door and had to look.

Clair Valens was rising to her feet from where she had been bending over the man Stahl knew as Belasko. There was a spreading bloody patch on Belasko's left shoulder. A flash of excitement surged within

Stahl. He *had* hit the man. He registered the slide on the Glock snap back. All he had to do now was to finish the bastard—and then the damned Valens woman.

His gaze moved back to Valens as he sensed something in her rising hand. It was the Beretta, its muzzle tracking in on him. The fleeting image of the muzzle vanished as Valens pulled the trigger and kept pulling it until the 3-round bursts exhausted the magazine.

The 9 mm slugs tore into Stahl's body, driving him away from the desk and into the corner of the room. He hung there until the weight of his own body pulled him to the floor, leaving a bloody smear on the wall behind him. His front was sodden red. The Glock fell from limp fingers. Stahl drew several shuddering breaths, expelling air that vaporized as swiftly as his thoughts of *his* America.

CLAIR VALENS leaned over Bolan and helped him to his feet. His wound was bleeding heavily. He leaned against the wall, watching as Valens located a fresh magazine from his jacket and reloaded the Beretta.

"Made a mess of your nice leather jacket," she commented.

"I'll claim it on expenses."

Bolan let her help him across the room to one of the armchairs. "Valens, you were close to the wire here."

"Yeah? But I was right about Stahl and his partner." She stared at him. "And didn't you come to get me out of trouble?"

He touched her bruised cheek. "Again," he said.

"Belasko, this is no way for us to keep meeting."

"Tell me about it. And it's Cooper now. Not Belasko."

"Really? We need to talk about this multiple personality of yours." She frowned. "Do you have a real name in there somewhere?" Bolan simply nodded. "I know, you're not going to tell me."

Bolan took out his cell phone and hit the speed dial number for Stony Man, and waited for Brognola to answer.

"Tell the Man it's finished. The main players have been neutralized. Tell him the general is fully retired and won't be drawing his pension. I'll leave you to suggest he needs to sharpen up things at his end."

Bolan heard Brognola relating the rest of the update, but he was starting to lose interest. It was a combination of the blood he was losing and his body giving in to the demands for a shutdown. He needed to rest, something he had been denying himself during mission time. The last thing he heard was Brognola telling him a federal task force was on its way to the Carson residence and would be on site shortly.

Valens took the phone from Bolan's hand and shut it down.

"Hey, soldier, time to take five. What the hell, take ten. In fact, we should both go for broke and have the rest of the damn day off."

Bolan decided that was not a bad idea. He heard her say something about going to fetch a towel to stop the bleeding. He didn't notice when she left him.

The room fell into shadows around Bolan. He let the exhaustion roll over him and he drifted into a sleep that was once visited by ghosts. Bolan recognized children, victims of the Brethren's bombs, drifting in and out of his conscious.

Only this time the troubled expressions on their faces

seemed to have faded, and though he was unable to see clearly he was sure there might have been the traces of gentle smiles there instead.

EPILOGUE

The Brethren was disbanded. Federal teams were able to coordinate operations, aided by the data found on Seeger's computer system. That data listed Brethren sites and personnel across the country. Arrests followed, including a number of people in local law and government positions.

The President, undoubtedly shaken by the revelations concerning military involvement in the affair, took steps to remove those involved. Behind the scenes there was a series of swift retaliatory moves. The White House was the scene of a spate of arrivals and departures, and the President's desk held a stack of letters of resignation, both military and civilian.

The President expressed his gratitude to certain individuals. Senator Vernon Randolph thanked the President for the offer to become a member of the White House staff and declined it in the same breath. He was, he revealed, about to retire from active politics, giving his advanced age as the reason. He later admitted to Bolan that a cushy job at the White House would probably kill him from boredom within six months.

Clair Valens, having to endure a severe dressing down from her superiors, did not lose her agency position. Although the fact was kept from her, a call from 1600 Pennsylvania Avenue, explaining her actions within a covert operation, went a long way to convince her department heads that she was too valuable to lose.

For Mack Bolan closure of a kind came from knowing that his efforts had at least provided some kind of justice for the innocent victims of the bombings. The ones who had died, not for a cause but simply because in the eyes of Seeger and the Brethren they were expendable losses. Bolan, as ever, refused to stand by and let that go unpunished. His ability to prolong his war against evil, in whatever form, would go on. His fight had to continue.

He had already gone that extra mile.

He would keep on going for as many extra miles as were needed.

That was his choice.

That was his destiny.

Don Pendleton's Mack Bolan®

Patriot Play

A violent group known as The Brethren have allied themselves with foreign terrorist organizations and are planning direct collision with the U.S. Administration. With federal agencies at a standstill, a determined President needs a direct, no-mercy solution and Mack Bolan is ready. Partnered with Able Team's leader Carl Lyons, Bolan returns fire on a relentless search-and-destroy mission against an organization driven by warped ideology to claim absolute power.

Available March
wherever you buy books.

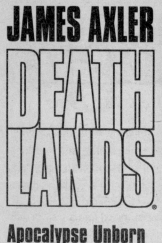

Look for

THE SOUL STEALER
by AleX Archer

Annja Creed jumps at the chance to find a relic buried in the long undisturbed soil of Russia's frozen terrain. But the residents of the town claim they are being hunted by the ghost of a fallen goddess said to ingest souls. When Annja seeks to destroy the apparition, she discovers a horrifying truth—possibly leading her to a dead end....

Available May 2008 wherever you buy books.

GRA12

TAKE 'EM FREE

2 action-packed novels plus a mystery bonus

NO RISK

NO OBLIGATION TO BUY

James Axler
Outlanders®
GHOSTWALK

Area 51 remains a mysterious enclave of eerie synergy and unleashed power—a nightmare poised to take the world to hell. A madman has marshaled an army of incorporeal, alien evil, a virus with intelligence now scything through human hosts like locusts. Cerberus warriors must stop the unstoppable, before humanity becomes discarded vessels of feeding energy for ravenous disembodied monsters.

Available May wherever you buy books.